Waking the Burning Valley

Ashes of the Past Saga, Volume 1

Christina Dickinson

Published by Christina Dickinson, 2020.

WAKING THE BURNING VALLEY

First edition. June 1, 2020.

Copyright © 2020 Christina Dickinson.

ISBN: 978-1952009013

Written by Christina Dickinson.

For Dad, Mom and Stephen

Thank you for raising me despite my best efforts to dissuade
you.

For Mrs. Sierra

Because in the seventh grade, I promised you I would.

1

~Khiri~

FOR AS LONG AS KHIRIELLEN Fortiva could remember, the hunting knife with the silver pommel had hung in the case on the shelf over her family's dining table. Her breath hitched as her father took the knife out and placed it on the table in front of her. Hesitating to reach for the weapon, Khiri gripped the empty sheath already strapped to her hip. Her own blade that she'd wielded since she was only nine summers was well worn, thinned out from too many sharpenings over ten summers of her novice use. That one was a poor cousin to the weapon that her father was nudging toward her. The moment Khiri's hand made contact with the handle, she felt a jolt, like the shocks that zapped her fingers in the winter when she put on new woolen socks. That happened sometimes, when she encountered new magic.

"Is it enchanted?"

"It is. The vines are stylized runes. That blade will never dull," Genovar Fortiva said. "It cannot be broken."

Khiri traced the vines along the single-edged blade, and an in-flight hawk shaped the hilt guard. The master's stamp at the base of the hilt indicated that it had never been in the hands of an apprentice. Her ear tips stung from the bite of the magic woven into the knife.

"My mother gave this to me on the day of my Name Breathing ceremony. I realize I'm a day early, but we already know you will be moving in with Micah by the end of tomorrow. I had to search for a long time to find my destined," some deep expression twitched at the corner of her father's lips. It may have been a smile. Genovar's love for Khiri's mother was a glowing example to all that the Name Breathing was never wrong.

"You're giving it to me?" Khiri asked, hardly daring to believe it. "Forest spirits..."

"Khiriellen Fortiva, watch your words!" her mother's voice came from the main living area. She had apparently returned from her expedition to the human camp a whole afternoon early. Khiri watched her mother duck into their small door and straighten to her full height. People had told Khiri all her life how much she resembled her mother. From the strawberry glint of her hair to the coppery sheen of her skin, there were only two things that really set the two of them apart. Her mother was tall for a wood elf, nearly the same height as a human, and had the tattoos of the Oak Wood Clan. Khiri didn't tower as high as her mother, but she was still taller than the average elven woman. She couldn't wait to receive her clan tattoos after the Name Breathing, when she and Micah made the formal announcement of their chosen village.

"I'm sorry, mother," Khiri said, slipping the knife into her old sheath. It fit better than she had expected, but she had too many other things to think about for the knife and sheath to occupy her long. Her father's dark eyes glinted with humor when they met Khiri's bright blue ones, though it was tainted by some other, darker emotions. Feeling something similar herself, Khiri pushed it out of her mind. Moving out of her childhood home was bound to be a little bittersweet. She smiled back at her father. It was an unspoken agreement that they never told her mother where she learned to talk like that. He let his silver braid fall over his shoulder as he rose from where they had been sitting.

"Welcome back, Leyani, my love," Khiri's father said in greeting.

"Genovar, dearest soul, what are you teaching our daughter now?" Leyani raised an eyebrow.

"Nothing, love. I gave her an early Name Breathing gift. She and Micah will be traveling to the River Willow Clan tomorrow, after all," Genovar rose on his toes to give his wife a kiss.

"Mother, did you do well with the human traders?" Khiri asked, trying not to sound too eager and failing miserably. The sole reason for her mother's trip was to help Micah find a joining gift. It wasn't necessary, but Leyani had told them stories about humans exchanging gifts during their bonding ceremonies. Khiri had been so enamored by the stories that Micah had requested Leyani's assistance to procure something special.

Leyani laughed, her voice trickling off the walls like rainwater. "You mean, did Micah find what he was looking for? You'll just have to wait and see, Starling."

Khiri tried not to make a face at her mother's use of the children's pet name as she shifted onto her knees and sat on her feet. Gently, she felt the warm place in the back of her mind where the name of her destined resided. *Micah Ulimani* echoed through her being, reassuring and constant. It was said that the humans did not have true soul mates and were born not knowing their own names, let alone that of their destined. Khiri occasionally wondered what that was like, and felt something akin to envy. No, that wasn't right. She loved Micah. As a soul mate should... At least, she thought she did.

Micah was two summers older than Khiri, and they had attended lessons together, played together, and he had attempted to tutor her in cooking when she helped him with forest lore. His Name Breathing had confirmed village suspicions that he and Khiri were destined, and the Council of the Clans had allowed them to go ahead and make the plans that would traditionally only be made after they had traveled the villages to find each other. They had chosen a tree to join and Micah had spent the last two summers building the house they would share. Tomorrow, Khiri would move into a fully furnished home settled in branches overlooking the waters of the Ota River.

Of all the Life Trees, the River Willow Clan's tree had the most diversity, being the closest to the human roads. It even had an inn nestled close to the trunk. Micah had wanted to stay in the tree that they were born and raised in, but had allowed Khiri to convince him that they would benefit from the distance from their families. It was as close to an adventure as Khiri was ever going to get.

Interrupting her thoughts, there was a hesitant tapping on the door. "Khiri? Are you home?"

"Micah!" Khiri sprang to her feet to greet her destined, though she wasn't supposed to kiss him publicly until tomorrow. Pushing her doubts back to dwell in the darkened corners of her mind, she willed the happy thoughts of newness and curiosity to show in her smile. "What are you doing here? I'm supposed to spend the day with my parents."

"And yet you loaned me your mother to run what may have been a full day's errand," Micah ducked into the house, smiling. "I only want to borrow you for half an hour at most."

Looking to her parents for permission, Khiri followed Micah as he climbed back out of the house. Khiri turned once through the door and studied the home of her childhood as though she had never seen it before. From this side, her house looked like a three room hut squeezed into a space between five large limbs, with a door that was greener than the surrounding leaves. It was a comfortable home, but not extravagant; a home fitting for a hunter and a merchant of modest needs. Khiri was to be a hunter like her father for her new clan, while Micah was already a journeyman fletcher. Their new home would be comfortable, too.

The walkways of the Life Trees hung suspended by braided vines between branches and limbs as thick as a normal tree's trunk, but were generally reserved for the village elderly, small children, or patrols. Khiri and Micah dropped down from the walkway directly onto a limb of the Life Tree and slid to a fork before jumping from branch to branch underneath the upper branches of the village. Below them, in the lower limbs and nearer the trunk, the market and guardhouse were swarming with activity. The Name Breathing was the biggest celebration of the year, and Micah and Khiri were minor celebrities this summer since it was uncommon for destined to know each other prior to the ceremony. Khiri felt sorry for the other two that were breathing names the next day. It wasn't fair that she was receiving special attention for a thing that was well out of her control. Many young elves looked forward to this day more than any other. They would speak a name that had been with them since birth, and then they would go on a journey to find their other half and begin their lives as full Clan members.

"Where are we going?" Khiri asked.

"I want to show you something," Micah replied as he grabbed a branch about as thick as his arm and swung to a secondary path. His light brown hair bounced in the dappled sunlight as he easily skidded and jumped down the paths that they had known since childhood. Khiri recognized the route to the lower canopy, where they had often snuck to stargaze in their youth.

"Micah?"

"Trust me," he said, recognizing her hesitation. The lower canopy was a place they hadn't gone in over two summers. Not since Micah's own Name Breathing. "We'll want to be well away from prying eyes when I show you what I found."

Her curiosity piqued, Khiri followed him, heaving herself onto the Sky Watcher's platform with the strength of her forearms. From here, the other six Life Trees could be seen; their branches rose above the forest like great reversed mountains. They were far enough apart that it was almost a week's travel through the woods to get from the Silver Rowan clan near the forest's heart to the River Willow clan. The midday sun made her squint after the shadowed paths inside the protection of the canopy.

"Ready?" Micah's eyes were a deep green, catching the light and glowing like chips of beryl.

Khiri studied him, taking in his bronzed, lithe form. She stepped in closer and brushed his hair away from his eyes. He was only about half a hand taller and she barely had to tilt her head to meet his lips. They started kissing three summers ago before they'd told anyone about their being destined, and it seemed well enough. Micah looked satisfied, and the name in the back of her head glowed a little more golden. Naturally, they had recognized each other the moment they set eyes on each other when he was six summers turned, and she was four. It wasn't that they were breaking any laws, but they were breaking tradition which was almost as bad. Pulling away from his embrace, Khiri smiled sheepishly and said, "Okay, I'm ready."

"Uh... What? Oh, oh yes," Micah recovered. "I went to see if the humans had something fantastic for our union token. This exceeded my expectations. I couldn't wait for tomorrow, I had to show you. I want to be sure it fits."

"Enough! Just show me!" Khiri laughed.

Micah reached into his small belt pouch and retrieved a ring. It was white gold shaped into several curved disks that melted into each other, with a great cabochon ruby set on the largest circle, like a drop of blood glistening in the sun. "Give me your hand," Micah coaxed.

For a fraction of a heartbeat, Khiri hesitated. The ring was large and gaudy, not at all something that Khiri would've chosen. It was a present from the man she was about to spend her life with, though. Khiri extended her hand, and Micah slipped the ring onto her left middle finger. She'd expected it to weigh her hand down with its size, but Khiri couldn't tell it was there except for an odd rush of warmth through her arm. The tips of her ears tingled much as they had when she'd been handed her father's dagger. "This is master level work. What did you trade for it?"

"I traded three bows and two quivers of arrows. They no doubt felt they got the better bargain, despite my work being a journeyman's," Micah shook his head, bending to kiss her hand. "It brings out the fire in your hair."

Khiri gazed at the ruby glinting just over her knuckle and tried to match her expression to that of her soul mate's, but those worried thoughts that she'd pushed away earlier were forming a knot of unease in her chest.

FOG DRIFTED OVER THE treetops of the lower forest, lending the air a crisp, dewy taste. The sky was gray with pre-dawn light and the birds were chirping both above and below the branches of the Life Tree.

Khiri's body quivered with nervous energy. She had already dressed in traditional cerulean robes for the Name Breathing. Though the ceremony was still an hour away, she was becoming increasingly agitated. Mentally, she caressed Micah's name over and over again, waiting for it to comfort her as it usually did when she awakened from a nightmare or when she was otherwise unable to rest.

Exiting the house as silently as she was able, Khiri made her way toward the Sky Watcher platform where the ceremony would take place. Maybe the Oak Wood Councilor would be there already and they could prepare.

As she pushed her way onto the platform, she found not the Councilor but Micah had arrived before her.

"Micah? What are you doing here?"

"Khiri!" Micah jumped. "I wasn't expecting anyone yet."

"I couldn't sleep. My skin feels as though it's going to crawl off my bones," Khiri said. Rubbing her bare arms, she found that she was coated in a thin layer of cool sweat despite the warmth that remained on a summer night, despite the fog.

"I couldn't sleep either," Micah sighed. "It troubles me that I have this feeling of unease on what should be the happiest day of our lives."

He didn't look at her, and Khiri felt a moment of kinship with him that was stronger than any of their clandestine rendezvous. She took his hand and squeezed it, trusting him to understand her in the way only he could.

"Maybe it's just that we have been looking forward to this for so long that we are making ourselves overly anxious," Khiri suggested.

"Perhaps," he said with a sigh. Micah gathered Khiri into his arms and held her to him. "I love you, you know."

"And I love you," she said, still feeling the knot of unease nested in her stomach.

They pushed away from each other as the noise of footsteps heralded the arrival of other villagers. Tylen and Illenia, the other two participating in the Name Breathing stood out in the crowd of brown leathers and the topaz robes of the village elders.

Councilor Rivinar, an elder woman with soft features, a white braid and skin that had once been tanned, made her way to the small dais that made up the eastern side of the platform. "If the participants would join me, we shall proceed."

Khiri gave Micah a nervous smile, then joined the other two as they knelt on the dais.

A brief spark of flame and the air was filled with the scent of burning incense. The smell was so heavy that it weighed on Khiri's tongue, making her fight not to gag. "Those of you that present yourselves, you each know a name that is not your own. That name has remained your secret, binding you to your adolescence. If you feel ready to reveal that secret, stand and face your families. Announce your secret, shed your bonds to childhood, and embrace your future."

Khiri rose with Tylen and Illenia to face the Oak Wood Clan. Leyani looked proud, though Khiri thought she saw a tear trailing down her mother's cheek. Genovar's mouth was set in a rather grim line, as though he'd like very much to delay this parting from his daughter. Micah tried to smile, but the intensity of their shared foreboding was still rising.

Illenia whispered into the sudden breeze, "Elvar Galantier..."

As the silence swallowed the last of her secret name, Tylen said, "Jamera Oltivian," as though it was sucked unwillingly from his lips.

The Counselor had warned the participants that they would have no control over their tongues while under the influence of the incense, but Khiri found the few seconds between Tylen's admission and hers unnerving. She reached for the presence of Micah's name in her mind as her mouth opened.

"Telgan Korsborn," she heard her voice say.

Her eyes widened as the hush turned from solemn to startled. Micah's expression melted from nervous anticipation to a grotesque mixture of pain and astonished disbelief. In a panic, she grasped for Micah's name, searching her entire being for that comforting, golden presence of her destined. Even though she could see him sitting next to her parents, it was as though he was lost, and she would never hold him again.

All she found, humming in his place, was the cold, gray name of Telgan Korsborn.

2

~Estan~

COLUMNS OF GOLD AND alabaster lined the Great Hall of the Temple of Taymahr, the Goddess of Protection and Loyalty, reminding those that passed of the goddess's glory and strength. Estan's polished armor weighed heavily on his shoulders, as though his pride in wearing it had made it lighter when he'd first been elevated into the goddess' service. It was traditional for his order of the Knighthood to don their ceremonial plate-mail when petitioning Taymahr. Estan had strapped on the less flashy, but more substantial field plate that he'd been wearing for almost a year. Still, one did not petition Taymahr in dirty armor, so he'd polished the field plate so that it shone almost as brightly as the silver stuff that had very little stopping power.

According to Shalora, the High Priestess of Taymahr, the Knighthood of the Protective Hand was needed in the war. Estan was unconvinced that his goddess would care about a boundary skirmish between Eerilor and Mytana, but had obeyed the word of the High Priestess. After all, he was a devout practitioner. Estan owed much to Taymahr, and her temple, and had been raised by those sworn to her service. Thought to hail from eastern lands, where the desert sun had led to people with darker skin, whatever had befallen Estan's parents and led to his being raised by the temple was known only to Taymahr herself.

This was his second summer as a shield-carrier, although he had been young to receive it. Most had to wait until their twenty-fifth summer before they were elevated to full knighthood. Because of his unique position, he had become a shield-bearer at only twenty-two. Maybe those that had opposed his appointment had been right, he thought, and maybe he had been overly young... Maybe there were divine reasons that were beyond his understanding. He didn't know, but the killing of dwarf and man over a river that no one had really cared about until recently left a foul taste in his mouth.

Clerics and scribes hurried out of the way as they saw him coming. The Knighthood of the Protective Hand was considered to be the hand of Taymahr in the same way that the priestesses were the voice of the goddess. Some of the elder knights took advantage of their station, demanding free services and favors from the rest of the temple staff.

With a deep sigh, Estan climbed the steps to the altar in the center of the hall. Anyone who sought a private council with Taymahr was allowed to climb these steps, but the goddess only spoke to the ranks of the priestesses. To contradict a priestess was to doubt his patron deity, but Estan had to question. He had so much blood on his hands at the word of one woman; a woman that he very much wished that he didn't doubt, but also hoped was wrong. The blood of people; men and women that fought because the temples or their nobility wished it. Knighthood had seemed glorious from afar, but the truth of it was a blight on his soul. Estan felt as though he carried the taint of a demon, like those creatures that he'd only read about in histories written of the Great War: *Flayers*. They still existed, of course, but he'd never been unlucky enough to see one.

Estan cleared his mind of all thought, as he had been trained to do when petitioning the Goddess.

"Holy Taymahr, I know it unlikely that you would speak to a lesser Knight of the Protective Hand, for why would you speak to me directly when you have let your will be known through your priestesses, but I would seek your guidance. When I was a child, serving you meant something. The Knighthood served the people, not the lords and ladies of the land. I don't understand why that has changed. Did my brethren not fight in the War of the Burning Valley against true demon-spawn? And now we are to turn our blades against humans and dwarves who were our allies against the dark legions? Why!" he demanded fervently.

Only the footsteps of other worshipers rang through the decorated hall, leaving Estan in his uncertain silence. He feared the Goddess might smite him where he stood, or could tell the priestesses of his blasphemy. Perhaps he wanted Her to, in the depths of his being. Maybe he should withdraw quietly from the ranks of the Knighthood before they could eject him publicly.

As he made his way back down the stairs, he resolved to talk to Shalora. Surely, she would have answers for him. She was the one responsible for his elevation after all, and the leading voice in their war efforts. It couldn't hurt to talk to her. Asking questions of the High Priestess of Taymahr could be no more insolent than demanding answers of the Goddess Herself, and he'd already done that today.

Shalora's apartments, including her offices, were located in the northern wing of the temple. Estan had to pass through the Hall of Reflection in order to reach the quarters of the priestesses, which was quite literally a hallway that was lined with mirror. Theoretically, anyone passing through the hall was purified, having to meet themselves in a never-ending series of reflections. Seeking answers in his own dark brown eyes was no help, and Estan's dusky features only scowled back at him as they did in the glass that hung in his own bedchamber.

Conversation met his ears long before he got to the end of the Hall of Reflection. He recognized the voices of Shalora and one of her highest ranking attendants, a woman called Inani that had always given Estan a feeling of unease. Though he couldn't see them, a door at the end of the passage was cracked just enough that he could see the lantern light dancing as though to caution him from moving forward. Estan slowed just enough that his feet weren't audible over the voices that were brushing their way down the corridor.

"How much longer do you think it will take?" the attendant asked.

"We've finally replaced all of the High Priestesses in all of the other temples. Honestly, I was starting to fear that old Shallel had actually tapped into something divine with her resistance to our machinations. Every deity from Taymahr to Oshyn is represented by our people. All recent recruits to the Knighthoods have been approved by Travin. There are a few outliers, but with the war, that can be fixed," Shalora sounded very confident, even as her words chilled Estan to his core. He froze in his tracks, and he could've sworn his heart froze in his chest.

"Twenty long years..." the attendant sighed wistfully.

"We haven't succeeded yet, Inani. By throwing the Knighthood of the Protective Hand away on this ridiculous excuse for a war, I've created the perfect atmosphere to get rid of the remaining true believers. Either they die in battle, or they expose themselves by coming to us with concerns and I denounce them as blasphemers," Shalora said. "The masses believe that the deities only speak to priestesses. It's lucky for us that the last of the priestesses that actually heard any of the Great Deities died or were struck deaf after the Great Devastation."

"What's to prevent another one from being tapped?" Inani asked.

"No one sends potential candidates to us, we search them out. Only unwanted children get sent to the temples, and the unwanted are easily controlled. Take that young Estan boy. He's my favorite project. He's a true believer that I raised from an infant, and he's never thought to doubt me," Shalora laughed.

Estan backed out of the hall in a hurry. He couldn't believe he had heard what he thought he was hearing. Shalora was subverting the infrastructure of the temples, along with every other High Priestess? Inani had mentioned that they had been working on this for twenty years; the War of the Burning Valley had ended roughly twenty years ago... And more damning still, Shalora had referred to the Great War as the Great Devastation. Only former members of the Gray Army spoke of it thus.

Shoving that line of thought out of his head for the time being, he tried to come up with a plan of action. The Knight Commander, Estan's foster father and the man who had taught him everything he knew about combat, would have some idea of where to start.

Estan ran as quickly as he could to the eastern wing of the temple, where he had been raised. The temple library, where he had snuck every night after light's out, was also in the eastern wing. He remembered a book from his youth which was the only recorded history of the War of the Burning Valley. Travin sounded extremely familiar, and he thought he remembered seeing it mentioned in the history. Stopping in the library, he found the book, a plain bound thing that was worn and smudged where there should have been an author and title. Estan only recognized it because of his many times sneaking it from the shelves and reading after hours as a boy. He leafed through the pages until he spotted the name, referred to as one of the five generals of the Gray Army. Tucking the book behind his breastplate, Estan continued running to the office of Knight Commander Jersal.

"Sir Jersal! I need to speak with you!" Estan breathed heavily.

Knight Commander Jersal set down the quill he had been scratching against the thick, rough paper of the tome resting on his desk. "Estan? When did you get back from the front lines?"

"Yesterday, sir," Estan said. "Look, Sir Jersal, I've just overheard something that I really feel you should know about."

The Knight Commander sat back in his chair, his iron gray hair pulling down into his eyebrows, making his look more and more like a festival mask with every word that Estan told him. Before Estan was able to pull the book out to show Sir Jersal the reference to Travin, the Knight Commander rose from his seat and came around his desk. He reached out and clasped Estan by the shoulder.

"Estan, I raised you as my own son, and I would dearly like to believe you, but these are some serious accusations that you are leveling toward a highly, highly respected woman. Now, are you sure that this was High Priestess Shalora?" Sir Jersal's blue eyes searched Estan's face, as though trying to assess the truth.

"I am very certain," Estan said, though his throat tried to close up over the words as he tried to push them out. As much as Shalora had been a mother to him, to find out that she'd only ever viewed him as a *project* hurt him in a spot that he'd thought had scabbed over. His parents were either dead or lost, and the family that had taken him in viewed him as something less than human. He swallowed around metal shards that were growing in his throat and promised himself a drink in the near future.

"And you heard her mention that all of the High Priestesses had been replaced with what she called 'our people' and you heard the name Travin?" the Knight Commander reviewed.

"Yes, sir," Estan said.

Sir Jersal's eyebrows drew even tighter, which was astonishing to watch even under the circumstances. He raised his hand and tried to push his scalp back into place, but it resisted, crinkling into an artist's rendering of grief. "I am very disheartened by this. There were signs, but I ignored them. I told myself that I had nothing to worry about. If I gave it enough time, then everything would work itself out. I never anticipated that you would put me in this situation, though," Sir

Jersal's hand tightened against the gleaming surface of Estan's pauldrons. "I am sorry, my son."

If Estan were still as green as he had been the previous summer, he never would've spotted the weapon in time. After his time in the front lines, his instincts were better honed. Estan jumped back as Sir Jersal stabbed at him with a wickedly curved dagger, trying to come up under the breastplate. Estan drew his sword, his eyes wide with disbelief. "Sir?" he couldn't keep the question out of his voice. "You're one of them?"

"The Gray Army was going to sweep the world clean. Humans, dwarves, elves, and whatever else is out there, we're all flawed. The gods don't care. They haven't cared for decades. Imagine it, Estan! A world with no crime, no war and no death! I am part of the foundation for a new future, and you can still join us. You could be a part of it," Sir Jersal coaxed, spreading his arms as though to encompass Estan with his arms. He seemed unaware that he was still holding the weapon he had just tried to impale his potential convert with.

"You're insane!" Estan backed toward the door. "What about your oaths to Taymahr? To the Knighthood?"

"You won't be persuaded then?" the Knight Commander shook his head, his eyes burning with flames of conviction. "You drove me to this. I wanted to keep you safe... I was going to teach you about everything, but Shalora was convinced that we could control you better if you believed in Taymahr. You had to poke into things, learn things, try things. I saw the signs." He flung himself at Estan, knocking Estan's sword away and plunging his knife into the middle of the younger knight's breastplate.

An emotional fog threatened to cloud Estan's vision as he swung his sword back toward the Knight Commander. He blooded the older man's bare arm. Even as his training screamed at him to follow through and pin his enemy, Estan only held his sword steady enough to cover his retreat. He couldn't bring himself to kill the man that had been his adoptive father. Sir Jersal cried out in rage and then tossed the clean dagger aside as though it, too, had betrayed him. Estan sent a thought of praise to any deity that was listening that he had worn his field plate, and tucked the heavy history book under his armor. The young knight slammed the door to the Knight Commander's office and ran for the Great Hall, hoping he could make it out of the temple.

He had nearly made it back to the library when Sir Jersal's door reopened. "Stop him!" the Knight Commander pointed at Estan, his arm dripping blood freely on the stone floor. "That man is crazed! He attacked me in my own office! Estan is a blasphemer and a demon sympathizer!"

Knights in residence started coming from their rooms and the mess hall, bearing their swords and maces. Blessing his continued luck that none of them had bows and arrows, Estan sprinted through the corridors. He passed through the Great Hall, glancing at the altar stairs as he ran by. He supposed that this, the betrayal of those that had raised him in the ways of the goddess, was an answer to the questions he'd come to ask.

Men that Estan had known most of his life were chasing him, hunting him. Feredan, that had tutored him with his numbers, was swinging a mace at Estan as though he were no better than a rat that had snuck into the food stores. Another, Restra, who had taught him how to string and shoot a bow, she was calling for his blood like he was a thief that had been caught stripping gold from the walls. Everyone that brandished a weapon had been family to Estan. He had no way of knowing which of these people were loyal to Taymahr and ignorant, and which were loyal to the High Priestess and Knight Commander. As far as it mattered to his immediate survival, there really wasn't a difference.

Tears burned at the edges of his vision. As he passed a candle stand, he flung it down at the feet of his pursuers. Without looking to see who it tripped, Estan dug his feet into the stone and ran for all he was worth.

IN HIS HURRY, ESTAN had rushed down a street that he was hoping would take him to the outer wall, but instead found himself in the weaver's district. It seemed that the luck that had been guiding his steps through the treachery of the day had finally dried up on him. There was no way that he could hide among the commoners long enough to ditch his pursuit. Soon, word of his blasphemy would spread to the other temples, and there would be more patrols looking for him.

"Estan?" a woman's voice said, timid and confused. "What brings you down to the dye stalls?"

Turning toward the voice, Estan found himself face to face with his first childhood flame. "Loni," he couldn't help the note of desperation that reverberated through his body. "Please, you know me. They are going to kill me as a blasphemer if I'm found. Please..."

The timidity evaporated from Loni's face and he glimpsed the same unyielding, fearless girl he'd known back when they played together in the temple stables. She was never the first to swing on a rope from the hayloft. That would've been himself or their friend Resmine, but Loni never backed down either. She grabbed his hand and yanked him into the stall where she'd been working.

"Loni, who is this? What's going on?" another woman in a thin gray dress demanded.

"Vessa, you never saw him. He was never here, the way that your special friend hasn't been here when your husband asks," Loni said, though it was almost a hiss.

"Oh, Loni... I didn't think you had it in you," the woman, Vessa gave Estan a flirtatious wink and moved on to a different stall.

Estan looked at her sadly, admiring her soft blonde curls and smooth freckled skin. He and Loni had been childhood sweethearts, meeting first when she was sent to the Temple of Taymahr to give her family's tribute during her eighth summer. They had remained friends even after she had married an apprentice baker in lower Seirane, though a part of Estan had never truly gotten over her. "I can't come back, and I can't explain. You and Jestin were planning to move once his apprenticeship was over. Stick to it... and stay out of the temples."

"There have been rumors in the lower city," Loni confessed. She handed him a towel and turned her back so that he could get out of the tub. "Many of the citizens keep private shrines now. The temples involving themselves with the recent war was a very unpopular move."

"They labeled me a blasphemer," Estan told her as he tugged on a shirt and pants. "It won't be safe for you to even let Jestin know that I was here."

"Rash," she shook her head without looking at him. "Whatever you discovered, it must be really bad. What will you do? Where will you go?"

"I need to find someone," Estan picked up the book he had smuggled out of the Temple of Taymahr's library. "I need to find the man that wrote this book."

Taking the book from his grasp, Loni looked at the cover and traced the puncture in the cover with one finger. "The author's name was damaged. Do you remember what it was?"

"No," Estan grimaced. "It was worn away long before this damage. But the author makes references to his heritage. He was an elf, raised in the Life Tree Clans. That's where I'm going to start."

As Loni opened her mouth to reply, their conversation was cut short by the sound of yells and wood being smashed. The sounds of angry dye merchants and their workers were undercut by the fierce bellows of trained soldiers that were following a trail. "Ash and waste! Someone must've spotted you," Loni hissed. "Nothing for it. Out the back!"

Estan ducked under the rear of the stall after Loni, nearly tangling in the stall's fabric as the edges of his pauldrons caught on the roughly hemmed curtains. They dodged down a narrow throughway that was barely wide enough for Estan's shoulders when he wasn't encumbered with his armor. Loni towed him through a stall that was filled with vats of green and blue dyes, her eyes darting this way and that as she tried to keep them hidden. Trying his hardest to stay quiet, Estan was having no luck. His armor would clank or creek in against the cobblestones or snag stalls. The sounds of yelling and clanking of other armor was drawing nearer.

Creeping across the walkway between the blue vats and another stall filled with red and orange vats, Loni plucked a hollow straw of snake grass that had worked its way into the city from under a paving stone that had come loose. "They're coming too fast, and you're too loud. Breathe through this," Loni said, she stuck the snake grass into his mouth and pushed Estan into one of the large, deep vats of orange dye. He stifled the urge to flail and clenched the grass stalk between his lips before the liquid closed in on him.

3

~Khiri~

FROZEN TO THE DAIS, Khiri's eyes were fixed on Micah in her panic. He would no longer meet her gaze; his face was contorted in pain, fear and confusion. Finding no solace from him, she turned to her parents. Her mother's eyes were welling with tears, while her father's face had turned rigid. There was no comfort to be found there, either.

"Child, are you certain you spoke true? Your tongue was anointed with the Incense of Honesty?" Councilor Rivinar asked. Her voice sounded as though it had been hardened in a forge of anger and tempered with a bath of befuddlement. Khiri couldn't blame the woman; something had gone terribly wrong and there wasn't anything that could be done to fix it or fight it.

"Yes, Councilor," Khiri's voice answered, ripped from lips that were still not hers to control.

"How long have you been planning to deceive us that Micah was your destined?" Councilor Rivinar hissed.

"I never planned to deceive anyone," Khiri heard herself say, the whispering voice of the ceremony taking on an eerie quality now that the villagers were starting to whisper amongst themselves. "I knew him, as all should know their destined."

"Your speech rings true, and yet cannot be," Councilor Rivinar's voice softened. "I will have to call a meeting of the Council of the

Clans. In the meantime, please stand with your parents while I finish the ceremony for these others, unless you would rather speak to the Council of the Clans on your own. I will want to speak with you and Micah both once I am finished here."

Still unable to stop the words spilling out of her mouth, Khiri answered, "I will stand and become an adult today."

The anger that flashed in Councilor Rivinar's eyes at that declaration promised nothing good would come of such defiance, but she did move on to the next part of the ritual.

Khiri did not actually hear the Name Breathing end. Illenia and Tylen were swarmed with well-wishers and congratulations while she was left to her unpleasant thoughts. Finally, Leyani and Genovar approached their daughter. Tears rampaged down her cheeks, leaving their coarse trails of salty water to tighten her skin. She didn't want to become an adult like this. Her hopes and dreams had all included Micah and the life they would share in the branches of the River Willow Clan's Life Tree. Micah already had his tattoos, declaring him a clan member. He had gotten them knowing that she would be following him to their new home... the home she had chosen for him.

"Are you alright, Khiri?" her father asked, placing a hand on her shoulder.

"I... I don't know," she replied, finally regaining use of her tongue. "Has this ever happened before? Why? Why...?"

"I'm sorry, dear one, but I... we have no answers for you," Leyani told her, exchanging a look with Genovar. Something passed between her parents with that look, something that would have sparked Khiri's curiosity on a normal day. Today, it barely registered. There was too much to wonder about already.

Her parents embraced her, giving her the first real sanctuary from the ill feelings that had plagued her since early that morning. They let go of her all too soon, but assured her that they would be waiting for her after she and Micah talked with Councilor Rivinar.

Micah would not look at her as they walked up to the Councilor. Khiri tried to touch his arm, but he flinched at her touch. The tears that had flowed down her face during the Name Breathing were joined by a fresh stream. She fought at the lump in her throat, concentrating on that discomfort in an effort to block out her urge to sob.

"Before I call a meeting of the Council, I should like to know the details. Tell me, when did the two of you find out you were no longer destined?" Councilor Rivinar inquired.

"When I said a different name... I did not know until the moment I spoke," Khiri said, her voice cracking with emotion.

"We both woke early feeling... uncomfortable," Micah's voice was hard and bitter. "I should have slept through today."

"Be that as it may," Councilor Rivinar sounded bemused, but sympathetic. "Did the two of you do anything unusual recently? Leave the safety of the Life Tree? Lay together? Lay with someone else? Attempt human or dwarven magic?"

Helplessly, Khiri shook her head. Micah did not move, his mouth tight. After several moments had passed, he said, "I went on a small expedition with her mother to the human trading camp early yesterday. All that I acquired was the union token that I was to give Khiri today after the Name Breathing. I was too excited to wait until today to show her, so I brought her here under the light of the sun and had her try it on. When I found it, I was compelled to trade for it. I got what I felt was a fair bargain, but I would have given anything to acquire it. I knew it was for her, as surely as I knew she was my destined...."

"I see," Councilor Rivinar held out her hand, "and may I look at this union token?"

Micah pulled the ring out of his pouch and dropped it reluctantly into the Councilor's custody. Her eyes widened ever so slightly in surprise and she let out a breath. "This ring is steeped in human magic. You found this at the human trader camp, you said. Did you inquire to its history?"

"The man who bartered it to me did not even seem aware that he had it until I pointed it out. It fell out of an herb packet that I had picked up to sniff," Micah said.

"One last question before I call together the Clan Council," Councilor Rivinar took a breath and held it for a few moments. "Micah Ulimani, what is the name of your destined?"

The skin around Micah's eyes tightened, and he looked up into Khiri's eyes for the first time since she had breathed another's name. "There is no name. I have no destined," he said, grief and betrayal lacing every word and making the statement weigh like an accusation.

Khiri felt like she had fallen from the upper branches to hit one of the lower platforms. Her chest ached as the knot in her stomach moved to her heart and started to twist. The blame in Micah's gaze was a bigger blow than losing her future with him. He had to know that she didn't want this for him. Even with a new name stamped in iron floating through her mind, Micah had been her best friend for as long as she could remember.

"May I give this to Khiriellen Fortiva?" Councilor Rivinar asked, still holding the ring out between them.

Hesitating, Micah's features softened for the briefest moment, and he nodded, "I bought it for her. I have no reason to keep it."

Councilor Rivinar turned and placed the ring in Khiri's hand. "Now, I must call to my fellow members of the Council. I will summon the two of you back once we've come to a decision."

"Excuse me, Councilor Rivinar, but I must speak with you before you call together the Council," Genovar said. Khiri hadn't heard her father's approach, but he was standing right next to her now. The comforting scent of her mother's soap and the oils that softened his hunting leathers made Khiri's heart ache. This morning, she'd thought that scent would be left to her childhood and she'd be on her way to something new.

This is not what I had in mind, she thought bitterly as she stepped off the dais and made her way to where her mother waited.

Micah left going in the opposite direction. He was probably going to the fletcher's workshop. That was where he normally went to blow off steam. It was unlikely he'd want to spend any time with his own parents after a day like this. They were not warm people, and would likely try to find a way to blame their son for the way things turned out, as little sense as that made.

Opening her mouth to invite Micah to come with them instead, Khiri couldn't get the words to come out. It was unlikely he'd want to spend time in her presence right now, either. She reflexively reached for his name in her head only to feel the sharp, metallic ridges of *Telgan Korsborn* waiting for her.

4

~Rivinar~

HAS IT REALLY BEEN that many summers? Rivinar thought as she watched Genovar Fortiva leave the Sky Watcher's platform. He had reminded her of a favor that she'd long since forgotten with the day to day duties of running her clan. Now that she'd been reminded, it was something she wished she could forget once more. It had seemed like a minor thing back when he'd asked it of her, but now, nineteen summers later, she regretted that she'd made the agreement.

She turned toward the sky, a brilliant sapphire overlooking a sea of clouds. The lower forest canopy was completely obscured in a blanket of white. It might even have been raining on the roots of the Life Tree. The other Life Trees peaked over the false ocean like great islands or mountains that someone had constructed upside down, with their great bases open to the sky. It was a good day for her voice to call the Councilors to session. Pulling a sachet of herbs out of one of her many hidden pockets, Rivinar gave it a sniff. She replaced it and tried a different pocket. Satisfied that she'd found the correct one, she withdrew a pinch of the herbal mixture out of the sachet and blew it into the wind. It was necessary to wait a few breaths to make sure the wind had noticed, but then she felt the mental tug that alerted her that it was time to speak.

One by one, Rivinar whispered the names of her fellow Councilors into the breeze. One by one, their whispers answered her call.

"Rivinar, why have you called on a Name Breathing day?" Teliv of the Pleasant Birch Clan asked.

"Yes, Rivinar," even though Rivinar had never seen her fellow Councilors, the scowl on Councilor Reshinel's face rang clear. He was the oldest of the Councilors and the most prone to taking offense. It had always struck Rivinar as somewhat fitting that he represented the Storm Grove Clan. "Some of us are actually busy tending to our new adults and their families. What nonsense would you draw us away?"

"Khiriellen Fortiva that was the named of Micah Ulimani..." Rivinar began.

"Yes, yes," Havelene of the River Willow Clan interrupted. "They're expected. I don't know why this warrants the attention of a full Council."

"Perhaps it has to do with the past tense in that statement," Elinastor of the Elm Thorn Clan said. "She said, 'was the named of Micah Ulimani,' and perhaps if we would let her finish, we may begin speaking as the elders that we are, and not a wayward bunch of children."

Despite the level of condescension that Elinastor brought to these meetings, Rivinar did appreciate that he was usually able to keep the others on point. *Spirits keep us from ever having to meet in person*, Rivinar thought. "Elinastor has the truth of it. Khiriellen Fortiva is no longer bound to Micah Ulimani, nor is he still able to name her. She spoke the name Telgan Korsborn, and Micah... He is unbound."

"Spirits of winter..." hissed Alitiar of the Sun Maple Clan.

"Councilor Alitiar!" Havalene admonished. She was constantly shocked by the language of her peers, despite having been on the Council for almost as long as Reshinel. It probably wasn't long before either of them returned to the embrace of the Life Trees. The thought saddened Rivinar momentarily. They were both irritating to work with, but she would miss them when they chose to sleep.

"How did this happen?" Kelinovi of the Sun Maple Clan asked. He was the youngest of the Councilors, at only sixty-seven summers. It was unusual for the position to pass to one that was not the oldest of his or her clan, but the Sun Maple elders had presented him before the Council upon his predecessor's return to the Trees. Rivinar had to admit that he had a presence of mind that deserved admiration.

"Khiriellen received a ring from Micah that was tainted with human magic, but I honestly don't think that was the cause, or at least, not the whole cause of this tragedy. I felt the ring myself, and it was nothing like strong enough to undo a soul bond," Rivinar said. "I called the Council to discuss what is to be done with the young couple now. Obviously, our original plans cannot happen."

"Why not?" Havalene demanded. "Why should this nonsense change anything? If we make them stay together, maybe whatever happened will untangle itself. Imagine depriving them of their real soulmates just because of some sort of fluke."

"Havalene, don't be selfish. If these two were heading for any clan but yours, would you even contemplate such as suggestion?" Teliv asked.

There was a breath of silence. For a moment, it felt as though Rivinar was alone with the chirping birds and the sun on the Sky Watcher's platform, merely enjoying the view. It was only a moment, though. Even while the other Councilors lapsed into a thoughtful silence, the situation weighed heavily on Rivinar's chest. To be unbound, without the knowledge of that one that completed your soul, it was unthinkable, and this had happened to a boy that she had known since birth... Khiri's situation was unfathomable as well, but the girl wasn't untethered.

"Have any of us ever heard the name Telgan Korsborn?" Elinastor broke the silence.

None of them had. It was an alien name, not belonging to the Trees at all.

"Then I think we must do what we have always done," Elinastor said. "We must send the girl to find her soulmate."

"Away from the Life Trees?" Havalene sounded aghast, and Rivinar didn't blame her. Being sent away, likely never to return, was a thing that only happened as punishment. Those that died away from the Trees had little to no hope of rejoining their ancestors within the embrace of the Soulwood.

Rivinar felt guilty for the rush of relief that she hadn't been required to offer the suggestion. She still couldn't fathom why a father would ask that his own daughter be sent away when the girl hadn't yet been born, but it had been a strange night. He had returned from parts unknown, and he requested that he and a very pregnant Leyani be permitted to change clans. There had been a Council called then, too, and once it was over, there had been a new family in her care. As soon as they were tattooed, Genovar had made her swear as his Clan leader that should it seem within reason, when he asked for his daughter to be sent away, that Rivinar do all she could to make it happen. After the Name Breathing, he had asked, and now the Council had suggested to remove her. All Rivinar had to do was agree.

Even that felt like a betrayal to the Councilor of the Oak Tree Clan, but she couldn't break a vow once spoken.

5

~Resmine~

THE ALARM BELLS WERE chiming. Resmine couldn't imagine what had set off the alarms for Temple Row, but it had to be something big. She tried to ignore it as she continued to shovel dung from the stable floor, as a true dullard might. *No curiosity, no visible thoughts,* she told herself, though it was less of a reminder than a mantra at this point. Just a few more months, and she would have enough cobbled together to make a real break for it. If only she could get her hands on some evidence so she could convince Estan to make a break for it, too, then she could have company on the road.

Not that she'd seen Estan since his elevation into the knighthood. It was a slightly bitter thought, but it had been for the best. If Estan had continued to visit her, the priests and knights in her own order would never have believed the act that she'd put on ever since the death of her beloved Syara. Syara had found them out, and she had confronted them. Resmine had begged her not to do it, but Syara was confident that the Grey Army's corruption couldn't go all the way to the top. *My righteous angel,* Resmine sighed. There wasn't a day that passed that Resmine didn't remember her beautiful, bold knight. All she had to fill the void was the hope that someday, she would be free from the false Temple of Locke, God of Beauty and Battle.

"Oy! You, there! Girl!"

Resmine pretended not to hear the call. People assumed that hearing and mental acuity were somehow linked, and so she always made those in the temple wait to be acknowledged.

"C'mon, girl! I've not got all day! Do you not hear the claxons wailing!"

Blinking, Resmine looked up at the knight addressing her as though she were surprised to see him. "What? Me, sir?"

"Who else could I possibly mean?" the knight growled. "Fetch me my gear! We're to ride this moment!"

"We are?" Resmine dropped her shovel and began walking toward the horses, as though she meant to let them all loose. She would, too, if it wouldn't gain her a beating. It would buy whatever poor soul that had drawn the ire of the entirety of Temple Row a few more minutes, assuming the knights were more concerned with catching their horses than the culprit.

"No, no, no! The knights must ride! You are to stay well away from us!" the man said.

"I thought you wanted me to fetch your gear?" Resmine kept the amusement out of her voice only through years of practice. She was skirting the line, now. It was a balance between too slow to be useful and too slow to bother keeping alive. Normally, she would've reined it in a bit at this point, but this time felt different. This time, she felt opportunity.

"Ashes, girl! Nevermind, just stay out of my way. That Estan boy finally outed himself as a traitor and I'll not be left out of the hunt!" the knight shoved his way past Resmine and hefted his own saddle from the post. If he hadn't been in such a hurry, he may have noticed that he pushed Resmine right into position to retrieve her shovel, and he may have remembered that he hadn't bothered to put on his helmet before rushing to the stables.

The clang was still reverberating in the rafters as Resmine rode out of the stables herself on Estan's own charger, a blue roan named

Catapult. Her gear had been hidden in the rafters for months and she had thrown anything else she could into the roan's saddlebags. She would have to drop the horse off outside the gates before returning to the market for some last-minute provisions, but Catapult would be better than a guard dog when it came to keeping what gear she had safe. Hopefully, Estan would be smart enough to make it out the gates on his own, but she couldn't worry about that now. Clubbing the knight over the head with a dung-covered shovel wasn't something she could come back from.

6

~Khiri~

WHEN COUNCILOR RIVINAR summoned Khiri and Micah back to the Sky Watcher's platform, Khiri felt her half-formed hopes break on the forest floor, yards below the false sea of clouds. The look on the elder's face was enough to make Khiri want to cry.

"Khiriellen Fortiva, I am so sorry. You must venture forth into the world and seek out the one who carries the name of your destined," Councilor Rivinar said, her voice cracking with grief twice as she delivered the news.

"Am I to be exiled?" Khiri asked, searching the Councilor's eyes. "Like a murderer?"

"If the name of your destined ever changes back, you will be welcome to return to the life you were expecting... Assuming you both revert to normal, that is." The Councilor dropped her gaze. Her bottom lip was trembling with barely contained emotion, but Khiri was having a hard time feeling for the older woman.

Before Khiri could protest further, Councilor Rivinar turned to face Khiri's former soulmate, "Micah Ulimani, what will you do? With no destined, you are free to move on to your new clan, stay here, or travel as you will," Councilor Rivinar said.

"I think I might enter my house with the River Willow Clan. I had arranged to start studying with their master carpenter once we... once I was settled," Micah looked down at the platform and would not acknowledge Khiri's pleading gaze. It was a bit ridiculous for her to expect anything else, but Khiri's hopes had sprung up of their own accord when the Councilor mentioned travel. To have someone from the Trees with her out in the larger world... Even if Micah was mad at her, couldn't forgive her, and blamed her for everything, he would've been welcome to join her. She was going to miss him almost as much as her parents; more in some ways. They'd shared secrets, stories, and adventures since they were children. No one knew her as well. It hurt that he couldn't even look at her right now, when she was effectively being banished from the Life Trees.

"Very well, I will let Councilor Havalene know to expect you."

With another deep breath, Councilor Rivinar turned to face Khiri. Whether it was the shock wearing thin, or just the sharp emotions lending the moment additional focus, Khiri couldn't help but notice how shear the elder elf's skin was, showing veins beneath that looked like wood grain. Just another reminder that life was bound to the Trees, and Khiri wouldn't be tied to them. "Khiriellen Fortiva, you have two days to make whatever preparations you must and to make your farewells. May the spirits of the forest guide your feet."

Micah turned and left so quickly that Khiri was starting to get angry. It was not as though she had hurt him on purpose. He had brought her the ring that had changed everything, after all. She was shaking as she descended from the Sky Watcher platform.

Her mother would know what she would need to travel into the world of the humans. She would speak to Leyani and figure out what advice her mother had to give. Genovar had already given her his best hunting knife, but maybe her father had an extra bow and quiver amongst his armaments. If not, she would have to go to the clan's weaponsmith. Khiri did not think she could take two full days of whispers and rumors, and decided to set out as soon as possible.

ONLY A FEW DAYS AGO, Khiri and her father had taken the spiral stairs around the great trunk of the Oak Wood Clan's Life Tree to descend into the forest to hunt together one last time before Khiri became an adult. That trip down the steps had been one of laughter and a few tears, but mostly happy ones. With each step Khiri took on this trip, her feet felt heavier, as though someone was filling her pack with rocks just to make things harder. Even so, she reached the bottom stair all too quickly.

Standing on the final step before the drop to the forest floor, Khiri felt like she was standing at the edge of the world. She had tried to say goodbye to Micah, despite his anger. The idea that she might never see him again had pushed her to try and make amends. Micah had refused to see her, saying that he was too busy with his own preparations. Her parents had been sad, but it was easier to part with them since they had already been expecting her to leave. None of them brought up the idea that Khiri might never make a return trip.

Bracing herself against the massive tree trunk, she inhaled as deeply as she could and prepared to make the ten-foot drop to the world's surface. The distance was designed to prevent predators and bandits from climbing unchecked into the village. There was a secret catch that an elven archer could shoot that would cause a rope ladder would drop. As this was the last opportunity Khiri would have to make the jump, and she'd always enjoyed the rush of the wind, she ignored it. Khiri had leapt down many times in the days that her father had taught her to hunt, but she had always known she would return home when the hunt was done. Her insides twisted at yet another bitter reminder that she wouldn't be coming back.

Before she could work up the gumption to make the drop, there was a crashing noise and the underbrush of the forest rustled violently in line toward the clearing at the base of the Life Tree. A man with dark brown hair and a slight tan, clothed in hard, dirty, dark leather armor, broke through the edge of the clearing and fell, scuffling his way back to his feet as though rabid bears were at his heels. He made it to the wall-like trunk and searched in vain for a hand-hold or foothold to make his way up. Khiri watched silently, curious that he had not seemed to see her in his desperation.

Three more humans emerged from the forest, wearing uniformly black attire that hid their faces behind cowls. One of them was holding a sword leveled toward the cowering stranger, one of them seemed unarmed, while the third held a glowing pebble in a throwing position. They did not seem to notice her any more than he did.

"Demon spit!" the man hissed. "How did you even find me here?"

"You are our prey. We were hired, we come. Nothing personal," the first of black clad humans answered. He was the one holding the pebble, and he threw his cowl back to reveal a pale, bald man with deeply sunken eyes.

"*Blood*," a second requested in a thin, whisper-like voice. It swayed slightly as it spoke, as though its words were being sung rather than sibilated. "*Red, flowing, hot, silky, copper blood… Rip, tear, shred, crunch, kill…*"

"All in good time, brother," the first one promised. "First, we must ask him questions. Our employer wanted answers before his death. Now, sir, what did you receive in Tenowa?"

"Go to hell!" the fugitive spat.

"Temper, temper," the bald man reproved. "My employer wants to know what it was that you were entrusted with. I confess, I find myself a bit curious why anyone would want you to guard something. You are possibly the easiest prey we've ever hunted."

"I have nothing to say to you, assassin. One of your allies is obviously a Flayer, and I can only guess at what your mother dabbled with," the fugitive growled. "If you're plannin' to kill me, have done!"

Khiri moved slowly, trying not to attract the attention of the assassins. The voice calling for blood had definitely been a Flayer, creatures formed when a human, elf or dwarf bound their blood to that of a demon in return for the demon's ability to grant a wish. The Life Tree Clans killed Flayers on sight, though there were usually three to four clansman per Flayer. Fortunately, not even a Flayer could make it up the trunk of a Life Tree and Khiri's arrows rarely missed their marks. She strung her bow and readied two arrows; drawing the first and leaning the second against the trunk of the Life Tree.

Without warning, she loosed the first and it plunged into the Flayer's chest. Before those below had a chance to react, the first arrow was followed by the second. The Flayer fell with an ear-piercing shriek as the creature began flailing and steaming as the demon blood forced itself out of a body that could no longer house it. Springing back toward the brush, the remaining assassins crouched into more defensive stances, their weapons now trained up toward Khiri's hiding place. She already had another missile cocked and ready, aimed for the heart of the bald man.

"Assassins have no place hunting here," Khiri stated with more confidence than she felt. Her leather armor was made for fending off animal claws and tree bark. It would not do much against a good blade. She trusted it even less to the glowing pebble, which she assumed was a rune. It had been a long time since her mother had told her stories about human mages, rune casters, and dwarven wonders in faraway lands. What any of those things were doing at the base of her Life Tree, she hadn't the slightest inclination. Once the assassins were gone, maybe she could find some answers.

The last assassin threw down her cowl, revealing a woman with short black hair and dark features that were contorted with rage. She started to rush the tree, mindless of the man still near the ground. Only the bald man's hand placed upon her shoulder restrained her. "How dare you threaten those of the Venom Guild!" she barked. "How dare you kill my brother!"

Instead of replying vocally, Khiri moved her aim for the woman's chest.

"I think the elf has made her point," the bald man said, assessing Khiri with hard eyes. "We will find you again later," he promised. "Both of you."

"What! She killed... Murdered..." the woman's voice faltered as she dropped her gaze from Khiri, "and he's right there! We can drop them both and be on our way before she finds the courage to loose that arrow!"

Khiri steeled herself. It had been the worst week of her life, and it was very tempting to kill the assassins just to relieve herself of some of her tension. Letting assassins live to hunt her later did not seem wise, but Khiri knew she was not a killer. If she were to become a murderer, she would never be able to return to the Life Trees, even if she found Telgan Korsborn the very next day. It would be different if they tried to kill her first, though.

As the bald man smiled, Khiri knew that he understood exactly what her limits were. "Patience, sister. She has us at a disadvantage today. There is always tomorrow," he bowed and faded into the forest.

Scowling, the woman waited until he was gone, then looked up at Khiri with a smirk that conveyed utter loathing and contempt. "This is not over, elf," she promised darkly.

With that, she also faded into the trees.

7

~Estan~

THE LIGHT OF ESTAN's campfire flickered off the surrounding trees as he scrubbed at his plate-mail with a rag and some polish that he had found in the bottom of one of his saddle bags. No matter how hard he tried to remove it, the orange dye had left a permanent coppery hue on what had once been silver.

His equipment and his horse had mysteriously met him outside of Seirane, including enough trail rations for him to stay out of cities and out of sight for a full week. Loni had bid him goodbye before he was out the gate. He hoped fervently for her safety. Though Estan had told her as little as possible, she was still guilty of aiding in his escape.

With an irritated huff, he dropped the piece of armor he had been working on. It was no use. On the other hand, maybe it was for the best that he was unable to restore it. He was no longer a Knight of the Protective Hand. Why should he toil to undo what was deemed by fate? A fallen knight should have fallen armor.

A rustling noise echoed through the underbrush, making Estan's internal grumblings cut short. He unsheathed his sword and rose slowly from the log he had been sitting on. The night had been clear of clouds, and so Estan had not bothered to set up a tent. His horse, Catapult, a blue roan gelding, twitched his skin nervously on the other side of the fire.

"I didn't think I'd catch up with you this quickly," a silhouette appeared out of the shadows of the trees. It was slender, and Estan got the impression that it was a woman.

"Who is it? Show yourself! I am armed," Estan warned.

"Estan, relax. It's me," a familiar voice said, as the figure entered the light of the fire, revealing a narrow face with high cheekbones and a mischievous arch to her eyebrows. Her hair was swept back in a high tail of light brown ringlets, where they didn't escape to hang loosely around a pair of hazel eyes that he struggled to place. "Resmine."

"Resmine?" Estan's mind flashed on a dozen images at once. Resmine and himself, about six summers old, covered in jam from when they had tried to sneak a pot out of the larder, and it had dropped and shattered on the floor. Resmine smiling mischievously at him when they were fourteen summers, just before they jumped into the sacred waters of Lake Reshin. She had been working toward becoming a shield-bearer for Locke, the God of Beauty and Battle, being raised by the members of that temple as he had been raised by the Temple of Taymahr. "What are you doing here?"

"Who do you think got you Catapult?" she said with a grin, her brown curls bouncing as she approached the fire. She didn't lower her hands as she strode toward him. She was covered in brown leather straps and buckles, the armor of a messenger and not the armor one in service of Locke. "Not your little girlfriend, though I will give you that she's got way more spunk than I thought."

"Loni hasn't been my girlfriend in years," he said, not lowering his sword. "Why are you here?"

"Estan, you are a piece of work. Do you really think that you're the only one who's found out about the temple infiltrators?" Resmine laughed, though the bitterness of her tone held no humor. "The reason they came after you was that you reported yourself to them."

"You knew? You know? How long have you known?" Estan demanded, lowering the tip of his sword.

Resmine walked over to Catapult and offered her hand. Catapult snuffled it, then bumped against her, insisting on an affectionate pat. "I've known since they tried to recruit me, just before Syara died. They test you out, try to figure how open you are to the idea of following a different set of ideals, and whether you would be an asset to them. I played dumb. The more they probed, the dumber I pretended to be. That's why I fell out of touch. You would've given me away."

Estan thought about it. He had not heard from Resmine since they were twenty summers old. Any time that they had gotten in trouble growing up, she had turned on a dumb-as-a-chicken routine that was incredibly convincing until they caught him gaping at her. Finally, Estan sheathed his weapon and resumed his seat.

"How did you catch up with me without a horse?" he asked.

"That was easier than you'd think," she continued to pet Catapult, scratching under his harness before moving on to check his hooves. The war horse seemed to take this as a matter of course, allowing himself to be moved and cosetted in equal measure. "I'm not being looked for, so I haven't had to avoid the roads. Now, where are we going?"

Hesitating, Estan studied Resmine. He wanted to trust her. She was one of his oldest friends, or at least, she had been. The way she had just dropped out of his life, and reappearing now, just as the whole world seemed to have turned on him. It seemed a little too convenient, and Estan had only recently learned the flavor of betrayal. "We? Why are you helping me? What are you hoping to get out of this?"

Resmine sighed and left Catapult, apparently satisfied that Estan hadn't neglected his horse in the space of one afternoon on the run. She wandered over to the fire and tossed another handful of brambles onto the embers. "I'm tired of playing dumb, Estan. I'm tired of hiding out in the stables of false temples and I'm tired of pretending I don't see it when people I know and respect disappear. People like you... People like her," the pain in Resmine's voice struck Estan like a physical force. Suddenly, he understood.

"Syara's death wasn't an accident. They killed her," Estan's eyes welled up with tears of grief. Syara had been five years older, and had been tasked with watching them when all of the adults were too busy. To him, Syara had been like a sister, but she and Resmine had been much, much closer. He had already mourned her parting, but knowing that she'd been killed by the same people that were out to get him made the pain of her loss fresh.

Unable to speak, Resmine nodded. Estan remembered the first day that Syara and Resmine had kissed, the radiant expression that Resmine had been unable to hide for days. They had become lovers when Resmine hit her seventeenth summer. Syara had achieved her knighthood and then Estan had not heard from her or Resmine for four or five summers. He had assumed they had just become too busy, as he had acquired more duties within the Temple of Taymahr. "I'm so sorry, Resmine," he rose and laid a hand on her shoulder. "You can come with me. I should have known I could trust you."

"No," she shook her head. Using the heel of her palm to wipe her tears away, Resmine forced herself to smile at Estan. It was a smile that was still a touch sad, but it was closer to the one he remembered from their childhood. "You are right to be cautious. Anyone connected with the temples could be one of the Gray Army. So... Where are we going?"

"I'm heading toward the Life Tree Clans," Estan said.

"The elves?" Resmine's eyes widened. "In all of the gods' names, why the elves?"

Estan picked up the rag and armor that he had been working with, and took them over to his saddlebags. He pulled out the book that had been his constant companion in previous nights. "An elf wrote this. It's the only written history the Temple of Taymahr had on the War of the Burning Valley."

Tossing the book to Resmine, he dug out a withered apple and bit into it. She studied the cover and lifted it up to point inquiringly at the punctured area that had protected Estan's chest. "I was lucky enough to be hiding it under my armor when my foster father tried to silence me," Estan shrugged.

"Fair enough," Resmine said. Flipping through the book, she opened it to the very end. She scanned the last few pages and snapped the book shut. "It sounds like he thought the Gray Army would not return, let alone infiltrate our society and corrupt it from the inside."

Estan grunted an agreement around a mouthful of sweet apple mush. "That book is written by someone that I know will work with us to clear the temples of filth," he swallowed. "I just hope that elf will believe a couple of renegades, and will be able to help."

THREE DAYS ON THE ROAD and Estan was starting to remember other things about Resmine that he had forgotten, like the fact that she had a bit of a temper. After a day's walking, she would get cranky and start griping about how stiff her feet were or how tired her legs had become. As soon as he distracted her with a word puzzle or a riddle, she would calm down, but he was already starting to miss being on his own.

It would be another two weeks before they reached the Life Trees according to his map. They would pass through Jarelton, a fortress city. Resmine's armor disguised her as a messenger, but Estan and Catapult looked too much like a knight and his mount, even with his armor stowed and oddly colored. They were approaching the northern gate when Resmine had a moment of brilliance.

"They are looking for a Knight of the Protective Hand that's escaping divine justice, right?" she asked.

"Yes. That's the problem we've been trying to figure out for the last few days," Estan said, feeling a bit testy himself.

"So instead of hiding that you are a knight, why don't we just say you are a Knight of the Battered Iris? They wear copper-plated armor. This far from Seinare, they may not look twice at the designs stamped into the plating. When they ask why we're seeking entrance to the city, we can tell them that we are hunting you," Resmine face was etched with the same mischievous look she would get when they were younger and about to get away with something.

Rolling the idea over in his mind, Estan was willing to admit that it was better than anything he had come up with. He pulled out his armor and started strapping it on. With the road dust coating his skin, he looked even darker than usual. He had stopped shaving and so he also had a few days growth of beard. It was unlikely anyone would recognize him at first glance.

Jarelton was situated so that it took up the majority of Mytana's western border. It only had three gates: one to the north, one to the east, and one to the west. Coming in through the north was chancy since it was the direction that anyone traveling from Seirane would take, but he was disguised as someone who had nothing to hide.

After much discussion, he and Resmine had decided to enter the city separately. She was going to wait within the forest for a full day after he made it in the gate, and then find him at a tavern somewhere in the mid-city. He would spend the day pretending to search for himself and gathering supplies before hunkering himself over a pint. It would give her the opportunity to search for him, while looking like she was there to deliver a message to a holy knight.

They spent hours going over the back-up plans in case something went wrong at any juncture. If he was caught at the gate, she was to try and find out where he was being held. Then Resmine would go on alone, find the elf and mount a rescue. Estan thought there was also the possibility that he may get captured while in town, attending to their supplies. If he disappeared quietly, and no one knew where to find him, Resmine was to get out of the city as fast as she could. Still, she would head to find the elf.

"Why always to the elf?" she demanded. "Surely there is someone else that we could find that would be loyal to those who fought the Gray Army?"

"I don't doubt that others exist," Estan sighed. He pulled out the battered book and ran his fingers over the worn bindings, tracing the spot that had taken a dagger for him. "But who are we that those people would trust us? Two temple brats on the run from our betters? We need a voice added to ours that they would trust. The elf that wrote this was one of the key players in turning the tide against the Gray Army. He was one of the seven that sealed away the Flayer Mage that all of the other generals in the tainted legion reported to, according to this. I know it's not a lot to go on, but it's the best lead we've got."

"Alright... We need the elf," Resmine surrendered. "Just... try not to disappear on me, okay?"

"I promise, I will do my best," Estan tried to give her a reassuring smile, but he couldn't keep the worry out of his eyes.

8

~Khiri~

SEVERAL MOMENTS OF silence lingered after the assassins had slunk back into the shadows of the forest. Khiri watched for any sign of their return, not relaxing her grip on her bow even after the sounds of insects began to return to the forest. Small game creatures began to resume whatever activities the Flayer and his kin had interrupted. The hunter in her told her the danger was truly departed, but still she hesitated to drop her guard. Her fingers were beginning to ache from the way the string resisted her draw; it was likely that her shoulder would hurt even worse in the morning. She debated whether to return to her father and warn him of what had just passed so that he could warn the rest of the clan. Perhaps that was really just her wish to prolong her time at home, before she left for good. If she had to walk the staircase to the forest once more, she wasn't sure that she'd make it down a second time. It had been hard enough the first time, and who knew what would be waiting for her when she returned. Maybe the assassins would be back, and maybe they would bring even more Flayers.

"My thanks," the man that had sheltered against the trunk of the Life Tree said. He was still tense, looking from where Khiri stood to the wall of underbrush that his hunters had vanished behind and back again. "What are you doing up there, anyway?"

"You interrupted the beginning of my journey. I was trying to find the courage to jump," Khiri lowered her bow, but kept her arrow strung. "Why were they hunting you?"

He laughed, sounding more tired than amused. "I owe you my life. I promise, I will answer any questions you have, just as soon as my heart stops yammerin' so hard that the entire forest can hear it."

"What are you doing out here? The human road is at least two days from here, and the traders wait for us at the designated camp site," Khiri said. "I don't think we've ever had a human visit the Oak Tree Clan."

"This is the Oak Tree Clan's Life Tree, then? I... An elf by the name of Genovar Fortiva," the man's eyes practically lit up despite the shadows cast by the limbs of the Life Tree above them. "I don't suppose you know him?"

Khiri's pulse quickened, but this time it was with the excitement of curiosity. Who outside of the clans would be looking for her father? She'd never heard of him having any human friends, but maybe he'd gone to trade with her mother a time or two before Khiri had been born. That would hardly account for the assassins, though. "I may," she said slowly. "Why do you seek Genovar?"

"Something about a danger to his daughter... A warning sent by a mage he once befriended during the War of the Burning Valley," the man said. "The mage said I could offer the daughter's name as proof, since none but friends know of her existence."

"Speak, then," Khiri said, feeling a little overwhelmed. Her father was in a war? When? How had he returned to the clans?

"Khiriellen Fortiva, daughter of Genovar and Leyani," the man said, like it was a password with no real meaning.

"Yes, that is my name," Khiri was beginning to feel light-headed. None of this made sense to her. A mage her father had met during a war knew her name, which meant that her father had been keeping secrets from her. Her mother must have known, too. She went to trade with the humans all the time, which made her mother the most likely point of contact with this mage person. Why wouldn't they tell her that they had contacts in the larger world? Especially when she was about to be thrust out of the clans? "What is this danger?"

He looked up at her with renewed interest. "That's you, huh? That figures. You said you were about to travel... maybe I should give you the warning instead."

"Whatever danger this mage friend was warning about... There's nothing my father can do about it now," Khiri sighed. "Look, friend, I'm about to leave the clans and I'm not sure I'll be returning. If this message you were to deliver had something to do with my Name Breathing, then you're too late. The damage has been done."

"Sounds like I'm in a difficult spot then, but as you are the daughter in question, it does make much more sense to pass this on to you," the man said. He dug out a slip of paper and waved it just far enough out for Khiri to see. He started to leave the safety of the Life Tree's trunk before jumping at the sound of a bush rustling on the edge of the treeline. A squirrel jumped out, chattered at the intruder to its territory, and then bounded across the ground as though the man had offered chase rather than nervous glances. "You know, if you're leaving this place anyway, I'd be glad for the company on the road. May even be able to help you get where you're going a might quicker. I was an army messenger back during the war. Learned most of the roadways and a few hidden tracks across the whole of Mytana."

Studying the treeline around the clearing, Khiri considered it. She couldn't stand on the steps to her former home forever. It was possible that whatever the missive warned about had not happened yet, or that the letter would have more information about the ring that Micah had given her.

"Fine. Do you think the assassins will return as soon as I jump down?" Khiri asked, trying for a jocular tone and missing. The encounter had shaken her more than she wanted to admit.

"They won't return until nightfall. You took out their Flayer and the Venom Guild always strikes in threes. It will take them that long to notify the guild that they need a new Flayer," the man said. He seemed much less jumpy than he had a moment prior. Perhaps it was because he found the idea of a traveling companion comforting, or perhaps telling Khiri about the Venom Guild's practices had reminded him that he was safe for at least a few hours. Khiri didn't even know the man's name, so guessing his moods was as useful as looking for stars from her current position.

Her excuses for staying on the stairs were wearing thin. She knew Flayers could travel through shadows, though only over land not above ground or across water. That was why the Life Trees were safe unless the Flayer was created inside the village itself. With a deep breath, Khiri swung the arrow back into her quiver, replaced her bow, and jumped. Wind slithered across her ears and wrapped itself around her limbs for a few brief seconds before the ground clapped against her feet. She rolled the impact into her limbs, letting the rest of her body absorb the pain that would've hampered her ankles had they been left to deal with the blow on their own.

"So, what should I call you? I know your name, already, o'course, but that's not the same as an introduction," the man said. Up close, she could see the gray hairs peppering his hair, the stubble on his jawline and his hazel eyes. He was easily two heads taller than her, which made her feel as though she were already at a disadvantage.

"Khiri... I go by Khiri," she said. She had no idea how human introductions were supposed to go, and she hadn't met anyone new since she was very young. From up on the stairs, this had seemed much easier. Now, Khiri wasn't sure whether she should bow, do something with her hands, or offer the man her waterskin.

"Fennick Worish," he stuck out his hand, "and my life is yours. I wasn't kidding about that. You did me a service and I am honorbound to repay my debt."

She looked at his hand reaching toward her and cocked an eyebrow. "What's that for?"

"It's called a hand. You grasp it with your hand and pump your arm up and down, usually two times unless you're feeling really insecure," Fennick chuckled. Khiri delayed for a moment of indecision, then took his hand and pumped as instructed. Fennick nodded in approval.

"Now, then... I believe we had an agreement," Khiri said. "The letter?"

Again, Fennick nodded. He handed Khiri the paper that he'd flashed at her when she'd still been aloft.

The letter was heavier than Khiri had thought it would be. Folded into an envelope, it was embossed with wax seal insignia that she had never seen before, but that was hardly surprising. Up until she'd reached the bottom of the Life Tree and encountered assassins and a stranger, there was a lot of the human world Khiri had never seen before. She touched the seal to check for enchantments, then drew her hunting knife and sliced the wax off, taking a small bit of the paper with it. The envelope spread out into the letter itself.

DEAR GENOVAR,

I hope this letter finds you well. You wrote me to let me know about your daughter's sensitivity to magic, and I originally advised you not to be overly concerned. I have new reason to believe that this could be a danger to her. There are spells that can target her sensitivity as long as she is untrained. She does not have to become a mage, but I do suggest that you send her to me. I can teach her to focus her potential enough to block these unfriendly forces, or at least make her aware of the danger.

Ever your friend,

Maleck Dorell

Khiri frowned and folded the letter back into its envelope shape. If this had arrived before her Name Breathing, things may have been different. Maybe she would have sensed the magical potential of the ring she now wore, or she may have insisted on testing the ring before letting Micah slip it on her finger. Councilor Rivinar had said she detected human magic on the ring, and Khiri had no idea where to start looking if left to her own devices... Maybe this Maleck would be able to help her with more than just her ear tingles.

"The mage that had you deliver this," Khiri held the envelope up between Fennick's eyes and her face. "Could you take me to him?"

Scratching his stubble, Fennick appeared to be considering her request, "I suppose I could do that. Are you sure that's what you want to do?"

"Unless you know where to find someone named Telgan Korsborn," she replied. Perhaps, if humans were as closely knit as the clans, this journey would be much shorter than she thought. A fledgling hope sparked in her chest as soon as she suggested the name, but it was quickly dashed as she saw the negative forming on the messenger's mouth.

"No, that doesn't sound familiar. This mage, though, he lives on the other side of Mytana.... Mytana is currently at war with Eerilor. It might be a little dangerous," Fennick grimaced.

"When aren't the humans at war?" Khiri said without thinking.

Fennick opened his mouth to protest and then gave her a good-natured shrug. "Fair enough, but you aren't up in your tree now. Human dangers are now dangerous to you too."

Her heart twinged with the reminder. She had already forgotten that this wasn't just a hunting trip, where she would be safely away from things like wars and Flayers by the time that night fell. Remembering the Flayer, Khiri reaffirmed her original decision. They had to get moving, and war or no war, Maleck was the only lead she had.

"Toward the mage is still my best option," she said.

"At least you don't lack for conviction," Fennick sighed. "Alright. You win. We best get moving... We're burning daylight."

FENNICK HAD CHOSEN to make camp under a cedar tree, insisting that the smell deterred insects. She supposed that was a human concern. Insects rarely bothered elves, except for the occasional ear buzz. He insisted on putting up a tent, even though the night was calm, assuring her that she would be happy that it was there by morning. Again, Khiri assumed this was a human concern, but didn't argue.

"How do we guard against the assassins?" she asked.

"Best we can do is keep watch," Fennick sounded uncomfortable. "We'll avoid building fires until we reach the road."

"Two watches, half a night each?" Khiri offered. Occasionally, when she and her father had gone hunting, they had done watches. Genovar had insisted that it was good practice for when she was part of a unit. Looking back, Khiri wondered what kind of unit her father had been thinking of... Elves rarely hunted in groups, and when they did, there were other ways to ward a camp. How much of her training was hunting, and how much had been due to her father's mysterious warrior past?

Her companion nodded. They had spent the day walking, often in silence. The man had a sense of humor that Khiri didn't entirely understand, but was patient when she had questions. In the sporadic conversations that had popped up now and again, she had gleaned that he was a retired army messenger from the country of Firinia. Instead of going mercenary, he had decided to become a private courier. It was more exciting than farming, and a lot healthier than fighting for a living, providing the news he delivered was good and no one objected to his carrying it.

It felt odd to Khiri, sitting underneath a tree instead of in its branches. She sat down on the ground in front of the small tent, really not more than a sheet propped on two sticks, and pulled out some of the food she had packed for her journey. Her father had a store of venison jerky that he had pressed on her, and her mother had given her a stash of hard cheese that Leyani had traded for during her last trading trip. Cheese was one of those glorious creations that Khiri's people simply hadn't bothered with until the humans had stopped dying from trial and error. Khiri also had some scones with cinnamon and raisins that Micah had made for them to carry to the new house. They smelled like home, and filled her with a longing to be back in the open-air kitchen with her family. Not that they ever encouraged her to cook. Not after the one time.

Fennick unpacked some of his own trail food, a few apples and some hard bread, as he sat down across from her. They were both positioned so that they could watch the surrounding forest, so long as they did not become too absorbed in their meal.

"We need some more companions," Fennick grumbled. "Half a night's watch, and this constant looking over our shoulders... It'll get old real quick."

Khiri did not reply, though she privately agreed. Tearing one of her scones into small bits, she thought about how long the road before them would be. They had yet to leave the lands that elves hunted. Tomorrow, they could count on reaching the human roads, and once there, they had to cross Mytana. According to Fennick, Mytana was not a small country. She was embarking on a quest that covered hundreds of miles, much of that in contested land.

"Why are Mytana and Eerilor at war?" she asked.

"Water rights, mainly. Eerilor, dwarven country, mostly—that means lots of smithies—decided they were going to build a dam to power their bellows. They don't pollute the river none 'cause they know that farmers use it to irrigate crops further down. Between that new dam and the farmers, not much of that river is making it down to Mytana anymore. That river, the Jaiya, was never a major water source for Mytana but they got their drawers twisted over it because they—mostly human folk—perceive it as an insult that Eerilor never asked their permission to 'steal their water,'" Fennick explained. "It's one of those silly details that people like to shed blood over."

"Oh," Khiri frowned. The idea of owning a river confused her. What was the point of claiming water that ran away faster than any game? Even the river's path changed over time, creating crescent lakes and tearing canyons into the earth. Her parents had told her of such wonders, though she had never before contemplated how they knew about them. The Ota River that ran beneath the River Willow Clan's Life Tree had created none of these things.

"What are the Life Trees?" Fennick asked. "Your people live in them, but they're too big to be natural. Fifty men could stand around the trunk of the smallest and not touch hands."

"They are the Life Trees. Arra had need of tenders, healers, and so it chose seven trees that stood just a bit taller than the rest. Power flowed into the roots, up into the limbs, and called the wood elves to existence. We were once immortal while the world was awake, but then the humans and dwarves came with their violence and greed. They robbed Arra of much of her life blood, and she slept. Our people, unable to draw upon her power, were introduced to death. Death is not really death among my people. We fall asleep upon the bark of the Life Trees that we were once called from and are reabsorbed, our energies given freely to grow and protect that which we called home in life. After centuries of our elven kin have passed, the Life Trees are what they have become. While we live on the Life Trees, we know no illness and the elements will not harm us," Khiri said, trying to ignore the sadness that was growing inside of her. If she died during her mission, her life energy would not return to its kin. Like a murderer, her energy would expel itself into whatever plants were nearby and become food for the grazers. "It is said that the voices of the sleeping elves can still be heard dreaming within the branches, if one knows how to listen."

"That's a heavy heritage. Why would you leave?" Fennick's brow wrinkled as he crunched into his last apple.

"Because I have to find Telgan Korsborn," Khiri said. "I breathed his name."

Fennick looked like he wanted to ask her more, but a twig snapped in the forest. He sprang to his feet, drawing a dagger from his boot. Khiri tried not to smirk as the deer, nearly as startled as the human, bounded from them into the thicker shelter of the trees. "I would have warned you, had it been a threat," she said calmly.

With a grunt, Fennick sank slowly back to his seat. "I'll take first watch," he offered, tossing his apple core into the forest.

In one nimble movement, Khiri got to her feet and scooped up her pack. She studied the tent, then looked up into the cedar. There was a promising looking crook between two of the larger limbs. With the ease of one who had climbed trees her entire life, she hauled herself through the maze of branches and nestled against the bark as though it were the embrace of an old friend.

"I'll wake you when the moon hits its peak," she heard Fennick say into the dusk.

9

~Estan~

THE GUARDS ON EITHER side of the drawbridge to Jarelton gave Estan a cursory nod; one beacon of order to another, just doing their duty. No dirty looks, no accusatory fingers pointed in Estan's direction, and no double-takes of recognition to make Estan hesitate or suspect he'd been found out. Just the dull eyes of the barely interested, making sure that no one coming into the city was actively murdering the other travelers on this stretch of bridge. Still, Estan hoped that the sweat dripping down his nose would be shrugged off as caused by the heat as opposed to his nerves.

Estan entered Jarelton only to find it a mad house of activity and stench. A sad, suffering breeze struggled to move fresh air into space occupied by the odors of animal sweat, sewage, unwashed people and produce, and other, less savory scents. Stalls and shops were everywhere, offering foodstuffs of every quality, runes and rune charging, clothes, weapons, tools, and trinkets. Seirane, in comparison, was a beacon of order and civilization. In Seirane, the stalls were only allowed to set up in specific roads, but Estan saw several stalls that blocked off entire streets. The stone streets and buildings that were accessible were ancient and narrow, crowded with people and filth. Estan moved his coin purse to the space between his chest and his breastplate after spotting a few pickpockets going about their trade.

"Come on, Catapult," Estan patted the blue roan's nose. It was comforting to have his horse with him in the strange city. Catapult had been with him through things like his first night in an army camp, his first solo scouting mission, and his first battle. It seemed only right that Catapult should be his companion in the first city he visited outside of his home.

"Knights always be talkin' to their horses or are you just crazy?" a small woman with copper skin and black hair asked. She was close enough to Catapult that Estan worried for her safety, but the horse barely flicked an ear.

"Uh..." Estan said uncertainly, embarrassment making his own ears burn and his cheeks flush.

"Ha! Look at that! Someone as dark as him blushin' like a virgin bride with her husband twixt her nethers!" the woman elbowed a man standing next to her that looked similar enough to be a relation. Her brother or cousin, perhaps. He merely nodded to Estan, as though this was an introduction and not mockery.

Estan ducked into the crowd to put some distance between himself and the two strangers. He hadn't thought anyone would hear him in the bedlam of the city streets. There were almost as many noises as there were odors.

Stopping to buy a skewer of roasting meat and vegetables, Estan tried to focus on his plan of action. He had to buy supplies. Between Resmine and himself, the food was running low. Neither of them were fantastic hunters, nor did they like to stop long enough to forage. They were trained for military travel, which did not include a lot of pauses. Eating was done on the trail, or not at all, with the exception of food cooked over a campfire in the very late evening or very early morning.

Looking for a shop or stall that carried jerky or salt pork, Estan moved on toward the center of the city. Along the way, he found a farmer selling apples and pears and another stall sold him some hard cheeses. Estan also started watching for a baker's shop.

Finally, he found a baker's shop called the Golden Crust that was located right next to a stall of cured meats that included everything from cow to fish. He went into the Golden Crust after picking his favorites from the jerky stall to find that the Golden Crust was more of a cafe than a shop.

Catapult was tied to a post outside with an employee of the Golden Crust watching him, not that Estan was worried about anyone trying to steal the fiery gelding. The last stranger that had tried to touch his lead rope had gotten a rather nasty bite on his hand.

"Welcome, sir," a man in a shirt and pants of good, sturdy material and light-weight vest. "Would you like a table?"

"I'm sorry," Estan said, starting to back out the door. "I thought this was a bakery."

"It's no problem, sir," the man assured him, still smiling. "We get that all the time, and do in fact sell breads and pastries. Would you care for a cheese pasty? We fold a thin crust around a creamed cheese that we sweeten with a strawberry glaze, when they're in season."

"I think I'm in the wrong place," Estan insisted.

"Feel free to come back any time," the man said, retaining his good humor even in the face of total rejection.

As Estan was walking back out, his book on the War of the Burning Valley fell out of its hiding place, having been dislodged by the frequent disturbances of his money pouch. Estan bent to pick it up and noticed that the man was watching him very intently.

"Excuse me, sir," the man said, his brow wrinkling. "What is that?"

"A history of the War of the Burning Valley," Estan admitted.

"The one by Genovar Fortiva?" the man asked, his voice taking on a quality close to reverence.

"I... I don't know," Estan held up the book so the man could see it clearly. "I'm afraid it's a bit damaged."

"May I see it, lad?" the man's voice lost its professional quality and took on an older, more world-weary tone. It was the voice of a man that had seen war and was trying to forget it. Estan handed the book to him, feeling a kinship with the man he now knew to be a veteran. Opening to the first page, the veteran read the first few paragraphs with an intensity that echoed Estan's own feelings for the work. "That's it alright. Genovar was an elf, you see. The only elf on our side of the lines. Genovar wasn't just a fighter, he was a natural-born leader. One of the best I've ever seen. The other elves wouldn't be budged from those Trees of theirs, but we only needed the one."

"Thank you," Estan smiled an odd, sad sort of smile. He was grateful for the shared knowledge; he now had a name, which would be much more helpful once he got to the Life Trees.

The man nodded, and then the moment passed and he donned the professional smile. Two more guests had entered the Golden Crust, seeking to be greeted by a friendly face, not a forgotten soldier.

RESMINE FOUND ESTAN contemplating a pint of lager in a tavern just off the main thoroughfare. He had ordered three before she had shown up, not really drinking them but nursing one until it was flat enough that it needed replacing. Once, another patron in a drunken stupor picked up the tankard in front of him and knocked it back before handing Estan back the drained pint mug with a happy belch.

Estan hardly noticed Resmine come in, he was so lost in thoughts of his book and satisfaction of finally having a name for his long-admired author.

"We've got trouble," Resmine said by way of greeting.

"I found out the name of the elf," he replied.

"That's great, Estan, but me first. Look what I found in one of the seedier places I ambled into to look for you," Resmine pushed a thick roll of parchment toward Estan.

Frowning, Estan gripped one edge carefully and unwound the poster. "Rogue Knight: Reward offered to anyone bringing information to the Venom Guild on current whereabouts of a missing brother of the Knighthood of the Protective Hand. He answers to the name of Estan and measures roughly six feet in height. Dark brown skin and eyes, no tattoos or missing appendages. The Venom Guild thanks you," he read.

"The Venom Guild... you know, assassins," Resmine said, dropping her voice to just above a whisper. "They've sent assassins after you. That means they aren't going to stop chasing us, even if we decided to lie low for a few years."

"We weren't going to lie low. You said it yourself; you are sick of hiding. If they send assassins, we'll fight them off," Estan shrugged. He brought his current pint up to his lips, before remembering that it was drained. With a sigh, he set the mug down. Burning through what money they had on cheap taproom ale was not going to do anyone much good, and it was time to return his mind to his mission. "I'm not the unblooded boy that pushed you into haystacks."

"These assassins employ Flayers," Resmine argued. "We won't know how much of a threat we're facing until they track us down the first time. How do you plan to prepare for something like that?"

Estan rubbed his chin thoughtfully for a moment. Flayers were a much bigger issue than normal mortal assassins. Even the low-level Flayers could move through shadows faster than a horse could gallop.

"We'll figure it out. There's only a few more days of travel between us and the Life Trees. In the meantime, I'd rather not carry this around." Estan rose and took the parchment over to the fireplace in the center of the room, crumpling it in his hand. He picked up a log and tossed it and the reward notice onto the flames, nodding to the barkeep. The man held up three fingers and pointed to the sign posted next to the bar that had ale, bread, and a few standard food items followed by prices. Dropping a coin that was only slightly too large onto the counter, Estan walked out the door.

Resmine had already started to untie Catapult. The horse whinnied a complaint that Estan assumed had something to do with being left in the streets of Jarelton for so long. Estan couldn't blame him; he was more than ready to leave the city as well. While Estan hadn't reacted very strongly to Resmine's news inside the warm light of the tavern's fireplace, the threat of Flayers was beginning to sink in.

Allowing Resmine to guide their way through the maze of Jarelton's streets, Estan rode Catapult toward the western gate. Soon, Jarelton would be behind them, along with the borders of Mytana. Soon, they would be entering the wildlands that surrounded the Life Trees.

DURING THEIR LUNCH time rest, Resmine had dug through Estan's mess of a saddlebag and produced a map that must have originally belonged to the Temple of Locke. It was wider than Estan's bed roll, and showed the entirety of Arra. At least, it showed everything that had been explored of Arra.

The map was unfurled and laid out on the dirt of the road, with large rocks placed at the corners to keep the winds from picking it up. Estan paced next to it, glancing down at it occasionally to make sure that his mental image was measuring up with the lines that the map displayed.

"I'm telling you, we should head into the forest now and make south," Resmine said. She was leaning against Catapult a small distance away on the shoulder of the road, no longer bothering to look at the map that she had brought along.

"If we stay on the road, we should go directly under the limbs of the nearest Tree," Estan said, for what felt like the thousandth time that afternoon.

"Do you see how big those things are? Map scale, they could hold the entirety of Temple Hill easy. Even if we go under the outer branches, it'll be a half-day's walk to get from the road to the trunk! We may as well cut through now," Resmine argued, petting Catapult's neck. She had become increasingly disagreeable with the weather changes that had blown in overnight, making the sky gray with clouds.

Estan picked up the map, aware that any moment could result in a storm. He wasn't very happy about traveling in these conditions either, but he was anxious to get to the Life Trees. They were so close that he could almost taste it. "We stick to the road," he said, his voice carrying the authority of a commanding officer. "There's no telling if the elves will take offense to a couple of strangers wandering through their forest."

"I thought they never left those Trees of theirs," Resmine mounted Catapult, making it obvious that if they were going his way that she intended to ride.

It was Estan's turn in the saddle, but he didn't argue. Catapult seemed to like Resmine and Estan liked to walk. It gave him an outlet for excess energy that riding a horse didn't, and Catapult tended to pick up Estan's moods much more easily than Resmine's for some reason. Estan resisted the urge to kick the head off of a nearby flower. Childhood friends were by far the worst travel companions, in his opinion.

Despite most of his armor being stored in the saddlebags, Estan wore his studded leather gloves and his padded under-armor vest. His undyed linen shirt sleeves and forest green pants seemed oddly light in the summer wind. After so much time away from the front lines, Estan thought he'd be used to wearing civilian clothing. Something about not wearing his armor was throwing him off, making him all the more irritable. Resting his hand on the hilt of his sword, he breathed long and low through his nose.

Catapult halted and neighed a challenge. Between one breath and the next, Estan had his sword in his hand. Resmine vaulted from the saddle to land on the other side of him, facing the three figures that were waiting at the edge of the forest.

"How odd that the Venom Guild should encounter you here, Sir Estan," the middle figure said, its face hooded by a black cowl. All three were dressed in black leather, too soft to truly be called armor.

One of them swayed slightly from foot to foot, chanting in a hissing voice, "*Ripping, tearing, licking, nipping, dribbling... Blood, sinew, flesh, bone...*"

"Our brethren chased a different mark to this forest," the middle one continued.

"Three teams of three," the last one agreed.

"But I think we will be unnecessary. We are free to hunt," the middle one stated.

"Come and try me then!" Estan's voice rang out clearly over the wind.

"With pleasure," Estan could hear the smile in the middle assassin's voice.

The chanting assassin, which Estan could tell was a Flayer, launched itself toward them, shrieking in a way that made his skin try to curl away from his flesh. The middle assassin lifted a hand and flung something at the ground. Whatever it was exploded with a flash and the assassin vanished in a cloud of smoke. Estan assumed it was a rune, but it wasn't one the knight had encountered before. The remaining assassin threw back the cowl to reveal a round, tanned, male face, that was so covered in tattoos that it was hard to tell where his eyes and mouth were situated. He began to chant, raising his arms level with his shoulders.

"Mage!" Resmine called, trying to interrupt the spell that he was casting. "Over here!" She uncoiled a whip and snapped it at the tattooed face.

Estan slashed at the Flayer, warning it without words to keep its distance. Catapult reared, kicking at the creature's head with his front hooves. The Flayer danced away, screeching in fury.

Knives shot out of the trees, making Estan jump to the side. He rolled on one foot to avoid running into Resmine, his ankle complaining bitterly about his antics. The Flayer lurched in, trying to take advantage of his unbalance. A flying hoof caught the Flayer in the side of the head, as Catapult continued to object to the thing's presence.

Estan searched the trees for the source of the projectiles. He couldn't see anyone in the nearby branches. Another barrage of missiles came from overhead and Estan brought his sword up to deflect the worst of them. Several darts pinged away, though one caught in the padding above his shoulder.

Resmine's whip had hooked its barbs into the mage's wrist and she was engaged in a tug of war against the tattooed man. He was trying to gather a spell in one hand, but the mage's concentration seemed to break every time she jerked the cord linking them.

Horse and Flayer were locked in a stalemate; the Flayer was unwilling to get close enough to get kicked again, and Catapult was unwilling to leave Estan's side. Estan closed with the Flayer, thrusting his sword at the thing's belly. The Flayer dodged to the side, its cowl getting knocked back as it scratched at Estan's extended arm. Catapult dropped his forelegs back to the ground and bit the creature's hand. The Flayer released another soul-wrenching scream and lunged angrily at the horse. With a neigh that sounded like a battle cry, Catapult reared back and let loose a bombardment of horse-shoe laden kicks that smashed the Flayer's nose and unhinged its jaw with a sickening crunch.

Estan fought not to throw up at the sight of the thing still trying to fight. It hardly seemed to notice its loosely hanging jaw, despite it being the kind of damage that removed a normal man from action. More missiles found their way down from the foliage, and this time Estan was able to follow their arc to its starting point. There, amongst the lower limbs, was a slight distortion to the air. "Rune user," Estan breathed. "I thought so."

The Flayer had moved away from Catapult again, trying in vain to gnash its teeth. Estan ducked around to the other side of the horse and pulled his bow off the saddlebags. "Alright," he said, stringing his bow as quietly as he could and shielding his actions behind Catapult. "We're willing to talk! What is it you want?"

The assassin in the trees laughed, helping Estan locate him within the concealment of the rune's cloaking power. "We want you dead, as per requirements of the contract," the assassin answered.

Estan knocked an arrow, then sprung up and aimed over Catapult's back. He loosed the missile. It cut through the wind like a lightning bolt and impaled itself into the center of the distorted bit of air. The distortion faded and the assassin dropped from the tree, arrow still embedded in one eye.

Dropping her whip, Resmine charged the mage, pulling her short sword out as she went. The tattooed man, free to focus, gathered energies into his hands. Particles of light and dark pooled into a ball, looking like molten metal covered in slag. As the mage raised his hands above his head to fling the spell at her, Resmine yelled, "For Syara!" and plunged her sword down through the man's collarbone, deep into his chest.

Knocking another arrow, Estan shot the Flayer in the chest. It dropped to the ground. Catapult dropped both hooves into the thing's head, bursting it like an overripe melon.

"I've got a sadist for a horse," Estan muttered, trying not to look at the goo that he was going to have to wash off of Catapult.

Picking her whip off the mage's corpse, Resmine bent down and cleaned her sword on the man's soft leather pants. "Three teams of three, he said. Think we'll run into the others?"

Estan considered the question as he slipped the string back off his bow. He looked down the road for a long time, and then into the forest that stood directly between them and the Life Trees. "Alright, you win. We cut through the trees. We move quick and quiet. Field signals from here on until the trunk of the Life Tree," Estan said.

Resmine signaled an affirmative with a cocky smile. They entered the treeline as the first drops of rain splattered against the leaves.

10

~Khiri~

WHEN THE NIGHT PASSED with no sign of the assassins Khiri was ready to relax, but Fennick advised that they become even more cautious. "If they haven't attacked again yet, it's for one of two reasons. Either they are still waiting for a new Flayer, or they've decided you are a real threat and want to take us flat footed," he told her in the dank morning air.

Though the clouds had moved on, the humidity was thick enough to swim through. Small buzzing insects, not generally a bother to inhabitants of the Life Trees, saw fit to leave one or two itching welts as they sampled Khiri's flesh. Even though she'd gotten bitten from time to time on hunting trips, somehow Khiri felt these welts reflected on the lack of protection from her people's home. Elves from other clans crossed their path once or twice, but when they saw that Khiri had no tattoos and was in the company of a human they dropped their calls of greeting and hurried on their way. Khiri was beginning to feel that if she were to return to the River Willow Clan and receive her tattoos, she would always be marked as an outsider. If Fennick noticed her despondency, he did not mention it.

It wouldn't be so bad on the human roads, she told herself. Humans probably didn't know that a lack of tattoos meant she was clanless, marked as an exile. She didn't know much about dwarves, other than that they have come from the bones of Arra much in the same manner that her people had come from the trees. Where her people had been its healers, they had been its shapers. They may or may not recognize that she had no clan, and they may or may not care.

About midday, she realized that she could hear footsteps falling in the forest that were synchronized with her own. She quickened her pace very slightly, just enough to throw the echo off.

Only one shadow, moving lightly... Khiri decided that the shadow would not be a problem. Flayers scared away the natural denizens of the forest and she could hear birds chirping in the nearby trees. *Interesting,* Khiri thought. *Maybe my father is seeing me safely out of sight of the clans? It does seem to be someone familiar with my rhythm.*

They passed the River Willow Life Tree and the shadow continued with them. Khiri debated telling Fennick about their fellow traveler, but he grew jumpier with every mile they covered. After the fourth time he went for his boot, he moved the sheath to his belt.

"Do you think the assassins are that close?" Khiri asked, resting her hand on her own hilt.

"I just have this feeling that they will try for us before we reach the main road," Fennick grimaced. "I've been hunted before. The Venom Guild are the best, and it's because they don't kill for the money. Their fees are nothing to trifle with, but they hunt and they kill because they like it. That's why Flayers join their ranks so often."

"There are that many Flayers?" Khiri's eyebrows rose.

"Everybody has a wish," Fennick said grimly.

The birds went silent, as though those words had been a signal. Standing in the center of the road, a lone figure in covered in black stood, swaying slowly from foot to foot. "*Kill...*" it said in its hollow, wispy voice. "*Sip, lick, drink... Blood... Sweet, sticky, hot... Taste, crunch... Kill...*"

"*Gushing, turning, flowing... Blood...*" came another voice from behind Khiri's back. She jumped to the side to keep both Flayers in her sight. Fennick was gripping his dagger hard enough to turn his knuckles white.

A third figure stepped out of the trees next to the first. "*Tear, crush, rip...*" it joined its voice with those of the other two Flayers. Khiri slipped her hunting knife from its resting place at her hip as gradually as she could. She remembered hearing that Flayers got excited when there was rapid movement. Sparing a momentary thought, she cursed the instinctual jump she had already performed. Their swaying was not a good sign.

The three Flayers threw back their heads and let out a soul-shattering wail that nearly made Khiri drop her knife to cover her ears. Their cowls dropped revealing their blackened, swollen faces, as though they had been beaten and bruised so many times that the wounds could no longer heal. One had once been a dwarf; the other two appeared to have been human. When Khiri met their eyes, she could see that their irises were spotted with rays of sickly yellow and their pupils were tiny, mere needle pricks.

For an instant, everyone stood frozen on the path. Even the air seemed too still to be natural. Time itself held its breath; and then the Flayers struck.

Khiri ducked beneath the grasp of one of the human Flayers and dragged her knife across its shoulder. It pierced the air with a shriek of pain and fury, swinging at her back-handed while the dwarf Flayer charged her.

She could see Fennick keeping the third Flayer at bay with wild slashes at the creature that weren't coming anywhere near it. The creature was playing with him, urging him into swinging, just to tire him out. There was no way she could help the messenger, though, and so Khiri sent him the briefest prayer to Arra for luck before ig-noring him completely.

The dwarf Flayer was gnashing its teeth at her midsection, a thin line of foamed spittle trailing down the corner of its mouth. Khiri kneed it in the stomach and slammed her knife into its back. It seemed subdued for half a breath, and then threw her backwards into the Flayer she had grazed.

Khiri fought as it wrapped an arm around her and brought its teeth down toward her neck. She found a firm stance just as its breath rolled over her skin and spread a coat of filth over her soul. Yanking viciously at the arm ensnaring her, she brought the creature over her hip and thrust her knife into its armpit. It hissed and fought against her hold screaming for her sweet, pulsing blood.

Two arrows blossomed into existence in the dwarf Flayer's chest. A death shriek erupted from its grotesquely swollen lips and it fell into a steaming heap on the ground.

Yanking her knife out of its fleshy sheath, she plunged it into the thing's heart and earned her own death scream as the Flayer started to sizzle in her grip. Disgusted, she flung the Flayer's wrist out of her grip as the final death call echoed into the underbrush.

Wiping her knife as well as she could on the soft leather wrapping the Flayer's remains, she looked at the arrows that had impaled the rest of its kin. Khiri's lungs burned with a mixture of hurt and hope. She recognized those fletchings, but how? Why?

Since the Name Breathing, her brain had shut down and refused to function correctly. All at once, it had gone into overload.

"Who's there?" she heard Fennick call. "Show yourself!"

When Micah stepped onto the road, Khiri started laughing, though nothing was particularly funny. It felt more like anger fueling her fit of mirth.

"I take it you two know each other?" Fennick asked, his eyes darting from Khiri's humorless laughter to Micah's expression of bemused embarrassment.

"Yes," Micah rubbed the back of his neck and glanced around at the carnage. "Maybe we should move on before we explain, though."

"But isn't it funny, Micah? How a ring that you gave me robbed me of everything, but then... when both our worlds came crashing through the light-blasted canopy... you decided to forsake all that we had been to each other and then blamed me for wearing the ring that you bought! I think that's hil-spawning-lareous," Khiri laughed harder, unable to stop. She turned on her heel, still chuckling and marched away from the bodies. Once her adrenaline wore off she would deal with Micah, if he was still there.

IT TOOK A FEW MILES for Micah and Fennick to catch up with Khiri. Micah took it in stride that she wasn't ready to talk to him. He didn't seem to mind her silence, chatting easily with Fennick about the best producers of cheese and wine and other imports that the elves had left to the humans and dwarves to perfect before sampling. They were on an impractical confection that Fennick swore up and down was even better than cheese. He called it "iced cream".

Khiri walked ahead of them, only half-listening to them talk. The anger that had erupted when Micah had arrived had cooled, but it had left Khiri with some questions. Wood elves were born knowing the name of their destined, but what determined that two elves were suitable for each other? Did the Life Trees pick out the names of their destined, or was it the sleeping Arra? Was the name the only thing that bound them together?

She glanced over her shoulder at Micah. It had hurt when he rejected her after the Name Breathing, but did she actually love him? Yelling at him about cutting her off had felt good, as though a great weight had been lifted from her shoulders, and yet... He had followed her into exile. *Shouldn't that make me happier, somehow? For nineteen summers, he was the only dream I had.*

Despite naming Telgan Korsborn as her destined, Khiri felt nothing like love when she touched his name in her mind. It was solid, immovable, and as cool as granite. Whenever she had touched Micah's name, it had seemed golden and warm. That feeling was gone, though. Thinking about Micah, seeing him, caused no rush of warmth. Khiri rolled it over in her mind, feeling as though there were something to it. Had she only loved Micah because she believed that she should?

Her parents genuinely liked each other, so maybe it was just her. Maybe she would love Micah if his name was still a part of her. It was possible that his reaction to her after the ceremony had shaken her image of him so badly that she could not look at him as the man she had loved, but that didn't quite feel right. A part of her insisted that something had always felt off when it came to their relationship.

Did others experience a thrill when they looked at their destined, or did it feel more like this stone name sitting in her mind? Was it supposed to be the way it had been between her and Micah: a flame with no heat? Perhaps they were terrified of meeting the person they were expected to stay with for the rest of their life.

"Oh, my. Look at that sun. That's a low sun, I think. Maybe we should camp for the night soon," Fennick said suddenly. "I'll find some wood for the fire. Why don't you two find some water, and set up a stew or... catch a rabbit?"

Micah exchanged a look with Khiri that he had always used in the past when someone, usually her father, had made obvious pains to be absent so the two of them could talk. Stifling a giggle, Khiri gave him a slight nod. It was past time for the two of them to talk.

"We can attend to camp. Are you certain you will be alright? Those other assassins are still out there," Khiri reminded the messenger.

"I'll stay within calling distance," Fennick assured her. He backed his way into the forest, nearly tripping over a fallen branch in his haste. Righting himself, he picked up the branch and examined it before tossing it back into the forest. The former soldier started tromping off with exaggerated steps in the opposite direction, picking up branches and fallen logs and discarding most of them. "Just stay put! Unless I need help, then come quick!"

Steeling herself, Khiri turned toward Micah. Unable to meet his eyes, she slung her backpack to the ground to pull out a travel cook pot that her mother had insisted would be useful. "You didn't go to the River Willow house," she observed quietly.

"Honestly, when you came to say goodbye, I was already getting ready to follow you. I just... I couldn't face you. I wanted to apologize, then. I'm sorry that I treated you that way. It was unfair," Micah said, his voice gruff with sadness. He knelt next to her and began clearing a space for the campfire. It looked as though the clearing they had stopped in was often used by a much larger group. All that was required was a bit of maintenance to a disarrayed stone or two and the pulling of a few stray clumps of grass.

They left the backpack behind as they took the pot in the direction of the Ota River. Neither of them had to ask which direction the river was, as the sound of rushing water had been with them for most of the day. Near the Life Trees, the river was gentle and wide, but this far north it sounded rapid and angry.

An uneasy silence fell between them as they headed toward the sound of running water. "Thank you," Khiri watched their feet move across the ground, out of sync and tentative. "I appreciate your apology. The past two days, all I could think to do was move forward. I couldn't stop to look back... I didn't even know I was angry with you until you showed up. The world was one big void of uncertainty. Things are still hazy, but I finally feel like I'm waking up. Why did you follow me?"

Micah reached out and held a low-hanging branch out of the way for her. "I couldn't stand the thought of living in that house, surrounded by things we had picked out together, while you were out here alone," a trace of bitterness found its way into his words.

"Where did you find this human, anyway? And how is it that you have assassins chasing you already?"

With a heavy sigh, Khiri told him about Fennick's appearance at the base of the Life Tree and how she had chased the assassins away, temporarily, after killing their Flayer.

The running water they had heard turned out not to be the Ota at all, but it was a largish tributary, frothing over mounds of stony riverbed. They could see the wider band of flowing silver laying across the landscape in the distance, and where their little tributary merged with the larger river. Micah examined the view, while she dipped her pot into the chill, crystalline liquid.

"You are destined for another man," he said into the stillness.

"Yes," Khiri said.

"Do you love him?" Micah asked.

"No," she admitted, looking down into her pot.

"Do you love me?" Micah's voice was soft and uncertain.

"No," Khiri answered just as softly. "Not like I thought I did. You are still important to me, but it's not..."

"It's not the same," Micah smiled at her, seeming more than a little relieved. "Thank the spirits. I was afraid that you would see me and expect... Well..."

"Expect things to pick up where we left off before the Name Breathing," Khiri finished. "I thought that would be where you wanted things to go."

"At first, maybe... I left a day behind you. A day's travel alone leaves a lot of time to reflect. The two of us have probably known each other better than any other pair of soul named before their majority, and yet, how often have we really talked to each other over the last five summers? Outside of picking out habitation and furnishings, I can't remember the last time we talked about anything personal," Micah let out a small, nervous laugh. "I wonder if this ring business didn't actually do us a favor."

"Do you think we'd still be in love if I had breathed your name?" Khiri asked.

"Probably... Or at least, we'd be convinced that we were," Micah said. "How would we have ever guessed otherwise? I think it may only be obvious now because we have a comparison."

As they started back toward the road, Fennick let out a whistle that echoed through the trees. "I got the firewood! Tent's set up and all!"

Micah turned to Khiri, his soft green eyes intent upon hers. "Will you accept me as a traveling companion, then? Are we friends?"

It seemed so simple for such a weighty question. Khiri could practically taste magical bindings forming in the air around it, even though they had performed no ceremony or ritual to imbue the answer with that kind of power. She thought about how to respond. Micah was not in love with her, but he was still willing to follow her into the unknown. They had talked about the assassins, and he was still offering to travel with her, to risk his life for her... He was offering her a bond that would preserve their past history, but free them from the past's obligations and expectations. "Yes," she said. "We are friends."

Khiri's step quickened, her chest feeling lighter than it had since her exile. She headed to the camp site determined to make her new friend do the cooking.

11

~Estan~

ESTAN, RESMINE AND Catapult reached the base of the Life Tree nearest the Ota River without any further complications. The other assassin groups had either found their prey and left, or managed not to cross paths with the knight's small party. Estan signaled the end of enforced silence.

"Finally," Resmine let out a great sigh of relief and shrugged her shoulders repeatedly, as though remaining mute for so long had strained something. "I hate being that quiet. It reminds me of having to play dumb at the temples."

Her comment barely registered in Estan's hearing, because his entire attention was taken up with awe of the Tree in front of him. Estan had never really thought about the odors put off by trees, but in this clearing, the scent of the Life Tree was overwhelming: part fruit, part spice, and soothing like a balm over sore muscles. It also smelled warm somehow, like sunshine in a meadow. The scent was nothing to the sight, however. From a distance, he'd been aware that the seven inverted mountains weren't really mountains, but the sense of scale hadn't really penetrated. Once they'd come beneath the outer branches, they just seemed to blend in with the lower forest's canopy. Never in his wildest dreams had he imagined the Life Trees would be so monolithic. This close, he couldn't escape seeing how the Tree towered above the canopy, seeming almost like a massive wall of bark stretching forever into the heavens. "I had imagined there would be a way up," Estan confessed.

Resmine pointed up and to the right, "There are stairs, if we can get to them."

Following the direction of her finger, Estan spotted the edge of the stairwell. It was roughly ten feet off the ground, with no visible means of ascension. Estan scoured the nearby clearing for any sign of branches long and sturdy enough to fashion a ladder. Resmine, seeing his intent, started looking over the wall of a trunk for a secret knot or lever. Both methods proved fruitless in the end, and Estan was starting to feel a bitterness creep up from his stomach. He'd come a long way just to be balked at the door.

"Maybe if we hail them, someone will answer," Estan said.

"Worth a try," Resmine hunched one shoulder in a halfhearted shrug. She wandered over to Catapult and began to loosen his tack, so the horse could begin his rest. Catapult began to lip at her arms, as though to thank her or beg for a treat. "If it doesn't work, we can always camp until someone comes down. There's plenty of space down here."

Gathering air into the base of his diaphragm, Estan gave a battle yard bellow, "HELLO!"

Holding her hands over her ears, where she'd apparently clapped them when Estan's roar had sounded, Resmine gave him a sour look. "Nicely done."

Estan gave her a sheepish smile. He leaned against the trunk to wait. Once Catapult had been combed, Resmine came and sat down next to him. Catapult grazed nearby, seeming unconcerned with what his companions were doing in this foreign place as long as he had grass to nibble. It occurred to Estan to wonder at the plentiful plant life at the base of a Tree that blocked the majority of the sun. It was dark enough this close to the Life Tree that he had mentally equated it to late evening despite the blueness of the sky showing through the cracks in the branchy ceiling.

Hours passed, and there was still no sign of an elf approaching. "Say we do camp down here, and someone does eventually come down. What do we do if they don't let us up?" Resmine asked.

Unwilling to let her know that he had been pondering the exact same thing, Estan shifted away from the Tree's trunk and tried knocking on it. No hollow thunks sounded, and no hidden doors opened. "Hold your ears," he warned Resmine. Filling his lungs with air, he bellowed "IS ANYONE THERE? TWO HUMANS SEEK-ING ADMITTANCE!"

Nothing happened for a long time. Another hour passed, in which Resmine had prepared a fire ring and gathered wood while Es-tan had stared at the Tree, willing someone to come down and see them. Estan made a stew for their lunch after Resmine promised to watch the stairs for him or burn his food. When someone did show up, it was from an entirely different direction. Out of the forest, a young elf wandered into the clearing. He seemed preoccupied and jumped practically a foot into the air when he saw them.

"Humans?!" he asked, seeming almost as intrigued as he was star-tled. Estan realized that the elf had probably never seen a human be-fore.

"We are humans, yes. We came to seek an audience with Genovar Fortiva," Estan said, trying to sound soothing. The elf was short, coming just shy of five feet. His hair was long and light brown, fash-ioned into an odd knot behind his head. The garment he wore was a robe that was dyed a light azure.

"Genovar? But he's... I think you'll want to see the Councilor of the River Willow Clan," the elf said. "That's the only Tree humans are allowed in."

"Where is the River Willow Clan?"

"Well..." the elf paused. "This is the right Tree, but I'm not a member of the Clan yet. I can't let you in."

Estan paused, digesting the information. This was not going at all the way he'd imagined it as he'd been riding across Mytana with his dire warning to speak with the war hero that he'd grown up idolizing. Somehow, this moment had always been much more dramatic in his head. "Alright. What if you go up and let them know that we are down here?"

"What are your names, humans?" the elf still seemed unsure.

"I am Estan, and she is..."

"Resmine," Resmine waved her spoon, barely looking up long enough to stop eating. That was when Estan realized that his friend had taken the opportunity of the elf's interruption to begin pillaging choice bits of meat and tubers out of his bowl. Stifling a sigh of annoyance, Estan returned his attention to the elf.

"I am called Tylen Otterwain," the elf gave a slight bow. "If you, Estan and Resmine, don't mind moving around the trunk far enough that you can't see me, I will take your message to the Councilor of this Life Tree."

Estan and Resmine exchanged a look. Resmine raised one eyebrow. Estan signaled her with an affirmative, and then gave her a move out gesture. She saluted him sarcastically, and threw a handful of dirt on their cookfire.

"TYLEN TELLS ME YOU are here looking for Genovar Fortiva?" Councilor Havalene, a squat, elderly elf with white hair that trailed down her back, questioned. She was a few inches shorter than Tylen had been and wore a bronze robe that reminded Estan of autumn leaves.

"Yes, ma'am," Estan found himself standing at attention, as though speaking to one of his superiors in the Knighthood.

Councilor Havalene studied Estan through narrowed eyes. The young knight felt as though he were being measured by a master carpenter. He wondered briefly which bits the Councilor was considering shaving off.

They were in the Heartswood Inn, a building in the very center of the Life Tree that seemed to have grown into the trunk itself. The main chamber was a soaring lacewood dome that looked as delicate as a dragonfly's wing, but had obviously stood for time out of mind. Small sleeping cubicles honeycombed the common area, and the only rooms that actually offered doors were the kitchen and a small, extremely cramped bathing area in which to clean and relieve one's self. Despite the ceiling being an easy seven to eight feet high, Estan felt the beginnings of claustrophobia setting in. Though this inn was supposed to welcome humans, most of the furnishings were made to elven proportions and Estan was tall enough that even their highest stool had his knees propped at an uncomfortable angle. Oddly, he wished that Catapult were with him, but it would've been impossible to bring the horse into the Tree. A group of young elves had agreed to take turns watching Catapult roam around the clearing, seeming as awed by the horse as Estan had been by the Life Tree.

"Genovar has gone through a lot already the last few days. What is it that you wished to discuss with him?" the Counselor asked. The lines around her mouth reminded Estan of wood grain wrapping around a knothole.

"I've come all the way from Seirane to discuss a matter of grave importance. I believe he wrote this," Estan pulled out the battered, dirty and damaged history of the War of the Burning Valley.

A look of revulsion passed over Councilor Havalene's face, followed by a look of utter regret. "Ah, yes... that. Genovar Fortiva and his destined, in their younger summers, were unready to be part of the Life Tree community. We woke up one morning to discover that they had disappeared. For five summers, we heard nothing. Then, the human traders brought news of a war, the Great War they called it then. Still, there was no news. The war was going badly, and we in the Council were starting to fear that it would find its way to the Life Trees. When the tide of the war changed, no one was quite willing to believe it. Slowly, the humans started talking about an elf that was making all the difference in this or that battle. Still, we weren't sure; he's not the only elf that's ever left, after all. It was a relief the first time we heard his name. Genovar's name started being mentioned often, with much respect. We heard that he was leading armies, that he was a general, one of seven, that was driving the demon-bound forces back. Back to where, no one seemed to know, but they were being driven back. The war ended, and it was renamed for its end battle: The War of the Burning Valley.

"Genovar and Leyani came to the Trees one night, after everything was over. He had a quiet weariness about him that no elf has ever matched. Even those that fight the occasional band of bandits don't acquire that look in the back of his eyes. The Council of the Clans held a special meeting concerning our wayward villagers, debating whether or not we would accept them back into our society. We were actually in the Chamber of the Clans, and Genovar came to see us.

"He stood, looking each of us in the eye, and told us, 'I have seen all that I set out to see. I have taken lives, for self-defense, in battle, but never have I killed without cause. Never have I lusted for the blood of my enemies. Leyani is with child, and I want our daughter to be raised within the Life Trees. We will return to our house in the Oak Wood Clan's Life Tree.' Those of us that were Councilors at the time could not argue. We left the Chamber of the Clans in utter silence.

"He and Leyani have lived in peace for nearly twenty years. I do not want to interrupt his life for something trivial like a young fan that doesn't even remember the Great War as anything more than a tale," Councilor Havalene said, meeting Estan's eyes.

Estan did not look away. "Ma'am, with the deepest respect, I have to talk to Genovar Fortiva because he is the only person on Arra I know I can trust with knowledge that nearly cost me my life to attain. It has robbed me of my home, my future, and the only family I ever knew. If you still feel that I am here to waste his time, I apologize, but I won't leave here without having spoken to Genovar Fortiva."

After several seconds of tense silence, Councilor Havalene peered deeper into Estan's eyes. "That look of quiet sadness. It's not as deep, but you have seen the darker side of the world. Very well, I will notify Councilor Rivinar. Bear in mind, Genovar may not want to see you. He has recently lost his daughter."

"I am truly sorry to hear that," Estan felt a lump start to form in his chest. "How did she die?"

"She did not die, but she has been lost," Councilor Havalene said cryptically as she turned to leave. "You are welcome to explore our village, so long as you respect the privacy of my people. Food and space will be available to you here at the Heartswood, for a fee, of course. Even should Genovar choose to come, it will take him time to arrive."

SIX DAYS PASSED BEFORE Genovar arrived. Resmine spent her time walking the suspended paths and talking to the villagers. She entered their stores, sampled their food and smiled and laughed at their stories. Estan admired that about her. His friend had an inner strength that shone through her eyes and lit her smile; she was as open with the elves as she had ever been as a child living on Temple Hill. In a lot of ways, she had been through more than he had, but he was not ready to laugh yet.

Estan spent most of his time waiting to meet Genovar on a large wooden surface that rested on the canopy of the Life Tree. The elves called it the Sky Watcher's platform, which made sense because there were no walls. Nothing blocked the sight of the other six Life Trees eating up chunks of the horizon. "Upside-down mountains," he said to himself.

"You know, my daughter always thought the same thing," an elf lifted himself onto the platform. Warmly tan and with a deceptive wiry build, he had a long silver braid and blue eyes that were so dark they almost appeared black. "She was constantly on the Sky Watcher's platform, too, though she thought I didn't know about that."

"It's gorgeous up here," Estan admitted. Every so often, elves came to check on him. He assumed it was so that they could be sure there was still a stranger among them. The elf walked over and stood beside him, sharing a quiet moment and drinking in the view.

"Beauty is often better appreciated in the midst of strife," the elf said, his voice low and smooth. "But I don't think you asked me to join you just to enjoy the scenery from another Life Tree."

"Genovar Fortiva?" Estan realized that he stood next to a living legend. His throat went dry and his voice refused to cooperate.

"Yes, lad. Or should I address you formally as a member of the Knighthood? I can't tell what order you derive from without your armor, but no mistake, you are of Temple Hill," Genovar smiled softly, though it did not reach his eyes.

"Sir, I was a knight. The temples... they..." Estan struggled to find the words. After such a long journey, it was embarrassing that he couldn't speak normally.

"Calm down, lad. I don't bite. Now, tell me your story," Genovar sat down in the center of the platform. "We can call your companion up if you wish, but she was the one who told me where to find you. She's a soldier, and a good one, but not the leading type. Too much responsibility, and too much pain..."

Taking a deep breath, Estan began his tale. He told Genovar about how the Temple of Taymahr had been infiltrated and corrupted by members of the Gray Army. Piece by piece, words tumbled out of his mouth, rebuilding the day he had been chased out of Seirane. Estan told Genovar about the price on his head and finally, he told the war hero about the assassins he had encountered in the forest surrounding the elves.

"That is troubling news. Very troubling..." Genovar looked out over the forest. "I had never wanted to leave my home again. I'd hoped... Well, my hopes are of little consequence."

"But, you understand why we need you?" Estan pleaded, aware that he was overreacting to what had not been a full rejection, but he was afraid that the responsibility of leading a march against the temples could end up in his less-capable lap. "The name of Genovar is still remembered. I ran into a veteran in Jarelton that spoke of you as though you were a living deity. Who am I that people will listen? I am labeled blasphemer by my former brethren, a barely blooded knight, that has only battled our former allies. This is too deep for me. Please!"

"I know you are dealing with a lot right now, and it's hard not to be emotional about this. My daughter is out there somewhere, among the Flayers and thieves. And now, I know she's also wandering in a world where the Gray Army is loose again. I've been in that world, and I never wanted it for her," there was an odd look that Estan glimpsed in the elf's eyes, but before the knight could recognize it, Genovar shook his head. "I will have to go home and prepare a few things."

"Sir?" Estan watched his hero. Hope took root within his chest.

"There were contingencies put in place between the other generals and myself. I'll have to contact them," Genovar said.

"I will go get Resmine, and we will be ready in—"

Genovar held up a hand and stopped Estan mid-sentence. "I will travel fastest on my own. Not even Leyani will be coming with me, this time. I've not earned the right, but I have a favor to ask of you, young friend. You have every right to refuse an old elf's request, but I must ask."

"Anything," Estan said. "Name it."

"Don't get ahead of yourself. You have yet to hear what I want," Genovar pushed himself off of the ground. "It is a very selfish request—I want you to find my daughter. Find her, and protect her, if you can."

"YOU AGREED TO WHAT?" Resmine's eyes were wide and her expression incredulous.

Estan rubbed his temples. Wind rustled the gigantic leaves of the Life Tree, permeating the air with their intoxicating blend of spiced fruit and safety. He was going to miss the brief respite that he had experienced with the elves. The Life Trees granted him a sense of peace that he hadn't felt since before his first battle. His irritation at Resmine cooled, and he said, "I agreed to find Genovar's daughter. She's nineteen summers and never been out of the Life Trees before. Apparently something went wrong at her coming of age ceremony, and they sent her out into the world. She's as much an outcast as I am, and I owe him for trusting me."

"Where are we even going to start looking for her? And did you forget that we're being pursued by assassins?" Resmine asked.

"So I'll trade in my armor when we go back through Jarelton..." he shrugged. "My beard's come in very nicely at this point and my hair's getting longer. I'll see about getting one of the elves to give it a few braids."

"What about Catapult? He's a little memorable. A mercenary would have to fight a lot of battles to get a horse like him, and you are not that old," Resmine pointed out.

"It makes the most sense for her to be somewhere in Mytana. We'll pick up her trail in Jarelton. We must have missed seeing her on the road out when we went through the forest to avoid the assassins," Estan said. He tried to ignore the question about his horse, not wanting to contemplate the possibility of having to give up his charger.

"Are you even listening to me? This is a bad idea. You should be making tracks from Mytana, not going back in," Resmine said. "When Genovar sets his contacts in motion, Mytana's going to become a hot zone the likes of which has not been seen since the Great War!"

Putting his hands on both of her shoulders, Estan caught Resmine's eyes with his and waited until she quieted. "I'm going back, and I'm going to find Genovar's daughter. I did not earn my shield to run when there was trouble, and I'm not able to help in any other way. You don't have to approve. You don't even have to come with me. I appreciate that you came with me this far." With that, he gave her a chaste kiss on the cheek, as though she were truly his sister and released her. He ducked into the Heartswood Inn and headed to his cubicle to start packing.

"I came with you to do something against those villains that took Syara away from me," Resmine followed him through the door. She started to slam it but remembered herself and the eyes of the elves that were watching them. Instead, Resmine contented herself with glaring at him. "We should be going with Genovar and knifing those bastards in their sleep."

"He's going to rally forces against the temples. We can't be a part of what he's doing. I know he's not telling me a lot, but I came to him because I trusted the elf that wrote that history. Now, whether you leave, or stay, or come, I've made my decision," Estan sniffed a dirty pair of socks and instantly regretted it. He tossed them in his pack to deal with later. "Do what you like."

Resmine scowled, not moving for a very long time. She left his cubicle and came back with an already packed bag while Estan was still making sure he had everything he had brought into his temporary quarters. "Of course I'm coming, you dolt. Someone's going to have to do the funeral rites when you get yourself killed," she muttered.

"Naturally," Estan tried to hide his grin and failed. Despite her temper, Resmine was his last true friend. He couldn't imagine embarking on the next leg of his journey without her.

12

~Khiri~

FROSTY MIST FILLED the air, stabbing Khiri's lungs with thorns of ice. A shadowy figure grinned at her, wielding a blade coated with a grisly, blackish-green light. In the center of the room, a gigantic shard of crystal lay on its side, pulsing like a heartbeat...

Khiri was jolted from her sleep by the sound of Fennick's rough laughter. He and Micah were sitting beside the campfire, sharing a game of cards. It looked as though the retired soldier was trying to teach her fellow elf a variation of a gambling game that had been popular when he was on the front lines.

"Micah, my lad, the point of a bluff is not to tell your opponent that you're cheatin' them!" Fennick guffawed.

Yawning, Khiri stretched her sore muscles. Sunlight was creeping its way into the sky, smearing the eastern horizon with soft pinks and oranges and exposing a sliver of painfully bright star. She loved seeing the sun each day, but she missed having a bed. Even elves could not sleep in trees indefinitely.

"What is this funny little man called?" Micah asked.

"That is the soldier," Fennick told him. "This is the priestess, and that one is the mage. The king is the one with the crown, and the queen has the scepter."

"Are you sure that's not a staff? Don't priestesses carry staffs?" Micah argued.

"I'm sure," Fennick said. "The priestess has religious sigils in the background. Soldiers wear armor and carry swords, no matter the gender, and mages are always in red robes."

"They all look like scribbles to me," Micah put his cards down and made a face. "People really play games with these slips of paper?"

"We aren't all as picky as you," Khiri teased. A warm breeze carried the smell of pine, birch and moss to her, but the memory of the icy dream made her shudder.

"About time you woke," Fennick smiled up at her. "Micah here found some eggs and wild mushrooms. I made some campfire omelets." He gestured to a flat stone over the fire's softly glowing coals that held a small lump of yellow and slices of brown. "When you're ready, we'll start out. I figure that we can set an easy pace today, and we'll still make Jarelton by sundown."

Khiri swung off her branch. It wasn't the ten-foot drop of the Life Trees, but she still enjoyed the momentary fall before her feet met the floor of the forest. Making her morning ablutions in the nearby stream, Khiri made sure to stay within earshot of her companions. The more she moved, the less her dream seemed to bother her. It was only a dream, after all. She shoved away the inner voice that reminded her the last time she had felt something like that dream, she'd ended up with a new soulmate's name in her head. It wasn't long before she was striding toward the fire and the promised food. "What is Jarelton?"

"It's the border city that we have to pass through to get into Mytana," Fennick said.

"What's a city?" Khiri asked as she took her wooden fork out of her backpack. She scooped a bite of Fennick's omelette creation into her mouth and very nearly spit it out again. The eggs were cold enough that frost had formed along the edges. She stuck the rock back in the fire, and tried to pretend she'd never seen anything amiss.

Perhaps I was imagining things. A bit of reheating, and it'll be like it never happened, she told herself.

THE FOREST FELL AWAY between one step and the next as the road crossed the tree line. From the comfortable blanket of the canopy and its carpet of underbrush, tying them to the ground and sheltering them from the breadth of the sky, they emerged into a world of grasslands, empty skies and vast expanses of openness.

Khiri's first thought was that it was a lot like being on the Sky Watcher platform, but there was no way to return to the safety of the foliage—no escape from the ever-present sun. In spite of having been on the ground for nearly a week, she felt as though she were too low. It was contradictory, but the sky that seemed much too close was also much too far away. She and Micah exchanged glances every few feet. He obviously felt it, too. They were too exposed out on this empty road through its empty fields.

Fennick had fallen into a brooding silence. It took him by spells. One moment, he was lively and talkative, trying to help them adjust by distracting them with tales of his past. He would tell them how he fought in the War of the Burning Valley, though he had been running messages and didn't spend much time with any particular unit. He never really mentioned what the war was about, but it was obvious that he felt strongly that his efforts were underappreciated by his superior officers. Other times, he would describe cities that Khiri had never heard of, from lands so far away that she couldn't believe someone would walk such a distance. Slowly, his animation and enthusiasm would dim and be replaced by a quiet, sullen mood that couldn't be broken by anything Khiri or Micah said.

As the day wore on, a long blotch of gray appeared on the horizon. The closer they got, the larger it became. Khiri watched the gray edge of the world approach. She was both intrigued and frightened.

It seemed as though the grasslands had been swallowed by an enormous, immovable storm cloud. As uncomfortable as the fields made her, she dreaded coming to the end of them.

The gray mass became more and more solid. It shifted before her eyes from an amorphous form into a barrier of stone. In all the tales Khiri had heard about the outside world, she had never heard about stone that formed itself into such a long, flat structure. She knew about mountains, and could even see them from the Sky Watcher platform if she faced south and the skies were particularly clear.

Strange smells and sounds started drifting toward them as they neared the smooth stone. There was a hole over the road that plunged through the edifice, and Khiri realized that she could see mortar and individual blocks. It was not a natural structure, but a created one. *A wall,* she realized, embarrassment coloring her cheeks. Relief that she hadn't asked anyone aloud about the stone did little to shake off the blush. *A gigantic wall, but just a wall. I don't know if I'm cut out for exile.*

Guards in chain mail and livery of bright orange, emblazoned with a large, intricate, silver knot, gazed at them without real interest as they wandered past. They held halberds in steady hands, as though the weapons were so much a part of them that they forgot that they held the long polearms. Bulky helmets rested on their brows, adding to the implied menace.

"Wait here," Fennick instructed. He made toward one of the guards that had a blue baldric draped across her chest and her helmet was missing. Khiri decided the baldric indicated that was the guard in charge. She looked over at Khiri, the sun shining off her dark skin, and nodded. The woman's hair was held in a short braid at the back of her head. The wisps that escaped were made of tight little curls. Her eyes were serious and piercing, glinting violet in the light reflecting off her mail.

Fennick slipped his hand into his pocket and handed the guard woman something. She looked back at him, and Khiri felt as though a weight had left her being. It had felt like the gaze her father had leveled on her once when she had dropped his favorite bow into the forest and told him that she didn't know what had happened to it.

A few more words were exchanged and then the guard captain nodded and gestured them through. Khiri felt the guards look her over with a renewed watchfulness. She jogged to catch up with Fennick as they entered the gate. "What did you say to that woman? She looked at me as though I were guilty of something heinous."

"I told her that I would vouch for your behavior while within the city walls. Mytana is not feeling very open toward visitors at present, seeing Eerilorian spies in every wagon. Eerilor lays against the northern border, but there are a few passes that would make it easy for a small party to make it down here. Jarelton is the only fortress along Mytana's western border," Fennick said. It was more than he had spoken in the last two days.

"But I'm of the Life Trees," Khiri protested. "How could she think I'm from Eerilor?"

"An elf traveler is uncommon enough for the captain to be suspicious. She's familiar enough with your clans that she asked about your lack of tattoos. I told her I didn't know the full story, but that you were the daughter of Genovar Fortiva and that you and Micah had saved my life," as he explained, Fennick was guiding the two elves through a dark arch that had metal spikes hanging by thick, black chains. Khiri could also see the outlines of thin windows interspersed along the walls. There was something ominous about those slits, but Fennick wasn't letting them linger long enough to really investigate.

"Just be sure to watch yourselves in these walls," Fennick said, pausing before they reached the end of the gate's hall. "If we are ejected from the city, we may not be in shape to walk around Mytana's border."

Micah scowled at Fennick. "What must we watch for? More assassins?"

"We'll stay at an inn tonight. I'm friends with the proprietor, and he's invested in several anti-demon charms. We should be safe from Flayers within the city limits, especially once we make it to the Scattered Winds Inn, but human assassins, yes. And there will be thieves... Others that don't like outsiders... Speeding carts and dishonest merchants... There is plenty to be wary of in a city," Fennick said, his voice thin and worried. "I have a few things to do while we are here. I'll get us set up at the inn, and you two can stay there while I'm about."

Khiri and Micah nodded. The smells that had carried outside the wall were stronger now, as were the noises. Fennick hesitated, looking them both over with a sigh. "There's no way to make you stand out less. You both reek of foreign parts. I guess it can't be helped."

With that, the human led them into a cacophony of shouts, clanging, rumbles, laughter, and chatter. Stench wafted through the streets, laced with spices, cooking meats and breads, tanneries, smithies, perfumes and unwashed bodies. Khiri's throat tightened at the sight of so many people, all in different colors and shapes of clothing, meandering down a street that was coated in stone. Walls on either side reached up toward the sky like trees, but they were made of even more stone. Other roads drew themselves away from the main street, paved with more stone, more people, and more noise.

"I want to go home," she whispered, hugging herself as though she were cold.

Plunging through the crowds, Fennick left the elves little choice but to follow or be left behind. After several minutes of dodging and weaving through the city streets, Khiri couldn't remember where the gate was anymore. Fennick led them deeper and deeper into the city, never slowing even when Khiri or Micah got distracted by a stall or window display.

They passed a stall that sold roasted bird legs and large pasties. The odors drifting out of the tiny establishment almost made up for some of the less appetizing aromas that Khiri had been subjected to since entering Jarelton. She realized that her party had not eaten since their breakfast that morning.

Though her stomach was growling its impatience, Khiri ducked back into the fray. Micah was ahead of her, and Fennick was somewhere ahead of him. Farmers lined this street with their crops, shouting their prices or negotiating with what would probably be their last customers of the day. The sun was starting to descend past the level of the walls, making shadows as deep as the forest ever saw.

Someone barreled into Khiri, throwing her into one of the darker alleys. Already disoriented, her breath was knocked out of her lungs as she slammed into a wall. Dizziness made Khiri's head swim as her assailant levered his arm under her throat and lifted her off the ground. "What have we got here? A little elf girl who's lost her way?" murmured the man in a rich baritone.

Struggling to get more air, Khiri squinted at her attacker. Tall, thick shouldered, pale and bald, the man's breath could curdle butter. His clothing was threadbare and so dirty she couldn't tell what color it had been originally. "An elf like you could fetch a pretty price if given to the right people," the man practically purred.

Kicking with legs that had been strengthened by a lifetime of climbing normal trees and uncounted trips up and down the Life Tree's stairs, Khiri made contact with the man's shin.

"Aach!" he shrieked. "You little bitch!" he dropped her, falling back to nurse his injured leg.

Gasping, Khiri squatted and massaged her neck. She glanced at her attacker and scrambled for the edge of the alley. "Micah! Fennick!" she tried to yell, but her throat was still too sore. She begged any spirits that could hear her in all this stone that her companions might notice her absence.

"Get back over here!" the man hissed. He caught her by the hair and yanked her back into the alley. Blocking the way out with his body, he flexed his injured leg and lowered the foot back to the ground. "Nothing broken, but that's going to leave one hell of a bruise. I ought to forget about getting paid and slit your throat myself."

Khiri gripped her knife hilt. If she killed this man, would she be a murderer and unable to ever return home... or would it fall into the more forgivable realm of war, bandits and Flayers? Given his general demeanor, she guessed he would fall under bandit. That was when the look that the guard captain had given her infiltrated her mind. She was in the world of humans, and their ways were not her ways. They might not take it well if they found an elf standing over one of their kind, no matter what defense she offered.

With a sigh, Khiri's fingers fell from her knife. "I'm going to have to do this the hard way," she said.

"That's better," the man chuckled roughly. "If you come quietly, I won't have to rough you up as much. You already forfeit any chance of getting out of here..." he cracked his knuckles, "unharmed."

Khiri looked around. The alley was thin enough that she could probably make it to the roof, if she could prevent Baldy from pulling her back down. Looking at his grim smile, that seemed unlikely, but she had to try.

Baldy took a step toward her and swung his fist at her face. She grabbed his arm and rolled back, hitting the ground and throwing him with her feet. He hit the stones hard as Khiri followed through the tumble, back into a fighting stance. Running toward the nearest wall, she scrambled up the surface and leapt toward the other wall. Back and forth she hopped until she clasped her hands on the smooth lip of the roof. If she could achieve the roof, maybe she would be able to spot her friends. She figured a lone elf on the run from a human would likely get apprehended by the very people she sought salvation from. Her experience was yielding far less benevolent humans than wicked ones, thus far.

By the time she was pulling herself up, Baldy was on his feet again. "You just don't know when to quit, pet," he rumbled, unhooking a whip from his belt. He lashed her ankle and pulled, using his superior mass to its fullest. With a yelp, Khiri lost her grip and smacked against the ground.

Sore muscles screamed at her as she drew her knife just long enough to free herself from the thick leather cord. The bald man seemed more wary of her now, but was still moving toward her. She forced herself to her feet, steadying her body with a hand against the nearest wall.

A sharp tingle in her ear tips alerted her just before a blue flare lit up the big man's face. He fell over instantly, snoring the deep snores of a dreamless sleep.

"Well, well, well... What's this? An elf? And it looks like our old friend, Reldan Jack," a female voice drifted through the alley.

"I think you're right, love," a male voice replied.

Two people wandered into Khiri's line of vision; one was of average human height, the other short for a human—about the size of Khiri's mother. The taller of the two was a man, clad in deep brown pants and a faded tan shirt. His brown eyes held a spark of mischief, and his lithe form spoke of a fondness for athleticism. Black hair was swept up into a tidy ponytail from a deeply tanned face. He seemed to defer to the smaller, darker woman, who wore a red shirt, black pants and a saber at her belt. Her hair fell loose and wavy over her shoulders. She held a bag that still glowed with invoked magic.

"Holding your own against Reldan," the woman raised an eyebrow. "No easy feat, love. Who are you, then?"

"Khiri," Khiri answered warily. She eyed the pouch with as much suspicion as either of the newcomers. What new threat was this, and could she get past these people before whatever magic they held took her? Her breathing still hadn't normalized from when Baldy had introduced her to the wall.

"I think she is a might put off by your pouch, Corianne," the man observed. "Danger's gone. Might as well be obliging, no?"

"Indeed," Corianne said, drawing the string. Immediately the tingling sensation in Khiri's ears receded, though it remained a faint irritation as the big, bald man continued to snore. "There you are. Safe as can be. I haven't a lick of magic on me own, but nothing's wrong with a fair bit of throwing, what?"

"Who are you?" Khiri asked. She was uncomfortably aware that she owed them thanks, but refused to let her guard down until she knew what they intended.

"My name's Corianne, and this is my brother, Evic," the woman said with a smile. "Thieves' Guild: Bronze Class. We're usually down in Deerun Flats, but the Queen has been detecting a might of skullduggery here 'bouts and next thing is we trusted lieutenants get dropped to nick the skinny of it."

"Queen?" Khiri asked. She had many more questions following what the woman just said, but couldn't think of where to start.

"The Queen of Thieves, lass," Evic said.

"I thought it was always a king?" Khiri tried to remember the bedtime tales her parents had told her of the Thieves Guild. There hadn't been many and she usually preferred others. With the large bald man snoring next to them, and the leftover dizziness and aches from her fight, the entire scene struck Khiri as being rather surreal.

"The King is dead, long live the Queen, eh?" Corianne shrugged. "We make no never mind, our allegiance is to the ruling class, and she's the class cut for crown. Cut it true, she did."

"Right across the throat," Evic nodded.

"So why did you save me? What do you want?" Khiri asked. She had exhausted herself against Reldan Jack. They seemed friendly enough, but if that was a false impression Khiri wasn't sure she was up for another fight.

"Reldan was the second in command of the up-and-coming usurper. My queen will demand his head or his heart, though neither might fill much space. He's more gut and meat than useful parts," Evic said.

"Aye, we're rattling on toward a full cask. Reldan, Steward Jels, and Tyronian Shedson shall all find their end, after their tongues cull their master, o'course. But there are two ways past gray to my thinking, and there's one that might trouble me some, should the bleeder Queen take her. You see, our sister, Dewin was a small part of the plot. Only ran a distraction gambit, once or twice, without knowing it for its truth, but she'd die every bit as dead.

"So here's what I'll offer... In exchange for a Thieves' Pass through the city, no more molestin', when you outsiders go, if you take our sister away. A year or two, she could come back, or no if she find other work more suiten'. Worst thief in the blood," Corianne finished. She stuck her hand out toward Khiri. "And a fourth to your band?"

Khiri rolled the words through her head once or twice, until she was pretty sure she understood what the thief was asking of her. "We are pursued by assassins. Your sister would still be in danger," she said.

"Bah... Assassins are a possible death, but an angry Queen, that's a surety. She'll still fare better with your lot," Evic shrugged.

"Flayers?" Khiri asked.

"Venom Guild, eh? Nasty buggers, love, but still a chance. You fight like a badger in a barrel and she's not useless. Quicker love with a hatchet you'll never cross," Corianne waved her hand impatiently. "Now, have we wagged our tongues enough, or are we charming squirrels from the stone?"

Nodding, Khiri wrapped her hand around the thief's and pumped twice as Fennick had taught her. "Where can I find your sister?"

"I will guide you back to your friends," Evic told her. "Tomorrow, we will send Dewin to meet you at the gate into Mytana proper."

13

~Estan~

"HAVE WE MET?" THE CAPTAIN of the guard squinted suspiciously at Estan. Her dark brown skin and single short braid gleamed in the dim torch light, and even in the dark Estan could tell that her lips were full and her cheekbones sharp. Estan caught the slant of his thoughts and he almost smiled. Her question had sounded like the kind of line that he had used in taprooms to strike up a chat with pretty women. Under other circumstances he would find conversing with her much more pleasurable. As it was, it was a dangerous question, and not one he wanted to hear from anyone wearing bright orange livery over their chain mail.

"I think I would remember," Resmine said, bumping Estan out of the way. Where Estan was hesitant to flirt in the face of danger, Resmine seemed to relish the challenge. She had a thing for women in uniform, and always had to Estan's recollection. They had grown up in the temples where most women were in a uniform of some kind.

The guard captain gave Resmine an appraising look, and then shrugged. "Might have been my imagination," she said noncommittally. "You two best hurry in. We're closing the gates soon. It would be most unfortunate to make it all the way here and then have to wait until morning."

"If I may I ask..." Estan paused, aware he was pushing his luck with the captain. She'd already come so close to recognizing them, but he had to know if they were actually going in the right direction. "Have you seen an elf recently?"

"Might have," the guard captain said, her mouth thinning visibly even in the limited light. "I don't think it's rightly any of your never mind. Move along."

As they hurried into the gates of Jarelton, Resmine let out an exaggerated sigh. "And to think, I was going to offer to bear her children. Oh well, can't win them all."

"Well, at least we know that an elf passed through here," Estan tugged on Catapult's lead rope and kept his voice hushed so it wouldn't echo as they passed through the gate.

"How do you figure?" Resmine rested her hand on the handle of her whip. Estan mirrored her casual grip on the pommel of his sword. In the dark hours of the city, thieves and worse would prowl the streets much more openly.

Entering Jarelton after nightfall had not been their original plan, but they moved at a steady clip. The entire way to Jarelton they'd been taking short two-hour naps instead of camping nights in order to close the distance between them and Genovar's daughter: Khiriellen Fortiva.

Estan looked over his shoulder to make sure none of the guards were following them, and then turned his eyes forward. "If she hadn't seen an elf, she would have said so. Instead, she told me to mind my own business."

"I see... affirmative evasion," Resmine tapped her chin with her free hand. "Does that mean she really wasn't blowing me off?"

"Uh..." Estan wasn't really sure how to answer that.

"Never mind," Resmine said. "We probably don't have time for a dalliance anyway. What's the plan?"

"Tonight, we find an inn. We spend tomorrow looking and listening for news about an elf wandering through town. It's bound to spark some gossip. When do people ever see elves, right?" Estan slipped a thumb over his sword hilt and tightened his grip on Catapult's rope.

"So, we're not in that big of a hurry anymore?" Resmine's mouth quirked up into a wicked grin. "I'm definitely going to find myself a dalliance. Maybe two!"

Estan sighed. Resmine punched his shoulder with her free hand to let him know she was just teasing.

The streets were nearly empty, though lurkers could be seen in the shadows of alleys. Stench rolled unchecked over the stone covered roads, no longer dampened by the mingling smells of cooking and produce that had been present in the city during daylight hours. It was so strong in some areas that Estan could taste the foulness. Torches hung in brackets along the walls of some establishments, lending their uneven light to those unfortunate enough to still be outside.

"Looks like we made it just in time," Resmine said. The sarcasm on her breath was thick enough to flavor the air beyond even the city's miasma. "Wouldn't want to be late to our own mugging."

Estan scanned the sides of buildings and spotted a wooden sign hanging over a door. He headed toward it, keeping an eye on the alleys around them as they walked. When they came close enough to make out the symbols, Estan read, "Talon Acre Inn..."

"Talon Acre? Sounds like a predator farm," Resmine grimaced.

"Look," Estan pointed at the door jamb. An anti-demon charm was etched into the stone. "We'll look into it. If it's unsuitable, we'll move on."

"You look. I'll stay right here with Catapult," his friend said. She took hold of the lead rope and slumped against the war horse's shoulder. Catapult stamped his hoof on the opposite side as though to re-assure Estan that he had things under control.

Estan wanted to argue, but shrugged. Catapult was more than capable of staving in a skull if needed. The image of the Flayer's head popping like a gourd thrust itself into Estan's mind, reminding the knight that his horse had done that sort of thing not long ago.

Pushing in the door of the inn, the young knight was accosted with the most horrible screeching sound. It reminded him of the sound of an injured Flayer, which he knew was impossible with the anti-demon charm in place. The screech was followed by a warble that made him squint, as though closing his eyes would aide in blocking out the sound. Despite the trepidation that was settling in his stomach, Estan made his way into the common room.

In one corner of the room, perched on a small stage was the source of the noise. He seemed to be a bard, though Estan could not remember the last time he had seen a dwarven musician, let alone a bard. The questionable bard's instrument of choice was a lyre played with a bow, though it seemed the dwarf had been taught how to best illicit music with the thing by a deaf carpenter.

Estan was approached by a rather stout woman with copper skin whose hair had once been an intensely dark brown, but was now threaded with gray. She had wrinkles in the corners of her mouth and eyes, and pronounced smile lines. Even as she approached him, her face split into one of the biggest smiles Estan had ever seen as she welcomed him into her inn. "I know Ullen's music is hard to get used to, but we welcome all strangers here," she said, her voice cutting through the din.

"Do you have stables?" Estan asked, his voice seemingly swallowed by a particularly hideous gurgle the dwarf chose to utter at that moment.

The proprietor nodded, "They're in the back, just through the alley to the right. And my husband's made a full meal this evening.

There's plenty, since there's been a lack of business lately. Ullen comes through every year about this time. We'd send him elsewhere with his talents if he and my husband hadn't been friends for so long." A fond quirk to her lips took the barb out of her words.

A sudden silence rushed in to fill the space vacated for what the dwarf had been trying to pass off as music. "If I were to play as I should, we'd never be rid of the riffraff," the dwarf muttered.

Holding up a placating hand, the innkeeper turned to the small stage. A handful of empty tables were between her and the dwarf, but she used the same level voice that had cut through the music with ease, "We dearly appreciate your efforts to save us from our customers, Ullen."

"Actually, things had turned for the worse as of late," she sighed, turning back toward Estan. For the first time since she approached him, the knight sensed real worry in her tone. "Things have been quieter with Ullen here. He tends to drive away friend and foe alike, and we're more grateful for his presence than usual. We've been having issues with the Thieves' Guild. There's a new Queen apparently, and some of the traditionalists are quite put out. They've been targeting our inn, since they know that the Queen was a friend of ours before she had to choose a Court. I can't guarantee that staying here won't make you a target for her enemies."

"I should go get my companion and see to my horse, but I wouldn't mind hearing more about this Thieves' Guild business over some of that food you were mentioning earlier," Estan said. "My name is..." he remembered the Venom Guild's wanted poster just before he let his name slip, "...Erdan."

"Pleased to meet you, Erdan," the innkeeper's smile twitched a bit, and Estan knew she had sensed the evasion. Guilt flooded him. He felt horrible about lying to his hostess, especially after how forthcoming the woman had been about her own problems. "You may call me Adela, or Madam Lysira, whichever you find more appropriate. Go and fetch your companions. More of Ullen's playing awaits."

Estan turned and fought not to wince as the screeching, wailing and gurgling noises commenced from the far side of the room.

Resmine jumped a foot off the ground when he emerged into the brisk night air. "Where have you been? The lurkers are restless. Something spooked them really well just as we arrived here."

"Place checks out, if our ears don't start to bleed too much," Estan told her. "Let's take Catapult to the stables and I'll fill you in."

TWO MEAT PIES, SIX stewed carrots, nine dinner rolls and several flagons later, Estan and Resmine were laughing at a story being told in equal parts by Adela, Ullen and Adela's husband, Ren.

"And so I sidle's up to him, real slow like," Ullen rumbled in his deep base.

"His attention has been on me this entire time," Ren added.

"Ne'er laid an eye on me... So I sidle's up to him and yanks real hard on his britches! Threadbare loin britches they was, too, so as soon as I has him up there..." Ullen said. Mischief and mirth danced in his eyes, and he was trying very hard not to laugh as he spoke.

"...the entire courtyard heard this ripping sound, and the vendor's face turned this very bizarre shade of puce. He started making the oddest expression," Adela laughed lightly, her eyes far away, as though she could still see the man's face in front of her.

"And then, he's on the ground, and I still has his trousers in me hand!" Ullen roared with laughter, which Ren joined, and they commenced to slapping each other on the back in what looked to be a ritual of congratulation.

Estan chuckled along with the others as he wiped up the last vestiges of gravy from his plate. The mood turned more somber as a few moments passed by with only the clink of Resmine's fork as she chased a pea around her dish. "So," Estan said, finally, "what's this about the Thieves' Guild and a Queen?"

"Ah, yes," Adela sighed. "I did bring that up, didn't I?" She looked at her husband and seemed to make a decision. "Dear, why don't you tidy up? You know how the dishes get crusty if you leave them too long."

"Indeed," Ren said, his mood seeming to shift. Adela watched him make his way across the slate tiled floor and waited for the kitchen door to close.

"He doesn't approve of my decision not to allow Ysinda to hold her Court here at the Talon Acre. We love her like a daughter, you see... I'm equal parts proud and concerned that she has become the first Queen of the Jarelton's thief population, but I cannot allow my livelihood to become dependent on her whims. The establishment that runs a Court for the Thieves' Guild is signing an unwritten contract that they will agree to close shop when the guild members need to arrange a more elaborate heist, and will hide those that are trying to escape authorities. That's not even considering the murders that occur in a Court..." Adela's expression turned grim, and all the glow of merriment fled her. It was the first time that Estan thought of her face as aged.

"Ren still sees her as the little girl that came to this city with nothing but the clothes she was wearing. We took her in... When she would let us. She came to us from time to time for a place to eat, maybe even sleep, if things got too rough. He doesn't realize she has grown into a woman that only holds us in esteem as long as we are not in her way... No, that's unfair... Ysinda does recognize a bond, but if we were to allow her to hold Court here, and I were to disagree with something she decided, I would be a liability," Adela studied her hands, as though her eyes were too heavy to lift. "That's a thing that I know, but Ren, bless him, just isn't willing to recognize. She's the closest thing we ever had to a child."

"This link you have, it's causing you trouble, lass?" Ullen asked, scowling into his tankard. His bushy brown eyebrows looked like hawk wings resting on his face. He had a pointy, well-trimmed beard, stopping just short of his collar, but his dark hair and mustache trailed down his chest, woven with red cords and beads. "Why didn't you and Ren tell me sooner?"

"Local opinion does not currently favor dwarves, old friend. I didn't want you getting involved," she told the bard.

"But you want to involve us?" Resmine asked, leaning forward in her chair so that she was propped on her elbows against the table.

"The two of you are a neutral party, outsiders... *Human* outsiders," Adela stressed when Ullen looked like he was about to protest. "All I request is that you keep an ear open for any news concerning the Thieves' Guild and bring it to me. That way I will know whether to hire guards, or if Ysinda has the situation in hand."

Estan considered the situation. He and Resmine were unable to track Khiriellen Fortiva further without ascertaining more information, which meant they would be grinding the rumor mill anyway. Adela and Ren were giving people; even with their troubles, they were barely charging Estan and Resmine enough to cover Catapult's care. "I think we can do that much for you while we're in town," he said. The knight made a private vow to do more if he could.

14

~Khiri~

TRUE TO HIS WORD, EVIC guided Khiri through the streets, setting a much easier pace than Fennick had. The streets were dark, but torches were placed on posts outside most of the shops, throwing puddles of light on their path. Khiri could smell the burning tar over the melange of other scents still lingering from the business of the day.

"Where did everyone go?" she asked her guide.

Evic gave a rough chuckle, "Didn't you know? The thieves come out at night. Timid mice seek houses when they hear owls hooting."

"You and Corianne don't speak the same way," Khiri said. "Aren't you siblings?"

"Half-siblings, actually. She was raised by her mother in the mountains of Eerilor and was roughly eight summers turned before our da brought her here, but Dewin and me... we were raised by our mother here in Jarelton. A bit o' it is usual thieves' patter, a dribble of nonsense, what? But most of it is pure Corianne. She can't stop bein' her anymore than I imagine you could," he said. With a gentle nudge to the right, Evic guided her down the next road.

"I'm sorry," Khiri said, realizing she had been prying.

"No harm. You'd have had it from Dewin eventually, love," he waved to someone in one of the alleys that they passed. A glint of metal flashed in the hand that waved in reply. "Now, an exiled elf is unusual, but in the company of an ex-soldier and another elf..."

Khiri studied Evic in the passing torchlight. "How long were you watching us?" she asked.

"Our people marked you the moment you entered the gate, love. We knew the traitorous blood lords would cling to your shadow like demon's piss," he met her gaze without turning his head. "Or didn't you wonder why that soldier of yours was running through the streets like his wife's mother found out about his camp followers?"

Khiri's stomach rumbled, reminding her of her earlier distraction. Evic threw back his head, his laughter echoing through the stone city. Several dogs barked in reply, adding their complaints to the softer night-noises. "I see," Evic said. "Even elves think with their stomachs on occasion. Don't worry, love. Inns usually have a small menu, even this late."

They walked on in a shared silence for awhile, Evic nudging or bumping Khiri onto the correct path whenever they had to turn. Khiri responded to his nudges without thinking. It was similar to the fashion that her father used when he guided her through training exercises on their hunting trips. It occurred to her after the third such turn to wonder why her father had taught her to follow someone's directions that way. Granted, it was harder for someone watching to follow the directions being given, but who would've been following Khiri on a hunt? How different was her training from the other hunters in her clan?

Finally, Khiri spotted a sign swinging in the torchlight. It depicted a compass rose painted with wavy lines overlapping the arrows. A smaller board hung beneath, with the words Scattered Winds burned into the wood.

"Before you go, I would like to thank you. I know we didn't give you much of a choice... but... well, thank you," the dark thief smiled warmly as he put his hand on her shoulder. Khiri felt as though Evic was granting her a special gift. She got the impression that his thanks were not often given.

"Thank you, and Corianne, for saving my life," she said. "That man would have killed me."

Evic laughed, but it was soft and barely registered in Khiri's ears. "I doubt you would have died alone, had it come to that. You would have had him, had you used your knife."

Khiri frowned. "My father taught me to fight when he taught me wood lore. I never thought I'd actually have to use those lessons... It didn't even occur to me to wonder where he learned it."

The thief's smile turned sad as he said, "Our parents keep secrets. Their generation had many difficulties. Most of that generation seem to feel the War of the Burning Valley never really ended, but they do not speak of it. I do not know much about it, love, but I'm sure your father would be proud of you if he saw you using the things he taught you."

He drew a necklace out of his pocket and placed in Khiri's palm. "Make sure you wear this where my people can see it. Dewin will meet you at the gate."

Evic turned away, raised his hand in farewell and seemingly evaporated into the night. He was very skilled at concealment, one of the best Khiri had ever seen. If it weren't for the lack of her ear-tingle that told her magic was involved, she would've thought he'd used some bit of sorcery. Khiri looked at the necklace in her hand and found it was a small charm made of polished bark, shaped to look like an open hand, and strung on a long leather cord. She tied the charm around her neck and entered the Scattered Winds Inn.

Micah caught her in a hug as soon as she was through the door. "Thank the spirits, Khiri. Fennick and I arrived shortly after night fell. He wouldn't let me go look for you. Something about being followed and elves standing out too much... He told me to wait here, in case you turned up," Micah said, refusing to let her go.

From her position in Micah's grip, Khiri got her first look at the interior of a human establishment. Round tables surrounded by ladder-backed chairs were spread over the main floor, while a counter took up most of one side of the room. The door next to the counter seemed to enter into the kitchen if the clattering sounds behind it were any indication. A set of stairs started near them and headed up to a second landing. Though it seemed like there were more doors upstairs, it was hard to tell. That area was partially blocked from view by the great stone chimney that rose from the fireplace set into the far wall. Wooden beams supported simple, sturdy iron chandeliers over the tables. Tallow, alcohol and warm food smells cast out the stink that inhabited the city streets.

"Easy, Micah," Khiri pushed him back. "I'm alright. Really. But I have to tell you both about what happened. Where is Fennick?"

"He should be back soon. After we got here, he made arrangements with the innkeeper and went back out to find you," Micah said, still agitated. He looked like he was ready to hug her again if Khiri gave him even the slightest opening. "The innkeeper said we could order whatever food we like in the meantime."

At the mention of food, Khiri's stomach gurgled in anticipation. "Good... How do we order?"

Escorting Khiri to a table, Micah signaled a barmaid to come to them. She sauntered toward them as though she imagined every eye in the dining room was on her. Next to Khiri's athletic build, the woman looked as though she had spent her life in a well-stocked kitchen. Though she wore a bodice designed to enhance her cleavage, it succeeded in making other bits of her anatomy jiggle as well. A big smile split her face as she approached the table.

"So you're the elves in town, huh? What'll it be, dearies?" she asked. Her voice caressed each word, drawing them out with extra syllables just so they'd last a little longer.

"What's ready?" Micah asked.

"Hot bread, fresh from the oven... And we got some chicken, potato chowder thing that Cook's been experimenting with. It's actually not too bad," the barmaid, played with one of her fiery curls. "I think it's got some sort of cheese in it.... And then there's mushroom pie, or baked potatoes."

"I'll try the chowder," Khiri said immediately, liking the sound of cheese in a soup, "and some of that bread, please."

"And you, cutie?" she turned to Micah, and placed her hands on the table, squeezing her bosom between her arms hard enough that Khiri was afraid she would pop out.

"I'll... uh... I'll have the mushroom pie," Micah stammered, trying to look anywhere else in the room, and failing.

"Sure, love. I will go get that right away," her lips curved up in one corner. She seemed smug about the blush she'd brought to Micah's cheeks. It was pretty impressive, actually, the way it was creeping all the way up his ears. "You two want something to drink?"

Khiri and Micah exchanged looks. Both of them had tried alcohol, but elves had a very low tolerance. This didn't seem like the type of place that served a lot of water. "What's on tap?" Micah asked.

"We've got a lot of home brewed... Ale, lager, and something Cook cooked up... He took an herb of some sort, brewed it. It's kinda sweet and sudsy, but it hasn't got a kick at all. Pretty popular anyway," the barmaid rattled off.

"We'll take two," Khiri said. "What's it called?"

"Sarsaparilla, I think he said," she tossed her hair over her shoulder and headed toward the kitchen.

The door to Jarelton swung open and Fennick entered, his face dark with frustration. He scoured the room until he spotted their table. Disbelief and relief warred for dominance across his features as he dodged drunken patrons and made his way to Khiri's side.

"What happened? Where were you?" he demanded, visibly restraining himself from touching her. Khiri wasn't sure if the former soldier wanted to shake her or hug her.

"I got caught by a man that wanted to sell me to someone," she admitted. "And then... well, the short version is that I agreed that we would take someone with us when we left the city."

"What's the long version?" Fennick asked. He crossed his arms and dropped into a chair, making it clear that none of them were moving until he heard the story.

So Khiri launched into the tale of her encounter with Reldan Jack, Corianne and Evic, and the deal she had made to get them through the city without any more trouble. She was interrupted when the barmaid brought out the food and drinks that they had ordered, and Fennick requested an ale and a baked potato. When she told them about the pass, Fennick dropped his gaze from her face to her new necklace.

"And that's how I came to be here," Khiri said.

Fennick and Micah picked at their food, looked at each other and sighed. "I suppose it could have been worse," Fennick said. "We'll see how bad it really is some time tomorrow, but in the meantime, we have two rooms with baths on the way. Khiri, you want to bunk alone, or do you want to share with Micah? I know it's traditional to give a woman some privacy, but I also know how hard it can be to be away from home."

Khiri swallowed the last of her third jug of sarsaparilla. Every time she thought it was getting low, a new one seemed to appear. She had put it on her list of excellent things from humankind after her first tentative sip. Having a familiar face with her in this place was appealing, but even with the agreement to be friends, she and Micah sharing a bed seemed problematic. It wasn't like she found him entirely unattractive, and he didn't seem unenthusiastic at the idea of sharing a bath and a bed, exactly, but she didn't think she could do it.

Thoughts of her parents, and their easy, loving manner popped into her head. That was what she wanted, and that wasn't something she and Micah could give each other. They'd stopped pretending it was something they wanted, and now it was just better to leave the possibility behind.

"I'll take my own room, if you two will be okay," she said.

The ex-soldier nodded, as though he were already anticipating her reaction. "That'll be just fine. Actually, I was going to entertain meself down here a bit longer, so Micah, if you want to head on up and show Khiri the rooms Twilla gave us..." Fennick caught the barmaid's eye and wiggled his eyebrows suggestively. Suddenly, Khiri understood the real reason he had offered to let the elves share a room.

Shaking her head to herself, she let Micah lead her up the stairs. It had been a very long day, and she hoped that the bath would make it before she fell asleep. Khiri desperately wanted to clean the smell of her altercation in the alley off of her skin.

KHIRI WOKE THE NEXT morning feeling refreshed. Her bath from the night before had been very different from those she'd taken in the Life Tree. They'd given her a tub large enough to sit in and the water had been heated! All of her muscles seemed to relax and even some of her troubles seemed to have melted into the bath water. The bed was not a kind she was familiar with, consisting of only a bed frame with a taut canvas stretched over the gap created in the center. It had been covered with a quilted pad, and an extra blanket had been draped across a chair in the corner.

Having never been to an inn before, Khiri didn't know how it compared but she was willing to wager that this was a rather nice one. She had slept heavily, feeling secure within the boundaries of the inn's anti-demon charms with the token of the Thieves' Guild around her neck. Human assassins could probably have made it in her room had they tried hard enough, but it looked like they hadn't bothered.

Stretching her arms over her head, Khiri started to notice the sounds from downstairs were getting louder. When she was just beginning to wake up, she had assumed that the shouting in the pub area was the normal bustle of the city. There was plenty of yelling and laughing to be heard during the night. This was different, though. There was a hostile quality to the voices she heard now that seemed out of place.

Cracking her door so only a sliver of light came through from the taproom, Khiri could hear individual voices clearly.

"You are harboring outsiders!" someone cried.

"This is an inn," another voice said, sounding as though it were weary of trying to reason with the unreasonable. "Outsiders are our stock and trade. There are only so many wives angry at their husbands on any given day."

A small wave of gentle laughter rippled through what sounded like a large crowd.

"This is war time!" the first voice insisted. "Outsiders are not to be trusted! How do we know that these are not Eerilorian sympathizers?"

"Two elves and a veteran of the Great War?" the second voice said. The skepticism in the voice was strong enough to dry Khiri's hunting garb after a good rain. "I would sooner believe my own mother a sympathizer. Now get off my property with your rabble rousing."

"We will not be ignored!" the first voice yelled. "Those elves are no better than the dwarves! They don't care one copper for humans or our ways!"

"One is the daughter of Genovar Fortiva, himself," a third voice said. "If you can't shut your mouth, those of us that remember such things will gladly shut it for you."

The mention of Khiri's father, so forcefully reverent, made her breath hitch. What exactly had he done in the War of the Burning Valley? She didn't even know who her father had been fighting against. Every time someone mentioned this war of the past, Khiri felt like she knew her father a little less. Why hadn't he ever told her that he'd left the Trees?

Chairs screeching across the floor alerted her that several people were getting to their feet. There was a tense silence for a few moments. Khiri hardly dared to breathe even though she was still in her room. All the feelings of contented refreshment that she had woken with were fading quickly. Khiri decided that she wasn't a fan of cities. Too many smells, sounds, and secrets surrounded by lifeless stone... and way too many people out to get you.

"Fine," the first voice said. "If she is Fortiva, I will not darken your doorstep any longer. The moment any of your guests makes a misstep, I will be back with the guard!"

A door slammed, shaking the chandeliers on their chains. Khiri felt a little shaken herself. What if the instigator found out about her agreement with the Thieves' Guild? Would that put this establishment at risk? At least she would be leaving soon... Back on the road to face more assassins, Flayers and spirits knew what else....

None of this would've happened in the Life Trees, Khiri thought, fighting back a sudden urge to cry. *I would be safe, and things would be...* She stopped herself. Things would be normal. Dull. She would be trapped in a life-long lie with a man she didn't love the way a soulmate should. Khiri opened her door and made her way down the stairs. She was hungry, and she didn't feel much like facing Micah or Fennick yet.

Silence met her in the taproom. It seemed as though the tension inspired by her presence had yet to ebb. Khiri was tempted to run back to her room and lock the door, but she held herself steady. It wouldn't do any good to appear frightened at this point. That would only make people wonder if she felt guilty.

Several people, hard looking men and women, turned their heads and studied her, as though they were trying to find her father in her features. Genovar hadn't passed much of his appearance on to his daughter, but she had inherited his temperament and, much more importantly, his skill. Her defenders deserved something, she felt, but what could she possibly offer them?

Evic's face flashed in her mind, and once more she felt the flash of warmth that fluttered in her chest when he thanked her for agreeing to protect his sister. Some might not consider the thanks of a thief to be much of a gift, but it had touched her. It was a bit of fire against the chill that existed so strongly outside the Life Trees.

Khiri met each pair of eyes that were focused on her, then gave a bow of deepest respect. As she rose, they were still watching her. "Thank you," she told them. "You honor me. I will let my father know he is well remembered."

One of the watcher's faces cracked into a wide smile. "Good to know the old boy's still alive," she said. "Come down, daughter o' Genovar. Tell us about your pappy!"

15

~Resmine~

IT WAS WELL AFTER MIDNIGHT when Estan finally lumbered off to find the bed that he'd been promised. Resmine watched her large friend leave with room with no small amount of relief. She loved Estan. He was the brother that she'd always dreamed about having. But he was also a pain in her ass. Volunteering to spy on a guild of thieves for people they barely knew wasn't something Resmine would've signed on for without more discussion, or some mention of payment. Still, Estan had agreed, so Resmine wasn't about to welch on the bargain. *In fact,* she thought, *I may as well get started.*

Knocking back what was left in her tankard, Resmine waited until Ullen also made his excuses and bade the innkeeper good night. Adela got to her feet and pulled a broom out from behind the bar. Ren was still sulkily scrubbing the counters and glared at his wife's intrusion. She grabbed one of his meaty hands and kissed it. For a moment, Ren's face bunched up with emotions: surprise, anger, frustration, affection, and acceptance all fought for control. They all fled just as quickly, leaving Ren with something gruff but less petulant than his former storminess. The exchange was so intimate that Resmine couldn't help but remember Syara. It was definitely time for a distraction.

Resmine plopped down her tankard with a loud *thunk*, hoping to remind the couple that they weren't alone in the taproom.

"So, this Thieves' Guild... Any idea where they hole up?" Resmine asked. "I think I may see if I can't get started on that listening tonight."

"You're going to seek them out on your own?" Adela's eyebrows shot up in surprise. "Forgive me sayin', but I was under the impression that you weren't all that keen on helping us."

It wasn't like the innkeeper was wrong, but Resmine didn't think that Estan would appreciate it if she were to cause any friction with their hosts. She just shrugged, "Estan's agreed to help you out, and I'm not tired. I may as well see what the night holds."

Adela bent to begin sweeping. Her expression was thoughtful, and her grip on the broom was tight enough to whiten her knuckles. Just when Resmine thought Adela had decided not to tell her anything, the innkeeper sighed. "The Two Beams," she said. "They're at the Two Beams."

WALKING ACROSS JARELTON when the sun was down was much different than it had been earlier in the day. The denizens of the shadows were much bolder than they were back in Seirane. One unfortunate drunk stumbling through the streets got mugged by two hooded men right in front of a guard. Resmine said nothing, only faded into the shadows herself. If Estan were with her, he would've taken off after them and won the purse back for the drunk after a brawl. He would've been appalled that she let the drunk get robbed.

That was the difference between her and Estan, though. Resmine knew how to keep her head down. She didn't have the slightest idea if she was enough of a fighter to take those two hooded figures on, and she wasn't about to risk it.

As reluctant as Adela had been to tell Resmine about where to find the thieves, Resmine hadn't expect much help with locating the tavern, but the innkeeper was much more forthcoming about the location. Two rights, a left, through the square market space, past the tax collector's office (which Resmine was supposed to recognize when she saw it,) and up the big hill. *How hard could it be?* Resmine thought ruefully. *Just all the way across a strange and hostile city in the dark... No problem.*

If she hadn't spent the last five years hiding herself from those in the Temple of Locke, she wasn't sure that she would've made it across Jarelton. There was one instant when she was passing a tall figure in the streets that Resmine had been dead sure that she'd been spotted. The figure stopped, turned toward where she crouched in the shadows, and leaned toward her. A knife gleamed in the moonlight, promising trouble for anyone that got in the way of this particular shade. Resmine held her breath, willing the figure to move on and leave her alone in the dark. Much to her amazement, it worked. The figure hunched one shoulder in a partial shrug and continued down the street. Not wanting to push her luck, Resmine stayed frozen in place and counted to five before moving on.

At the door of the Two Beams, Resmine hesitated. Turning back toward the street, she debated whether to return to the Talon Acre Inn. What if the thieves killed her just because she was an outsider? What if they threw her back out into the streets? She wished she hadn't been so impulsive when she decided to come here alone. It was rash, and she knew better than that. Why had she been so certain that this was something she should do without Estan?

Because Estan is Estan, Resmine reminded herself. *He'd do something stupid and/or heroic the moment he walked in the door, and they'd know we were spies. He's going to get one or both of us killed someday with his hell-bound sense of honor. Whereas I can blend. I'm just crooked enough to do this...*

Her determination refreshed, Resmine pivoted on her heel and found that she was no longer alone.

"Hello, love," dark eyes danced in the torchlight, framed by a trim of inky black bangs. The rest of the raven hair was tied up in a horse tail, exposing a neck of smooth caramel skin. Resmine bit her lip to resist the urge to lick the woman in greeting. She hadn't been this attracted to anyone since... Well, since Syara.

"I... that is... Um, hi," Resmine stammered. *Real smooth*, she winced. It was like she'd never flirted before.

"Never seen you around before," the young woman said. Her smile revealed a dimple in one cheek. "Not a place you'll be wantin' to lurk in without so much as a by yer leave from her Highness, neither. Not without a host. My name's Dewin."

Resmine's mouth felt horribly dry. She swallowed a few times, hoping to clear the dust from her vocal chords. What was wrong with her? "I... My name's Resmine," she said. "I don't suppose you're volunteering to show me around?"

Dewin's expression flickered for a moment. If Resmine hadn't been watching so closely, she might have missed it, but she was having a hard time pulling her eyes away. Dewin's features settled back into a smile and she said, "I think I might be."

The young thief dragged Resmine into the Two Beams Tavern and past the bustling taproom. Resmine had been anticipating a night of bitter ale and sour looks, but the moment they entered the hallway, Dewin's sweet lips were all she could taste.

16

~Khiri~

WHEN MICAH ENTERED the pub, Khiri barely noticed. Her defenders had peppered her with questions about her father, never giving her a chance to formulate her own questions about his past. They laughed when they discovered her fondness for sarsaparilla, and harder when she treated the offer of a cheese plate like a religious experience.

Micah also seemed amused as he elbowed his way into the crowd she had gathered and told her that Fennick had left early to run errands before they left. They were to meet him at an armory on the far side of the city just after midday.

"Do you know how to find it?" she asked Micah. A scowl turned down the edges of her mouth and a dimness was cast over her earlier mood. She wasn't sure she wanted to go out on the streets alone except for Micah. Her first time through the streets of Jarelton had left a bit of a mark.

"He gave me the name and said pretty much anyone could direct us there," Micah shrugged. "The Thorn and Rose Armory... Apparently, it's got a great reputation."

"Finest leather and chain smith this side of eternity," one of the men agreed, lifting his mostly empty tankard in a salute.

"Here, here!" three or four others raised their own mugs.

The innkeeper, a man with a thick, black mustache, long black hair and a barrel chest, brought a pitcher over and refilled several tankards. He had been a part of the group surrounding Khiri for a good part of the morning, but had removed himself when more customers started to appear. "I can have one of my boys take you. They'll be eager for a chance to escape more chores," he grinned at Khiri. "I like you, lass. You're good for business."

Khiri felt her cheeks flush. It was one thing to be praised for skills that she'd earned, but she didn't feel like she'd done anything to deserve the innkeeper's compliment. It was really praise meant for her father. Somehow, someday, she hoped she could inspire the loyalty of an entire bar full of people on her own.

THE PROMISE OF RAIN clung to Khiri's skin the moment she and Micah walked out of the tavern. Tarick, the innkeeper's son, was pelting through the gray stone streets as quickly as his little legs could carry him. Khiri and Micah were running after him, though they were having an easier time of it than the day before. Many farmers and merchants had not bothered to set up their stalls, more concerned about the damage rain could do to their wares than getting a few sales done before the downpour.

"How much farther?" Micah called out to their guide.

"Only a bit," Tarick stopped to let them catch up, and then darted forward again. "There's no way I'm going to make it home before the sky splits," he grumbled.

"Hey, Tarick!" Khiri said. "Wouldn't the rain give you an excuse not to rush home? Didn't your father say you were excused from your chores until you were done with this errand?"

"Yes!" Tarick exclaimed, halting altogether. He looked at Khiri with bewildered astonishment. "You're smart for a grown up! Maybe it's because you're not so tall... Okay, we can walk from here." His pace became much slower, more of a saunter, as he kept just ahead of the two elves. The boy started skipping every other step and darting back and forth across the street as things in stalls and store windows caught his attention.

"Soothing the wildlife, I see," Micah heaved a sigh of relief. "I don't know how you do that."

"Intuition," Khiri said. Her head twisted as she spotted a familiar street. She realized with a start that they were passing the alley that she had gotten jumped in. Shivers danced down her spine. It had crept up on them without her realizing they were even heading toward it. How did the roads look so much different without the crowds? Relief was never so sweet as when Tarick turned into a new section of the city and the alley passed out of sight.

Small, stinging pellets of rainwater were just starting to drop as they reached the Thorn and Rose Armory. They hurried into the shop's covered patio, a space decorated with clay shingles and potted plants that opened right into the heart of the building. Petrichor and the sharp tang of tanned hide mixed in the air thick enough to threaten Khiri with a headache. Leather breastplates and studded shields of all sizes and shapes hung from pegs and rafters. Fennick was waiting for them, leaning against the lone patch of open wall available in the entire store.

"I see Burson took a liking to you. What ho, Tarick?" the messenger bent down and roughed the boy's hair in a familiar and friendly manner.

"I brought your friends here all by myself, I did!" the boy said.

"So I see," Fennick said with all seriousness. "And they look like you've taken very good care of them. Here's a coin for a bit of iced cream. I believe there's a vendor just next door who would love to part with some."

Tarick's eyes became as wide as some of the bucklers hanging on the wall. He stood for a moment, staring at his prize, and then took off even faster than he'd been running before the rain started.

"You two only have hunting leathers, I've noticed," Fennick said, looking over first Micah and then meeting Khiri's eyes. "I've made a fair bit of coin this past year, running messages, doing favors, and the odd wager here or there. In gratitude for savin' me hide, I'm going to buy you both more road-worthy armor. Maybe a bit of chain, if it catches your fancy..."

"You're outfitting us?" Khiri asked, feeling oddly uncomfortable.

"Sure am," Fennick replied. "This is not entirely unselfish, I assure you. The two of you fight much better than I do, and I want you to be well protected so that you can continue to protect me. I am at your service, taking you to the mage you seek, but I want all of us to live long enough to see it through."

Still uncertain, Khiri scowled. She wasn't entirely sure how much Fennick was offering to spend, but Leyani was a trader and had talked to her daughter about how to tell the value of something. This offer seemed overly generous. A kernel of unease was forming when it came to Fennick, and Khiri wasn't sure if she'd done the wisest thing in tying herself to the first human she'd met. "If you are determined..."

"I am," the messenger said.

Micah was already looking over displays and asking the shop attendant about a pair of bracers. The attendant was a petite woman with spectacles and honey colored hair that she had pulled into a tight bun. She wore samples of some of the merchandise; her vest of splinted armor was shaped from a solid piece of leather that had large metal rings fastened on, and she wore a pair of strategically padded and reinforced leather pants. Grinning shyly at Micah, she helped strap one of the bracers around his wrist.

Fennick crossed his arms and ducked his head so that he could speak next to Khiri's ear, "You aren't at all jealous about the amount of attention that he's been getting since we got into town?"

The question almost distracted Khiri from her concerns about Fennick's generosity, but not entirely from her concerns about Fennick. She thought about the conversation that she and Micah had almost a week before. It had been a necessary conversation, but it had been mostly instigated because Fennick pushed them. He'd tried to push them again at the tavern. "You've been asking about our relationship an awful lot ever since Micah showed up. What is it to you? Why are you so interested in what we are to each other?"

"The way you yelled at him that first day, it was obvious that you two had a connection. You were mad at him for abandoning you, but he came after you. I thought that meant you two were involved. I've been pretty confused about that since we hit the city, though... He's been eyeing every woman that glanced his way, and you've not fussed even a smidge. Now, either I'm wrong, or the Elven clans could teach a bordello a few things about loose morals," Fennick said, not seeming to care if Khiri found this offensive.

Glaring at the former soldier, Khiri debated whether to say anything. It wasn't Fennick's business if she and Micah were lovers, friends, or just people that enjoyed hunting ducks in the same pond. On the other hand, if the former soldier knew what had happened, maybe he would stop trying to leave the two elves alone together. Maybe that was part of what had happened the day before, when Khiri had gotten jumped. She stilled her doubts, and decided that she was going to tell Fennick her tale.

"Micah and I are just friends. We were meant to be more once... Our kind are born knowing the name of our soulmate, and during our coming of age, we tell our families and friends the name. Micah is two summers older, and so everyone knew we would be together even though I hadn't yet reached my maturity. Then, the day I was to name Micah... Something changed. His name was no longer in me, nor was my name in him. We're no longer bound. I'm bound to a stranger somewhere out here, and Micah's not bound to anyone. So, no, I'm not jealous. I don't begrudge him his new freedom. If anything, I think I envy him," Khiri said. Micah was free of his bond. He had no name to replace hers, so he had the liberty to flirt and tease as he would. While the Life Tree clans had always considered that sort of behavior lowly and base, Khiri was beginning to find that she craved that freedom. *Telgan Korsborn*, the space in her head insisted.

Fennick stood in front of her, one eyebrow raised quizzically as though he had heard her internal monologue as well as her explanation. Khiri didn't move, the silent anticipation of Fennick's judgment weighing down her feet. Even though she didn't think she liked the man, he was her touchstone for this new society. It scared her that humans might try to cast her out, too.

Finally, Fennick dropped his arms and hooked his thumbs through his belt. "So that's the way of it. No wonder you two are wound up like frustrated rabbits!" he laughed. "C'mon, lass, if ever there was a cure for an ailing heart, it's preparation for a good fight."

17

~Ullen~

ULLEN KICKED HIS BLANKETS aside and rolled over for what felt like the hundredth time that night. He wanted them back the moment they fell off the bed. With a sigh, he climbed off the thin straw mattress and tossed the covers back into position. Jarelton was never really warm, even in the summer, but the temperature wasn't really the problem.

Some secrets were easy to keep. Ullen had been keeping some of his secrets for decades. It only seemed fair to let other people keep one or two from him. But it irked him that Ren and Adela decided to trust the stranger that wandered into their tavern before they'd even mentioned their problems to an old friend like himself.

The strangers had temple training. It was obvious to someone as old and welltraveled as Ullen. He didn't look anything like his eighty summers to the moth-sized lifespans that were humanity or the elves, but Ullen was a dwarf. They came from the Stone, or so the stories said. Stone was long lived and so were his people. Barring accidents or worse, Ullen could look forward to another three hundred years or more. Long lives needed long memories, and Ullen had traveled with Knights before. He would lay money that the male stranger, *Erdan* as he called himself, was a shield bearer. What the man was doing in Jarelton when the temples were making war on Eerilor was something the dwarf very much wanted to know. Was this knight trustworthy? Would he actually follow through on his promise to help Ren and Adela?

As tired as he was, Ullen couldn't bring himself to climb back into his bed. He knew there was no rest waiting for him tonight. His body was willing, but his mind wouldn't allow it. Laying the matter of Erdan and his friend aside, there were rumors that there were elves in the city. It had been ages since Ullen had seen Genovar Fortiva and his mate. Of course, there was no guarantee that any elf leaving the Life Trees would be Genovar, but if it was... Well, that wouldn't be good. Genovar had said that anything that brought him out of the Life Trees would likely mean that Irrellian Thornne had succeeded, despite their best efforts.

That thought sent a chill through the dwarf's body that had nothing to do with the bite in the air. *Irrellian Thornne*, the name seemed to reverberate through Ullen. One of those secrets that Ullen kept: the method used to defeat the Flayer Mage and end the War of the Burning Valley—if the Gray Army ever learned what they had done, it would be undone in a heartbeat. The Flayer Mage could never be allowed to get free. It would be the end of everything. Everything.

Ullen turned away from his bed with a shudder and began pulling his pants back on. It was no use. Thoughts of the Great War always put an end to his attempts to sleep. There was only one other topic that kept him up nearly as well, and that... Well, that didn't bear thinking about when he was already this agitated. He decided to return to the taproom and leave all his thoughts in the dark room with his blankets.

It was almost a shock to him when he found Adela still sweeping despite the late hour. There hadn't been much cleaning left when Ullen left to find his bed, and even Ren seemed to have gone to bed. "Lass, what ails yer spirit? Sommat I can help with?"

"Ullen!" Adela said with a start. She apparently hadn't heard him enter the room. "I... I'm sorry, old friend. My mind was elsewhere. The woman, Resmine, she... She left for the Two Beams."

"In the middle of the night?" Ullen asked. His eyes went to the door involuntarily. "Why would she go out on the streets in the wee hours?"

"I... It may have been my fault," Adela sighed. The broom was starting to shake in her hands. "I could've chosen not to tell her where Ysinda holds court, but she asked... and then she called Erdan 'Estan,' and I started tryin' to remember where I'd come across that name. When I remembered, the Two Beams slipped out of my mouth... Oh, Ullen, what if she comes to harm because I went and said?"

"Easy, lass, easy," Ullen took the broom away from Adela and set it against the wall. He guided the innkeeper back to her favorite chair and drew her a pint from the tap. Once his friend was settled, he drew a second pint for himself. "Yer two guests are adult enough to decide when to be about. It's dangerous out there, to be sure, but they made it here from wherever they were coming."

"Seirane, if the one upstairs is really named Estan," Adela said, swirling the ale in her mug absently. She seemed more interested in watching the bubbles than actually drinking. "That's what the poster said. He's wanted by the Venom Guild on the authority of Temple Hill."

Since when do the temples ally themselves with the likes of the Venom Guild? Ullen wanted to ask, but he was too used to keeping things like that to himself. Instead, he tried to guide the topic away from Flayers. "Are you mad at the lad for lying, then?"

"I was never mad at Ysinda," Adela said, with a hint of a smile. "But you knew that."

"Would you like me to try and find the lass before she gets into trouble?" Ullen offered.

Adela shook her head in a hurry. "I'd not ask that of you, Ullen. I meant what I said before. It's dangerous for strangers in the city right now, especially those from Eerilor."

That was met by one of those moments of silence where both parties hold still, wishing that the words had not been spoken. Maybe if no one spoke, if no one moved, maybe the words would evaporate and everyone could forget about them. Ullen knew that Adela didn't mean to convey anything but concern for his well-being, but she was one of the few people that actually knew what Eerilor was to him. It was too late to erase it, so Ullen did the only thing he could think to do.

"I think I will go look for the lass," he said, leaving his pint on the table unfinished and Adela's half-formed apologies unheard.

He knew it was unwise to travel the streets of Jarelton in his state of mind, so when Ullen's vision suddenly went dark, he almost thought he deserved whatever came next.

18

~Estan~

CARRYING HIS SADDLEBAGS down the quiet city streets made Estan uncomfortable. In the bustle and business that normally clogged Jarelton's arteries, he'd been hidden among the masses, but being one of the few souls out in the open felt very much like leading a parade. The morning carried the promise of rain, and many of Jarelton's denizens elected to stay indoors rather than risk getting wet. Those that were out were heavily hooded and cloaked, unlike Estan. He only had one shirt worth wearing after so many days on the road, and it was bright orange. It happened to be the one he'd worn under his armor during his dye bath on the way out of Seirane. Multiple washings hadn't dimmed the color at all.

One good thing about the rain was that it gave Estan the opportunity to trade in his tell-tale armor without the eyes of the city watching. Adela told him that Resmine had volunteered to find a good tavern near the Court of the Thieves' Guild and keep an ear open while he was gone. She also asked him to keep an eye out for Ullen, since the dwarf had also left some time during the night.

Estan suspected that Resmine was trolling for a promising flirtation. It wasn't as though the knight would mind finding someone himself. The last time he'd been with a woman, he hadn't yet been to battle in Eerilor; that had been nearly three full seasons ago. Maybe he would find a willing bunk mate here in Jarelton while they looked for Genovar's daughter. Even the thought made his trousers seem a bit tighter, and Estan made himself concentrate on other things. The request to keep an eye out for Ullen seemed a bit odd, but if the mood toward dwarves was as bad as Adela thought, Estan could oblige.

Wooden signs clacked in the wind of the approaching storm. Estan hurried his pace. There had to be an armory that specialized in plate-mail somewhere in the city. He had passed several leather work armories and a few weaponsmiths, but had not seen any plate armor hanging on display.

"I may have to make do with splinting or studs," he said with a sigh.

As Estan turned a corner, he found himself on the outer edge of a crowd of people. In the center of the crowd, on a hastily erected platform, a man dressed in deep crimson shouted and pumped his fist into the air. "The Eerilorians hold no respect for Mytana!" the man spoke with such zeal that spittle flew from his lips with almost every word. "They steal the waters that bring life to our fields! They would eat the grain that belongs in our bellies! Eerilor feels nothing for us but contempt, we who fought for them during the War of the Burning Valley! We were the power that saved the world, and they see us as pigs!"

Estan gave the group surrounding the rabble rouser a wide berth, trying to walk around them. With the temples looking for him, the last thing he needed was to attract this kind of attention, but to completely ignore such blatant saber-rattling went against his grain. Risking another glance at the make-shift stage that the man was standing on, Estan stopped. There was something up there that he couldn't turn his back on.

"Well, today, we take our revenge on these fiends!" the man held up a bound and gagged dwarf that Estan had no trouble recognizing. Even if the dwarf hadn't been someone he knew, Estan didn't think he could've walked away, but those red ribbons woven into the black whiskers told the knight that this was the same Ullen he'd agreed to look for. "Today, we will make one suffer for all that we have suffered!"

Scattered shouts from the crowd met the man's pronouncement, most calling for blood. With a quick curse, Estan dropped his saddlebags where he stood. He knew he was probably never going to see those bags again after he dealt with this crowd, but it was a small price to pay compared with what his soul would bear if he left Ullen to his fate.

"Drop that dwarf!" Estan yelled.

"Who dares speak for this wretched filth?" the man in red asked. A knife appeared in his hand.

Pushing his way into the center of the crowd, Estan climbed onto the small stage and unsheathed his sword. "I do," he said. "As a blooded campaigner for Mytana, I vouch for the dwarf you hold. Release him."

"Blooded campaigner, you call yourself, and yet you draw steel against another Mytanan?" the man spat. "You deny us revenge against our wrong-doers and threaten your kin!"

The crowd started muttering amongst themselves. Estan was relieved that the crowd still seemed uncertain enough to be swayed. He would only have to deal with the man in red for the time being.

"My kin? My kin are men and women who kill to protect their homes and families. My kin are those who draw blood of necessity, not for sport and not to satisfy their own egos. If that dwarf is your enemy, why have you trussed him up like a roast? A true protector of Mytana meets his enemies on the field. He doesn't jump them in the marketplace," Estan's contempt grew as he spoke. He hadn't intended to make a speech when he'd climbed onto the stage, but every word that sprang from his lips carried the weight of truth.

An honorable foe shouldn't try to stab without warning, Estan thought as fury built within him. An honorable foe wouldn't kill someone just because it was convenient.

A smattering of cheers arose from the edges of the group surrounding them. They were drawing more watchers, and the man in red was growing more and more incensed. "You wish me to meet my enemies head on? Fine. I will show you what it means to be a true Mytanan!" the man released Ullen and charged Estan with a scream of pure rage.

Estan dodged the man with the ease of one that's been trained for most of his life, and brought his pommel down on the back of the man's skull. The man collapsed like an overstressed bridge, landing belly first on the slats of his bedraggled dais.

"Alright, loves! 'Nough seen and heard to satisfy your jigger itchin' louse heads! Heard the man, right enough you did! The dwarf's Mytanan as me, and I ain't heard a word o' complaint since I were high enough to wee in a privy! Bout your business!" a woman in a black outfit with flashes of purple trim chivied those closest to her away. When she got close enough that Estan could see her coppery skin and black hair, she bent down and untied Ullen with two quick jerks of her wrist.

Men and women started to wander away; some talked in groups and others went down the street in silence, seemingly lost in thought.

"Lovely bit o' talk," the woman said as she assisted Ullen with removal of his gag. "Twas palmin' a rune for a throw and a mad dash, myself, what? But I never could make my tongue dance a mob's tune worth a lick. Quick and hard, strikin' quietly from the shadows with a smith's hammer, right, love?"

Estan blinked in confusion, "I'm sorry. I have no idea what you just said."

"Lass is praising your speech, lad," Ullen said, pulling the gag out of his mouth with a scowl. "I'd like to thank you for intervening.

That crowd could have gotten very ugly, very quickly. I should'a listened to Adela last night, but I figured I'd been passin' through Jarelton for the last twelve years. People here know me, like Corianne fer instance. Didn'a cross my mind that street filth would sucker punch me durin' a morning stroll."

The dwarf began to massage his wrists, where the ropes had been drawn more tightly than those that had been tied across his thick leather boots, or his multiple layers of clothing. Estan couldn't remember what Ullen had worn the day before, but now he had on at least three shirts: blue, striped, and the top layer was a dusty yellow, all three of which opened enough at the neck to display the rough V of Ullen's chest hair. "Bastards broke my lyre in front of me after they drew the lashes tight. Then a group of 'em went to search the other taverns and inns for 'strangers'. Hope to Arra's bones they don't find any."

Corianne, as Ullen had named her, grimaced and helped the dwarf to his feet. "What're you plannin' now, love? Could mayhap nick you a new one, but it'd be fair chancy. I've no eye for singin' wood, and they're a might bigger than the usual bits."

"Naw, lass, I shan't be playin' a lyre no more. To tell the truth, I wasn't never much good, even when I played it proper. Until this war dies down, I think it's back to my old vocation," Ullen made an effort to smile, but it looked weary and false.

Corianne took the ropes that had been holding Ullen and used them to tie up the man in red. Estan stepped down from the elevated platform and began to search for his dropped his saddlebags. He was amazed to find them only a few feet away from the stage. Lifting the flap, Estan performed a quick inventory and found nothing missing at all.

"Every trinket in its all, yes?" Corianne called from the dais. "I was gonna nick 'em from you, fair and even, but then you had to cut dice with this git and I ended up standing watch o'er your lot instead."

Picking up his baggage, Estan walked back toward the stage, though he didn't climb up again. "Thank you for watching my stuff," he said. "My name is—"

"Oh, I recognize you, knight. Your blushing bride cheeks is fixed in my mind, sure as the knowledge of pickin' my way into a second-floor balcony," she laughed. "Shouldn't bandy your name about, what with those who're lookin'."

"Erdan's a knight?" Ullen asked, though his expression didn't look entirely surprised. "Awful young, aren't ya?"

"Erdan! That's a right fine alias, love. I think I'll use Collianne, next time I need to prance about in front guards with aught but my rune bag!" Corianne laughed harder, holding her stomach.

"Uh... I—I... Heh," Estan stammered. He looked at Ullen searching for the words to explain, but the dwarf waved it away.

"Later, lad. When we've no more audience," the dwarf said. Then Ullen got to his feet and jumped off the stage, "I think I'll tell ya about it on the way to wherever we're goin'. Where are we goin'?"

"I was hoping to find a place that swaps, sells, or buys plate armor," Estan shifted his saddle bags and their contents so that he could carry them more comfortably. His armor was heavy enough when it was strapped on. He wasn't sure how someone as small as Corianne had managed to move the bags as far as she did.

"I know just the place." Ullen assured the knight. Turning back to Corianne, the dwarf gave her a warm smile, "Find us later, lass? I believe you need to take care of sommat."

Corianne's laughter subsided. She nudged the unconscious man with her toe, "Aye, this be Tyronian Shedson. Picked up one of his conspirators yesterday. Rate we're takin' the rats, Queen'll start to call us her cats. Outsiders make the best bait, loves. You lot wander about emitting pungent aromas that rats cannot distinguish from jam."

"Wait, you said Queen?" Estan stopped and turned back to the woman.

"Can't talk now, love," she waved one hand at them while the other dug into a pouch at her waist. There was a blue glow that surrounded her like an aura, and she hefted Tyronian Shedson over one shoulder as though he weighed no more than a bed roll. "Later, we will slaughter a pint and paint the breeze, eh?"

As Corianne walked away from them, the rain that had been threatening started to fall.

Ullen and Estan watched her slip around a corner, then Estan adjusted his saddlebags to prevent them from falling down while he walked.

"So... What was your old profession?" Estan asked the dwarf.

Ullen fell into step beside the knight and began to tell Estan about his time as a professional tattoo artist.

"...AND THAT'S WHY YA NEVER want to deal with a masochistic bleeder," Ullen explained, nodding sagely at his own wisdom. Water dripped off the corners of his long mustache as they trod through the heavy drizzle.

"Thank you for that," Estan said, praying to any deity that would listen that the story he'd just heard would not haunt his dreams that night.

"Had to cauterize with a hot—" Ullen tried to continue.

"I don't want to know," Estan interrupted.

"He screamed like a—" Ullen said. He seemed to enjoy how uncomfortable Estan was with this subject.

"Enough!"

The dwarf laughed and slapped his knee. "By Arra's blood, Corianne was right! Yer red enough to see through the rain!"

Before Estan had the chance to regret saving Ullen from the man in red, Ullen pointed to a building labeled Stolen Jug Armory. A metal chest plate with a heavy clay jug dangling under it told Estan that this was exactly the kind of place he'd been looking for; he likely wouldn't have found it without the dwarf's help.

Once they were inside, the proprietor, an older gentleman whose craggy features were nearly ebony, looked over the armor Estan offered for trade.

"Straight up trade, one piece of mine for every piece of yours," the proprietor said. "It's good work, well maintained. Oddly dyed, but that's easy enough to fix."

Estan shook the man's hand. Even though he knew his armor was higher quality than anything that was hanging on the shop's walls, there weren't many smiths that were willing to negotiate a straight trade. Nothing in the shop was badly made, and the danger of having someone recognize him due to his armor's markings was much worse than the danger of new armor giving out on him. Until the temples were back in the hands of the truly devout, Estan couldn't take wearing the armor of his service for another day.

While he was making his selections, Ullen watched him with darkly thoughtful eyes. Estan didn't know what was going through the dwarf's mind, but he didn't want to ask in front of the shop owner's wary gaze. He suspected that it had to do with Corianne's revelation that he was a knight and his name wasn't Erdan.

Placing each new piece on the counter as he chose it, Estan soon came to the agreed upon amount. None of his new armor matched: the chest plate was bare of decoration, the gauntlets had woven knotwork stamped into the cuffs, and the wolf's head shaped helmet was more leather than metal, but each piece was sturdy. His new breastplate had the added benefit of lacking a hole puncture just over the heart. Armor was made more to deflect glancing blows than piercing, but Estan still didn't like how easily his former captain had planted his dagger through the metal. Estan suspected that his old captain used a magic blade. It seemed the only sure guard against an enchanted weapon was enchanted armor of similar strength, something Estan didn't have the coin to procure. The vendor measured out the pieces side by side and gave a grudging nod.

Back on the street, the rain was falling harder, making the roads slick beneath Estan's boots. Ullen waited until they'd put some distance between the Stolen Jug Armory and themselves before he said, "After Corianne told me what ya were, tweren't nothing to put together. You be the one that the Venom Guild is after."

"I'd appreciate that staying between us," Estan said, his brows drawing together.

"To be sure, to be sure," Ullen agreed. He tugged on his mustache, still seeming troubled. "Something smells wrong, lad. What are you doin' in Mytana? Why are you not leagues away? And why would the temples be so worried about one man, when they are busy fightin' a war? A war that's no business of the deity's at that..."

"Those are some very good questions. I promise, I'll explain myself when we get somewhere dry," Estan felt a pang in his chest. Parting with his armor, with his past, was harder than he'd anticipated. He shoved the uncertainty away, under the shield of numbness that had placed itself between his heart and his head.

"And the both of you could suck on a wooden teat, for all the good it'd do you," Corianne said from behind them. "I could've dropped you both without so much as a breath and a bolt. What's more," she lowered her voice to a whisper, "I'm not the only one that's found you, love."

The blue glow of Corianne's rune pouch as it opened cut through the gloom like a torch lighting a beacon. Three figures in soft black leather dropped from the walls, surrounding the knight and his two companions. For a moment, Estan thought that Corianne had actually signaled the assassins, but then the attacker in front of the knight lunged and the time for thought was over.

Estan threw himself backward, dropped his saddle bags, and blocked the assassin's dagger with his sheath. He barely had time to get his blade two inches out of its scabbard before the arm bearing the dagger swung at him again. "Taymahr, blast it!" he cursed, as the assassin pinned him against the wall.

Corianne tossed an exploding rune. It missed its intended target, but the burst of magical energy caused a stone to fall out of one of the nearby buildings and hit the unlucky assassin over the head. With a groan, that enemy fell over, either dead or stunned. Corianne turned away and found herself face to face with the last assassin. He too, was a rune thrower. In what almost looked like the opening steps to a dance, they both tossed down runes that popped shields up around them. They paced the edges of their shields like caged animals, experimenting with the other's shield by tossing runes charged with everything from ice to lightning. Ullen seemed to have disappeared from the scene, running as quickly as his stout legs could carry him.

Metal bit into Estan's arm while he was dodging a blast of ice from one of the stray runes. Immediately, his arm began to go numb... and then it started to burn. "Poison," he spat.

With a cocky twirl of the bloody dagger, the assassin gave Estan an affirmative salute. Estan used the opportunity to pull his sword free, though his reflexes were alarmingly slow. Whatever poison the assassin used, it was alarmingly effective. Estan was struggling to hold his sword up. His wrist shook more with each strike. He was unable to step back because the way was blocked by Corianne and her assailant. An odd tangy coat seemed to form on his tongue, making it hard to swallow.

The assassin tried to thrust his dagger in for the killing blow, but missed Estan's chest. The very same ice that had distracted the knight earlier managed to save his life. He slipped and fell to one side, ending up with his back against one of the surrounding walls. Pushing off of the ground, Estan spent the last of his energy to hurl himself at his enemy's stomach. The flat of his sword was braced against his good hand, more like a metal board than an edged weapon. It was enough to send the black-clad person flying into the wall on the opposite side of the rune casters. He hissed as the movement sent a new burning wave of pain through his injured arm.

A large purple flash alerted him to something changing in Corianne's fight. She stood behind her glowing blue shield, looking quite smug. The other rune caster was missing except for a pile of leather that sizzled in the rain.

"Estan!" he heard Resmine's voice, as though it were coming from far away. His eyes felt like they were getting heavy. Fighting to keep them open, he saw a swarm of people flood the space around him and the fallen assassins—his opponent and the stunned assassin that hadn't moved since taking a rock to the head.

"All human," Corianne's voice reported.

"Unusual for the Venom Guild," one of the crowd commented. "They were after this guy?"

"He saved me from Tyronian Shedson this mornin'," Ullen told them. "I dunno if they took exception to that, or sommat other, but I owe him my life."

He kept my secret, Estan thought as blackness settled in. *I should thank him.*

19

~Khiri~

RAIN CONTINUED TO THRUM on the roof of the Thorn and Rose Armory the entire time Khiri and Micah tried on and tried out breastplates, bracers, greaves and bucklers. The regular shields were too big for elves, having been made for humans, but Micah was rather fascinated with the idea of having a shield fastened to his arm.

In the end, Micah had a vest much like the one the shop attendant had been wearing, only his was dyed a deep green, and a pair of black leather pants that were much heavier than the ones he'd worn out of the Life Tree. He had picked out a pair of gloves with a wooden buckler attachment that could be removed and replaced, though it was sturdy enough to block one solid blow. At Fennick's suggestion, he had also found a new pair of boots that matched his new ensemble.

Khiri refused to try on any of the dyed pieces that were brought to her. She watched Micah make his selections without regard for Fennick's coin. Micah's vanity was something she'd never really noticed before, but it was becoming harder to overlook. When they'd been furnishing the house that they were supposed to live in, their taste didn't often overlap, but Khiri had been too thrilled at the thought of adventure to question it. Her excitement when he'd brought her the ruby ring had been genuine, but not really because of the ring. She had liked it because it was a present from her destined to celebrate their joining. At least, that's what it was intended to be; neither she nor Micah could've anticipated what had happened after she put it on. Khiri wondered just how much of Micah's picking it out had been compulsion, and how much had been his desire to own beautiful things. When they had been destined, had Micah seen her as a possession? She wasn't sure she wanted to know the answer.

Her new armor consisted of a reinforced, but still flexible, breast plate. It had been stained and pressed with a leafy vine pattern on the pauldrons, but was otherwise undecorated. Khiri would've stopped there, but Fennick refused to leave the shop until she was fully equipped.

"You need protection out there," he said. "Stop worryin' so much about what I'm payin' and just pick things out!"

After a quick discussion with the shop attendant, the girl had brought out a set of pants that Khiri had found acceptable. They would've been baggy on her, but they laced along the sides like a bodice and stopped at the top of her boots. Her thighs were covered by an extra layer of leather that hung in flaps that the attendant called a kilt. Nothing she had picked out restricted her movement, nor did it weigh much more than her hunting leathers had.

"Tell you what..." Fennick said when the attendant was figuring a total. "Khiri, will it make you feel better if you had a hand contributin' to the purchase o' this lot?"

Khiri nodded immediately. She didn't like feeling indebted to Fennick. It wasn't like he'd given her reason to doubt his intentions, and she was starting to feel a bit guilty that she was doubting him without cause. Still, guilt or no, there was something in her stomach that wasn't able to unclench when it came to the former soldier.

"Would you be willing to trade in your hunting leathers? They're a new design to these people, and could deduct a fair amount in the barter," Fennick told her.

My hunting leathers, Khiri felt stunned. Without her tattoos, her leathers were really the only thing still marking her as a member of the clans. If she were to return one day, would the Life Trees recognize her in her human attire? *Don't be absurd,* her more rational side chastised her. *Your father came back to the Life Trees, and you don't have any idea what he wore. You are yourself no matter what garment you strap on. Would you rather drag these all over the world, or would you rather get to work?*

"I'm willing," Khiri said, though she couldn't bring herself to watch the garments disappear across the counter.

The eagerness with which the shop attendant agreed to the trade erased Khiri's concern that Fennick was trying to trick her. Micah added his own leathers without batting an eye, and the attendant scooped those out of view as well. Fennick only set a few of his coins on the counter when all was totaled, though they were silver coins and not the coppers that Khiri had seen him use at the tavern.

After a return to the Scattered Winds to gather their bags and a lunch of cold meats and cheese, Fennick said it was time to be on their way.

"But it's still raining," Micah protested. "Shouldn't we stay here where it's dry until the weather clears up?"

He looked at Khiri for support, but she was used to hunting trips with her father below the elevated canopy of the Life Trees. Hunting didn't wait for good weather, and she wanted to be free of Jarelton. "I made that agreement with Evic, remember? I told him we'd be leaving today."

Micah's dark grumbles were hard to hear over the tautophony of raindrops smacking the dark stone of the city. It was hard to hear much of anything over the constant barrage, actually. After nearly losing sight of Fennick as his long strides took him through the blurry world of gray, Khiri started to regret not backing Micah's idea to stay an extra day in a warm, fire-lit tavern. She was holding her talisman from Evic to remind herself exactly why they were leaving when an arm shot out of the dark and looped itself around her throat.

"I've got a knife to your back, love," the voice was that of a young woman's, but pitched low to sound gruffer. "Don't move, or you'll be a pretty smear."

After having been jumped the day before, Khiri wasn't really in the mood to play nice with yet another attacker. "Let go of me," she warned. "I guarantee you won't like what happens next if you don't."

"Big talk for one as been taken so easy," the young woman said. Her arm tightened around Khiri's throat. Khiri couldn't actually feel the point of a knife in her back, but her new breastplate was being poked by something. For the first time since she'd allowed Fennick to purchase the new armor, Khiri was truly grateful that he'd insisted on the upgrade.

"Yer one to talk, girl," Fennick said. It was impossible to see what he did from Khiri's position, but he had the arm that had held the elf tangled in his and wrapped behind the young woman's back. Micah grabbed the woman from the other side. If there had been a knife, it got lost in the tousle.

As Khiri massaged her throat, the young woman thrashed in the grip of Khiri's friends. She had the same black hair and dark complexion as Evic and Corianne. "You are brutes to be sure, and ain'ta goin' nowhere with the likes of you bunglers! Can't even see a love behind you in the rain..."

"Let me guess," Fennick sighed, releasing the arm he held. "This is Dewin, the innocent thief we're to rescue."

She collapsed to her knees, almost taking Micah with her. "I didn't mean it before, love," she whispered, looking at Khiri. "I just thought to scare you out the gate. Iffen you lot left me, then my kin would've maybe let me stay. The Queen's not so bad as to kill me for unknowingly playing the blind! Please, tell them you won't take me! I pulled a knife on you! You can't trust me in a fight!"

"Dewin," Evic said as he melted out of the shadows, his tone saturated with disapproval. Khiri wasn't even sure how long the thief had been standing there watching his sister's antics. "That is enough. We already told you that we would send for you when it was safe, love. Until then, you are in this woman's custody, and you will treat her as though she is kin. Don't be shamin' Corianne and me. Khiri did us a fair turn, both flushing out a lunk of a rat, and now takin' you on."

He hauled his sister to her feet. In hiss of a whisper that Khiri was certain she wasn't supposed to hear, Evic said, "More than ever, you need to be out of Her Majesty's eyes... What were you thinking, bringing an outsider into sleeping chambers without permission?"

Dewin's dark eyes closed, acknowledging the rebuke, but she offered no explanation. Her shoulders sagged in surrender.

"I'm very sorry for Dewin's behavior, love," Evic reached out and squeezed Khiri's shoulder, an echo of the thanks he'd given her during their initial agreement. It was that more than anything that made Khiri's anger evaporate. "She's not happy about the situation, but you know how it is, being displaced."

Evic and Khiri exchanged a silent moment of perfect understanding. She was an exile, and he was a thief. Neither of them truly belonged to society, and neither of them could escape what they were. They could be accepted, ignored, mistrusted, or rejected according to their nature, but only others who had gone through it would understand. Dewin was not at that level, and Corianne and Evic knew that. Sending her with Khiri, they hoped to protect her from becoming one of them.

"Keep her safe," Evic said.

"I'll do my best," Khiri promised.

Dewin did not cry. She hugged Evic and took the pack that he pulled out of the alley he had been hiding in. Her head hung with dejection as she proceeded to lead Khiri, Micah and Fennick out of Jarelton.

20

~Estan~

THE HAZE THAT HAD DARKENED Estan's vision seemed to be lifting. His eyelids felt less heavy, and the tang gluing his mouth shut began to ease.

"Easy, love. You got yourself kicked in the teeth with a lethal dagger bite. Luckier than a tavern wench that you had a knowledgeable rune thrower within spittin' distance," Corianne told him.

"What happened?" Resmine's voice followed Corianne's through the fog engulfing Estan's brain. He wondered when she'd returned and how long he'd been out. "Is he going to be okay?"

Frigid rainwater soaked through everything Estan was wearing. He wanted to move, to stand. Struggling against the hands that were holding him down, he tried to rise. "Don't listen to well, do you, love?" a male voice asked him. A face that was a slightly lighter copper than Corianne's lowered itself into his vision, seeming somehow familiar.

"Evic, I think this one is even clumsier than the friend we made not long ago," Corianne said. "You were rather fond of Khiri, no?"

The man smiled, "Good fighter... Strong woman. Hard to dislike that combination, love. Reminds me of my sisters."

"Khiriellen Fortiva?" Estan barely forced his mouth to cooperate. The words seemed to be stuck behind the lump in his throat. Stale water flowed into his lips from a cloth. He almost choked before he remembered how to swallow. More water eased the foul taste that still lingered. "Elf?"

Surprise registered on the man's face before it withdrew from Estan's sight. "You two know Khiri?" the man asked, apparently directing the question toward Resmine.

"It's a long story," Resmine sighed, speaking softly. "We've never met her, but her father sent us to find her."

Estan realized that he was on his bed at the Talon Acre Inn. He struggled to get up again, only to be pushed back down by a firm dwarven hand. That was when he realized that Ullen was also in the room. Just how many people were in here watching him anyway?

"Easy, lad. Corianne knows what she's about," Ullen told him.

"He's wanting to be rid of the damp. Didn't reckon on his coming to before we had off his drawers," Corianne said. "Barely shoved him twixt the sheets and he's lively as a randy rabbit. Well, the lot of you, out. Except you, love. He'll want someone close that he trusts."

Resmine's chestnut curls bounced around the shadow of her head. Estan couldn't tell, but he thought she looked worried. "Just a scratch," he croaked.

She forced a bit of a laugh and then began to help Corianne pull his clothes off. Estan didn't much care that they were going to get an eyeful of his flesh. All he wanted was to sink back into the dark place where he didn't have to think about the throbbing of his arm.

"So tell me more about why you're after Khiri, love?" Corianne said, tugging on one of Estan's boots. "Does it have sommat to do with us havin' to knick you from the Two Beams before'n Her Majesty rose this morn?"

Resmine slipped the other boot off easily. As a squire for the Knighthood of the Battered Iris, she had a lot of practice stripping a knight of things like boots. Remembering Syara, Estan guessed she probably had a lot of practice stripping a knight of other things as well. Thoughts of Syara brought him to thoughts of Loni. He wondered how she was, and whether her connection to his escape had been discovered. Hoping Loni was alright brought unbidden thoughts of loneliness. How long had it been since he'd had a proper relationship? Was it the aftereffects of the poison or the realization that he'd nearly died that made it so hard to focus?

"How much do you already know?" Resmine asked.

Corianne let out a rough chuckle that was somehow also musical, and Estan felt a tugging around his injury. His pain level increased so sharply that it filled his mouth with heat and daggers, and then the intensity vanished altogether. All he felt was a dull ache, like that of a bruise.

"That should ease you a bit, love..." her voice was very close to Estan's ear. He wondered if she was close enough that he could turn and kiss her. Anyone that was that good at chasing away pain must have been sent from the gods.

"Evic and I saw this one pass through as one of the Knighthood, and then pretty as a May posy, the Venom Guild blows through with reward lots. Then we sees him again, tryin' his hardest not to look like the same knight we sees before. Tweren't much to add two to two and come up with him bein' in a fair spot o' nip. We'd be in a way to make a coin on him, but three things. First, you lot stayed with the Talon Acre Inn, which is not Court but is protected. Then this bloke stands up and speaks for Ullen, who is looked on fondly by me and mine. Lastly, and mayhap the biggest bug in the nap sack, Venom Guild ain't welcome in Jarelton. Thieves need to make a livin' and we can't hold Court when the royals could be plucked by outsiders. They start huntin' civil folk, rats will get ideas...."

"You lost me a little toward the end, but it sounds like you've pieced together enough. It started when..." and Resmine proceeded to tell the story of how they fled Seirane, met Genovar in the Life Trees, and the agreement that had brought them back into dangerous territory.

Estan fell into a light doze and lost their conversation to a whirl of vividly colored, nonsensical dreams.

BRIGHT SUNLIGHT BEAT against the knight's eyelids, insisting that he had been asleep long enough. Estan sat up in his bed and flexed his injured arm. It felt as though a lump of stone was pressing against his muscles hard enough to bruise. He explored the white bandages with the fingers from his other hand. There was a small spot of darkened blood showing through the wrapping, but it was no longer damp. It felt as though there was a rune tucked into the folds of the cloth.

"About time for that one to recharge," Corianne said from a chair across the room. "Shouldn't be any poison left, but better to wear wool and sweat than linen in the snow."

Wincing, Estan tore the knot on the bandages loose. "Thank you, for all of this... If it hadn't been for you, that attack would have killed me. You saved my life, twice over," he sighed.

She came to him and stopped his hand. Heat passed through their joined skin, and for a moment, Estan forgot everything. The injury, the fight, his mission... It was all background noise to his suddenly hammering heart. Corianne dropped his hand and the moment was over. The thief woman cleared her throat and began unwrapping his gauze, "I'll handle that, love. It's not all charity. Resmine told us that you are goin' to aid the elf, and we just sent her along with our sister. If you are helping to protect Khiri, you'll be helpin' Dewin."

"I have a price on my head," Estan argued. "Helping me reach them will likely put them in more danger."

With a smile that lacked humor, Corianne shook her head. "Won't make much difference," she said. "The elf's already bein' hunted. They haven't a price on her head, so whatever she's done, they're takin' it real personal."

Estan jerked just as Corianne tied the knot on a fresh bandage. "She's already being hunted?"

The thief nodded. "Khiri's got two companions; one is an elf from her home village, while the other is a message runner, ex-soldier. That one's been through the city many times, but never bore the glance of a butterfly. Saw her fight. She's a fair bit of flash without a dagger, only touched her knife once."

A chunk of rock was building in Estan's stomach, "In other words, she's probably the best fighter they have and there's no harm in adding my assassins to hers."

Corianne walked back to the other side of the room and grabbed a pair of pants off the back of her chair. She tossed them to him without looking. Estan noticed that they were not originally a pair of his, but he didn't argue as he yanked them on. A sense of urgency had overtaken him, and he wanted to be out of Jarelton. He practically punched his arms into his spare shirt, and in his haste, nearly tore his healing flesh. As much as it rankled Estan to do so, he made himself slow down.

"Maybe one night before you run yourself broken, what?" Corianne said, her expression one of wry amusement. "Ullen wanted to throw a few words your way. I'll send him up with your dinner." The thief exited the room before Estan could protest.

Laying back on the bed, Estan considered his wound. If half a day of nursing had taken him from near death to his present state, it would probably be better to wait a full night; however, the idea that Khiriellen Fortiva was just a few hours away was hard to ignore. They could probably catch up to her before full dark, assuming Estan could keep his seat on Catapult.

Ullen ambled in carrying a tray that held a bread bowl full of some sort of stew. "Lad? They sent me with sommat to help ease you."

"I'll take that," Estan rose, took the food laden tray with his good arm and placed it on the bed. With slow, deliberate movements he sat down and started spooning the hot savory broth into his mouth.

"Uh... Lad, I'm sorry I didn't... I couldn't... I was unarmed, low to the ground, and took the only course I saw open," Ullen muttered. The dwarf looked like he was about to start scuffing his feet on the floor, like a child caught stealing pies. "I'm ashamed that I couldn't do more than run for reinforcements."

Still pondering whether he was leaving as soon as he could, or waiting until the next day, Estan dropped his spoon onto the tray. It took him a few moments to digest the dwarf's apology; it hadn't even occurred to Estan that Ullen might feel responsible. He certainly hadn't begrudged Ullen when he'd run from the fight. If anything, Estan felt a bit guilty that he hadn't bothered to think about it at all. After having saved the dwarf from a mob, he'd just assumed that Ullen wasn't a fighter. "Don't worry about it," Estan said. "We're both alive, right?"

"Some of us more so than others." Ullen coughed and looked pointedly at Estan's bandaged arm. "Actually, I wanted to discuss the possibility of going with you. If you let me come along, I may be able to pay you back one day."

Estan studied Ullen with an appraising eye, reassessing what the dwarf offered in the sense of military strengths. Even though he had never seen Ullen touch a weapon, the dwarf had a lot of raw power. "Do you fight? What weapons do you use?" he asked.

"Quarterstaff... Not much use in city streets, but very good for a traveler," Ullen answered. "And I've a few tricks I've picked up while travelin.'"

Between Resmine's whip and dagger and his own sword and warhorse, they already had an admirable force to add to Khiriellen's party. If they added Ullen's quarterstaff to the mix, they would be able to protect their flanks from the assassins' three-man system and then some. Assuming the dwarf was any good. If Ullen proved a liability to their party, they could always part ways later on down the road.

"I'll take you up on that offer, Ullen, on two conditions," Estan said, ripping a piece of bread off of his bowl and offering it to the dwarf.

The dwarf took it, placed it in his mouth and chewed it carefully. "What conditions, lad?"

"Number one, on the road, I am the commander. If I make an odd request, like 'stop and look at those cows', we stop and look at the cows," Estan ripped another piece of bread from the bowl.

"Aye, lad," Ullen nodded and leaned against the door frame, "I can do that. And what's the other condition?"

Popping the salty stew-soaked bread into his mouth, Estan sighed, "You have to talk me out of leaving tonight."

21

~Khiri~

JARELTON'S EASTERN gate opened onto more grasslands, which Khiri found a welcome sight after the stone of the city. At least in the grasslands there was life in the soil. The ground was softer on the feet as well, and Khiri broke out into a run, greeting the rain, the mud and the grass as though they were old friends.

Micah's laugh sounded right behind her, also reveling in the freedom of the sky after the harsh lines of the buildings and streets.

Khiri held herself back, unwilling to get too far ahead of Fennick and Dewin. The thief was still very unhappy that she'd been forced to leave the city. Fennick was trying to cheer the young woman up, pointing out the line where the clouds ended, and chuckling loudly at what he called an "elven romp".

Slowly, the rain drifted away from them, darkening the western edge of the horizon and blending with the gray stone ridge that was Jarelton. Dewin started to come out of her funk as the sun ignited the landscape. They were heading into an area surrounded by orchards, and the smell of peach and apple blossoms permeated the air. Khiri took the young thief into the rows of trees to begin teaching her the fundamentals of wood lore. Already, there were signs of wildlife stirring from the shelters that they used to wait out the rain.

"My first memories are of when Corianne came to live with us," Dewin said, unprompted. She looked like she was about to cry. "If

I've ever been away from Jarelton before, 'tweren't long enough to make a lasting impression. Corianne was the one, you know, that taught us to knick and tussle. Evic was the first to get caught, though Corianne put him up to it. He never ratted on her, even when the guard gave him five days in a cell. I don't think we ever stole anything until she showed up... But it was all her, knowin' and thievin', that kept us alive when our mother passed on. I only ever wanted to make her beam proud an' all."

Khiri wasn't sure how to respond. Back in the Life Trees, she hadn't really made friends growing up, Micah excluded. Her father spent most of her free time on training, even before she was old enough to apprentice as a hunter. When she was old enough to start desiring more of a social life, her peers had already spent years getting to know each other and doing things without her. They had inside jokes and stories that Khiri didn't know, and he attempts to get closer only made her feel more like an outsider. Khiri wasn't planning to speak when she heard herself say, "I was an outsider long before I was ever an exile."

"So we're well match for company, you think?" Dewin gave the elf a tight-lipped smile. "Still, the timing was something awful. Had me a new sweetheart, I did. Would've liked to pursue that."

IT WAS CLOSE TO EVENING before the pleasant feeling in the air started to dim. The sounds of wildlife faded, and then stopped altogether. Khiri halted in her tracks. Using the hand signals that Genovar had drilled into her over the years, she instructed those with her to freeze before it occurred to her that they may not understand.

"Well, look what's crawled out from under the bedrock," a familiar voice said. The assassin woman stepped out from behind a tree, her sword reflecting the pink and violet of the setting sun. Khiri felt the woman's acidic gaze on her; if someone's eyes were able to peel off skin, the assassin wouldn't need her sword.

"Indeed," the pale, bald assassin melted into existence behind them. "We had not hoped to recount this pleasure so soon."

"Who are these brutes, love?" Dewin asked, her voice barely more than a hiss. "Those are assassins' cowls, yes?"

"*Bloooooooooooooooooood*," came a long whispering demand from behind them. The Flayer did not delay for niceties, but plowed into them at full charge. Fingernails like claws raked Khiri's exposed arm as the Flayer bounced off of her and slammed into Fennick, pushing him to the ground.

Dewin let out a fierce war cry and flung herself to one side, reaching for her belt. Half a dozen darts appeared in her hands and she flung them toward the bald assassin with the sunken eyes. Micah reached for his bow and began to string it. He was trying to keep Khiri between him and the remaining assassin, but he needn't have worried. The woman was focused on Khiri with a hatred so savage that the rest of the world could've been on fire and the assassin wouldn't have spit to dampen the heat.

"You killed my brother!" the assassin yelled, swinging her weapon at Khiri as though she held an ax instead of a sword.

Khiri blocked with her knife, attempting to twist the sword out of the assassin's grip and failing. "I killed a Flayer," the elf corrected.

"That Flayer was my brother!" the woman took another swing, the rage building up into tears. "All he wanted was to have the power to protect me, and you killed him!"

"He was a Flayer. Flayers don't protect, they just destroy," Khiri said, even though she knew it was useless. She blocked another wild sword strike, stepped into the woman's guard, and elbowed the larger woman in a sensitive part of the forearm. The assassin cried out in pain, but refused to drop her sword. Instead she kicked Khiri away and mustered herself for another attack.

One of Micah's arrows found its way into the back of the Flayer that had Fennick pinned. It screamed, a sound that caused everyone fighting to pause and cringe. Micah's shot had missed the vitals of the creature. It reached as far back as it could, groping and scraping to pull out the arrow. Fennick rolled the creature to the side, smashing it against a tree. Again, the Flayer yowled in pain.

Dewin was dancing away from the hollow-eyed assassin, pelting him with darts when she got an opening. The man was not impressed. If anything, he seemed to be toying with her. She drew the hand axe that she kept on her belt and charged the assassin, knocking his blade out of the way with blunt side of her weapon. Instead of fighting the movement of his sword, the assassin allowed it to be batted away and danced after it. Instead of Dewin's swing meeting his collarbone, the axe whiffed through empty air. "Naughty, naughty," the pale man taunted. "What's a thief doing connected with such people?"

"None of your business, love," Dewin snarled.

The woman Khiri was fighting caught the elven woman's wrist in one hand and held the knife away from her body. Khiri strained and twisted as the assassin raised her sword for a killing strike. A crazed hunger filled the woman's eyes as she licked her lips in anticipation. "One less elf, just another notch on my blade...."

Khiri kicked the woman in the knee, causing the assassin to jerk. She twirled into the arm holding her wrist and ducked under the other woman's armpit. The assassin released her grip, shrieking with rage.

Fennick had gotten ahold of a rock in the road, and was smashing it into the Flayer's face. Micah was out of arrows; he was approaching the Flayer from behind, his hunting knife drawn. Bloody gashes decorated Fennick's arms above his gloves.

Malice shown in the pale assassin's eyes as he evaded Dewin's descending axe and nicked her arm with his sword tip. "It's different when we're all on the same level, isn't it, elf girl?" he taunted Khiri while he fought the thief.

Blood sprayed everywhere as Micah dispatched the Flayer, slicing through its neck. Steam and sizzling sounds began rattling the corpse as it shredded itself into ash. Rolling away from what was left of the body, Fennick was finally able to pull his sword free of its sheath. "Let's see how well the two of you fare against four," Fennick said.

Khiri kicked the assassin woman in the butt, propelling her toward her companion. The pale man barely had the time to lower his blade to prevent impaling his partner. With a speed that she didn't know she possessed, Khiri dropped her knife and strung her bow, knocking an arrow before the two assassins could untangle themselves.

"Run," she breathed.

Both assassins looked as though they wanted to kill her where she stood. The bald assassin pushed his partner away in disgust. "Perhaps your threat level should be reassessed, elf. Make no mistake, though. We will kill you, and anyone that swears you allegiance. You've made this... very personal."

In response, Khiri pulled the bowstring tighter.

Without further delay, the assassins melted into the orchard, taking the very last rays of sunlight with them.

BUBBLES ROILED IN THE stew pot that Khiri had set over the campfire what seemed like a lifetime ago. She tossed a hunk of dried meat and sniffed at one of Micah's herbal packets. It just smelled like a bunch of herbs to her. Tossing those in, she began chopping something orange into smaller pieces like she'd seen Micah do on occasions when he did the cooking. It looked more like a carrot than anything else, so she figured that it would go well enough with the boiled venison meat. Micah was too focused on crafting more arrows to offer much advice, so Khiri decided that he'd be happy that she volunteered to cook for once. The stew was starting to smell a bit like food, if one was imaginative. It smelled better than some of her previous attempts, anyway.

Fennick was stitching Dewin's wounded arm. He had already produced a small vial of wound-cleanser and smeared it over the scratches that he and Khiri had acquired from the Flayer.

"I thought they were hired to chase you," Khiri said, looking at Fennick. "Why were they directing all of their threats toward me?"

"My guess is that they took your interference real personal," Fennick told her, not looking away from Dewin's arm. "The Venom Guild's not used to being thwarted, and you've just succeeded in surviving a third attack."

"They're hurting their cause with these Flayers," Micah observed. "From what I've seen, Flayers are creepy and evil, but they aren't very strong. They also don't seem to have any mental power."

"Ow!" Dewin yelped as Fennick broke the thread he was using to sew her gash. "They probably will use the tougher ones soon, love."

"There are tougher ones?" Micah looked up from the feather he was splitting.

"My aunt told me, during the War of the Burning Valley, there were legions of Flayers and they all looked alike but they weren't equal. The chanters, those that do nothing but say things about blood and death and ripping and what, they are the lowest of the low. Weren't much to them before the change, and even less after," Dewin explained.

"Aye, there were many Flayers in those days," Fennick agreed. "Some of the smarter ones pretend to be the lesser ones. I'm surprised that your aunt knew different."

"You knew these were lesser Flayers?" Khiri asked. She poked at her stew with one of Micah's large wooden spoons. It looked lumpy, which she didn't really understand. Maybe the lumps would boil out. "Why didn't you mention that we might have to face something stronger?"

Fennick began putting away his mender's kit. He placed the needle in a small bottle which he sealed with a cork. Winding the end of his thread carefully, the messenger seemed to avoid looking at the elf as long as he could. "I was hoping it wouldn't come up," he said.

"It took two of us to face one of the lesser Flayers. That bald man outmatches any one of us in single combat. The woman I fought nearly had me toward the end of our bout... If things escalate, we're in real trouble," Khiri sighed. "We got off easy. Scratches and stitches are child's wounds; they will not satisfy a true blood lust."

An uneasy silence fell over the camp. Flames whispered into the quiet, inviting those surrounding it to gaze into the fire's hypnotic destruction. Micah took the stirring spoon out of the stew and blew on a chunk of mushroom that came out with it. He slipped the mushroom into his mouth and attempted to smile. "I think the food's ready," he said. "For those brave enough."

There was not much discussion as they each spooned stew into their bowls, and then commenced to spooning it into their mouths. Dewin made a small exclamation of surprise after trying one bite, but the noises of the fire and the local wildlife soon overpowered the brief interruption. Khiri wondered if the others were racking their brains for a solution, or if their minds were swallowed by the sense of impending doom. She brought her first spoonful of stew to her own mouth, and started to reassess whether the doom had already found them.

"Training sessions," she said when she managed to swallow. If she was going to continue eating, she needed to distract herself with other problems. "If they are going to rise in skill, we need to as well. Before we leave out each morning, we will put in an hour of practice.

Exercises in reflexes, flexibility, endurance... We will need to start sparring."

"Will that be enough?" Micah asked.

"It's a start, lad," Fennick helped himself to a second serving of stew. Dewin and Micah both watched him with utter disbelief. Their own bowls were still almost full. Khiri couldn't even make herself do more than a few bites at a time. "Like army drillin', you don't start out knowin' all the moves, but you do them often enough and they ingrain themselves."

"Instead of final watch waking us for breakfast, we rise with the sun," Khiri said. "And none of you should let me do the cooking ever again... This is vile."

Fennick grunted in agreement, but still managed to drain a third dish.

KHIRI DUCKED UNDER Dewin's practice hatchet, which was a stick about the same size as the real weapon. The elf was facing her opponent unarmed, as she had been unable to find anything that resembled her knife in length.

Dewin made a second sweep with the stick, again swinging wildly after failing to make contact.

"Smaller strokes," Khiri suggested. She circled behind the thief and kicked Dewin in the rump. "Like a figure eight."

With an angry grunt, Dewin spun around and tried to bring the stick down on Khiri's head. Khiri caught Dewin by the wrist and threw the larger woman over her hip. Proving surprisingly spry, Dewin landed on her feet and managed to regain her balance, using the excess momentum to throw Khiri away from her.

"Not bad, eh, love?" Dewin smirked.

Instead of responding, Khiri stepped in and thrust her foot into the thief's face. Scrambling back, Dewin cursed and threw her stick at the elf, landing a glancing blow on Khiri's forearm.

"Now what?" Khiri demanded. "You're unarmed."

"So are you!" Dewin said, frustration evident in every line of her face.

"The difference being that Khiri's trained to fight like that, whereas you are a self-taught street brawler," Fennick pointed out. He was officiating for the final sparring match of the morning while Micah stood watch. "But, if you feel the need to make a dash at it... continue."

Khiri took a stance and waited for Dewin to gather herself. Taking a deep breath, Dewin charged in and started flinging random punches at Khiri. Blocking anything that would do real damage, Khiri rolled with the punches, letting the ineffective ones hit her where they would. Dewin started to grin, her emotions dwelling on her face. The thief obviously thought she was doing extremely well.

Letting Dewin get carried away would not accomplish anything, so Khiri grabbed the thief's arm as Dewin swung wide overhead. Ducking through the thief's armpit, the elf twisted Dewin's arm up behind the thief's back and held her there.

"Surrender?" Khiri asked.

"Let go!" Dewin demanded. She tried to struggle against Khiri's hold, which caused Khiri's grip to tighten. "Ow!"

"Surrender," Khiri repeated, no longer asking.

"Alright, alright... Damn, love. Near twisted my hand off my arm," Dewin stumbled away and rubbed her wrist with a sour look on her face.

As the match broke up, the three of them went back to what remained of the campsite. Micah dropped from a nearby tree to join them. Dirt was thrown on the leftover embers, and they scuffed the ground that had been under the tent to make it look like an older site.

Within half an hour, Khiri and her friends were on the road again. The scents of fruit-bearing blossoms danced through the hot summer sun, promising a good harvest in the fall. Khiri walked in silence, feeling as though this beautiful world was a lie. It was full of assassins, betrayals, and vengeance.

She looked at her companions. Micah, her one-time love, was deep in conversation with Dewin. He was trying to flirt with the young woman, though the thief seemed immune to his charms. Fennick was watching the trees pass by, his face hard. The ex-soldier had sunk into one of his dark contemplations that had earlier baffled Khiri. The longer they traveled, the more Khiri felt she could understand Fennick's need to brood. Though she missed her dreams from her days of innocence, every step they took made her that much different from the Khiri that she'd been back in the Life Trees.

They stopped for lunch just before the edge of the treeline. Micah got out some of the food stores and began making sandwiches. Khiri offered to search out some wild lettuces or herbs, but Micah shook his head and told her not to worry. He'd already spotted some red lettuce off the path, and he ran off to fetch it.

"How far will we go today?" Khiri asked. It didn't seem likely that Fennick would answer her, given his mood. Still, he surprised her on occasion.

Fennick turned his head, his expression not changing as he gazed down at Khiri. For a few uncomfortable heartbeats, that was all he did. His expression was unfathomable, almost angry. Khiri felt that if she could read his thoughts, she'd learn the worst secrets in the world, but then the moment passed and Fennick was back to normal. The ex-soldier responded to the question that Khiri barely remembered asking, "We'll be able to reach a trader's inn tonight: The Tilted Donkey. It's midway between Jarelton and Illesdale. We'll turn north tomorrow, after we pass through Illesdale, and then it will take us five to six days through the Eisessi mountains to reach Harish. From Harish, we travel northwest for two days. Mage Maleck Dorell resides in a tower there."

"Roughly a fortnight on the road," Micah said. Khiri's friend had his arms full of red lettuce and a few tomatoes. He set down his finds and returned to his sandwich making. "That's not bad."

It was obvious that Micah hadn't returned in time to see the odd moment that Khiri had just experienced with Fennick. A glance at Dewin told Khiri that the thief hadn't noticed anything, either. Dewin's back was turned on her companions and she was looking wistfully back in the direction of Jarelton.

"It wouldn't take that long, but we have a mountain range to cross between Illesdale and Harish. There is a pass, but it is too far to the east. Traveling there would add almost a week, and we'd be camping the whole way. It's closer to Seirane, and the roads there are crowded with soldiers and members of the Knighthood, guardians of the human temples," Fennick told them.

Talk ceased as Micah pronounced their sandwiches ready. It would take nearly two more weeks to find her father's mysterious friend, and find out about his secret past. She retained the hope that Maleck Dorell would be able to help her find Telgan Korsborn, though there was no certainty that one mage would know another.

After lunch, they returned to the road. The peppery aftertaste of the red lettuce stayed on Khiri's tongue and made her mood shift slightly toward more pleasant things. There were aspects of traveling that were very enjoyable, including the discovery of many foods that were not common among the Life Trees. Her cooking duties had been lifted after the stew incident, and it was nice to have more companions than just her father at a campfire. During their many hunting trips, Genovar didn't spend much time telling stories or talking to his daughter when they'd shelter for the night. It was more advice, more lessons, and more about the training they were doing. Occasionally, the mood would lighten and they would joke about something that had happened during the trip, or Genovar would teach Khiri things like curse words. Her father promised that all the greatest hunters knew how to swear. But something had been missing with her father's company, and Khiri thought she was beginning to find that missing element out here in the human lands.

Without warning, the sounds of wildlife went quiet and a Flayer collided with Khiri, knocking the air out of her lungs. It snarled savagely; its bruised and deformed face snapping its teeth inches from her eyes.

22

~Estan~

CORIANNE AND EVIC ESCORTED Estan's party to the gate. It was as much for the safety of the travelers as it was to keep an eye open for the Venom Guild or someone called Steward Jels. Estan felt his eyes drift toward Corianne a bit too often to deny that he found her attractive, but she was a thief and he was still a Knight of Taymahr in his heart. He walled off the part of him that longed to say something, to act. True, she had saved him, but he was leaving town in pursuit of another woman. The momentary ember would smother out in a few days' time. It wasn't long before Evic and Corianne were left behind, along with the city's interior.

Catapult was excited, breaking into a trot any time he felt Estan's attention wander. The blue roan had not enjoyed being left in a stable for two days, with only short walks in the stable yard for exercise. He had nipped at the stable hand and taken a bite out of Estan's sleeve. It had taken Resmine and a handful of apples to calm him enough to be saddled.

Ullen and Resmine had begun a conversation about Ullen's days as a professional tattoo artist, and Resmine was inquiring about the oddest tattoo that Ullen had ever created.

"So many, lass... Two headed drakes, large men wanting lace patterns over bits of their bums, the odd sea creature on a land-locked duffer, and people who don't rightly know what they want, just know they want ink driven into their skin," Ullen shook his head, laughing under his breath. "I wouldn't know where to begin with which was the weirdest tattoo. Now, the weirdest person I ever tattooed, that's another question altogether!"

Estan tuned them out. Until the most recent assassin attack, the danger posed by the temples had seemed distant; he thought he'd managed to shake the worst that Temple Hill had to offer. The brush with death from the day before made him all too aware that the temples weren't finished with him.

Jarelton's gate opened into a sky still rosy with the breath of dawn. Grasslands stretched into a low treeline—the orchards that made Mytana famous among traders. Apple and pears grew in abundance in the lower regions of the country.

Khiriellen Fortiva was ahead of them, somewhere. The knight could almost feel her, calling to him, summoning him as though he were a lodestone and she were the north. He didn't understand it. Her father, Genovar, was also out there drawing together an army to fight for Estan's home, honor, and his very beliefs. Logically, he should be agonizing about his inability to help in any real fashion. Instead, he marched on, through risk of life and limb to try and protect an elf girl that he had never met and knew very little about.

"I'm coming, Khiri," he whispered. "I'm coming."

LONG BEFORE NOON, THEY crossed into the shade of the orchards. Estan had pushed them with a pace that bordered on brutal. He made Ullen ride with Resmine on Catapult while Estan jogged next to the horse after it became evident that the dwarf's shorter stature made it impossible for him to keep pace. Dappled shadows fluttered over fresh footprints, two sets of which were small enough to belong to elves.

They spotted a poorly concealed campsite that was just a few feet off the road around midday. Dirt had been spilled over the fire pit, but the air had not fully whisked away the last heat from the dead embers. "They were here this morning," Estan told the others.

"Won't tonight be quick enough to catch up to them?" Resmine asked, irritable with her fatigue. "They can't possibly get that far away from us if they camped here last night."

"I can't explain it," Estan wanted to run a hand over his tightly bound hair, but he was prevented by the wolf helmet that was firmly strapped in place. "I feel like she's in danger. We have to catch up. I have to be there."

Ullen humphed from his place on the horse, "Well, lad, we'll do our best. Tweren't never much for riding, but Catapult here's got as even a gait as ever I've seen. We'll make it."

Estan held the stirrup of the saddle while Catapult cantered through the evenly spaced trees. Even with his lighter armor, the knight was beginning to tire. Within an hour's time, they heard the sounds of a struggle ahead.

A woman that resembled Corianne and Evic, armed with a hatchet, flanked a Venom Guild assassin, while a tanned male elf with golden hair menaced the black clad figure from the opposite side. The man that had been described as a former soldier was being held within a rune shield. Though he was fighting to free himself, the red, glowing barrier did not show any signs of giving. It took Estan several seconds to locate the female elf that was sprawled on the ground, struggling to keep the Flayer on top of her from getting to her throat.

With a gruff war cry, Ullen launched himself off of Catapult and landed on the assassin between the thief woman and the male elf. The dwarf twisted the assassin's neck, and there was an audible crack of bone as the Venom Guild assassin collapsed to the ground.

Resmine yanked the bow off the side of the saddlebag and strung it, knocking an arrow and aiming toward the trees. She appeared to be looking for the rune thrower.

Estan unsheathed his sword as he ran, charging the Flayer that had its teeth mere inches from the skin of Khiriellen Fortiva's neck. He kicked the creature off of her and brought his sword down, slashing the leather on its back. It continued to roll away, springing to its feet as soon as it was out of his sword's range.

The creature released a fierce, inhuman cry, sending shivers of fear through Estan's very core. He gripped his sword's hilt more tightly, and considered the Flayer in front of him. It had been a woman at one point, one with skin even darker than his and short black hair. "*That elf... It will be... mine...*" the Flayer said, its voice rasping like the wind. "*She...was... my wish.... Her life... is... mine....*"

"Not today," Estan growled. He brought his sword up into a guard position and kept his eyes on the Flayer.

Khiri climbed to her feet behind him, breathing heavily as though she had her wind knocked out. "I... I know you," her voice sounded strained. It took Estan a few seconds to work out that she was addressing the Flayer. "You were that assassin with the Flayer brother."

"*I... was.... Now... I am... much greater.... You will know... absolute... suffering.... I will... taste... your flesh....*" the Flayer hissed. Estan was certain that voice would haunt his dreams for years to come. "*My name was... Liren.... Once my...wish...is granted... even that... will be lost.... You... destroyed... my... family....*"

"If your brother was a Flayer, he was already gone," Estan said, still keeping himself between the creature and the elf. It stepped into a shadow and reappeared in a shadow behind him, flowing toward Khiriellen like a gust of wind.

Khiriellen tumbled out of the way, coming up behind the Flayer with her knife unsheathed. The creature spun and lashed out at the elf, knocking her to the ground again. *"You... cannot strike... against me.... My... wish... was for... your... life.... You... cannot... touch me...."*

A pale bald man, the rune thrower, was tossing exploding runes at Ullen and the thief girl while evading Resmine's arrows. The male elf knocked an arrow on his bow and aimed at the pale man. It struck the pale assassin in one arm, right in the meat of his muscle. An anguished cry of fury erupted from the man. His eyes darted from the arrow to all of the new players on the battlefield, and then the assassin slammed a rune into the ground before vanishing in a blur of smoke.

Estan interposed himself between the Flayer and Khiriellen once more, thrusting his sword at the center of the creature's chest. It twisted away from his blade, but not far enough to remain entirely unscathed. His sword sunk into the thing's right breast. It let out a shriek of frustrated desire and furious agony.

"This is... not finished... elf girl..." the Flayer stepped into a shadow, which flowed over the thing's skin like living oil, and then it too was gone.

Collapsing against a tree trunk, Estan shook with exhaustion, his sword falling to the ground. He felt as though he had run all the way from Seirane, instead of the three or four miles they had covered since discovering the campsite. Khiriellen Fortiva picked up the fallen weapon and approached Estan cautiously.

"Thank you for your intervention, but... who are you?" the young elf woman asked. Her strawberry hair fell in gentle waves where it had fallen out of her ponytail. Estan looked into her steady blue eyes. Even though she looked nothing like Genovar, the knight felt he would recognize her as her father's daughter even if he had met her within the Life Trees. The way she carried herself was with a similar confidence, one that bespoke a trained and tested fighter.

"Name's... My name's Estan," he managed to gasp after a few seconds. "I'm sorry. We left Jarelton at dawn. Didn't think we'd reach you... so quickly."

"Alright... Estan... but why are you after us?" Khiriellen asked.

In the distance, Ullen and Resmine were having a similar conversation with the thief and the ex-soldier. The other elf was tending to Catapult. It sounded like Ullen and the thief were old friends, which Estan supposed made sense. Oddly, though, Resmine and the thief girl also seemed to know each other. His tired brain wouldn't let him focus on two conversations at once, though, so he made an effort to concentrate on Khiriellen.

"Your father sent us. The rest is a very long story," he said.

"My father?" Khiriellen's eyebrows rose in surprise. "You've met my father? But... you are not old enough to be a veteran of the Burning Valley, surely."

"Uh, no..." Estan rubbed his neck with one hand. "I am not a veteran of the Great War. I am—was a Knight of the Protective Hand. I, um, I sought your father out because I needed his help. You see," he met her eyes again, and felt the blood rushing into his cheeks and ears, "I read his book when I was young. He was something of a hero to me, and when the temples turned on me, I—"

Khiriellen held up a hand, hushing him. "Is my father well?" she asked.

"He was when I last saw him," Estan nodded.

"What color are his eyes?" she still held the sword toward him, not seeming to notice that her companions had accepted the others and were sharing food and drink. Estan felt himself swallow. He couldn't remember the last time he had taken a swig from his water bag, and his throat was parched.

"Deepest blue, almost black," he said. "His are the wisest eyes I have ever witnessed."

She flipped the sword around and offered it to him. Taking it carefully, Estan rose to his feet, then cleaned and sheathed the blade. The elf woman untied her own water skin from her satchel and tossed it to him. "Welcome, Estan," she smiled. "You may already know my name, but it feels wrong not to introduce myself. My name is Khiri."

Estan felt his knees turn to mush at her smile and tried to hide his reaction behind taking a long pull from the water skin. She thrust her hand toward him. When he took it, she pumped her arm twice, very deliberately, as though it were a foreign ritual that she was attempting to do with utmost decorum.

Shaking himself, Estan reminded himself that he was there to protect her, not to court her.

"We have time for your full tale later. Mine is simple enough... Micah over there was my destined soul mate, but the name of my destined changed. Now, I am looking for a friend of my father's to help me determine where I can find this Telgan Korsborn, and get my sensitivity to magic under control," Khiri sighed. "But then, my father probably told you about the exile and name-switch when he told you to find me."

Feeling worse than he had during the fight with the Flayer, Estan felt the flush leave his cheeks. "No," he admitted. "He didn't mention it."

ONCE THEY WERE TRAVELING, it became obvious why Estan, Resmine and Ullen had been able to overtake Khiri's party so rapidly. Despite Fennick, the ex-soldier, having military experience, Khiri was clearly their leader and she set a very easy pace. She allowed frequent rest breaks, and stopped them long before the sun was down to let them set up camp. They had exited the orchards shortly after joining forces, and come into grasslands that were similar to those on the far side of Jarelton.

Micah, apparently the appointed cook, set up the fire and began sending people to forage through the grass for wild onions, potatoes or other tubers, and mushrooms. Fennick volunteered to go for water, while Ullen and Dewin, Corianne and Evic's sister, searched for firewood.

Resmine sidled up to Estan while Khiri was arguing with Micah. It seemed like a friendly disagreement about the merits of pork versus fish in whatever Micah was planning on cooking. He had rested two flat rocks next to the fire to warm them before setting them directly on the flames.

"Dibs on the elven cutie," Resmine said.

"She's on a quest for her soul mate. His name is Telgan Korsborn," Estan said, trying his best not to sound sullen. "Besides, I thought I saw you flirting with that Dewin girl."

"I knew it," Resmine smiled in triumph. "You do like her."

Estan glared at Resmine, "I find her attractive. It's not the same thing."

"Not yet, but we're looking at a lot of time on the road with these people," Resmine reminded him. "You may want to think about that, before we decide that we are committed to traveling with them."

"That Flayer I kicked away from her, its wish was her life," Estan said grimly. He turned to lead his friend away from the campfire. As soon as the elves stopped talking, they would be able to overhear his conversation. Estan didn't want to trouble Khiri at this point in time, though he would have to discuss it with her eventually.

"Damn... The Third Hell just erupted on that idea," Resmine sighed, hugging herself as she walked. "She can't kill it?"

"Can't even touch it. It's up to others to protect her whenever that one shows up," Estan confirmed. The smell of sage drifted past. He looked around and found a large patch growing around their feet. Gathering some of the herb as an excuse for their absence, he turned and found Resmine staring at him.

"What?" he scowled.

His oldest friend in the world gave him a knowing smile, "You do like her already. By Locke, I would swear you're already in it deep." She laughed softly, and clapped Estan on the shoulder.

"This is a mission for me," Estan told himself as much as he was telling Resmine. He sniffed the sage and breathed out. It wouldn't be hard to ignore his attraction as long as she showed no signs of reciprocating. "There won't be a problem. I just want to protect her."

"If you say so," Resmine said with an expression of smug satisfaction. "If you say so...."

23

~Resmine~

IT WAS A MISTAKE, HER night with Dewin. Resmine could see that now. Every time her eyes met those of the younger woman, Dewin's sparkled with anticipation. Yes, she still stirred something in Resmine's chest, but there was also guilt. Syara had been Resmine's everything, her entire world in one luminous package. When it had seemed like one glorious night, losing herself in the arms of someone she could dream about when dreams of Syara hurt too much, it had made all the sense in the world. The next morning, Evic and Corianne bursting in and rushing Resmine out had made breaking things very clean and easy. Resmine thought that had been the end of it.

Then she learned that Dewin was traveling with Khiriellen and the others that Estan was rushing toward. Eagerness...that had been her immediate reaction. She couldn't wait to see the young thief again. Of course, that earnest eager moment was what triggered her alarm bells. Resmine wasn't ready to fall for anyone. There was a chance she might never be ready.

Dewin's greeting had spelled everything out for Resmine. The thief girl's lips practically begged to be kissed, but Resmine resisted. Giving in to her urges would've given Dewin the wrong idea. Had already given her the wrong idea. In a last-ditch attempt to exit the situation, Resmine had approached Estan after the fight, only to learn about her friend's feelings for the she-elf.

As much as she wanted to avoid it, it looked like she was going to need to talk to Dewin about some things.

Pulling Dewin aside as the stars began to emerge, Resmine's heart ached. The night was clear and bright and beautiful. This was the kind of sky that begged for lovers to bare their skins in a meadow, not break the heart of someone that under other circumstances could be a lifelong romance. "I need to speak with you, away from the others..."

"Sure thing, love," Dewin's smile was radiant. It made Resmine's determination waiver, but it wasn't enough to make her resolve crumble.

"I... We should never... I can't..." Resmine shut her eyes. This was much harder than she thought, and she hadn't guessed it would be easy. "I'm not looking for anything serious, and I never was. When we tumbled into your bed, I figured I was in for a night of fun. I never thought we'd run into you down the road. That night, I barely knew your name. I... I hope you understand."

Dewin's smile faded and her eyes darkened as she looked away from Resmine. In that moment, Resmine wished she could chase down the words she'd just spoken and jam them back in her mouth. She would have swallowed them and never let them pass her lips again, but they were out there now. All she could do was wait for Dewin's response.

"You're sayin' that even had I stayed in Jarelton, we'd never be more than just bunkers," Dewin's voice was soft to the point of nearly being inaudible. "Maybe you'd have sought me again, when journeys had you in need of someone comfortin', but I'd never be your only love. This is for true?"

Resmine sighed. Despite it being the height of summer, the air felt like it was plunging into late autumn. She didn't like this conversation. Why had things gotten so complicated so fast? "It's not like that, either. I... was involved with someone. She was my all, but she was... She died. I've never been serious about anyone since. I wasn't looking to be."

For the space of almost fifteen breaths, no one spoke except for the crickets. Resmine felt her mouth fill with the spice of trepidation. She wasn't sure what she was dreading since she'd meant to break things off with the thief entirely. This conversation wasn't going the way she had planned.

"I'm not sure what you're askin' of me, to be quits entire, or if you're wantin' to continue some sort of night visits without the ties, but I went in knowin' you for a beautiful stranger. When you figure out what you want to be, let me know so I don't go gettin' any more ideas!" Dewin said. With that, the young thief turned on her heel and marched back to camp, leaving Resmine alone in the moonlight.

That should be the end of it, Resmine thought. She wanted... She was no longer sure what it was she wanted. If Dewin had just stayed in Jarelton, things would've been much easier. Then Resmine wouldn't have warm, wet tears trailing down her cheeks. *I don't think I want this to be the end of it.*

It seemed like Dewin was right, and Resmine had more thinking to do.

24

~Khiri~

MORNING PRACTICE BECAME much more intense with the addition of the former knight and his companions. Ullen, the first dwarf Khiri'd ever met, had done a great deal of traveling, including some time spent with an old hermit that had taught him about a unique method of unarmed combat. He enjoyed showing off his brawling skills, though most of what the hermit had taught him required the dwarf to be higher off the ground than his natural height would allow. More often than not, the dwarf used a staff that looked like it should've been three times too long for him.

Estan and Resmine were also very skilled fighters, specializing in armed combat and speed. Watching them spar was like watching a lightning storm. Flashes of metal caught the morning sun as they set up a rhythmic give-and take sequence of choreographed moves. Khiri found herself counting off with their pattern, even though they were silent.

The day had started out with Fennick and Ullen having a bout, followed by Micah and Dewin, and Estan and Resmine were about to finish their practice. Khiri had her choice of anyone who had already gone. The addition to their group had given them an odd number of participants, which made it necessary for one of their number to either sit out entirely, or go twice.

"You're up, Khiri! Who's it goin' to be, love?" Dewin asked. "Don't say me. I fought you yesterday." The thief sat back and started to sharpen her hatchet. Her mood had been sour since the arrival of Estan and his friends. Most of Dewin's ire seemed to be directed toward Resmine, but neither the thief nor the squire seemed very interested in talking about it.

Khiri ran her fingers over the silver pommel of her knife. She studied the vine-like runes, and thought about the day her father had given it to her. Had Genovar suspected then that her life was about to go awry?

"I choose... Estan," she said. The knight impressed her. His dark brown eyes were intense, focused, and intelligent. The way his smooth leather-brown skin slid over his muscle was enticing to watch, though she couldn't allow herself to truly appreciate it. She tried not to smile as his braids bounced around his ears. "If you're feeling up to it," she challenged as she got to her feet, "Knight."

"Oh, I'm up for it. The question is, can you handle it?" he grinned at her.

Resmine made a coughing noise, which caused Estan to grimace and look a bit sheepish. Khiri wondered if she had misconstrued their relationship. The night before, they had disappeared alone for a time. Perhaps they were lovers?

As Resmine struck up a conversation with Dewin, Khiri disregarded that notion. The thief didn't seem at all displeased by the older woman's attention. Something intangible passed between the squire and the thief that reminded Khiri of her parents. Micah was watching the two of them with something like disappointed understanding. Relief seeped into Khiri's being, as she realized how easily her camp could have erupted into a mountain of drama. She wasn't very versed in matters of the heart, but even the Life Trees held lovers' spats.

"I'm ready," Khiri said. "Weapons or unarmed?"

"You can do unarmed?" Estan raised an eyebrow, seeming impressed.

"Name your preference, Knight," she stepped toward him, even though her head barely came to his chest.

"Willing to go head to head with real weapons, or did you mean the wooden practice pieces?" he asked.

Khiri rested a hand on her knife hilt, "This is an enchanted blade. It never dulls. If I accidentally injure you, it will go deep."

Instead of arguing further, Estan scratched his thin beard in thought. "Resmine, may we borrow your dagger? It's about the same size as Khiri's knife there, right?"

Hefting her dagger, Resmine tossed the weapon, still sheathed, at the knight's feet. It sent up a small puff of dirt as it hit the ground. "Should be close," she responded.

Estan picked up the dagger and offered it to Khiri, "Think you could use this?"

Taking the weapon from him, Khiri removed the sheath and tested the weight. The smell of cleaning oil was strong. It was a well-cared for blade. The balance and weight seemed comparable to her knife, though the point was slightly longer. It was very important not to underestimate her reach, or she could end up hurting Estan anyway. "Are you sure this would be better?" Khiri asked.

"You can use your enchanted blade, if you're concerned. I just thought it might make you more comfortable," Estan shrugged.

After a moment's thought, Khiri tossed the dagger in the air and caught it again after it had flipped twice. "This should do. My knife is actually shorter than the one I used to take hunting," she said.

"Shall we?" the former knight gestured toward the clearing that had been hosting their practices all morning.

Khiri stretched her arms over her head, arching her back and rising to her tiptoes. The knight turned away from her hastily and headed into the flattened ring of grass. Before Estan had taken his position, she darted past him and sank into a fighting stance. He stood across the circle from her and drew his sword, his face unreadable.

Micah positioned himself at the edge of the ring to work as the fight's supervisor. "Ready?" he asked, meeting both of the combatants' gazes.

"Ready," Estan acknowledged, saluting with his sword.

Nodding, Khiri barely shifted her eyes from her opponent. There was a nervous energy building in her stomach, both like and unlike the fear that she had experienced when facing Renald Jack in the city. She did not think that Estan was there to kill or capture her, as the thief had been, but there was a confidence about him that made Khiri both anxious and excited.

"Begin! Micah yelled.

Estan did not hesitate. He thrust his sword toward Khiri as though she really were an enemy. Ducking beneath his blade, she ran under his attack and slashed at his hands while she kicked for his belly. The knight spun to the side, lessening the impact of Khiri's foot. Her dagger scrapped harmlessly over the studding on his gloves.

Kicking at her, Estan tried to knock Khiri back into optimum range for swordplay. She caught his leg and used his force against him, spinning him so that his back was momentarily facing her. Khiri leapt onto the knight's back and scrambled to get a proper hold on his neck. Estan twisted in her grasp and managed to throw her off of him.

Khiri tumbled across the ground, holding the dagger well away from her body. With his sword raised, Estan hurried after her. She reversed the direction of her roll and collided with Estan's legs. Lashing out with her foot, she caught him in the nethers. He groaned in pain and stumbled a few steps, giving Khiri a chance to scramble to her feet. She brought herself back into a ready stance just as Estan swallowed enough of his pain to rejoin the fight.

Keeping his movements tight, Estan began one of the complex patterns that Khiri had watched him practicing with Resmine. She threw herself to the side of one pass and found the weapon coming back at her. Blocking the larger blade with the dagger, Khiri slid in and grabbed Estan's wrist with her other hand. Dancing under his arm, she put the arm she controlled between her and his free hand.

Breathing heavily, Khiri tried to plan her next move. Estan struggled to knock her hand away. His height and strength were against her. He began to raise his arm high enough that Khiri's feet started to leave the ground. Shifting her grip on the dagger, she punched the pommel into the knight's armpit.

"Yaaah-hah!" Estan screamed, dropping her. "Alright, I yield. You've landed two solid blows to my nothing. I'm willing to withdraw before either of us gets seriously injured." He sheathed his sword and held up his hands in a sign of surrender.

"In a real match, I'd be dead," Khiri argued, kneeling on the soil and sheathing the dagger.

The knight rubbed the spot she had hit with a wry smile. "I don't think so," he said. "You were holding back. The only time you used the edge against me was a hand shot."

"I've never killed a person," Khiri confessed. "Only Flayers... If it comes down to a death match, I don't know that I have it in me." As soft as her voice was, she wasn't sure if Estan even heard her confession.

Helping her to her feet, Estan clapped a hand to her shoulder. Khiri could smell the salt of his sweat overcoming the combined scent of their leather armor. It reminded her of training sessions with her father, when he would insist on working with her until they were both drenched.

"You have it in you," Estan assured her. "I have met many soldiers, many fighters, and I have worked with knights that don't have your spirit... your drive. Not one of them would have tried to match me sword to dagger, let alone had the gall to make it a decent fight."

Khiri offered the knight a weak smile. She decided this was as good a time as any to broach a certain subject. "I... I was curious about something. You mentioned that you had read my father's book..."

"Yes?" Estan prompted. His expression was one of patience and curiosity. She wasn't sure what it was, but there was something in his bearing that made Khiri feel she could trust him.

"I didn't know that my father had written a book," she said.

"Oh..." it seemed whatever the former knight had been expecting, Khiri had surprised him. "Would you... like to borrow it?"

Relief flowed through Khiri, easing a soreness that she hadn't known she was feeling. The road had been filled with so many people that had known her father in a way that she never had. While she was growing up, Genovar was her guardian and her mentor. Even when teaching her to hunt and fight, she had never thought that Genovar Fortiva was anything more than a member of her family and her village. The farther from home she had traveled, the more of a stranger her father became. "I would really appreciate that, thank you," Khiri replied. "There's so much I never knew about him."

A tormented shadow of dark emotion swept over Estan's features as they reentered the campsite. "The man I considered to be my father... Well, I guess I never really knew him either," Estan said.

Resmine and Fennick had already done most of the packing while Dewin practiced throwing her hatchet. Micah and Ullen seemed to be having difficulties with Catapult, the horse deciding that he would rather play than be saddled. Estan turned his head and laughed as his steed picked the dwarf up by the back of his collar. Seemingly the shared moment of introspection was over.

"Here! Put me down, devil horse!" Ullen cried. The dwarf was turning purple with embarrassment as he flailed his arms and legs, trying to loosen Catapult's grip on his clothing.

Uncertain and hesitant, Micah was trying to duck around Ullen to calm the blue roan. Catapult used Ullen as a shield, or a weapon, blocking every attempt that Micah made to get past.

Unable to help herself, Khiri also started to laugh. At the sound of her mirth, Ullen ceased his thrashing and scowled at her, "I'm in a right state, and all the she-elf can do is giggle! Estan, come and liberate me from this creature!"

No longer blocked by flailing dwarven limbs, Micah ducked past the horse's defenses and waved an apple within Catapult's sight. "Look what I've got, boy. It's a nice and juicy, but you'll have to release Ullen if you want it," Khiri's oldest friend breathed on the fruit and rubbed it against his chest.

The warhorse considered the bright red apple for a moment, rocking the dwarf in his mouth back and forth a bit as though to see if he could start up his victim's tumult again, and then dropped Ullen on his rump in the dirt. Crunching into the offered delicacy before it could be taken away, Catapult allowed Estan to saddle him without any further difficulty.

"I don't know whether you think you're a war mount or a dog," Estan told his horse as the knight retrieved his bridle from Micah. Even though the dark moment had passed, Estan still had an echo of his earlier discontent lingering on his features.

Not wanting to press him for more of an explanation in front of the entire group, Khiri made note of it and stored it away for later conversation. Estan was the first person she had encountered that seemed willing to speak of the War of the Burning Valley, and she intended to find out all he knew about it and her father's role in what had occurred.

"SHAME WE DIDN'T MAKE it to The Tilted Donkey last night," Fennick lamented. "Have to admit, I was lookin' forward to a bit of a tumble with a wench I met there last spring."

"You wouldn't be meaning Roserra, now, would you, lad?" Ullen raised a thick, black eyebrow.

"I did, in fact," Fennick's fond smile turned stormy. The ex-soldier had not taken to the new recruits very well, and was especially hostile toward Ullen. Khiri had tried asking Fennick about it, but the messenger refused to discuss his discomfort with her. If anything, her questioning him had only made him more irritable.

"No need to look at me as though I just trampled your vineyard," Ullen rolled his eyes. "Roserra ain't exactly a one-and-only kind of lady; well, not to the likes of us wanderers anyhow. She up and married 'bout two months back. Her husband took her off toward Dormin, capital of Firinia," the dwarf informed the scruffy ex-soldier.

Thoughts seemed to roll around inside of Fennick's eyes while he tried to sort them out. All at once, the ex-soldier's demeanor shifted, and he regained his easiness and good-nature. "Well, I expect that she is well and truly stolen from us, jewel of a woman that she was," Fennick gave Ullen a conspiratorial smile.

Hesitating at this sudden change in attitude, the dwarf tentatively returned the smile.

Watching Fennick, Khiri felt troubled. His gruff manner was friendly enough, most of the time, and Micah even seemed to like him. Dewin's opinion was unclear, but then the thief hadn't really taken to anyone until the appearance of Resmine, with whom she seemed quite taken. Now that Fennick and Ullen were becoming more comfortable with each other, it felt like Khiri had lost a potential ally. Something about Fennick didn't seem to add up, but Khiri couldn't explain what it was she mistrusted about the man.

"We could stop at the inn for lunch anyhow," Fennick suggested. "Then, on toward Illesdale...."

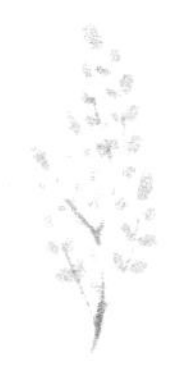

25

~Estan~

TO CALL ILLESDALE A city would be like equating a regular old pecan tree to one of the Life Trees, Estan decided as he walked through the muddy streets. Oak, pine and birch trees grew in small lawns, sheltering the town's houses which were all made of the same white plaster and dark wood. More planks of that dark wood jutted out of the houses to create elevated porches inhabited by the elderly, most of whom observed the village children as they played on the grass and in the trees.

Estan watched the elves as they looked around at the tree-littered town with pleased curiosity. Illesdale was on the edge of the Eddergrim Wood. It was nothing like the growth that had surrounded the Life Trees, but it was a natural forest. After days surrounded by grasses and the falseness of man-planted orchards, Estan thought he could understand a bit of how they felt. He was glad to be out of the wilderness and in something approaching civilization, even something as tiny as this village.

Though he enjoyed his time on the road, Estan was feeling pangs of homesickness. In his rooms within the Temple of Taymahr, he could smell rolls being baked in the morning and had a fine mattress stuffed with lambs' wool that kept him warm in the cold of the night. The Knighthood was not allowed to use blankets within doors, because it was a sign of disrespect to the Goddess of Protection. Estan wondered whether that was the real reason, or if it was one of the ways that the infiltrators kept the devout controlled. Infiltrators would only have to stay awake and see who was shivering in the cool winter drafts rather than running the risk of insulting Taymahr, and dispatch them later. *Maybe it made us weaker, and easier to manage,* Estan's mouth twisted at the bitter thought.

"Are you alright?" Resmine asked, keeping her voice low enough that he had to lean toward her to hear it.

"Fine," he sighed. "Just felt a little homesick, and then…"

"Memories bit you," she nodded. "Used to happen to me all the time. Still does, I suppose."

Estan saw Khiri steal a glance toward him out of the corner of his eye. As soon as he looked toward her, she averted her eyes. He felt a twitch of hope pull at his chest, even as he tamped it down. All that she had shown for him was a bit of respect, and the offer of friendship. Her sharp elven hearing had probably caught the hurt in his voice.

"Where do you lot hail from?" one of the elder women asked, her voice thin with age. "Can't never recall having seen such a group. Not since the Great War."

"Recognize the dwarf, I do," a plump old man with wispy white hair said. "That's Ullen, that is! Are you here to play for us, Ul?"

"Naw, sir, I'm 'fraid I be a bard no longer. Ye see, while I was in Jarelton, my dearest lyre was smashed before my eyes, and I think me fingers shall never recover the loss," Ullen said with a grin. "But if my companions should suffer it, I think we could stay for a meal and I may weave a tale or two for yer pleasure."

Even Estan found his gaze locking on Khiri to ask her permission. She was completely oblivious to the fact that their small band had elected her leader. Khiri only saw Ullen's questioning gaze. "My mission isn't so urgent that we require to press on tonight," she shrugged. "We did miss getting to stay at The Tilted Donkey."

Micah let out a whoop of happiness and gave Khiri a hug. The two elves shared a kinship that reminded Estan of Loni. There was a loss between them, but they enjoyed each other's company and understood each other in a way that few others were able to comprehend. Out of respect for Loni's husband, Estan had stopped spending time with his one-time sweetheart, but with the exception of Resmine, he couldn't think of anyone else that would've helped smuggle him past his hunters like Loni had. Another thrum of homesickness ran through the knight, and he wondered how Loni was doing.

"It's a good night for strangers," the wrinkled reed of a woman that had spoken first told them. "Festival of Petora is tonight."

His breath leaving him in a rush, Estan felt his knees weaken and he was exceedingly glad that he had a grip on Catapult's lead rope to keep him steady. The Festival of Petora was the event of the year in Seirane, celebrating the emergence of the phosphorescent acolyte moths that lit up the sky for one glorious night. They mated and laid their eggs in the space of one day, honoring the goddess of fertility and light. Estan had spent many festivals in his youth watching the moths dance from his window. As he grew, the Festival of Petora had become filled with other, less innocent activities.

Time on the road had certainly dimmed his senses if he'd forgotten that the Festival of Petora was approaching! It surprised him that such a backwater place as Illesdale celebrated Petora. The elderly citizens of Seirane had their own events if they did not feel up to the liveliness of the younger crowd, though it was not unheard of to see a wrinkled body wandering the streets wearing nary a stitch. Estan didn't want to think about the porch dwellers surrounding him in that context.

"We have a feast, and there'll be music and dancing for the unwed. There's a good many acolyte moths that emerge. It's quite the sight; bright as the moon, and thrice as pretty," another elder interjected.

"I've never heard of this festival," Khiri said. Her intelligent blue eyes darted from one face to another, inquiring without words. Estan felt his cheeks heat as her gaze locked on his. "What is it celebrating?"

"The emerging of the acolyte moths," Resmine came to his rescue.

"Best time of the year to take a tumble," Fennick added. "The goddess Petora considers no union sacred on her night, so many a man or woman has woken in a stranger's bed and ambled back to their beloved the next day. If the pairing honors the goddess, then all's fair."

Khiri looked perplexed. Estan wished he knew where her thoughts led her. If she wanted to participate, he was eager to volunteer his services.

"Humans have very strange customs," was all she said.

Ullen laughed, "Aye, lass, but 'tis no stranger than your Name Breathing is to them that's not born knowin' who's right for 'em. We dwarves are like humans in that."

"In the Life Tree Clans, we are taught to view those without destined as practically soulless," Khiri said, the shame evident in her voice. She looked apologetically at Micah, whose happiness had ebbed. He tried to smile at her, but it was morose.

"Cheer up, love," Dewin told him. "Illesdale isn't half as small as she looks, and there'll be plenty of girls looking for a toss from someone exotic as yourself."

"Take you myself, were I a generation or two younger," one of the porch denizens cackled. "Demon spit, but I'd take the lot of you!"

Estan cringed all the way to the main crossroads, where all of the village's inns and taverns lay.

THEIR GROUP WAS TOO large to stay at one inn; it seemed like all of the nearby farmers and shepherds had come into town for the festival. Dewin and Resmine had offered to take Khiri for the night, but she declined after they also invited her to join their festivities. Micah, Ullen and Fennick had agreed to share a room with the provision that if any one of them made it there first, the others would sleep outside if they didn't find more willing pillows. After finding the one tavern in Illesdale that still had stable space, Estan offered his room to Khiri, knowing that he sounded awkward and hopeless. She was brushing Catapult while he tended to cleaning his saddle and harness.

"I mean, it's just that everyone else is going to be busy... Not that you can't be busy, if you wanted to be. You're a very attractive elf-person, and... I don't mean that. Well, I do mean that, but not in that way! What I mean is..." Estan scrunched up his face in frustration. "I don't even sound sane anymore, do I?"

Khiri laughed at him, a light, musical sound that drifted past his ears like a breeze. Her hands were coated in blue-gray horse fuzz, which stuck to her forehead when she tried to wipe away a trickle of sweat. "You can relax, Estan. I won't jump down your throat if you accidentally flirt with me. I just can't look at anyone that way. Not until I know if this Telgan Korsborn is the person that I am destined to be with." she told him.

Making a valiant attempt to hide his disappointment, Estan gave Khiri an embarrassed grin, "Yes, well, what I mean is, you can stay with me. No strings, just a room."

Khiri's brow furrowed as she stroked Catapult's flank in silence. Estan was starting to wonder if he had pushed too hard and offended her despite her assurances to the contrary, when she answered softly, "Actually, I would like that.... You lent me the history that my father wrote, but there are place names that I don't know. He uses language and terms that are not part of my culture. I can hear his voice and I see words written in his hand, but it's like a foreign language."

"I see," he rubbed vigorously at particularly stubborn bit of tarnish on one of the buckles. He decided to attempt a joke to lighten the mood. "You are emotionally unavailable, but you want me for my brains."

"Ha ha," she stuck her tongue out at him. "Maybe I'll just stay in a tree. They're more comfortable, anyway."

"Of course I can help you decipher the history," Estan said hastily, fearing that Khiri really would walk away. "But I do insist that, destined or no, you see the acolyte moths and maybe engage in a dance or two. Even the most studious of the priestesses and clerics take a break to watch the moths."

Khiri paused in her brushing to pull matted fur out of the brush's bristles. With a grimace, she finally noticed how much of Catapult's hair clung to her. "Do these priestesses and clerics smell like horse? I'm going to speak with the tavern owner, and see if they'll set a bath up for me."

As she left, Catapult started to nicker and huff. The blue roan was unhappy that his brushing was over. "Who ever heard of such a needy war horse?" Estan shook his head and continued mending his tack. "You wouldn't carry on like this for Resmine, traitor horse."

Even after he was finished with his work, the knight sat in the stable for a long time. Thoughts were running through his head; he and Resmine had lost their homes and the only families they'd ever known, Khiri had been banished from her former life, and even Dewin had been forced to leave her city. Micah had not been banished, but he had suffered a loss even deeper, if Estan understood the culture of the Life Tree clans correctly. Fennick and Ullen hadn't shared their past with anyone within Estan's hearing, but they had been traveling far longer than their companions.

The coincidences and parallels between Estan's experiences and the occurrences that had proceeded the War of the Burning Valley were starting to bother him. Before the War of the Burning Valley had begun, hostility and unrest had erupted between Mytana and Firinia concerning a missing diplomat. Strangers were met with hostility on the roads, and the Flayers had increased in number roughly ten-fold.

Since he'd left Seirane, Estan had encountered more Flayers than he had in the whole of his previous life. Combining that with the number of Flayers that Khiri and her group had encountered before they'd joined parties, well, Estan didn't like it.

One passage from Genovar's book kept repeating in Estan's head: "Though the Great War had not yet officially started, we were living in a war state. Trust was an expensive commodity, most often paid for in blood."

Estan shook his head, trying to replace his brooding with excitement about the coming festivities. He sent a brief prayer to Taymahr that the remembered passage was not a premonition.

Since he didn't know if Khiri had been allowed to bathe within his room or was bathing in the kitchens, the knight left word with the bartender that he would be spending some time with Ullen and Dewin. If there was drinking to be done, they were the pair to do it. According to one of Ullen's many, many stories, the thief could drink him under the table. Estan wasn't about to get drunk himself with the possibility of spending an evening with Khiri at stake, but he would gladly fund someone else's imbibing.

He had barely taken three steps out of the tavern's front door when he felt a tap on the shoulder. As he turned, a fist met his lower jaw, clicking his teeth together sharply.

"What in all the heavens...?" he exclaimed, recognizing his assailant. Tan skin, long blonde braid, three wavy lines tattooed above the right eyebrow and only about four feet and seven inches of elven muscle uncoiled from under his chin.

"That's for all the doe-eyes you've been giving Khiri since we got into town," Micah said, rubbing his knuckles. "I don't stand a chance in a fair fight against you, but I'd be willing to try if you pull anything."

"Do you really think that was necessary?" Estan worked his jaw, trying to assess any real damage. "She'd clock me herself, and probably do a better job of it. You need to come up from the hips, not rely on your arm power." The knight shook his head as he realized he was coaching the elf on how to hit him better. Maybe the punch had knocked his brains loose...

Micah glared at Estan, as though daring the knight to make the next move. "Khiri is special to me, even if we aren't meant to be together. I thought you should know that she's not alone out here, and I wanted to make sure I had your attention."

Cocking his head to one side, Estan met Micah's stony gaze and really looked at the elf man. Behind Micah's green eyes, there was a layer of hurt and betrayal that confused the knight. That look wasn't there when Micah was with Khiri or any of the others. Either the elf wasn't as over his former destined as he claimed, or... "You're jealous," Estan realized.

"I'm not jealous!" Micah scoffed. "Khiri and I—"

Estan held up a hand to stop Micah's protest, "Not of Khiri and myself. Which, if it makes you feel any better, she has already dashed my hopes pretty thoroughly..."

"Yeah, she's good at that," the elf said.

"...but you're jealous that I was sent by her father," Estan finished his thought as though Micah had not interrupted.

Several people had stopped to watch after Micah had smacked Estan in the face with his uppercut, but most had continued on their way when it became obvious that no fight would follow. The elf turned his glare to the stragglers; while Micah wasn't very intimidating, they also began to move about their business in the muddy streets. Vendors were starting to construct shoddy booths in preparation for the Festival of Petora, which was due to begin at midnight.

"That could be," Micah said. "I was very close to both her mother and father. My own parents were...distant. On the day of Khiri's Name Breathing, her parents came and offered her comfort, solace. I know that I can't expect them to place me on equal footing with their daughter, and that day was hard on all of us, but... They didn't say anything. Even when I went to their house to apologize to Khiri for my... overreaction... Genovar and Leyani barely spoke to me."

"Come on," Estan looped an arm over the elf's shoulders. "I think we could both use a drink. Let's go see if Dewin really can outlager a dwarf."

26

~Khiri~

SOAKING HAPPILY IN her bath water, Khiri let her tension ease into the rich, velvety warmth that caressed her skin. The only thing that caused her discomfort was the way the water infiltrated her ears when she dunked her head to wet her hair. Bathing was a much different experience the human way, and she savored it each time there was an opportunity.

In the Life Trees, all baths were taken with collected rainwater, which was refreshing in the summer months and uncomfortably cold in the winter. The process involved two largish wash basins, one full and the other empty. While standing in the empty basin, one had to lift the full basin and dump it over their head. Soap was applied, and the process was repeated until all of the soap, dirt or water was gone. Khiri didn't miss it.

A knocking at the door hammered through her solitude. She assumed that it was Estan returning from the stables, or wherever he had been waiting for her. "The door is barred," she called. "I'll be there soon."

Trails of water ran down her legs, fleeing the refuge of her hair for the tub it currently called home. Little did it know that it would soon be pitched from a window or doorway. She toweled off the more complacent drops and was in the middle of pulling on her armored leather pants when the knocking started again.

"Who's there?" she asked. Estan didn't strike her as the impatient sort, and whoever it was didn't like to wait.

"It's me," Fennick called. "I wanted to discuss something, before we hit the road again."

Pausing in the act of tugging on her breastplate's straps, Khiri's feelings of warmth and comfort started to dissipate. Her dislike of the former soldier only seemed to grow with every passing day, and she couldn't explain it. It wasn't like he went out of his way to be dis-likable; Micah seemed to like Fennick very well. The messenger had gone out of his way to outfit them for the trip and took his shifts on watch without complaint. He wasn't doing anything wrong that she could tell, and no one else in the group seemed wary of him. If she could only figure out why he bothered her, Khiri could figure out what to do about it.

Fennick reminded her of a hunting trip she had taken with her father during her sixteenth summer. They'd encountered an old rac-coon that was rabid and the creature had bitten her hand. Genovar had put the raccoon to rest, and the trip had been cut short. Her fa-ther had rushed her back to the healing protection of the Life Trees. The poisonous illness had been leached from her body, but Khiri still remembered three painful, aching nights of fever and nightmares while her father tried to carry her back to safety. Like that raccoon, she was sure that Fennick would bite her and this time Genovar wouldn't be there to rush her back home.

"I'll be right there," Khiri said as she finished strapping her gear on. She tugged on the rope pulley system that lifted the thick plank that served as a lock.

Pushing his way in the door, Fennick strode into the room as though he'd been invited. He took in the small fireplace, the lone lad-der-back chair, single paned window, and finally his eyes rested on the wash tub as he sat on the double bed. "So that's what took ya," he rumbled, reclining on the headboard. "Small room, but I imagine you and the knight'll work it out."

"What was it that you wanted?" Khiri leaned one shoulder against the door frame and crossed her arms, trying her best to look casual instead of irritated.

The ex-soldier peered at her, scratched his speckled brown and gray stubble, and gave her a wry smile, "Look, you don't like me, I can tell... And that's alright. We're only together until you find this mage friend of your father's. All the same, I'm your senior travel companion, second only to your friend Micah, and I'd like to offer ya a bit of friendly advice."

"I'm listening," Khiri gave him a slight incline of her head. She didn't bother to deny that she didn't like him. If anything, it felt good to know that it was out in the open.

"Ditch the knighthood gang," Fennick said, picking at his nails. "Between you, me, Micah and the thief girl, we should be able to fend off the worst of the assassin attacks."

"Odd advice from someone who was willing to fund new armor sets to keep himself safe," Khiri pointed out. Even with the door open, the room felt small and tight with the ex-soldier's presence.

An uncomfortable pressure seemed to weigh on her for a moment, building from her chest and rising to her ears. She instinctively fought against it, mentally tamping it down, away from the place that she usually sensed power. The pressure subsided all at once, leaving her feeling a little unbalanced.

"We only have Estan's word that he was sent by your father," Fennick said as he shrugged one shoulder. "According to Resmine, she never actually met with Genovar and she was against the idea of coming to our aid in the first place."

"What are you implying?" Khiri's head began to ache. It was difficult to keep her eyes locked on Fennick's hazel gaze. All she wanted to do was rest and maybe find a mug of willow bark tea. *And listen to Fennick*, the thought seemed almost alien. That certainly hadn't come from her own head.

"How much do we really know about the knight? Estan claims he is being hunted by assassins because he witnessed several key members of his temple talking about their ties to the Gray Army. Assuming that's true, how do we know his own loyalties aren't for the people that raised him?" He shifted from his casual perch on the bed to lean forward and rest his elbows on his knees. His fingers intertwined and locked together, and Khiri swore that the gesture was followed by an audible snap. "I just think it may be possible that he's hunting you so he can buy himself safe passage back onto Temple Hill. Think about it... he's lived there his whole life. Those people, they were his family. If he handed 'em the daughter of one of their greatest enemies, he could go home."

Fogginess shadowed Khiri's vision, but she still didn't agree with Fennick's logic. "I... I'll think about it," she said. "Now, if you don't mind, I would like to rest before the festival starts."

A smile twitched at the corners of Fennick's mouth. "Fair enough. I'll leave you to your contemplations," the ex-soldier stood and sauntered past Khiri, taking most of her headache with him.

Khiri closed the door and lowered the plank to prevent more visitors. Despite the haze that still clouded her mind, she had to get out; she had to find a place where she could think clearly. A place more like home.

Estan's room had a small window that opened toward the Eddergrim Wood. Between the tavern and the wood there was a rocky green slope that seemed treacherous even for elven footing. Khiri unclasped the latch, swung the glass open and stuck her head out. A thin edge of roof led onto a larger, flatter bit of shingling. The view practically invited her to pull herself out of the room and climb carefully over to the flatter surface. She edged her way over to the flat bit and then laid down, facing the sky. If she ignored the wall of the second story and the noises of Illesdale, she could almost believe she was back on the Sky Watcher's platform of the Oak Wood Clan. Maybe the poisons would leach out of her system even in this human place.

THE SCENT OF RIME, sharp and metallic, hung in the air. Thick frost crunched beneath Khiri's feet, reminding her of crushing bones. The large pulsing crystal in the center of the icy chamber seemed to beckon to her, even as a thin cackle rolled off the walls. She held a knife that was not her father's....

Shaking, Khiri's eyes opened onto the dimming sky of a summer evening. *Telgan Korsborn,* her mind told her when she reached for comfort. His name was heavy, leaving an aftertaste like iron in her mouth. She rose slowly to her feet and climbed back in the window to Estan's room.

Someone was tapping on the door, a much different sound than the harsh banging that had been Fennick earlier that day. "Khiri? You alright in there, love? Estan said you was bathin' but it's been nearly two hours," Dewin's voice carried through the wood.

Khiri let the thief in, "I'm okay. I was just... napping. It's supposed to be a long night, after all."

Dewin's coppery features were twisted into a small scowl. She seemed unsure of whether to believe Khiri or not. Her black hair was down, hanging soft around her shoulders. The thief was wearing a pale pink, sleeveless shirt and a darker, rose-colored skirt. Compared with the dark leather that the thief usually wore, the contrast was shocking. It made her look older, and somehow highlighted the similarities between her and Evic more than those she shared with Corianne.

"You aren't going to celebrate looking like that, are you?" Dewin asked, looking at Khiri's leather armor with disdain.

"I haven't anything else," Khiri shrugged. "It isn't as though I'm trying to attract anyone."

The thief sighed, "Love, you are a dense one. It's not about attracting someone, it's just about feeling pretty. We could rustle something up. Come on, then. You and I are doin' a run on the town to find you sommat suitin'."

Grabbing Khiri by the wrist, Dewin towed her out the door and down the street. It became a blur of colors and fabrics, as the thief thrust her into the dressing rooms of garment shops and tossed clothes at her from what seemed to be every angle.

Every item came with a rapid explanation, as though the thief was trying to impart her knowledge of fashion on a student. "This blue will highlight your eyes, love," or "No, no... That won't do. This is a winter and your coloring is all summer. Don't know what I was thinkin', love," and off she would go to throw something else at the confused elf.

In the middle of the third or fourth shop, Khiri managed to ask where the rest of their party was hiding.

"Resmine got roped into a drinking contest with Micah, after I refused to get into it with Ullen. Damn dwarf can out drink an army. I got the best of him once, but I had the 'keep in my pocket with a thickly greased palm. My ale weren't much more than water, and Ullen's was laced with a sleeping draught. Don't be rattin' on me, though. Was the only way I could get him to remember me as Dewin and not 'that sister o' Corianne's'. He was fair smitten with my sister, but it didn't work out. She found out that he was already involved with two other women in town, and a few others about the country besides," Dewin said. Tossing a light brown skirt of a very light, relaxed fabric at Khiri, the thief girl shewed the elf back into the changing room. Dewin threw a rich indigo bodice-style shirt with some sort of shimmery, fluttery sleeves over the top of the stall.

"And Estan?" Khiri asked, fumbling with the shirt's laces and grunting in irritation when her hair got caught in the eyelets.

"He's funding the drunkards," Dewin's voice took on an amused note. "Why the interest, love? Got sommat to do with the two of you sharing a room tonight?"

Khiri emerged from the room she had been changing in and spun around slowly, the way that the thief had taught her to during the course of their mad dash around Illesdale. "Not really," Khiri said, waiting for the inevitable uttering of dissatisfaction that had always come from Dewin after seeing the effects of whatever she had picked out for the elven woman.

Most of the items were originally intended for children. They fit poorly in addition to being the wrong color or style. This particular ensemble had neither of those issues, having been made for the maker's daughter when she was about thirteen summers but had blossomed into womanhood early. The girl had outgrown the pieces quickly, and the tailor had decided to display them since they were practically new.

"Khiri, love, I think we found what we're lookin' for. Not that you aren't a sight most days, but that... you'd move the heart of a mountain, you would," Dewin said, her eyes sparkling with satisfaction. "Sure that you won't change your mind about an evenin' with me and Resmine?"

"So we can stop shopping now?" Khiri slumped in relief. She felt exhausted, as though she had never taken a bath and a nap that afternoon.

Dewin laughed, "Aye, love, we can stop shopping now. I'll take that as a no to my invitation as well. No harm in askin'... Though, if you don't mind my curiosity, why did you accept the knight's offer?"

As Khiri gathered her leathers from the dressing room, Dewin haggled with the tailor and then money exchanged hands. Human coin still confused Khiri. She couldn't tell what was worth how much. Trading in goods or services made more sense to her, but then, her people only ever dealt with merchants that came to them. They took elven goods elsewhere and would make their barters with the elves without changing money at all. Many of the weapons and armor pieces that her people made were probably traded for coin after the merchants left... The realization made Khiri seriously consider learning more about coin. She wondered how much elven goods were worth in the wider world.

Khiri thought about Dewin's question concerning Estan. She couldn't deny that he was easy on the eyes, and she was comfortable with him. Estan possessed a quiet strength and his mind was as sharp as his sword. If it weren't for mitigating factors, such as Telgan Korsborn, she might be tempted by the idea of spending a romantic evening with the knight. But under other circumstances, he still wouldn't have been an option for her. If Telgan Korsborn's name had never appeared in her head, she would be committed to Micah and she wouldn't have met Estan. "I don't think I gave it much thought," she told Dewin. " I mean, I trust him... and I wanted a chance to talk to him about my father."

"It never occurred to you that he could have been anticipating a much different activity for the evening?" the thief persisted.

"Well...no. He said that he wouldn't bother me for more than a dance or two," Khiri said. She frowned at the way that the skirt brushed against her legs as she walked. Resting on her hip was the knife her father had given her, and at least the skirt was not tight enough to hinder her flexibility. Should the need arise to defend herself, she thought she could still fight in her new clothes.

The thief walked her back to Estan's room where they found the knight sitting on the windowsill, reading her father's book. "Ah, that's where you got to Dewin. We had all started.... started to... um..."

Khiri had dropped her leathers unceremoniously into the corner and was adjusting her belt. She looked up to see what was causing Estan to stammer, and was shocked to find him staring at her with a warm longing in his eyes. A blush rushed into her cheeks as Dewin's probing suddenly made sense to her.

"Uh... The, um, the lanterns are being lit. Festivities will begin soon, though the moths won't make an appearance until around midnight," Estan said, recovering himself.

"I'm off to locate Resmine, then, loves. Estan, you behave yourself. Khiri'll knock you flat on your ass in a heartbeat, and we've all seen her do it," Dewin parted with a wave over her shoulder.

Letting the surprise of her discovery wash off of her, Khiri responded in the only way that she occurred to her: she ignored it. She offered Estan a hesitant smile and said, "So, now that it's just the two of us, can you finally tell me about the Great War, and my father's part in it?"

27

~Estan~

"HOW DID YOU WANT TO go about this?" Estan asked. He gripped the abused leather cover of Genovar's book with both hands and hoped he didn't accidentally tear the book in two through sheer nervousness. "I could give you a brief overview and then we could take it by chapter, or would you prefer to read it and ask me questions as you go?"

Khiri seemed to think about it. Her festival garb didn't really reveal anything that her normal gear didn't, but for some reason, Estan felt like he couldn't stop staring any time he made eye contact. Even though he had been aware of his mounting attraction for her, he had never been quite this aware of her hips. Also, the shirt hinted at her cleavage in a way that Estan found very distracting. He was going to strangle Dewin the next time he saw her; she had definitely done this on purpose, the little minx.

"I suppose an overview would give us more time at the festival," Khiri decided. "And it's not as though we have to cover everything tonight..." A dark cloud of concern seemed to pass over the elf woman's features.

"Are you alright?" he rose off the window's ledge and lost his grip on the book. It clunked its way across the floor as Estan rushed to scoop it back up. *There went what little dignity I may have retained,* he thought, sighing through his nostrils. "You look troubled."

Soon, they would need to light the fireplace in order to see anything. The sun had already set, and the last vestiges of light were retreating across the horizon. It was becoming hard for Estan to read the features of Khiri's face while he waited for her response.

"I'm sorry," Khiri sighed. "It's just... Fennick said something earlier and I think it may have gotten to me a bit more than I had anticipated." She sank into the room's only chair and pushed a stray hair back behind one of her delicately tipped ears. "Would you ever consider using me as a trade to get back into the temple?"

"Never," Estan responded. It struck him in the core of his being that she would feel the need to ask such a thing. Reminding himself that they hadn't known each other very long, he forgave her the question, but his ire toward Fennick rose. "I am a man of honor. Even if you were a complete stranger, I would not exchange another's life for my own... And I've studied the War of the Burning Valley. I'd never join with the Gray Army."

With a relieved nod, Khiri gave him an apologetic smile, "I didn't really think you would. My father wouldn't have sent you to me lightly."

Estan pulled his flint and steel out of his saddlebags and tossed a few logs into the small fireplace. He kindled the fire, breathing deeply as he worked to regain his temper. There were few things that hurt him as much as the accusation of being dishonorable, and he had been through a lot of that recently. With his growing affection, the last person he wanted to lash out at was Khiri.

"The War of the Burning Valley," Khiri prompted, and the moment passed. Estan was once more in control of his temper.

"In the early days, people didn't know they were entering what would be called the Great War, and now the War of the Burning Valley. They were dangerous days, but for the most part, it was still safe to travel in groups as long as it was no great distance.

"A minor border skirmish of a war was taking place between Firinia and Mytana, with neither side gaining nor losing ground. Lord Erish of Mytana hadn't even bothered calling for extra forces from his neighbors, it was that small," Estan felt his voice taking on the teaching cadence that he had used to tell squires and pages about their duties during orientations.

"Lord Erish?" Khiri inquired. She picked up the book from where Estan had set it so that he could strike the fire and flipped to the pages that described Mytana's nobility. "Okay, so he's one of six lords, and they each rule one city on the borders. Who rules Jarelton?"

"Jarelton is Lady Ilamar's jurisdiction, though she is getting on in years. Between her husband and their three offspring, the city could end up in contention, though I've heard that her youngest son would make the best heir," Estan pointed at the page where Ilamar was described. "One of the oddities of the Great War was that the seven generals that led the Unified Army to victory weren't lords, royalty, or even of the Knighthood. Every man and woman among them was common as clay. It made the nobility wary of their people for a time, mostly for the good... But I'm getting ahead of myself," Estan cleared his throat, and attempted to begin again.

"Many consider the true beginning of the War of the Burning Valley to be the birth of the Flayer Mage. His name was Irrellian Thornne, and unlike any other Flayer, he retained himself," Estan paused for effect and was rewarded with a small intake of breath from Khiri. Nodding, he continued, "The general knowledge on the formation of Flayers is that the more powerful the mind, the more powerful the demon that bonds with you. Irrellian Thornne was nothing short of brilliant. What's more, he was well liked in many social circles. No one suspected that he would become the Flayer Mage, leader of the cruelest, most bloodthirsty army that the world had ever witnessed."

"What was his wish?" Khiri asked. Her bright blue eyes glinted in the fire light, as intrigued as any child of six summers.

"No one knows," Estan scowled down at the book. It was a question that he had often wondered, too. "Most believe that he was just power hungry and went too far. Your father believed it was something much deeper than that, though he never wrote more than hints at his suspicions. All I've really gleaned from my years of study is that Genovar didn't think that Irrellian Thornne ever meant to become the leader of an army. That was all his bonded demon's doing."

"The Flayer Mage possessed a demon so powerful that he was able to unite the lesser Flayers in a way the world had never seen. Scarier still, he drew followers that weren't demon-bound. One conversation, your father says, would sometimes be enough to convince even the most ardent believers. Maybe they professed more loyalty to good than they felt, or maybe they were weak-willed. Either way, the Gray Army held as many untainted beings as it did Flayers. The unbound make much better leaders. They retained their minds, which made the Gray Army very powerful—a many-headed beast.

"Your father was actually not a part of the war for the first few years. He was living in one of the dwarven cities of Eerilor. Early chapters of this book show his fascination with dwarven technologies. Have you heard about the recent hostilities between Mytana and Eerilor?"

"Something to do with water rights?" Khiri said, though she sounded uncertain.

"That's right. The dwarves of Eerilor, and some of the humans, refer to themselves as engineers. They diverted the river to create a cooling system for their forges. In turn, the steam from that is captured and pumps the very same bellows. It's quite ingenious, really. If Mytana weren't diverting Eerilorian resources, the engineers could be working on other uses for this steam power of theirs. They already have a system for their city lamps, where the steam is charging flame runes encased in glass..." Estan smiled, realizing he was getting off track, but unable to contain his enthusiasm. A pang of guilt rang through his soul; the memory of slaying those same engineers in the name of his temple, only to learn he had been misled, haunted him in his dreams.

"Anyway, Genovar was living in Tenising, a city on the western edge of Eerilor, when he received a vision. He saw himself standing before a vast ocean. When he raised his arms, tremendous towers of water rose in response. A gray fog began to encroach on the ocean, eating away at it. Six figures rose out of the waters and took on the shapes of humans and dwarves. Each figure added their strength to the struggling towers of ocean water, and slowly, the smoky fog was pushed back. The six figures joined hands and invited him to join with them. They rode on a wave of water, and extinguished the fiery heart of the haze.

"Genovar recognized that he had been tapped by a deity to unite and lead the factions that were being overcome by the Gray Army. Mytana was the center of the conflict, and so he traveled here to begin his efforts. At the time, he had only whatever skills your people teach to their hunters and some minor experiences with road skirmishes. He joined the Mytanan army at the basest level and worked his way up, with the help of visions sent to him through the deity. Once he became a Captain, he began to meet with the other figures from the vision, and they recognized him as well.

"That was when the tide of the Great War began to shift—" Estan's voice was cut off by excited laughter and shouts of merriment.

"Sounds like things are picking up at the festival," Khiri said. She started shifting positions and stretching her legs. "Are you still planning on making me dance? I've never learned."

"Well..." Estan looked down at the ragged tome between them. The pull of its history was strong, but he didn't want to miss the Festival of Petora. "Yes, I suppose that is a decent place to pause our discussion."

Khiri rose a skeptic eyebrow, "With my father being directed by an unknown entity?"

"Deity," he corrected, pushing himself to his feet.

"Alright, deity. Why would an elf get tapped by one of your gods though? We are direct creations of the Earth, and we don't recognize human gods," Khiri frowned as she reached out for him to help her to her feet.

"That, I don't know," Estan said. "Your father never mentioned which of the gods tapped him, and never explained why he was picked in the text. The lack of curiosity makes me think he knew the reason." He took the offered hand and savored the warmth of her skin touching his. It was so tempted to press his luck with another offer of something more than dancing, but Estan had promised the elf that his room was a safe space.

"But enough of this... You need to see the acolyte moths," the knight said. He kept his grip on the elf woman's hand as he escorted her out of the tavern.

ESTAN TOWED KHIRI THROUGH the streets of Illesdale, until he found a spot where music permeated the air, punctuated by laughter. Bouncing, sweaty bodies in their festival finery made two rows that converged and fell back, matching the rhythm of several stringed instruments and a set of pipes. None of the playing was professional, but that somehow made it better.

The elf watched in fascination, experimentally following the steps from the edges of the crowd. Estan pulled her into the lines before she could protest. Khiri was a fighter, which meant that she knew how her body moved. Her stances were a bit awkward, but within a few rounds she managed to stop running into people. She grinned at him as she began to move with the rhythm and Estan's own cheeks hurt from smiling so much.

"The acolytes!" someone shouted.

Stillness began to fall on the town's people. One by one, the instruments grew quiet, and the dancers paused in their jubilation. Shutters were drawn on the lamps, and for a moment it looked as though utter darkness had fallen over Illesdale. Not even the stars dared to shine.

Estan's eyes darted back and forth as he scanned the sky for the first tell-tale hints of the acolyte moths. He heard an intake of breath from Khiri, and then spotted it. A tiny, fluttering of green, yellow and blue glowing against the blackness of the sky. One or two more colorful specks appeared in other parts of the sky's dome, and then a few more. Within minutes the sky was a canopy of dancing color and brilliance, almost bright enough to let him see Khiri's face. It wasn't hard to imagine that the goddess of fertility and light had called the moths to being out of the fringes of her favorite cloak, as the old legend said.

A few of the braver moths ventured down toward the crowded streets, alighting on roofs, shoulders and open palms. Estan stretched out his hand, inviting Petora's blessing. One friendly little moth landed on his outstretched fingers and tickled its antenna against his skin. He gently brought his hand down so that Khiri could examine the pattern of the green, yellow and blue speckles on the creature's wings more closely. The insect leapt toward the elf woman and seemed to kiss her nose before returning to dance with its own kind.

Slowly, the quiet began to be broken by whispers and murmurs, and then talking and finally the music started up again. Lanterns were opened to renew the light on the streets, though they were only half as crowded as before.

Turning to ask Khiri what she thought, motion at the edge of his vision caused Estan to freeze. The elf woman turned as though moving through a thick chowder. Uncertain screams filled the air as a fog rushed over the streets, obscuring the dance of the moths. Estan stood, unable to move, even as Khiri broke free of her trance and dashed away from him into the mist.

28

~Ullen~

DEWIN, RESMINE AND Micah left Ullen to his pints after he won his third drinking contest. The festival had other sights and activities, after all, and they were all out in the world for the first time in their young lives. Ullen had bade them a cheerful farewell and returned to his drinking.

From time to time, one of the village women would occupy the stool next to him and inquire about his availability for a dance, a drink, a bit of conversation, or something a bit more interesting. Each time, he turned them away. It wasn't that Ullen had anything against Petora, it was just this feeling he had in the pit of his stomach. There was something off about the night. No matter how much he drank, or how much he pushed the feeling away, it was nagging him.

The dwarf was about to push himself away from the bar and try another form of distraction, when he saw the silver gleam of a familiar set of pauldrons. Ullen slid down the stool as gracefully as dwarf could—which, admittedly, wasn't very—and made his way through the crowded tavern.

"By the Stone, if it isn't Quinton Ilyani!" Ullen said as he clapped a heavy hand over the startled knight's shoulder.

"Taymahr's grace! Ullen? Ut'evullen Dormidiir? What in Arra are you doing way out here?" Quinton's face was much older than it had been twenty years before, and his fiery red hair had darkened into an iron gray. The years were equally unkind to his face, which was windburned and ruddier than ever. Still, Ullen knew Quinton as surely as he knew his own toes. There are some ties that never fade.

"Easy with my full name, if you please," Ullen cautioned. "I know it's been awhile, but there are still those that would recognize it and given the current war..."

"Sorry," Quinton said. "I didn't think... I've been on the front lines of this stupid conflict, and still..." the Knight of the Protective Hand broke off with a sigh. "I'm very sorry, old friend. These last few years, nothing seems as easy as when we last saw each other."

Ullen waved away the knight's apology. "I don't think anyone here heard, but had you made that slip in Jarelton... Well, they already tried to kill me once this year. It was a close thing, too, but someone managed to talk the crowd down."

Quinton's grizzled eyebrows drew together as the corners of his mouth twitched into a frown, "That seems extreme for such a minor altercation. Even those on the riverfront aren't taking this war that seriously."

Ullen glanced around, making sure the happy villagers were still keeping their distance from the table. Quinton's mood seemed to be throwing its own sort of barrier between the festivities and their conversation. It was almost surreal to see such merriment only a few feet from this dower reunion, but Ullen felt a brush of nostalgia, too. Clandestine meetings in the midst of the unknowing masses. He almost felt sixty summers old, again. "Genovar's on the move," Ullen kept his voice low.

The look on Quinton's face sharpened. "He said he wouldn't return."

"He said he wouldn't return until—"

Screams from the outside cut through the cheerful drunken chatter, calling the two old friends to action. Quinton evaporated into the night as Ullen sprinted upstairs for his staff as quickly as his stocky legs could carry him.

29

~Khiri~

KHIRI DIDN'T KNOW WHERE she was running, only that she must run. She unsheathed her knife and plunged it into the neck of a passing Flayer. Flayers were everywhere, lurking within the unnatural fog. Some of the town's people had rallied, gathering whatever was at hand for weapons. Others mulled about in confusion, unaware of the danger.

"To arms!" Khiri yelled. The dancing had been awkward and stilted, though she had been picking up some steps toward the end, but this... This dance was one she knew all too well.

"*Blood...*" one Flayer said in its sing song whisper. "*Rending, tearing, sweet and salty flesh...*"

"*Bodies writhing, gnashing, spewing...*" another chanted. Everywhere, the whispers joined their voices to the hissing song of desire, and still Khiri ran, downing the Flayers that got in her way.

Screams of pain flooded her ears, driving out whatever siren's call beckoned her. Two Flayers were huddled over a collapsed body while a boy of eight or nine summers kicked at their ankles and smashed a lantern over one of their heads. "Leave Mother alone!" the boy demanded.

The creature turned, oil dripping down its bloody face. With a hiss, it launched at the boy. Khiri's foot slammed into its face, throwing it to the side. "Run, boy!" she instructed.

"I won't leave my mother!" he snapped back, running toward the other Flayer with his damaged lantern.

"Arra preserve me," Khiri swore, bringing her knife down into the chest of the Flayer she'd kicked. She hurried after the boy. He'd already smashed the broken lantern into the rear of the second creature.

It turned with a howl and gripped the boy by his throat. As the boy struggled to free himself, Khiri thrust her blade into the Flayer's shoulder and down, renting a long, deep gash over the creature's ribs. An unearthly screech echoed through her bones as the thing dropped the boy and began to reach for her.

In an instant, the boy was back on his feet and smacking the Flayer's face with his lantern again. Impressed with his determination, Khiri gave the boy a small comrade-in-arms smile as she grabbed the creature's reaching arm and threw it to the ground. She dealt it a finishing blow, then turned to the boy who was standing over his mother.

"How is she?" Khiri asked.

"I... I don't know..." tears streamed down the boy's cheeks. "She's not moving... And there—there's so—so much blood..."

Khiri knelt next to the woman that possessed such a loyal son and examined her. There was a great deal of blood coming from a gash in the woman's arm, and another from one of her legs, but most of the blood on the woman's face and torso had been spread or dripped from the other two wounds. A shallow rise and fall from her chest reassured Khiri that the woman still lived.

"Do you know someone who can bandage her?" Khiri asked. The boy nodded solemnly, and darted off before Khiri could instruct him further.

"Oh, Locke... Barah!" a man appeared out of the grayness. "My sweet girl, what has happened to my daughter!" He knelt beside

Khiri and examined the woman much in the same way Khiri had. "Thank the heavens, it's not serious. Where is Railen?"

"Her son?" Khiri asked. The older man nodded, even as he began to bandage his daughter. "He ran off to find a healer."

The boy came back panting with a woman in tow that had a little black bag of needles, thread and salves. Khiri couldn't restrain herself a moment longer, for the strange need to run had overtaken her again.

People were gathering into groups; stronger fighters circled around the weaker members of the village, defending those who were unable to fight. They reminded Khiri of the deer that she had once hunted with her father. Others were dashing wildly around the streets of Illesdale looking for family members, or loved ones. Bodies lay in small bloody masses, some of them people and some of them Flayers.

Still Khiri ran, sometimes stopping to help or calling instructions as she passed. The number of Flayers thinned and the fog drifted away with them. Finally, Khiri ran over a threshold.

It wasn't a physical doorway, but that was the only thing Khiri could think to call it. One moment, she was running through foggy streets laden with fear and carnage, and the next, she was in a bright sunny meadow.

"You came," a voice filled with music and light said. "I wasn't sure you would be able to. I am only a minor goddess, after all."

"Where... where am I?" Khiri asked, looking for the source of the voice. "Who are you? What's going on?"

A woman stepped into the verdant grasses, casting the light that Khiri had mistaken for sunshine from her body. Despite the brightness, Khiri's eyes did not hurt to look at her. Golden skin shone beneath a dress and cloak that gleamed with tiny striations of color, the same colors as the wings of the acolyte moths. The woman's hair was a deep, rich black or midnight blue, with soft white beads that clung to her gossamer tresses like stars. "I am Petora, and this, this is my corner of the heavens. It is lucky for us that you were attending my festival, or I would never have been able to bring you here."

"What about the Flayers?" Khiri asked.

"They were already retreating. Unlike those allied with the assassins that pursue you, this was one of the bands that remained after the War of the Burning Valley. No leadership, but they hunger. Now, Khiriellen Fortiva of the Wandering Life Tree Clan, I brought you here to warn you," the goddess frowned and spread her hands toward the ground. Several acolyte moths sprung from the edges of her cloak and fluttered before Khiri.

Images started to form; abstract pictures became sharply defined the longer that Khiri watched them. "The heavens are on the brink of war. We are torn, between beliefs that no longer grant us power, and lack of our leaders. Some among our numbers would have us turn against humanity, and others wish to withdraw from the world and start fresh with a new place. I am of a minority that wants to help in what promises to be the next Great War," as Petora spoke, the moths showed Khiri a table that was surrounded by other deities, shouting at each other, raising fists and thumping on the massive structure that was both wood and stone. An image of the Arra that Khiri knew hung between them, fracturing more with every argument.

"What can I do? My father was a war hero, but I'm just on a quest to find out what happened during my Name Breathing," Khiri protested.

"Laws were established long ago that prevent me from interfering on too grand a scale," Petora sighed. "All I can tell you is that your quest is not what it seems. You will soon find yourself to be the fulcrum on which the world shifts. Only by igniting the darkness, will you find the light."

Khiri watched the images on the moths' wings as they showed the same icy cavern that she had been dreaming of ever since she had touched the ground outside of the Life Trees. "I have no idea what you mean," she felt the confusion and frustration of her journey shift itself from her chest to her shoulders. Khiri's entire being was slowly being crushed with the fate of a world that she hadn't known for more than a month.

"I know," Petora said, sounding truly apologetic. "There is much I wish I could tell you, but it will make sense once you find yourself in the coldest place you have ever been."

"My father," Khiri tried to duck past the conglomeration of acolyte moths so she could see Petora's face again, "he was once tapped by a deity. Do you know which it was?"

Petora shook her head, her midnight hair seeming to float as though it were suspended in water. "Even should I know, I couldn't tell you. What I *can* say is this: it was one of the seven High Gods. Ask your friends, Estan and Resmine, for more information about their beliefs. It may be a bit skewed, but they will have a base understanding. Our time here grows short. I can only bend the rules for a short time. My power begins to wane as the acolyte moths leave your realm. You should go, before the threshold falls," the goddess made another gesture and the acolyte moths that she had called into being returned to her cloak.

Turning back the way she had come, Khiri only saw stretching fields of gloriously green grass and the most vividly colored wildflowers she had ever had the pleasure of witnessing. Steeling herself, she marched ahead. The effect of crossing the threshold in this direction was less jarring, a fact that Khiri pushed away to be thought over later.

The last lingering tendrils of fog were evaporating into nothingness as the cool hissings of Flayers quieted and then vanished. Khiri hadn't known that they could carry a fog with them, but maybe it was an ability belonging to those too weak to travel through shadows. It was something to ponder, but at a later date. Tonight she still dealt with thoughts of her father and what Petora had told her.

And then there's Estan... a small voice in the back of her head reminded her. That, she could definitely set aside until later.

"Khiri! Forest spirits be praised," Micah ran up to her, panting as though he had been running for miles. "Estan said that you ran off into the fog. We've all been looking for you... You were gone half of the night."

"Is everyone alright? Is the festival over?" Khiri asked. "I have to talk to Estan and Resmine." Her body began shaking like the victim of a lightning rune. She'd been given quite a few shocks in a very small amount of time; it didn't surprise Khiri in the least that her body was starting to protest its misuse.

"Come on, Khirs. We'll see about getting something hot into your belly, and you can tell me what happened. The others can come to us, just this once," Micah took her arm and wrapped it around his shoulders.

Khiri couldn't find the voice to protest. His presence was comforting, and he smelled like home. The Life Tree Clans once produced children the way that humans and dwarves did: unlimited offspring. Over the centuries, as the Life Trees became bigger and deaths more infrequent, the elven couples rarely bore more than one child. Despite this, elven children raised together sometimes became extremely close and longed for the bonds of siblinghood.

As this crossed through her mind, Khiri's eyes wandered over Micah. The two of them had explored the Oak Wood Life Tree's secrets and shared a childhood. He'd followed her into exile, even after realizing that she could offer him nothing but friendship. Micah was no longer a soft, shining golden name in the back of her mind, but he resided in her heart almost the same way that her mother and father did.

"Micah," she started before her throat closed with emotion. It was harder to ask him than she had anticipated.

"Yes?" he turned to look at her. Micah's eyes were the soft glowing green gemstones that she had known her whole life. There was an affection, soft and easy, reflected within their depths. The places where their skin touched offered no excitement, only a steady comfortable warmth.

"We've been through so much together... A lifetime in the trees, and what feels like as much among the ground walkers. You were once destined to be my mate, and we agreed that will never happen," she tried to explain how her thoughts had formed, aware that her words were clumsy and formal.

"Yes..." a questioning note entered his voice, hesitant and a little alarmed.

"I'm not retracting what's already been said," she hastened to reassure him. She felt his tension ease again under the muscles in her arm. "What I'm trying to say is you are like family to me. Will... will you be my bonded brother?"

Stopping so suddenly that Khiri nearly tripped over her own feet, Micah stared at her untattooed face in disbelief. As she was becoming nervous that perhaps she had presumed too much, a wave of pure elation swept over the older elf's features. "Truly?" he asked in disbelief. "You want to become siblings?"

Khiri nodded, the beginnings of a smile quivering at the edges of her mouth.

Micah laughed as he spun to pick her up by the waist and twirl her through the air. He sobered almost immediately, putting her gently on the ground and embracing her as though they'd not seen each other in several years. "I can hardly believe it, Khiri. I always wanted to be part of your family. The day... That day... I lost all of you.... I never thought that..."

Townspeople passed by, and Khiri felt a tug on her skirt. Turning to see who it was, she found the boy, Railen, standing next to her. His mother and grandfather were a short distance away, his mother's wounds wrapped with clean linens. "Thank you, elf lady," Railen said. "You saved my mum."

"Is there anything we can offer you?" the boy's grandfather asked.

"Not really," Khiri shrugged. "I didn't do much more than the boy was doing on his own. He's got a fire spirit dwelling inside him, I'm sure," she smiled at the lad, aware that he wasn't much shorter than she was.

"Perhaps when he is of age for an apprenticeship, you would consider taking him?" Barah, Railen's mother, suggested. "According to my son, you fight like the winds of a storm."

"Uh..." Khiri was speechless. She didn't consider herself a master of anything, and the idea of an apprentice following her around was more than her stunned mind could handle. "I... I'll have to think about it," she said after an uncomfortable moment had passed.

The boy and his family took their leave, extracting a promise from the elves to stop in for a visit the next time they were in town. While Khiri was still waving to Railen, Micah frowned and leaned toward her. "Before we were interrupted, a thought occurred to me," he said softly.

"What's that?" Khiri asked. The shakes that had plagued her before were finally subsiding, and the last of the acolyte moths was making its way across a sky full of stars. A late moon was rising in the east, shining down on the ground below so brightly that it almost seemed like overcast daylight, making Illesdale's leftover lanterns rather superfluous.

"If we do the sibling bond, what happens if our destined names ever switch back?" Micah asked, his worried face clearly visible in the moonlight.

Khiri turned the thought over in her mind as she held up the hand that bore the ring that had changed everything. Studying the big, staring ruby and interlocking disks, she bit her lower lip. It seemed unlikely that the name of her destined would change again; however, it had been unimaginable the first time it occurred.

"I guess we'll just worry about that when and if it happens," she said. "I'd much rather have you as a brother than as my destined, though, and I think Arra would consider that."

30

~Estan~

A FLAYER LUNGED FOR Estan's throat and managed to skewer itself on his blade. The knight didn't even remember drawing his sword. Estan sent a quick prayer of thanks to Taymahr that his lifetime of training enabled his body to act on its own with no conscious urging on his part.

The demon-bound were everywhere, but they seemed to be having very little impact. These were very old Flayers; even the extended life a demon gave its host faded with time. Abilities gained through a bonding depended upon the strength of a person's will, but after the initial wish was granted, the demon blood fed on sacrifice. Flayers hunted to fill their demons' needs, but when a Flayer's hunts went poorly, the only body it had to sacrifice was itself. Powers lessened as the body deteriorated, which made it more difficult for a Flayer to find prey; finally, the demon took whatever of the original host remained, leaving nothing but a lumbering husk. At least, that was what Estan's books said on the subject.

Torn between helping the citizens of Illesdale and pursuing Khiri, Estan took two steps in the direction Khiri had gone before he heard Resmine calling for him in the opposite direction. His hesitation evaporated, and he pivoted on his heels. Khiri was a skilled fighter, more than capable of protecting herself in the mists of aged

Flayers. Resmine was also skilled in combat, so whatever had her calling for him had to be urgent.

Rounding a muddy corner, Estan stumbled in surprise. Resmine was fighting back to back with a Knight of the Protective Hand. It was a man that Estan recognized. The last time he'd seen this man was on the front lines; it was the same man that had hauled Estan through the line of fire during an Eerilorian ambush, saving the younger knight's life. The older man had lost his helmet in the battle, Estan remembered, and rivulets of sweat had been running from his iron-gray hair down his ruddy weathered cheeks. "Quinton," Estan breathed. "Quinton Ilyani..."

The circle of Flayers surrounding Resmine and Quinton was nearly five deep. Estan waded in, his sword hacking through the aging Flayers like paper. What the older Flayers lacked in strength, they made up in numbers. There were so many limbs reaching out that it was impossible to dodge or block them all. Estan felt claws shred through his festival shirt and graze his skin before he stumbled into the perimeter that the knight and Resmine were holding. Dewin was between them, lying in a crumpled heap on the worn roadway.

"Resmine! I'm here! Is Dewin okay?" Estan asked. Everything in him was urging him to check on their fallen friend, but that would leave too much of a gap for Flayers to come in behind him. Instead he took a third position facing out into the ring of hissing demon-bound bodies.

"I don't know," Resmine said, her voice breaking like she was holding back a sob. "We were laughing about something one moment, and the next, she was on the ground and these demon-sput were everywhere. If it weren't for this guy, I'd be down by now."

"Quinton Ilyani of the Protective Hand," Quinton corrected. "I know you know me, urchin. And I have much to discuss with your friend here, once the battle is over."

"Hopefully that means you're not here to arrest me," Estan parried a Flayer's claws and took another's head. Several Flayer bodies sizzled away into ugly mounds of remains, creating a ring of heat around the fighters.

"No."

There was something about Quinton's delivery that made Estan's stomach drop. It should've been good news that his comrade in arms wasn't here to take him in, that he wanted to talk. Instead, the chilly fingers of dread caressed his spine. "Why are you here, Quinton?"

The older knight struck three Flayers with one swipe of his broadsword. Flayers in the back of the crowd were beginning to drift away in search of easier prey. That would've been the end of the fight if Dewin hadn't chosen that moment to moan from the ground and renew the Flayer's taste for her suffering. "Taymahr's grace take you!" Quinton swore at the endless horde. In short bursts between sword strokes, he hammered out an explanation, "I wouldn't tell you this here, but you must hear it. The temples have laid new charges at your feet, Estan. I... Anyone that knew you couldn't have believed it, but they offered proof of your misdeeds. I came to see if I was... If you were the man I thought I knew."

Estan felt his stomach squeeze in on itself until it became one solid mass of stone. Immediately, his mind latched onto the worst thing he could imagine happening. He couldn't breathe, but he had to hear it. There was still the slightest possibility that his suspicions were wrong. "What did you see? What am I supposed to have done?"

"Loni Ashfield," Quinton said. "She's gone. Disappeared three days after you escaped. Temple Hill is claiming that you killed her, but there's been no evidence of her body. They burned a pyre, and gave her husband the ashes... They said it was to spare him the pain of seeing her that way."

"No..." stunned tears burned at the edges of Estan's vision. "She can't... They didn't..."

"There's no way to know right now," Quinton said. "Loni's always been capable. She may yet be in hiding."

Estan barely heard Quinton's heavy voice anymore. Even though the older knight was doing his best to be reassuring, Estan feared the worst. Despite everything that the temple had done—turning on him, the betrayal of Temple Hill's leaders, his near-death at the hands of assassins, and Resmine's loss of Syara—somehow he'd believed that Loni, soft and sweet Loni, would be safe as long as he stayed away from her. They couldn't have traced him to her, or they would have caught him before he ever left Seirane. His body continued fighting mechanically, even for a few strokes after the remaining Flayers fell back and the mists started to retract from the streets.

"When did you find out? When did you return from the front?" Estan's voice echoed through his body, as though he were hollow inside.

"Three days after the Knight Commander called for your arrest, they tell me," Quinton replied, still waiting for one of their remaining opponents to charge him. "I was summoned from the lines to help in the hunt for you. I think they hoped I'd be angry enough to slaughter you myself...but it's obvious to some that they've lost Taymahr's path."

Flashes of memories kept playing in Estan's head: a young Loni coming into the temple for her first offering—Loni at her wedding feast, glowing with happiness—holding the body of her beloved dog after it had passed, tears streaming down her freckled cheeks—Loni laughing with straw in her hair and sunlight playing over her bare skin. She was so vibrant, so full of life. It seemed impossible that Quinton could be telling the truth, but there was hardly any reason the older Knight would lie to him.

His eyes met Resmine's. Her features were etched with pain and understanding, but not surprise. Estan wondered if she had known that Loni was gone or if she only expected the worst from the temples and was therefore prepared to accept it.

It was hard to make himself come back to the reality of the Flayer raid and what he had to tell Quinton, but Estan knew he couldn't shut himself up inside his memories. There was too much left to be done.

"They haven't just lost the path. Temple Hill has been infiltrated by the Gray Army," Estan shuddered. Every time he had to say it, his throat felt a bit more raw, like he was scraping the truth out with a knife. "I discovered them, and that's why they want me dead."

"That's a strong claim," Quinton said, his voice turning hard. Even the Flayers nearest the older knight took a step away from the cold fury that suddenly saturated the air. "I'm willing to believe the Temple of Taymahr has fallen away from the Goddess, but falling into the hands of the Gray Army is no joking matter. Thousands died to quelch the fires that fanned the Gray Army's flame."

Another wave of Flayers thickened the mist that surrounded the fighters. For a few moments the conversation was halted as Estan lost himself in the dance of thrusts, dodges, and strikes. Steel flashed, demons hissed, blood dripped, and sweat rained. Through it all, Estan wondered what he could possibly say to make the older man believe him. It had seemed so easy when he told Genovar Fortiva. Impossibly easy. The elf hadn't even questioned him, really. *Why did Genovar believe me?* Estan wondered.

"It's true, Ser Quinton. Syara discovered them, too, may her ashes find peace," Resmine said once they recovered some breathing room. She flicked her whip into the ring of Flayers, wrapping it around one demon-bound throat. With a tug, the Flayer stumbled into arm's reach and Resmine dispatched it with her dagger.

The ring of Flayers broke entirely, as though they'd received some ethereal signal that was beyond mortal hearing. Dewin mumbled something into the dirt and curled into a ball. It looked more like she was sleeping than in pain at this point. Resmine knelt to begin nursing Dewin's wounds.

"How is it that you've found your tongue after so many years, urchin girl? You were struck dumb after..." Quinton's features started to thaw, frozen hatred melting into waxy confusion.

"After the love of my life died under dubious circumstances," Resmine finished for him. "She discovered the same secret that Estan did. "

"And I'm to believe you? A woman who's apparently been living a double life for years?" Quinton scowled, but Estan could see the man's mind working now. He wasn't ready to believe them yet, though he was willing to listen.

"Resmine did what she did to survive. She wasn't a knight, and she had nowhere to go. If she hadn't been there when I needed her, the temples would have caught me already," Estan said. Meeting Quinton's eyes, Estan made a decision. Genovar could deal with whatever was thrown at him. The elf was a war hero, and more importantly, Estan had no idea where he could be. Unlike Khiri, Genovar would be traveling alone and harder to track.

"I've met with Genovar Fortiva. He believed me," Estan said. "Resmine and I travel with his daughter at his behest."

"He requested that a knight being pursued by the Venom Guild travel with his daughter?" Quinton shook his head, but Estan felt it wasn't a rejection so much as the older knight's attempt to sift things into place.

Someone screamed in the distance, breaking through the illusion that their fight was over.

"I swear, on the altar of Taymahr, I will explain everything over a pint. But first, there's still a city full of Flayers that require our attention," Estan said.

Quinton's dark eyes fastened on Estan, weighing him with the same mysterious silence that had once measured him over an army campfire. "Then we have little time to waste," the older knight gave a slight nod, before turning on his heel and disappearing into the waning night.

"Are you okay?" Resmine asked. She grabbed Dewin by one arm and tossed the prone thief over her shoulders, using all the muscles that years of stable work had toned. A lazy smile tugged at the corners of the unconscious woman's mouth as she murmured a string of nonsense and a giggle.

"I don't have time not to be..." Estan tried to smile, but thoughts of Loni were still swimming to the surface. "I'll be okay, but you'd better get Corianne's sister to safety or we'll never hear the end of it."

Estan escorted his sister-in-arms and her charge to the nearest open tavern before charging back out into the streets to lend aid to Illesdale's villagers. Grieving was for campfires and tankards, and this was a battlefield. Estan felt his resolve stiffen like a shield around his tattered emotions. Before he could process his feelings about Loni's disappearance, he had to deal with a horde of aging Flayers and get Quinton to believe that the Gray Army was back. Releasing Resmine from his grip, Estan cleared his mind of all but the fight. The vengeance that he couldn't take on the Temples would temporarily be paid in Flayer blood.

ESTAN STEPPED INTO the taproom of the last tavern that Quinton could possibly be in. Most of his party were still looking for Khiri. It seemed like just about everyone in the village had seen her running through the battle like a wildfire of carnage, but she seemed to have evaporated into the mist that left with the Flayers. He wished he could join them, but his sense of duty would no longer let him avoid meeting with his former comrade-in-arms.

The tavern, a place called Wooden Wings, was crowded with those who had been injured during the fighting. People were nursing their bandaged wounds and drowning their pain. It was a festival night that would be long remembered for all the wrong reasons. Estan breathed in the smell of poultices and alcohol, thanking Petora for bringing so many safely through the night that should have been devoted to her glory. It didn't take long to spot Quinton, the lone warrior in blood-splattered silver armor, hanging his head over the bar.

"I can hear you back there, you know," Quinton said, not turning his head away from the pint he nursed. "You've a warrior's step."

"Not that I was hiding it," Estan sighed. A new thought had occurred to him while he'd been out fighting on his own. True, Quinton had seemed furious when Estan had said the Gray Army had taken over Temple Hill, but what if that fury was over the discovery and not the accusation as he'd claimed? "How am I to know that you aren't a trap sent here by the Grey Army?"

The older knight turned, fire burning the edges of his eye sockets as it leaked toward Estan. "I should cut your tongue for such slanderous implications. Would too, if a young whelp like yourself hadn't already invoked the name of Genovar Fortiva. You say you travel with his daughter. Where is she?"

"She ran into the Flayer mists. The rest of my company is still looking for her," Estan said.

"You trust too easy, boy," Quinton Ilyari spat. "And for that matter, so do I. Here I sit, lured by an old name and a tale, while you use names that are best left unsaid."

Wishing that he had brought Genovar's book with him, Estan sat on the stool beside his brother-knight and summoned the barkeep. Not a word was spoken as the slender old man, with more mustache than face, placed a fat tankard of amber liquid in front of the younger warrior.

"Sir Jersel himself tried to knife me before I fled the Temple of Taymahr," Estan told his drink, not daring to meet Quinton's eyes just yet. "I suppose it didn't really teach me much. I was still happy to see you... until I heard why you were here."

"Assuming that's true," Quinton said, also to the mug in front of him, "I'm sorry. I know what it's like to be cast out by a parent. Enough of this, though. You promised me an explanation... So explain."

With a deep breath and a quick chug of courage, Estan launched into his story. He began with the conversation he had witnessed between High Priestess Shalora and her attendant, detailed his escape through the city and Loni's aide, told of the journey to the Life Trees and his plea with Genovar, his experiences in Jarelton, teaming up with Ullen, and finished with his meeting of Khiri. "That's the whole of it," he finished.

Quinton had sat quietly during Estan's testimony. Sometimes scowling, his face had remained largely impassive. Estan sat quietly, willing the older man to believe him.

As Quinton opened his mouth to respond, either favorably or not, the tavern door swung open with a bang. Micah sprang inside, seeming unaware of the solemn atmosphere and smiling as though the festival had never been interrupted.

"Estan! Khiri and I have been looking for you everywhere! She's asked me to be her brother! Hurry! Before she comes to her senses!"

"Her brother?" Estan repeated dumbly.

With a gruff laugh, Quinton clapped Estan's shoulder. "Alright, I believe you. The gods themselves could not have timed that lad's appearance better. Take me to see Khiriellen Fortiva. I'd like to pay respect to the daughter of my old friend."

Blinking in bewilderment, Estan turned from Micah back to Quinton. He felt like his mind had completely skipped the last few seconds and he was trying to fill in the gap, but nothing fit. "Wait... What?"

31

~Khiri~

"TAYMAHR'S GRACE!"

Khiri was still adjusting the lacings on her bracers as she walked back out of the tavern she and Estan were staying in when she realized the exclamation was directed at her. A strange knight stood between Micah and Estan, his eyes wide enough to be visible in the dimness. He sank to one knee, drawing his sword with barely a whisper of blade against leather. Thrusting the tip of the weapon into the soft earth as he knelt, he was like a living statue of supplication. Blood-splattered silver armor glinted in the torchlight. The man's hair looked darker than her father's hair, but still held a bit of a metallic shimmer.

"What's this?" she asked, not sure what to make of the knight kneeling in the dirt at her feet.

Before either of her friends could answer, the strange knight had risen to his feet again. His sword was back in its sheath as though it had never been drawn. "I fought beside your father in the valley itself," the knight told her, an odd smile playing on his lips. "You have his bearing, his knife, and more's the wonder, his gods' mark."

Khiri felt the frown tugging at her mouth, but it evaporated with sudden understanding. "You were one of the six... The others from my father's vision..."

The man smiled. It was an expression of relief, the sharing of a secret that had been almost forgotten. "There is much I would like to discuss, Khiriellen Fortiva, but there is little time. If your father is on the move, so must I be."

"I... Of course, but, who are you?" Khiri blinked.

"Quinton Ilyari, Knight of the Protective Hand," he grasped her hand tightly, as though she were her father. "Former avatar of Taymahr."

Estan broke into some sort of coughing fit. His eyes were wider than Micah's buckler as he stared at the older man. "But... avatar? That's..."

"A story for another time, I'm afraid. Estan, you told me yourself that the Gray Army has set its foot on Temple Hill. I must go."

Without another word to any of them, the Knight Ilyari turned on his heel and left, presumably to do work that would aid her father. Khiri watched him go, thinking over his assertion that she too was touched by the gods. Her thumb slipped to touch the troublesome ring that had changed her world and started her on this quest.

Gods touched, she pondered. Given her run in with Petora earlier that same evening, it was worth considering.

"That was bizarre," Micah said, cutting into her thoughts. "I found Estan. Will he do as a witness?"

"What exactly are you wanting me to witness?" Estan asked, pulling his attention back from the direction that Quinton Ilyari had left in. He raised an inquiring eyebrow at Khiri. She gave him a small shrug in return. The knowledge that the man had been one of the six standing with her father at the end of the Great War had been instinctual, and was hardly something that need further attention in the middle of the street.

Micah was still pointedly ignoring anything that didn't have to do with becoming her bond-brother. Khiri let herself smile. Even in the midst of mystery and turmoil, gaining a sibling was exciting. The ritual called for a witness and a guide. The witness was there to make sure that both parties were willing, but the guide...

"Who could we ask to be a guide?" she asked.

"Guide to what, exactly?" Estan said.

"I told you before," Micah crossed his arms and tapped his fingers against his buckler, "Khiri asked me to be her brother. We need a witness, someone we both trust, to see that our bond is honored. We also need a guide... Someone who knows what makes blood call out to siblings..."

"Dewin has Corianne and Evic," Estan suggested.

"True," Khiri sighed, "but I don't know that having siblings is enough. Normally, the process is guided by the Elder Council through their bond with the Life Trees themselves. It may require a touch of magic, and Dewin's not gifted that way."

Running through the inner list of companions, Khiri felt a certain tug toward one in particular, and she didn't like it. Still, if he agreed, it would confirm a growing suspicion that lurked in the dark corners of her being. As long as he didn't suspect her reasoning, there was no reason not to ask. Estan was the one standing guard over the ordeal, and next to Micah, she trusted him most of all.

"Fennick may have some talent with battlefield enchantments. Enough to handle magicked equipment on the road anyway. Perhaps we should ask him," she suggested.

Before Estan could voice a protest or maybe even an agreement, Micah had bounded off like an excited puppy to collect the veteran messenger. Khiri maintained her silence as she and Estan followed in her soon-to-be-brother's wake.

When she and the knight had caught up, Micah had the rest of their party gathered around him while he explained their need. Hoping her face showed more of her shared happiness with her fellow elf than her misgivings, she trotted toward the group.

Before Micah could inquire about Fennick's participation, Ullen burst out with a rough chuckle. "A bonding ceremony! I haven't done a guiding in years, but if stone and wood ain't made from Arra's bones, I'm not a dwarf!"

Smiles and hugs were passed around the group along with feelings of congratulations and relief that they had all made it through the night. The sibling bond was scheduled for the next evening, after camp had been set up. Ullen insisted, with good reason, that a tainted festival night was no place for a blood union.

Trying not to appear troubled, Khiri stole a glance toward Fennick. That odd pressure in her head from before the Flayer attack... His mistrust of Estan... Even the letter that had determined her course... She was beginning to suspect they were all somehow connected. None of it seemed harmful, but at the same time, she wondered; if it was all connected, what was the purpose?

CAMP HAD GONE UP QUICKLY that night. Catapult was grazing between the treeline and the stream that cut through the glade that Ullen had deemed appropriate for the ceremony. A few boulders scattered the landscape, calling to his heritage, even as the nearby forest called to Khiri and Micah. On the not-so-distant horizon, the mountains that they had been pushing toward rose against the sky, biting into the clouds like jagged, earthy teeth.

"Through that range, and just past Harish," Fennick said softly. Khiri hadn't heard him approach, but she wasn't really surprised at his intrusion on her thoughts. He had been trying to talk to her alone since early that morning.

"Is it just me, or have we picked up speed since we acquired more people?" she asked, trying to relax her shoulders. The messenger's presence was growing increasingly uncomfortable, but so far he still hadn't really done anything to provoke her increasing reluctance to be near him. It was just a feeling.

"We're definitely making better time," he confirmed. "I didn't figure we'd make it to the foothills for another three days, but we'll probably enter them tomorrow if we match today's pace."

Khiri looked back at where Ullen and Micah were arranging the fire pit and a small stone altar. Unconsciously, she ran a finger down the length of her arm that would be cut during the binding. If things went as they should, the wound would only last for a day or two, but she would no longer be alone. She would have a brother. A smile wedged its way onto her face, despite her present company.

"Did you think about our talk from last time?" Fennick asked. His tone was lazy, but she caught an underlying hardness in his eyes. They were not focused on her, though she knew better than to assume his attention was elsewhere.

"It was my father's wish that Estan travel with me," Khiri said cautiously. "Despite your concerns, I feel that he really did speak with my father. How else would he have even known to look for me?"

With a silent plea to the natural spirits around them, Khiri willed Fennick to accept her answer. That odd mental pressure from before, she was sure was meant to make her more pliable to his suggestions. Was it really him using a hidden power, or was he in possession of a rune like those Corianne had used? Or was it just Khiri's imagination?

There was so much of this world that Khiri still didn't understand. Since Fennick was still her guide to find Maleck Dorell, it would be counterproductive to ask him to leave. Fighting the urge to bite her lip, she hoped that he was trustworthy and all of her suspicions were unfounded.

After a long pause, the veteran soldier's stiffness melted away. He gave a slight shrug and said, "Fair enough. This is your quest, so it's your call. Just... Be careful, eh?"

Fennick turned and headed back to Resmine and Dewin, who were arguing playfully about who was stuck cooking while Micah's attention was elsewhere. Khiri turned away and continued to watch the mountains themselves. They seemed very serene, wearing their long, green cloaks of forest that left bare their bald, grassy heads. A pang of homesickness threatened to take root as she studied the way they brushed the sky.

Micah called her over for the final preparations and she gladly left her thoughts of Fennick and home for later. Tonight was special, after all. In only a few hours, she would have a brother.

32

~Estan~

SITTING OPPOSITE OF Ullen, Estan watched the dwarf as he carefully placed Khiri's knife on the altar. As had been explained to the knight several times, there was very little talking during a sibling ritual. The Guide and Witness roles were added after the rest of the ceremony had already been in practice for nearly a century, but the process had occasionally proven fatal when the delicate balance of wills wasn't achieved.

Most of the ceremony was still a mystery to Estan, as he had never studied much in the way of magic. At one time, the High Gods were more powerful and their knights were gifted with miraculous powers, but that had been long before his elevation. The last known knight with such abilities had died before the War of the Burning Valley had even taken place.

Khiri and Micah placed their hands together on the knife's hilt and said their bit in unison:

"Spirits of nature, gods of man, and blood of Mother Arra, hear our oath. From this moment on, we are kin; flesh of flesh and bone of bone."

Ullen placed his hand over theirs, and nodded to Estan to do the same. Hesitating only a moment, Estan added his hand to the stack. A node of warmth seemed to be forming in the hilt of the knife, accompanied by a steady golden glow that was showing through the gaps between all of their fingers. Like liquid fire, the light flowed down the blade and strengthened until the metal itself shown like a star.

Estan took his hand away. Relief washed over him with the knowledge that his part in the ceremony was done. All he had left to do was watch.

The dwarf picked up the glowing knife carefully, as though it were fragile enough to crumble in his grip. Khiri and Micah extended their opposing forearms, their faces etched with a strained sort of longing. Ullen guided the knife's tip down the outer edge of Khiri's arm and back up the outer edge of Micah's, leaving a thin streak of light rather than blood welling up along the lines he had traced. The weapon's glow faded, having passed its light to the elves.

Khiri and Micah pressed their arms together.

Brilliant white banished Estan's vision, and for a blood-curdling moment, he thought he had been blinded. Blurry shapes started to swim their way back into focus, slowly sponging away the sensation. He saw the two elves sharing an embrace, their faces still seeming alive with the light of the ritual. A smile of his own tugged at his lips in sympathetic happiness.

He should've known that the light would draw attention.

Two men and a handful of dwarves charged out of the treeline, howling war cries and bearing down on their small party with all the anger that was normally accompanied with a long trek away from home in enemy territory. Estan's war-honed instincts automatically reached for his sword, as he saw Resmine and Dewin moving to respond to the sudden threat.

"HOLD!" Ullen's voice boomed over the clearing. The voice held such authority that even Catapult stopped mid-canter, only walking a few more paces toward Estan as his momentum petered out.

The invading Eerilorians paused, uncertainty weighing over the field. They teetered on their feet as though still considering making use of their weapons, despite the element of surprise being taken from their advantage.

"Hold, People of Eerilor. These are allies of peace," Ullen continued. It was then that Estan realized Ullen's usual cant had been smooth throughout the entire ceremony. More secrets... What else lurked in Ullen's past?

"Who are you to speak of allies, Dwarf?" one of the two human soldiers demanded. "You may be Eerilorian born, but you travel in Mytanan company."

Ullen walked forward, putting himself between the Eerilorian force and Khiri's camp. With great flourish, he removed an iron medallion from some hidden pocket within his sleeve. "I am Prince Ut'evullen Dormidiir! I speak for my father's House!"

Awed whispers flowed out of the lips of the invaders. Estan only caught a word here or there, as he was also caught in a state of utter astonishment. His mind raced back to his initial meeting with the dwarf and the crowd that had called for Eerilorian blood. Had they suspected that the ill-dressed bard had been the second son of the current ruler of Eerilor, or had it just been chance...?

Estan stole a glance at Khiri, who had moved up behind Ullen, subconsciously putting her own authority behind the dwarf's assertions. She watched the newcomers with a calm, confident curiosity. Had she somehow known or guessed, the way she had with Quinton?

One by one, the invaders dropped their weapons into the grass and knelt.

"Forgive us, Highness," the man who had snarled at Ullen before said. "You have not been seen within the borders of Eerilor in so long, there were rumors that you no longer lived. We have standing orders to accompany you to the palace, should we encounter you."

"Has something urgent occurred that I have not been aware of?" Ullen asked, his tone dripping with regal condescension. Estan fought the urge to make a face. Hearing Ullen use this haughty, proper language seemed... vulgar. Like he was seeing the dwarf naked, instead of facing down a handful of trespassing Eerilorians.

"Well, your Highness," the man sighed. His hair was the tattered hay blonde of a man no longer in his prime, and his voice was hoarse with the utterance of many battle cries. "There is the war."

"Trivial, at best," Ullen said dismissively. "Hardly worth my return to the palace. However, I can't have it said that the second son of House Dordimiir shirked their duty in the face of battle."

New Ullen, Prince of Eerilor, turned to face Khiri. "Your thoughts, Khiriellen Fortiva?"

The invaders again exchanged a round of awed whispers. Their lost prince, traveling in the company of a Fortiva. It was impossible that they would remain silent about this encounter.

"We are close to our current objective," Khiri said cautiously. Her tone was that of someone who dared not give anything away. Estan suspected she was more concerned with the possibility that Ullen would leave them than she was with the Eerilorians knowing her business.

"Then, we will reach a compromise," Ullen stated. "This company will return to its current mission. We will return to ours. In one month's time, I will meet you in Grimson's Pass and you will escort me as our queen has requested."

"Understood, your Highness," the man said. The apparent commander rose to his feet and signaled to the others. With a silence that Flayers would envy, they collected their equipment and faded back into the night.

Estan watched them go, his instincts at war with his better judgment. It hadn't been that long ago that he had been on the front lines of the war that those soldiers were still fighting, and on the opposite side. Eerilor wasn't the real enemy though. The Gray Army had tricked him and those like him into fighting so that both Mytana and Eerilor would be weakened, making both countries easier targets for whatever they had planned.

Still, it felt wrong to watch a foreign strike team pass through Mytana unmolested. He turned to where Khiri and Ullen stood, continuing to watch the forest.

"You'll be wantin' an explanation or sommat?" Ullen said, the regal tone noticeably absent once more. His face was impassive, his chin set.

Micah was hovering near the ritual altar, while Resmine and Dewin were pretending to be absorbed with sharpening their blades. Fennick was on his way back into camp, holding a string of trout. "Did I miss much?" the ex-soldier called lazily.

Estan's scowl deepened. He was aware that the former soldier didn't like him, and had heard from Resmine that Fennick was trying to rouse suspicions against the knight. That was especially galling, seeing as the veteran apparently had absolutely no nose for trouble. Estan asked Resmine to help him watch the former soldier for any other odd behavior.

"We've got a month," Khiri said softly, her voice barely reaching Estan's ears. "If you feel need to share before then, by all means. As far as I'm concerned, you'll always be Ullen, whatever your vocation."

Something like relief shown through the dwarf's eyes before he eased back into his usual swaggering stance and ambled toward the fire. "Nothin' better than a celebration with fish and beer! Mayhap I'll even pleasure your ears with a song!"

Dewin let out an exaggerated groan, while Micah laughed and collected his new sister to help him gut and clean Fennick's catch. Things had progressed from tense to normal in only a few moments. Estan crunched his way through the thick grasses and ran his hand over Catapult's back.

Blessed Taymahr, he sent his thoughts out into the night, *if only this could last.*

It was an empty hope, what with the Gray Army gathering and the Venom Guild on their heels. In their race against the past, Estan had a feeling they were losing ground.

AROUND NOON, THE SMALL band of travelers made it past the foothills and started the climb through the Eisessi mountain range. Seemingly gentle slopes disguised treacherous footing, and several members of their party nearly took a tumble as scree slid loose. Steeper, less-inviting paths were hidden beneath swathes of grass and brush.

Planting his foot into the gravelly incline, Estan pushed himself to follow Ullen and the two elves. Catapult was balking behind him, disliking the stones that threatened to lodge in his shoes even more than his rider.

Khiri paused and studied the war horse. "Perhaps we should find a better route. We can't leave him behind."

Estan let out a breath he had been holding. He hadn't wanted to be the one to mention his difficulty, as he already felt stripped of his authority in the camp. Conceding to Khiri had come easily, naturally even, but it embarrassed him when he remembered the promise he'd demanded from Ullen before they'd left Jarelton. It was even worse now that he knew Ullen was really a prince of Eerilor. Maybe it made sense at the time, but if he'd known just how presumptuous...

Resmine petted Catapult's nose and made sympathetic noises at the war horse as Dewin caught her breath by sitting on a boulder. Fennick kept moving, as though he hadn't heard any of what just passed between the rest of the group.

Micah stopped the older man with a hand on his shoulder. Fennick started and looked at everyone he had just walked by, seeming confused. "Are we taking a rest, then?" he inquired.

"We need a path for Catapult. He is not a mountain horse," Khiri said. If she was irritated at having to repeat herself, Estan couldn't hear it. He admired her restraint. The ex-soldier had been becoming more and more preoccupied as of late, and it was starting to be something of a nuisance.

Staunching his thirst with one of the water skins, Estan wiped his brow with the back of his arm. The patch of ground they were currently on provided little shade, and the sun was already heating his skin a few degrees past uncomfortable. The heat wasn't helping his mood.

Fennick gazed at the horse and Estan for a long time, saying nothing. He looked back at the mountain and further down the range. The Eisessis lined the sky as far as the eye could travel in either direction. Finally, Fennick sighed, "There should be an easier path down that'a way, 'bout half-day's march. She'll cut into our time a fair piece, though."

"We can spare it," Khiri replied. "We're already ahead of where we should be, and no one's likely to expect us."

"Except for the Venom Guild," Fennick reminded her. "They'll likely be watchin' the road of which I speak. It's the best way through, barrin' the pass proper."

Silence struck, bringing a bitter chill into the heat of the day. The teams sent by the Venom Guild were outnumbered, but with a Flayer that Khiri couldn't touch, no one much wanted to encounter an ambush.

"Khiri..." Micah only said her name, but that one word carried all of his fears for his sister and her safety.

With a steadying breath, Khiri seemed to be weighing the dangers of the Guild and their current concerns. Catapult was the only one that chose to contribute to her internal debate, huffing into the heavy mountain breeze. Her eyes hardened. "If I am to alter my course to avoid one Flayer the rest of my life, how can I call myself a Fortiva?"

Estan smiled, "Spoken like the daughter of a war hero."

"Aye," Ullen echoed. "Lass has a point. Far better we have it out with their lot and done with. 'Tain't right, living with a mark on yer head."

Shaking his head, Fennick turned back and began leading them toward the road. "I think it's a fair mistake, but seems I'm the only one," he grumbled.

Khiri followed right behind him, flanked by Micah and Ullen. Estan turned, holding Catapult's reigns, partially for balance and partially to help guide his furry companion. The war horse flicked his tail, seeming very pleased that people had listened to his input.

Resmine stepped in to Estan as he guided Catapult past where she and Dewin had watched the latest development. "I think you're right," she hissed. "Something's off."

"Think his concern is really about the Guild?" he asked softly.

Dewin tugged off one of her boots and pretended to remove a stone. "Can't rightly tell, love. He's a slippery sot, sure as rain seepin' through socks."

"Right," Estan let his breath out slowly. He'd hoped that voicing his rising trepidations to his oldest friend would've eased his worries. Instead, Resmine echoed his suspicions and invited Dewin into the fold. The thief's perspective only made him more anxious. "Not much we can do about slippery."

"We'll keep an eye on him," Resmine promised. She flipped her tied hair back out of the growling wind and gave him a sly wink. "You keep an eye on your flame."

Estan felt the blush rise up in his cheeks. He looked down at the ground, using the excuse of moving on to hide his embarrassment. His eyes traveled over the rocky terrain to Khiri's back.

She and Micah were talking quietly. Micah was increasingly agitated while Khiri seemed determined. It wasn't hard to guess that Khiri's new brother was unhappy about her decision to face her Flayer.

"I'll do my best," he muttered into the wind, uncertain that Resmine had even heard him. "I just hope it will be enough."

33

~Khiri~

THREE DAYS INTO THE Eisessi mountains, and they still hadn't encountered the Venom Guild. Khiri supposed she should be relieved, but each mile brought on more tension. More expectation. More... Desire.

Perhaps desire is too strong, she thought. *I just want to get it over with.*

Golden rays of light dappled the landscape, making the rocky crags showing through the trees appear magnified. The taste of the mountain air stuck in her throat; thin and chalky. Maybe she was just antsy. She was a child of wood stuck in yet another world of stone. Despite the forest that clung to the rock, the mountains choked her even worse than the human city of Jarelton.

Thinking back to her time in the Life Trees, Khiri felt as though she wouldn't know herself if she met the person she had been at the beginning of her journey. She missed the Life Trees fiercely, but even if Telgan Korsborn appeared in front of her around the next bend, she wasn't certain she could go home. Flicking her eyes toward Estan's broad shoulders, she stamped down whatever reaction her inner voice was prepared to offer. No matter the reason, the Life Trees were a place that she revered, but couldn't belong.

Micah had taken Dewin into the forest to teach her more about survival and foraging. The former thief was an apt pupil, and almost

250

as good a cook. Khiri dropped her pace to match that of Resmine, sensing an opportunity to learn more of her background... No other reason, she told herself firmly.

Telgan Korsborn, the iron weight of her Life Bond's name was such that she could practically taste the metal. No other reason, she mentally sighed. Even if she wished to, there was no use fighting her destiny.

"You and Dewin seem close," Khiri ventured.

Resmine's face twisted, a mixture of fondness and regret battling her over her delicate features. "I like her, sure enough," Resmine smiled sadly. "I can't give her what she wants, though."

"What does she want?" Khiri asked. This was her first real conversation with the woman, but Resmine seemed eager to talk. Given the nature of their group, Khiri figured that travel made friendship stronger or more freely acknowledged. Whatever the reason Resmine was so willing to share, Khiri felt she was equal to asking.

"She wants love," Resmine said. "She needs it. Deserves it, truth be told. But I feel... If I give it to her..." Her voice trailed off into the songs of birds and the rush of wind through branches. Khiri was beginning to wonder if she was as ready to hear this as she had originally thought.

When Resmine found her voice again, Khiri wasn't sure she was still the one the warrior was talking to. "Would it be a betrayal to love again?"

After a long pause, Khiri prompted, "Love again?"

"Syara was a... friend to Estan and me, growing up. Older. Full of fire and stronger than Catapult. She could kick a man's pelvis into pudding in one go, but she was soft and sweet as honey butter. In all the world, she was my... My breath. Dewin's amazing, but she's not Syara. And she never will be," Resmine sighed. "I don't get serious anymore. Haven't since the Temples took Syara away. Dewin's not asking, but I can see it in her eyes. She wants more..."

"Have you told her about Syara?" Khiri asked.

Mulling things over as she watched the ancient beds of pine needles pass underfoot, she was startled to see some similarities between her situation and the predicament Resmine faced. True, her beloved had not died, but their romance had. If Micah had been less forgiving, or if she had been more angry, he wouldn't be a part of her life now. That loss, not anything like as strong as Resmine's, had still left a scar. Khiri couldn't imagine how much pain Resmine still carried.

For the first time, she appreciated how strong the woman standing next to her really was. Khiri had assumed that Resmine's jocular nature was the normal way of things. Now, she wondered how much of that was an act, intended to keep her feelings hidden.

Sensing the road that Khiri's thoughts were taking, Resmine looked up and gave a slightly forced smile. "Don't feel bad for me, Khiriellen Fortiva. It doesn't look good on you."

"As for talking to Dewin," she sighed, "I tried once. It didn't go very well... But maybe it's time I tried again. Thanks for listening, trite as it may sound."

Before Khiri could form a reply, Resmine bounded up to Estan and thumped him on the shoulder. The two of them exchanged a few words before he threw back his head and laughed.

Watching them, Khiri rolled the conversation with Resmine around in her head, like a sweet that she was sucking on for flavor. Somehow, Resmine's reluctance to love again reminded her of Telgan Korsborn and Estan, or maybe someone else that she hadn't met. How could she even begin to think about someone else when she was bound by destiny? And yet... Fate had already changed once. Could it be altered again? It was thought provoking.

She added it to her mental list of questions to pose to Maleck Dorell once they made it to him. Her ear tips were starting to itch just thinking about it.

The sensation persisted for another hour before Khiri realized there was more to it than her anticipation of meeting the mage. Magic was active nearby. Judging by the way her senses were progressing from mild irritation to feeling like her lungs were on fire, it was getting closer. Her temples were throbbing in a way that seemed... familiar.

Khiri struggled to stay calm. Nothing smelled off to her more mundane senses, and she couldn't spot anything abnormal. The path was rising into the clouds, but there was no sign of a Flayer fog. Estan and Resmine were still conversing. Fennick, ahead of them, was watching the trees around them, but didn't seem alarmed. Dropping back, Khiri pulled even with Ullen.

"Does anything seem off to you?" she asked without preamble.

The dwarf rose one of his dark eyebrows, the beads in his hair clacking as he leaned against his quarterstaff like it was an over-large walking stick. "Off how, lass?"

"I'm not sure," Khiri swallowed. "There's something brewing. A storm or...something... only, unnatural."

"Can't say as I've noticed aught, but that's not to say you're wrong. Could be sommat you're in tune with that's beyond the lot of us. We're goin' to see this mage fella on account of your abilities, I understand."

Khiri nodded once, a sharp jerk of her head, still scanning the thin stretch of valley behind them and the brief incline ahead. It wouldn't be long before they crested the top of the ridge. "Keep your eyes open. Something's wrong, and it's getting closer."

She quickened her pace so she could alert the others to stay alert as well. Dewin and Micah caught up with them over the ridge. The wind, which had been constant across the other mountain tops, died down entirely. Khiri sent a quick prayer to Arra and any nearby forest spirits. A craggy mountain face bare of trees was no place for an ambush, but the feeling wouldn't wain.

They were descending the final mountain of the Eisessi range into a foreign forest, which was comprised almost entirely of birch trees. Leaves shimmered like a sea of golden mirrors, reflecting the sun in glorious cascades except where the small puffy clouds cast shadows. It was a breath-taking vista. Somehow it made Khiri feel like a bug, small and insignificant. Easily squished.

At the forest's edge, the pulse of magic throbbed so strongly that Khiri felt she would collapse. She cried out in pain, instinctively clutching at her father's knife.

It was like plunging into an icy river, the numbness that cut in when the sensation ceased. Khiri fought to stay on her feet, even as the world began to spin. Estan reached to steady her, but his hand was knocked away by Dewin. The knight looked at the thief in confusion as an ugly hiss escaped from Micah's lips.

Micah tore Khiri away from the rest of the group, flinging her to the ground. For a moment, all Khiri could do was stare at her brother, her life-long friend, trying to comprehend the rising sense of betrayal.

Dewin's face began to melt away as she struggled to fend off Ullen's staff. Catapult was kicking toward the thief from the opposite side, when a sphere of blue light appeared, encompassing the person left in Dewin's place.

Khiri turned her attention back to Micah, whose features were also beginning to melt into another face. One that had haunted her in dreams. Resmine stepped between Khiri and the false Micah, her whip and knife cutting through the air. "Khiri, run!"

Her feet were moving to follow the command before her mind even had time to decipher it. The Flayer that desired Khiri's destruction had found her. She had to find a way to fight without actually touching the thing.

What had happened to Micah and Dewin? Had the Guild already killed or captured them? Were they waiting in the Eisessis somewhere for a rescue? Khiri stopped, noticing she was almost halfway back up the slope of the mountain.

Resmine still struggled to retain the Flayer's attention, while Estan and Ullen were steadily moving in on the mage that had taken Dewin's place. Khiri couldn't see Fennick, but she didn't feel that the ex-soldier would be much help. Pulling her bow off of her pack, she slipped the string into place. If only they had gone deeper into the forest, she may have been able to bank her arrows off of the surrounding trees. As it was, all she could do was try to distract one of the attackers.

Knocking an arrow, she let out a deep breath... and felt something yank her back foot away from the ground. She fell forward, somehow managed not to fall on her own arrow, heard the snap of wood or bone with her whole body, and began rolling downhill. Grabbing onto a thick clump of grass like it was a rope, she slowed herself enough to regain control of her downward tumble.

Laying on the ground, Khiri's eyes darted back up to where she had been tripped. The skinny, bald assassin that played the part of the Flayer's leader stood there, covered in dirt and plant debris, as though he had just climbed from an earthen grave. He was shaking his head with a smug smile of reproval. "Shouldn't let your guard down like that, Fortiva. It's most unprofessional."

Pain lanced through her wrist as Khiri climbed back to her feet. She ignored it, keeping her eye on the rune thrower while attempting to not turn her back on the fighting below. There was only so much Resmine could do against a Flayer with an ungranted wish.

"Sorry to disappoint," Khiri grumbled. "I do so wish to be a professional target."

The rune thrower bent down and picked up the remains of Khiri's bow, snapped in half when she had landed on it. He flung the pieces away, down the side of the mountain, seeming to pocket something as he did so.

"My colleague down there, once known as Liren, had quite the future ahead of her. Well, as much of a future as one of our ilk can expect. Now, even if I allow her to succeed in her wish, the most she can expect is to be completely consumed one day. I thought I should let you know, the Venom Guild has elected to hold you accountable," he dusted off his hands and smirked.

"I merit a whole guild now, do I?" Khiri drew her knife and shifted her balance, testing her footing on the mountain's topsoil. "Lucky me."

Sprinting up the road, she charged at the bald man. When she made easy throwing distance, he loosed a rune in her path. The earth began to shake and shift, threatening to toss her back down the side of the mountain. Khiri fell to one knee and clung to the tufts of mountain grass with her empty hand. By the time the quaking stopped, the rune thrower had vanished.

Unfortunately, he hadn't left Khiri alone on the mountain. In his place, Liren the Flayer stood, her hungry eyes scouring Khiri's flesh. Khiri hurried to regain her feet, keeping her knife up in a useless gesture of defense.

Daring to look back where the Flayer had been, Khiri saw that Resmine had become entangled with a black net of sticky tar stuff. Fennick, now visible, was tag teaming with Ullen against the bald man. Estan and Catapult were still dealing with the mage. They had him backed against a tree and seemed to be holding their own. Khiri sent another hopeful thought out for the real Micah and Dewin to be safe wherever they were, and then her reprieve was up.

"*Blood!*" the Liren Flayer cried, all vestiges of humanity now wiped from her voice. She flung herself down the mountain at Khiri, a cold, menacing smile twisting her already deformed features.

Waiting until the last possible moment, Khiri stood her ground. She latched onto the Flayer's outstretched arm and pushed back, rolling into the creature's momentum. Even the protection of a demon wish couldn't prevent the Flayer from being rocketed off the mountain's face. It crashed back to the ground with enough force that a mortal being would have been severely injured, if not killed.

It being a Flayer, the thing picked itself up and hissed, immediately racing toward Khiri again. Determined to make the Flayer earn every inch in this fight, Khiri pelted her way down the mountain face, vectoring away from the creature and toward the nearest tree stand. She hadn't made any plans, but maybe the forest spirits would recognize her as a child of Arra. It seemed better for her to take action rather than stay on the slope and wait for her demise at the hands of a demon-bound moron.

Shrieking with rage, the Flayer realized that it wouldn't catch Khiri on foot when it was running across the flatter ground while the elf was hurtling down an incline. Khiri pumped her legs with renewed vigor, her battle-fervor fueling her need for survival.

Then the sun was snuffed out by a passing cloud.

"Spirits!" Khiri half-swore, half-prayed. The Flayer cackled as it faded into the passing shadow, seeming to sink into the ground at a full run. Trees that had beckoned with promises of shelter now seemed riddled with menace.

Unable to stop herself, Khiri plunged into the treeline. There were shadows everywhere. Using the last of her forward momentum, she scaled one of the birches, swinging up onto a thick branch that was nearly eight feet off the ground. She clutched at her father's knife, waiting for some sign that she was not alone.

Leaves rustled in the underbrush beneath her perch. Shifting her grip on her blade, she readied herself to jump.

The motion beneath her stilled. Not a sound was uttered by the forest; no bird, no beast, and not even the wind decided to add its voice. In the quiet, Khiri felt like her heart was beating loud enough to be heard back in Illesdale. Every moment of silence brought on a new wave of tension.

At what was surely the brink of her sanity, something struck her from above. Sharp talons pierced her leather armor, biting into the flesh of her shoulders. She fought to roll away from the Flayer's grip before they both hit the ground, but to no avail. Only a lifetime of falling out of heights kept her from breaking anything vital, but the Flayer's weight drove the air from her lungs even as the thing's claws thrust deeper into her back.

Hot, rancid breath coated the back of her neck as the thing leaned into its grip, savoring her pain. "*Your life... is mine...*" it whispered with triumph-hardened finality.

A thin, screechy whistle and a wet *thwuck* accompanied a sudden sense of freedom. Khiri rolled on her back, ignoring the way her wounds were already protesting. Much like her wrist, they would have to wait. Rough gasps of air rushed into her battered lungs and threatened to pull her into unconsciousness, but she had to spot the Flayer.

It was only a few paces from her, snarling with rage as it wrenched an elven arrow from its side. The missile had been enough to knock it away from Khiri, but not enough to stop it. Khiri skittered backward, attempting to put some distance between them before it turned its attention back to its prey.

"Leave her be," Micah's voice came from over her shoulder.

"Oh good," Khiri could hear the quaver in her voice, but under the circumstances, she was glad she could speak at all. "You made it."

"Couldn't let you have all the fun," her brother tried to grin, but it was more of a grimace. Another arrow was already drawn and aimed at the monster.

The Flayer glared at both of them, swaying in a breeze that only it could feel. "*I'll not be denied, elf boy. That one is mine. Her blood calls to me...*"

Micah loosed the arrow. It flew straight at its target, the center of the demon's chest, only to be batted out of the air like an irritating fly. There was a brief pause as the Flayer seemed to smirk at the paltry attempt. It wasn't much time.

But it was enough.

While the creature hesitated, Micah rushed forward and took up the knife that had fallen out of Khiri's hand when she'd hit the ground. He managed to put himself between the Flayer and Khiri right before the monstrosity charged.

"Micah! NO!"

Khiri watched in horror as a reddened Flayer hand popped out of Micah's back, spraying the blood of her newly bound brother in her face. Tears broke from her eyes, not waiting for the unreal sensation to dissipate. She ran forward, her need to get to Micah overwhelming her sense of self-preservation.

The Flayer was chuckling, an unnerving sound that made Khiri's skin prickle. Micah was clinging to life. His hand trembled but still gripping the knife handle that was stuck in the Flayer's abdomen.

"Useless, elf boy. You'll be drained soon, and then nothing will save her... Too bad you missed," it taunted.

Through the misery that was already engulfing her, Khiri wondered why the thing was taunting the already-fatally-wounded Micah instead of moving on. Then she saw it... The enchanted knife her father had given her was holding the Flayer in place. It couldn't pull its arm out of Micah's stomach as long as he kept his grip in place.

Swallowing back her grief, Khiri moved forward to do what had to be done. She placed her hands over Micah's, careful to stay on the side of the Flayer it could no longer reach.

"What...No...NO!" The Flayer that was once Liren realized Khiri's intentions and struggled to free itself from the knife's embrace.

Putting everything she had into the effort, she shoved Micah's hand up, through the thing's ribs, until the knife found the Flayer's heart. Micah let out a pained gasp as the Flayer screamed its death cry, cursing the world that had betrayed it one last time.

Khiri caught Micah as the Flayer's steaming arm released him. His bronzed skin was pallid with beads of sweat forming even as she watched. A trickle of red stained the corner of his mouth.

"Micah... I'm so sorry..." Khiri barely managed to get the words past the lump in her throat. "If only you hadn't... If I could've..."

His eyes fought to focus as he grasped for one of her hands. "Khiri, you are... always have been... my kindred..."

"Don't leave me alone," Khiri pleaded. Her tears were like trails of coal, burning their way down her cheeks. "Don't go..."

A rueful smile flickered over his features between spasms of pain. "My sister... I won't... You'll never be alone," he promised.

One final heaving gasp shuddered through his body, and then he was still. Bird song and breeze sounded like thunder as they entered the forest where Khiri knelt holding onto Micah. His being was about to return to the wood, and there was nothing she could do.

With reverent hands, she lay him fully on the ground, making her pleas to the spirits that somehow his life energy find its way to their ancient elven home. She turned away, sobs jerking her every breath, unable to watch Micah, her dearest and most loyal companion, fade into the surrounding trees. Stumbling toward the place her knife had fallen, Khiri felt an odd sort of numbness set in. Sinking to the ground, she let herself cry until her legs started their protests of discomfort.

When she had finally regained herself enough to recover her weapon, Khiri turned back to the spot that Micah's body had been. In its place, a remarkable bow stuck out of the ground, looking for all the world as though it had grown there. The wood was the same golden hue as Micah's hair and it was the exact size of the one that Khiri had lost to the mountain. A dark mark etched into the wood above the handle was the symbol of the River Willow Clan: Micah's tattoo. She reached out to touch it and Micah's final words echoed in her head.

"You'll never be alone."

34

~Estan~

ESTAN HAD LOST SIGHT of Khiri when she'd dashed down the hill with the Flayer chasing after her. Dewin arrived shortly after, knocking the mage out from behind and allowing Estan to join the fight against the bald rune thrower.

Despite the numbers stacked against him, the rune thrower seemed to be playing with his adversaries, biding his time. He activated an armor rune that Estan's sword wasn't even close to cutting through and Ullen's staff bounced off. A swarm of beetles burst forth from the ground underneath Fennick with one flick of the rune thrower's wrist.

An inhuman scream echoed through the trees.

Even the beetles swarming Fennick seemed to freeze in place as the scream reverberated against the walls of stone. As the last echo faded, the bald man drew himself up out of a fighting stance and gave a polite bow. "That's my cue to leave. Until next time, gentlemen. Ladies."

His gaze turned to the unconscious mage. "Do let Kal know when he comes to that he has failed one time too many and would do well not to cross my path again, won't you?"

The bald man brandished one final stone and slammed it to the ground beneath him. Smoke and fire burst forth, cracking the ground around the man in a pattern reminiscent of shattered glass.

Estan and Ullen jumped back to avoid being scorched, while Fennick's beetles scurried through the fire with abandon.

"Illusion!" Estan snarled, rushing forward again only to swing through open air. The rune thrower had vanished entirely, as if he had a Flayer's shadow step. Cursing under his breath, the knight sheathed his sword and turned to deal with the aftermath.

Dewin bound the unconscious mage and emptied his pockets of various bags of powder and scraps of paper. A silvery cast to the man's pale skin and his light gray hair made Estan pause. His build was tall, maybe a few inches higher than Estan, and lithe. It had been a long time, but Estan thought he had seen people like the assassin before.

"I'll be buggered," Fennick said, stepping up next to the knight. "He's an Odlesk!"

"Don't everyone help at once!" Resmine yelled. She struggled against the tar that she'd been trapped in, but it didn't budge. Ullen and Dewin moved to begin chipping Resmine out of the now-solid tar net.

With a shrug, Fennick went to help release her. Estan kept watch over the once-assassin. Despite what the assassin's leader had said, it didn't seem likely that the mage would accept their word about his superior's dismissal. More likely, he would bide his time. Maybe he would answer some questions before it was necessary to dispatch him, though... Like who was the bald rune thrower? He was no average ranked Venom Guild flunky, as Estan had previously assumed. Why was Khiri their priority, when Estan and Fennick both had contracts out?

Once Resmine was free, she helped Estan lift the trussed-up mage over Catapult's back and tied him to the saddle. They still had plenty of daylight, as long as Khiri and Micah returned soon.

"Dewin," Estan called. "Micah went to help Khiri, right?"

She nodded, "He did. We weren't sure what was going on, but someone laid a trap for us out in the woods. Wire and runes... Nasty bitta work. It took us long enough to get free; but then we heard Resmine yellin' at Khiri to hoof it, and Micah practically jumped the trap altogether. Tells me to find you lot as soon as I'm able—which as far as we'd gotten, only took a blink."

"It's been awhile since we heard that Flayer scream," Estan said with a frown of concern. "I'm going to see if I can find them."

A mixture of twigs, white flakes of birch bark, and gravel crunched underfoot as he started in the direction Khiri had taken when she disappeared through the trees. A sense of foreboding grew in his chest as he approached her entry into the forest. Something must have happened, or the elves would've been on their way back by now.

When he saw Khiri approaching, Estan's relief was short lived. An unfamiliar bow was clutched in both of Khiri's hands and her face was caked with blood and tears. He didn't know the specifics, but her expression told him everything he needed. Micah wouldn't be coming.

Not sure whether to approach her or not, he waited for her to come to him. Khiri plodded her way to him, each step heavy with grief. When she drew even with him, Estan placed a hand on her slender shoulder. She drew the bow in closer to her chest and shuddered with a small, fluttering sob—the kind that only came after many tears had already been shed. Neither of them spoke on the way back to their companions.

It only took one glance for Resmine to utter a sharp gasp and rush to Khiri's side. Ullen and Dewin were only seconds behind her, and the three of them enveloped the elf in a massive hug. Estan wanted to join them, but he felt too awkward, having already walked her out of the trees with only his rough hand on her shoulder. He reached to grab Catapult's reigns, but his horse dodged around him and lowered his massive velvety nose into the circle of mourners.

That left Estan standing on the outskirts with Fennick. The former soldier met Estan's eyes, and for once, it didn't seem to have that edge of hostility.

CAMP THAT NIGHT WAS quiet. Solemn. When Estan received the news that Loni was missing, it wasn't a loss shared by the entire group. Micah had been a friend to everyone to some measure. Dewin braided a small lock of hair behind her ear and tied it with a small bit of black ribbon that was barely visible in the dark waves of her hair. Resmine was staring into the fire; she was doubtless recalling Syara, as she did with every new wound. Fennick and Ullen were taking turns tossing back a thin flask of something that smelled vile. Khiri sat away from the fire, still clutching the bow she had retrieved from the forest.

Cooking fell to Estan, which he didn't mind for once. It helped distract him from his own morbid thoughts.

The captured mage was now conscious, but he hadn't chosen to speak to anyone yet. He just glowered at them from the tree he'd been tied to for the evening.

Catapult was the closest thing they had to an assigned guard at the moment. That would have to be fixed before too long. The silence couldn't last forever, but no one wanted to be the first to speak. Breaking the spell of silence that wove around the campfire would be like admitting that Micah was gone. Somehow, it seemed like as long as no one spoke, he was still there.

"Do you intend to mope all night, or is this some sort of deranged torture?" the prisoner demanded, shattering the collective muteness.

Khiri stood, setting down her bow for the first time since they had left the mountain side. For the first time, Estan saw a mark above the grip. Her hand had covered it during the day, and he hadn't really tried to look. It was Micah's tattoo... But... That couldn't be. How would such a thing be possible?

"What is it to you whether we ignore you or not?" Khiri asked. Her voice was soft, dangerous. She radiated with cold anger, seeking a target.

"If you would like to kill me, get on with it. The fact that I'm here means my life is already forfeit," the Odlesk man chuckled grimly. "Not that it was ever much of a life to begin with."

For a long time, he and Khiri locked eyes and said nothing. Unlike the shared quiet of before, this silence was volatile. Sparks of lightning seemed to pass between the elf and the prisoner. Neither one gained, and neither one lost. Estan hadn't seen many commanders maintain such an intense exchange for such an extended period.

"What are you?" Khiri asked. It was one of her classic non sequiturs, dropping the tension flat on its face.

Her question seemed to catch the mage completely off guard. "I was an assassin..." he said, bemused.

"No, I mean... I'm an elf. Catapult's a horse. Ullen's a dwarf. They're all human. What are you?"

"I'm an Odlesk. More precisely, I'm half-Odlesk, half-human," he answered. "My mother fell in love with a man in a nearby town and I was the result, much to my grandfather's chagrin."

"Oh," Khiri paused, confusion still playing over her face. "What's an Odlesk?"

"A people born of the Lake Echar, like you un' I are of tree and stone, lass," Ullen said. His voice was steady, despite the liquor he'd been swallowing for most of the evening. Firelight danced over the dwarf's stern features as he sat forward, placing his hands on his knees. "Twas 'nother of Mother Arra's whims, so the stories go. Moonlight glowed such that she wanted to keep it. Summoned the Odlesk from the glimmerin' and when they go, they go to the water as we go to the stone and wood."

The mage tugged at his restraints, returning the camp's attention to him. "As fascinating as my heritage might be, I'm sure it's not why you people chose to keep me. Now please, end me or interrogate me, whatever you wish, but may we change the subject!"

"And we're to trust any information that you give?" Fennick asked, nowhere near as steadily as Ullen had managed. "You'll tell us whatever you think'll get you freed. End him! End him like he wants," the messenger's tirade ended with a hiccup.

The pot chose that moment to start boiling over, drawing Estan's attention guiltily back to the food preparation he was neglecting. Sizzling broth on the coals made the entire clearing smell of boiled rabbit and tubers.

"Uh... I guess the soup's ready," Estan muttered, his cheeks growing warm. His cooking mishap reminded everyone once more that all was not as it should be.

Khiri turned from the prisoner and sullenly gathered her bowl and spoon from her pack. "We'll decide nothing tonight..." she paused and looked questioningly at the mage.

"Kal," he supplied without meeting her eyes. "My name is Kal."

"Tomorrow, Kal, I would speak with you when everyone is..." she paused again, glancing at her bow, "...when everyone is more themselves."

After that, Estan would have welcomed the cold anger that Khiri had possessed before. Anything was better than the emotionally numb shell of an elf that sank to the ground and fiddled with her soup spoon like a child poking a wound to see if it still hurt. He turned from watching Khiri to watching the captured assassin.

Kal's eyes, like a cat's or an owl's, had no whites. Large round pupils reflected the light of the fire and the moon, making them seem to hold a glow all their own. That unnatural seeming gaze was fixed on Khiri with a keen interest that Estan found unsettling.

Double guards tonight, he decided. Unless, of course, there was a way to ensure the prisoner couldn't try anything. Robbing their diminished numbers of half a night's rest, especially with the emotional exhaustion most of them were experiencing, didn't seem fair.

War wasn't fair. Like it or not, their little group was at war. Micah was the first casualty on their side. They were no longer mere fugitives... Taking a prisoner, killing the unbeatable Flayer, Khiri being the primary target for no reward; all of these pointed at one thing. The Venom Guild no longer viewed them as a normal contract, or even an interesting diversion. They'd become a genuine threat.

Estan took his bowl of stew over to the Odlesk man and leaned against a neighboring birch. He took a bite or two, careful not to look at the mage. In his peripheral vision, he could see that the man's unusual eyes had moved from Khiri and were fastened on the up and down of Estan's spoon.

"Would you like some?" Estan asked.

"Just ask your questions. This taunting is useless," the prisoner turned his head away. He rocked his wrists in their bindings, only to succeed in tightening the ropes. "I'm not sure what you expect of me, anyway. Do you think showing me mercy is somehow going to sway the Guild? I'm about as welcome there as a rabid rat with fleas."

"We knew that when the bald rune thrower told us that you were out. Apparently, you would do well not to cross paths with him again," Estan said. He held a spoonful out toward the prisoner, "Sure you won't have any? It's pretty awful, but at least it's filling."

"If you know I'm useless, why am I still here?" Kal demanded.

"Khiri said you'll be here until tomorrow. None of us are going to argue with her. Not when her brother just died," Estan shrugged. "There is one thing I wanted to ask you. It's not much. Not sure if it's really that important..."

The prisoner swung his head around, the sheen of his silvery skin making him look sweaty despite the cool bite of the night air. "Finally," he smirked. "I knew you'd want something."

"I just want to know the name of your bald companion," Estan said. His stew bowl was already cooling in his hands this far from the fire. He fought the urge to look over at Khiri. If he turned her way now, Kal would turn his attention back to her as well.

A low, husky laugh started in the mage's throat and carried down through his chest. The chill Estan had noticed before seemed to intensify by several degrees. "Oh, by the waters and all of the gods of my father! That's too much! You really don't know?"

Resmine and Ullen looked up from where they'd started dealing out a deck of cards. Dewin's spoon paused halfway to her mouth. Drunken muttering came from the far side of the fire, where Fennick had fallen over. Khiri barely even looked up from her dish, though she was obviously listening.

"No idea," Kal continued to chuckle. "The entire Venom Guild on your heels, scraping every informant from Jarelton to the Eastern Reaches just to find out... Undines surround! That's the head of the Guild! Arad Rhidel!"

Estan choked on the spoonful of rabbit he'd just scooped into his mouth. "The Venom Guild's leader has been after us for the last few weeks?"

Kal continued to snicker to himself while Estan tried to absorb this particular nugget of information. The knight shoved his bowl into the other man's lap, stood and walked toward the area where his horse was grazing. Catapult huffed at him. Estan imagined that the war horse was chastising him; as though somehow Catapult would've told him the same thing that he'd just learned from the assassin, if only Estan would occasionally listen.

Khiri appeared next to him, Micah's bow firm in her grasp.

"This is bad," he said.

"He told me he would hold me personally accountable for Liren's death," Khiri's voice was all but a whisper. "It was like he knew I would walk out of that fight. If he knew that, then he also knew why..."

"Khiri..."

"No, Estan," her voice was hard. "The Venom Guild sent us a message. Next time, we'll send them one. I'm not going to take this lying down."

Estan studied Khiri's face in the starlight. The plains of her face seemed sharper than before, but still young. He thought about how much they'd been through in such a short time. Whatever her decision, he was with her, heart and soul.

"If I'm responsible for Liren, he's responsible for Micah."

35

~Khiri~

PACKING UP CAMP THE next morning, Khiri slung the bow-that-was-also-Micah into the harness in which her old bow had resided. During her dreams, she and her brother had talked for a long time about what it meant for him to be a weapon at her side. It had been so vivid, so *real*, that Khiri wasn't sure it had actually been a dream.

No Flayer could ever again use a wish for her life as a shield. An arrow knocked on her new bow was now a strike from Micah. Even in death, he would continue to stay by her side, and there was no need to wear out his wood with her palms. He wasn't about to wander off.

Kal posed another problem altogether. If they left him behind, he might strike at them on his own. On the other hand, taking him along was like keeping a poisonous spider on your shoulder. Sooner or later, it may bite. No matter what Khiri thought about doing with him, the answer seemed to be the same—she didn't trust him.

Fennick suggested killing him. Often. Every five minutes, he pointed out that they "were overlooking the safest solution".

"Just because it's safest, doesn't make it right," Resmine snapped.

Estan looked at his friend in surprise. "That's not what you said before we got to Jarelton," the knight said as he threw Catapult's saddlebags over the war horse's gray-blue back. Catapult stomped his hoof twice in agreement.

"Fine. You were right. Happy now?" she struggled to tie her hair into place. It seemed determined to defy her, two curly strands falling out her grip even as she spoke. "But if you were right back then, that means I'm right this time. I don't think we should just kill the man."

"We're not going to kill him," Khiri said. "I'm not out to become what we're fighting against."

She strode over to the prisoner and crouched in front of him. Kal stared at her, giving her that odd penetrating gaze that he had given her the night before. In the daylight, his pupils had narrowed to vertical shards of black, surrounded by blue-green irises. Khiri met his gaze without flinching, attempting to get a read on him. Everything about him was so... shadowed.

"You refuse to kill me. You can hardly let me go. What will you do? Toss me over the horse like a sack of potatoes?" he asked, his voice seeming to brush against her ears despite the fact that he was still tied flush with the tree. The odd sensation gave Khiri an even odder thrill that seemed to originate in the small of her back and skitter along her spine. She felt a bit tingly.

"If I have to," Khiri stood back up. Letting the assassin know that he got to her wouldn't be a good idea, no matter how it looked. For all she knew, he had been planted in their camp on purpose, either to spy or as part of a long-term attempt to gain her trust.

"In that case," he said, his voice returning to a normal cadence, "put me under."

Drawing one of her hatchets, Dewin stepped up behind the mage and positioned the butt to strike him over the head. "Mind you, be a love and don't wriggle, or might being you lose sommat more'n your mind," she told him.

"Undines surround! That's not what I meant!" Kal struggled with his ropes, ducking away from Dewin and her bludgeon. "For a peace-loving lot, you're awfully quick to bash skulls!"

"Then what did you mean?" Estan asked.

"Probably somethin' like this," Fennick muttered, pulling a rune out of his belt pouch. "I found it on the ground after our fight with that Arad fella'. Figured it may prove useful."

"Yes! That! That, I'll agree to! Now please," Kal pleaded, "Call her off! I swear she almost split my head open last time..."

Khiri nodded at Dewin and motioned for Fennick to apply his rune stone. She watched as the ex-soldier pressed the rune against the mage's forehead, appreciating the irony that the man she had long mistrusted was the one she was asking to safeguard the man she newly mistrusted. Not for a moment did she believe that the rune they needed just happened to be dropped by the Master Assassin. Arad Rhidel didn't strike her as the sort to carelessly leave his weapons in the field for others to find.

"Now, we tie him down like a sack of potatoes," she told the others. "On to Harish, and spirits help the next distraction."

STOPPING FOR LUNCH and a rest, Khiri pulled Fennick aside. "Revive him," she nodded to the mage, sprawled across Catapult's back. "We still need to talk, he and I."

"I wouldn't'a listen to a word out of the hornet's mouth," Fennick spat. "Best we just leave 'im be."

The ex-soldier stooped down, picked off a grass stalk, touched it to his tongue and tossed it into the air. It spiraled down to the ground, drifting slightly to the west. Fennick's rough face twisted into a grimace and his eyes darted over the landscape, "We shouldn't'a dawdle about. Sure as we stop, there'll be rain tonight. Thunder too. Cold'll hit us like a fury."

He wandered away from the clearing without pulling out the rune. Khiri watched him go, and then saw Dewin remove herself from a tree to follow after him. It made her feel better to know that someone was watching Fennick. What was he hiding that the sleeping assassin might know about?

Estan, Ullen and Resmine were busy with slicing bits of bread and cheese while debating whether to start a fire or make do with cold meats. Ullen was halfway into an anecdote about his time with a traveling theater troupe. Echoing a question of her own, Estan asked the dwarf just how many vocations Ullen had accrued over his travels.

Despite her curiosity, she crept over to Catapult and studied the mage. There had to be a way to rouse him without the rune. She sensed that he would speak to her, wanted to speak to her... Kal was sent to kill her, was a member of the group responsible for Micah's death, and yet... And yet.

"Enjoying the view?" Kal whispered.

Khiri jumped, startling Catapult into dancing a couple of steps away.

Estan turned toward her. He started to get up, concern written in his eyes. Kal hadn't moved, and there was no way his voice had carried to the others. Making a pacifying hand motion, Khiri stilled Estan's intervention.

"Been awake long?" she asked in an equally hushed voice.

"Long enough," the mage grinned, an expression that would've been more sly if he hadn't been roped to the back of a very tall horse. "You wanted to talk to me. Here's your big chance."

Climbing to a branch that was near-level with Catapult's back, Khiri took out an arrow that Micah had been working on and began trimming it with her knife. She didn't have the skill Micah had possessed with wood-crafting, but it gave her something to do with her hands and drew less notice from the others. "First question," she said. "How is it that you're awake?"

"Runes only work on mages once in awhile. It's more a matter of power than skill... Something to do with inert magics and overcoming saturation of the spirit," Kal answered. "I was rather hoping that any rune your lot would possess wouldn't work, and I was lucky enough to be right."

Digesting this new information, Khiri paused mid knife-stroke. The headache she had experienced, first the conversation with Fennick, and then before the last Guild attack. "Are there side effects to rune usage when they don't work?"

"Ever try hanging off a horse when your head's already killing you?" Kal responded. "I don't recommend it."

"Prior to your attack, what rune was Arad using?" Khiri asked, struggling to keep her voice steady. She wasn't entirely sure if the emotion growing in her chest was anger or excitement. It was important; of that, she had no doubt.

"I couldn't begin to tell you Arad's business. I've never been very high in the Guild's ranks. My talent as a mage is limited, and my talent as a killer was undoubtedly worse," the mage looked up, his eyes locked on hers. "Honestly, though, is that all you wanted to talk about?"

"What do you mean?" Khiri asked. His gaze was strong enough to pin her to the tree. A brief sensation, like warm bath water, brushed against the side of her face.

"I've never met anyone like me before," he said, his voice going husky. Despite the way he was tied down, Kal suddenly seemed dangerous in a wholly different manner than Khiri was used to.

Telgan Korsborn, her thoughts reminded her. She bit back the sudden metallic taste in her mouth. For once, the reminder didn't bother her so much. It helped her regain her emotional balance. "Like you?" Khiri raised an eyebrow.

"Born of the Mother's creations and the mortal gods' children," Kal's own brows drew together. "Surely you knew?"

Her regained stability melted away like so much iced cream. Khiri knew that her father had a number of secrets; over her travels, she'd learned that he kept a lot from her while she was growing up. But... One of her parents? Human? How could a human have lived in the Life Trees all this time?

Memories rushed through her. All those times her mother had ducked into the front door of their home, Leyani's being "tall for an elf" often eliciting remarks, her mother's hair being carefully braided so that her ears were always partially hidden, how her mother was almost solely responsible for trading with humans that came near the village... And Khiri's own sensitivity to magic—human magic. Genovar and Leyani lived in a different Life Tree than either had grown up in. She never thought to inquire why she'd never met her grandparents when she was a child, despite other elven children knowing the parents of their mother or father. As curious as she was about everything else, why hadn't she thought to ask that question? Unless...

Unless on a certain level, she already knew.

Had she ever seen, really *seen*, Leyani's ears? She couldn't remember.

"You didn't know," Kal sighed. "I'm sorry that I mentioned it then. I just thought, perhaps, I had finally found someone who understood what it was like."

"What what was like?" Khiri asked, surprising herself with how vehement her voice sounded. She sheathed her knife and dropped from the branch, Micah's arrow still grasped in one hand. It was an anger that was almost entirely directed at her parents. They'd both watched her during the Name Breathing, knowing that she was different, and neither one had thought to warn her that her duel heritage might possibly be problematic. Perhaps they hadn't known? *They still should've told me, by Arra.*

"Growing up alone," the mage said, sinking against Catapult's flank.

The despair in Kal's voice called to Khiri in a way she didn't fully understand. Those same instincts that wanted her to get as far away from Fennick as she was able, urged her to trust this man. She reminded her instincts that he'd tried to kill her, not even a full day ago. That didn't seem to matter as Khiri looked at Kal, his long body awkwardly draped across Catapult's back. *I must be crazy*, Khiri thought. *Why do I feel like I trust him?*

Despite Khiri's maelstrom of conflicting emotions, she placed her empty hand on Kal's, under the guise of petting the warhorse. Catapult flicked his tail, seeming unhappy with his part in the deception. "You may have come to the right group," Khiri told the mage. "I just lost my brother. Estan and Resmine lost their home. Dewin's here because it's safer for her to be on the road with me, of all things. We may not have grown up alone, but we're all we've got. I can't say why, and I certainly can't make it official yet, but I have an urge to welcome you to our little band."

The Odlesk raised his head just enough to meet her eyes. Khiri felt her breath catch, suddenly aware of how close together they were. *Telgan Korsborn*, the name inside of her insisted. She barely noticed.

"When your group decides to pull me down, I'll be ready to accept whatever welcome you care to give," Kal breathed. A chill-edged wind blew between them, causing his gray hair to dance toward her.

Gripping the arrow, Khiri drew away, a mixture of relief and regret coloring her cheeks. "Don't let the others know you're awake just yet. I'll make sure you're given a chance for food when we camp for the night. For now, it's the best I can do."

"Still don't trust me? Should I be hurt?" Khiri could practically feel the sarcasm as it rolled across her skin.

On the other side of Catapult, she saw Fennick's feet approaching the others. Micah's bow seemed to vibrate in response to her growing sense of wrongness. What had started as a mild dislike had started to take form into something bigger. Almost palatable. "It's not you I'm worried about."

WHEN THE RAINS CAME that night, as Fennick had said they would, Khiri couldn't help but be disappointed. Not to mention, *cold*. Compared to the dreams of the frost-filled cave, it was practically warm, but it was hard to remember that when every inch of her was soaked through.

Trying to pile seven people into the only tent was uncomfortable, especially when most of them were attempting to avoid sleeping near their prisoner. Estan suggested that they place the assassin outside, under Catapult. Testily, Khiri suggested that Estan switch places with his horse, since Catapult was bound to be more quiet.

"You have met my horse, haven't you?" Estan retorted, though he did let the subject drop.

Ullen and Dewin took turns throughout the rainy night creating their own thunder, which threatened to drown out the actual storm's noise.

Eventually, Khiri ducked out of the tent herself and sought the war horse's company. He was below an oiled blanket that Estan had spread between two branches to try and provide the animal with some shelter from the unfriendly damp. The blanket did seem to be keeping the worst of the storm at bay, that which made it through the trees in the first place.

Her wood lore told her that the trees were not the safest place to weather this kind of storm, but given that they were in the middle of a forest, there didn't seem to be much choice. She and Dewin had chosen a campground beneath the sturdiest trees in the area, free from already-dead branches and rotting timber. The only thing to do now was wait out the volatile spirits.

"Couldn't sleep?" Estan asked, shaking the storm from his boots as he also entered the tiny horse sanctuary.

"I doubt anyone could, but those two," Khiri muttered. "You?"

"I did manage a few nods, before they woke me," he said. "Battlefield experience."

"Ullen and Dewin could wake the stones," Khiri nodded.

"Not them," Estan moved to his horse's side. Khiri noticed that he had a brush hooked to one hand. The blue roan stamped an appreciative hoof into the dampened forest bed beneath him. "The ghosts of people I killed. In the war with Eerilor."

"Oh," Khiri said, feeling awkward. The mention of killing reminded her that Kal was an assassin. Somehow, she had a hard time picturing the mage taking a life. Was it because he had convinced her that the two of them were more alike? She watched the knight move the stiff-bristled brush over Catapult's hide in long, smooth strokes.

Estan was a capable man. Strong, fierce, loyal, all of the qualities that she found admirable. He liked her a great deal, despite the fact that she had been careful to keep a distance between them. How did she feel about him, or how would she, if Telgan Korsborn's name wasn't throbbing behind her eyes? She didn't know.

A flash of Micah's face lifting away from hers the first time they had kissed on the Sky Watcher's platform filled her vision. At the time, what seemed like two hundred summers ago, it had felt so... awkward. Warm and soft, the golden name had fluttered in response; but the rest of her had been oddly disappointed.

Khiri pictured the same kiss with Estan, and felt her blush warm her face against the cold of the rain. The image in her head changed, unbidden, to Kal's lips replacing Micah's and she felt her color grow stronger. Hiding her reaction by tucking her head into her cloak, Khiri huddled against a tree, pretending for all she was worth that she was alone with the horse and the storm.

36

~Estan~

HARISH WAS A WELCOME relief to Estan's city bred senses after so long out in the wilderness. It wasn't quite so vast as Seirane or Jarelton, but it was a good sight better than the village of Illesdale. The buildings and houses were all suspended above the ground on large stilts and bits of scaffolding that made the town look larger. Well-traveled roads led between the buildings on the ground while bridges spanned the air in zigzags and arcs. A spiked stone wall surrounded Harish, making the town resemble a fort, which was probably a necessary precaution this far from the other major cities of Mytana.

Despite the usual bustle of people that gathered in cities, there was a definite lack of the overcrowding that had flavored Estan's time in Jarelton. It felt more like the Seirane that he remembered from his youth, before Syara's elevation and Loni's betrothal. He turned to Resmine to see if she was having similar memories. He saw her reach out for Dewin's hand and felt a sense of relief. Finally, she seemed to be moving out of the shadow that Syara's ghost had cast on her life. If only he could duck past his own ghosts...

His eyes wandered over to Khiri. The elven woman was much quieter since the incident with the Flayer. *The incident*, he thought sardonically. As though calling it an incident made it hurt less. Estan rubbed his jaw where Micah had sucker-punched him during their time in Illesdale. There was not a second in the last three days that passed by without a reminder that their party was missing the sun-filled elven man. Ullen's stories were less boisterous, Fennick's manner less friendly, and even the food was blander; granted, that was because Micah had been a fantastic cook. He probably could've made a pine cone taste better.

Also, Micah probably could have talked some sense into Khiri about the assassin. Each night, Khiri had requested him awakened so that either Ullen or Estan could escort the Odlesk to relieve himself, and then she made sure that he was fed something from their communal pot. Initially, Fennick tried to point out that a magical sleep didn't require such niceties, but when she refused to be dissuaded, there was little any of them could do. She was so determined that Estan had no doubts that she'd wake the mage, this *Kal*, on her own with sheer stubbornness.

Each time they woke *Kal* up, Estan liked him less. He was trouble. Estan was certain that the Odlesk was a sleeper agent, just waiting for a chance to get Khiri alone. Why else did he watch her like he did? Well... No, that couldn't... *No.* With a shake of his head, Estan banished the thought. It did him no good to dwell, anyway.

Khiri turned to Fennick, one hand resting next to her knife, as it often did now. "Where to?"

"We should probably start..." the former soldier trailed off with one hand still scratching at the stubble of his poorly shaved chin, when he was interrupted by the arrival of a newcomer.

"Welcome, friends! Welcome to Harish!" a tall, barrel-chested man in finely sewn, thickly woven, wool greeted them. Coarse, dark hair covered his scalp in silky waves that curled around his ears like it was afraid of blowing off of his head. He had a purple shirt, a green surcoat without sleeves and black breaches that flowed into supple thigh-high boots that were dyed to match his coat. "We don't get many visitors in Harish. Do you come to trade? Or perhaps..."

The man paused and shook his head, "But I forget my manners. I am Brel Rethos, Lord of Harish. Who... Ah! Fennick Worish, I didn't see you there. Are these people with you?"

The messenger strode forward and clasped hands with the nobleman. They exchanged a warrior's hug, each thumping the other once, strongly on the back before releasing each other. Estan tried to remember if he had ever heard anything about a Lord Rethos. Harish... No, Harish had sprung up after the Great War. It wasn't mentioned in Genovar's book.

"I think it's fairer to say I'm with them," Fennick said, his smile looking more genuine than Estan had ever seen it. "Traveled with this young lady all the way from the Life Trees on 'ta other side of Jarelton. We picked up a few along the way."

Lord Rethos glanced at Catapult's load and let out a low whistle. "Seems you picked up some odd company. Hope you're not looking to trade him. You know we've no room for slavers within Harish."

"Nothing like that," Fennick assured him. "He's not a great traveler. Asked us to put him under and wake him when we got to our destination." Estan was impressed with how smoothly Fennick deflected the question. It wasn't even an outright lie, since Kal had asked them to put him to sleep rather than knock him out. Of course, Kal had also asked them to kill him and get it over with, but that was hardly something to bring up to a random nobleman.

"Not much out here besides Harish. Where are you headed?" Lord Rethos asked.

"The mage's tower. You know... Maleck Dorell's place," Fennick said.

Color drained from the young lord's face and the welcoming smile seemed to freeze. Slowly, the man's expression morphed and tightened into a grimace, "In that case, I have some unfortunate news. Maleck Dorell has passed on. His staff has mostly moved on or found new vocations."

"Passed on?" Khiri's voice sounded empty, hollow.

For almost three breaths, no one said anything. The silence was loaded with frustrated tension. They had traveled across the whole of Mytana with one goal, just to have things end here with a single sentence.

"You are welcome to travel on to his tower. It still stands, though I'm sure it's probably been hit by every looter in the area by now. In the meantime, how about I treat your party to dinner. I don't often get company, and there is more than enough room for you all to stay the night. Please, say you'll stay!" Lord Rethos said, his enthusiasm already returning.

Everyone turned to Khiri, deferring to her as their leader as they always did. Estan wondered, too late, if it was wise to let Rethos know that they all relied on her that way. What if this nobleman was untrustworthy? Not that there was really any way of hiding Khiri's heritage. Elves from the Life Trees were either criminals or Fortivas.

"I suppose one evening would be alright," Khiri said hesitantly. She glanced from Rethos to Fennick, and the look on her face told Estan that she wasn't sure about trusting someone that was that fond of the ex-soldier.

"Gods preserve me, after you go and introduce yourself, I up and forget to return the favor," Fennick chuckled, either ignoring or not noticing the look Khiri had given him. "This lady, to whom I owe my allegiance, is Khiriellen Fortiva. With us—Estan, Resmine, Dewin, Ullen, and I think the lad on the horse is... Kell? Kol? Something like that."

The lordling bobbed his head at each of them in turn. "It's nice to meet all of you. Now, there's a nip in the air, so if you all don't mind accompanying me to my estate, we can get you settled."

They fell into a loose formation behind Lord Rethos and Fennick, who seemed to be catching up on local events. Khiri took point, followed by Ullen and Resmine, Estan pulled Catapult along, and Dewin guarded them from the rear. The city of Harish rose around them on all sides, in equal parts friendly and imposing. Citizens were bold enough to call out greetings to the group's host, and he responded to each of them with a wave or a nod.

Estan's initial relief at finding himself out of the wilderness was short-lived. Somehow the relaxed nature of their stroll through town and the benevolent nature of their host seemed false. Not that Estan had seen any cracks in the facade, nothing to point at as entirely wrong. It was, if anything, too right. Harish seemed like the type of place where nothing bad happened, or would ever happen. The bright, friendly faces were a little too cheerful, a little too friendly. Armed strangers were walking into town and not one citizen looked in the least concerned.

Walls and stilted houses weren't generally built without a reason. Estan hoped they might leave before they found out what Harish was hiding.

Much to Estan's surprise, Lord Rethos led them out of one walled town node into a second one. This node was much like the first, only there seemed to be structures built into stilts as well as on top of them.

"Excuse me, sir," Khiri ventured. "Why is the city partitioned like this?"

Lord Rethos glanced over his shoulder and seemed to be gauging the elven woman. "As I understand it, your people live according to a clan structure. It's similar here. One side of town is made up of survivors from one side of the Great War, the other side is made up of survivors from the opposing army. All of those that had nowhere to go when the war was over gathered here."

"Which side do you reside in?" Khiri asked. Ullen stifled a giggle, muttering under his breath about the girl's stones.

A hint of a smile quirked the edge of Lord Rethos's mouth, "My estate is actually in its own partition. Can you tell which section of the city is which?"

For a moment, Khiri was silent. The lordling seemed smug, knowing that they hadn't seen anything that could really differentiate the two city nodes. "I can tell that the next section is yours," Khiri answered.

Rethos started laughing, "I suppose I deserved that. Most who travel through Harish are very reluctant to accept our lifestyle. Many of our residents have stopped adhering to the walled system, living on whichever side they feel more protected."

"Protected from what?" Dewin asked from the rear.

"Here we are," Lord Rethos announced. Estan wasn't sure if the man was pretending not to have heard Dewin's question, or if he'd genuinely missed it. "My home!"

Estan nearly forgave the lord for not giving them an answer. The man's estate took up the entire city node. Instead of stilts, it was raised on an enormous slab of rock, suspended from the walls by monstrous chains. The path up was something like a drawbridge except that both sides of the bridge-like platform moved. A huge wheel was in the center of the platform and it required at least two guards to crank the mechanism. Even with Catapult next to them, the platform lifted the entire group with ease, but then, they probably made the thing to accommodate all kinds of livestock and goods.

They ascended through a hole in the elevated slab of stone that was twice as thick as Estan was tall. It was then that Lord Rethos' estate became visible. The entire disk that the estate was situated on was coated in gardens. Packed dirt paths were lined with river stones, while flowers and small trees were carefully spaced and labeled. The buildings were constructed of timber, but gleamed with white plaster where the boards normally would show, much like the houses of Illesdale. Estan imagined it would be easy to forget that they were close to fifty feet off the ground if it weren't for the monstrous chains that connected the gardens to the outer walls.

Drawing closer to the Main Hall, a full story taller than any of the other buildings, Lord Rethos took a path to the right. Estan guessed that Rethos was guiding them to the guest rooms that they had been offered. Lord Rethos passed by a stable and beckoned to one of the grooms to collect Catapult, which meant that Estan had to pick Kal up off the horse and carry the lanky assassin over his shoulder. The path wound close to the edge of the disc, and that was where they came to a long hall that was all one level. It was almost quaint compared with the Main Hall, but Estan thought that it could probably house an army as easily as a handful of guests.

"I'll let you get comfortable. You're welcome to any of the rooms in this building, and feel free to wander the gardens," Rethos said, his voice seeming to carry across the entire disk unaided. "I will send for you at dinner time."

The guest hall proved to be one long corridor with five rooms on each side. Each of the guestrooms had at least one bed, but some of them had bunks or spare beds. None of the rooms were very extravagant, but they were comfortable and well-stocked with blankets. Khiri took one of the rooms that had stacked bunks, while Dewin and Resmine took a room close to the end of the corridor. Fennick chose one on the opposite end of the hall from the women, while Ullen chose the door right across from Khiri. Estan chose a room with one large bed and an opposite bunk where he could deposit the assassin. While he didn't really want to sleep in the same room as the Odlesk man, he didn't like the idea of no one keeping an eye on the mage.

Khiri appeared in Estan's doorway. For a moment, Estan felt his heart leap, but she was focused on the assassin. "It's about time for us to wake him up," she said.

"There's no reason to have him up an' about an' loose here in Harish!" Fennick pushed his way into Estan's room, though Khiri didn't take up much of the door. "We should leave him be. His lordship ain't gonna miss the assassin comin' to dinner, and we canna exactly explain his holdin' a spoon between his tied hands at the Main Hall!"

"I said nothing about bringing him to the Main Hall. I said we should wake him," Khiri's jaw was set, but privately, Estan agreed with Fennick on this occasion. It made no sense to let the assassin out of his magical coma in a place that could provide for his escape, or somehow turn their hosts into their captors.

"You seem to be confused about something here, lass. Let me illuminate it for ya. This here git is a full-fledged member of that society that took your beloved bond-brother's life. He don't merit the pity and protection you been showin' him," Fennick hissed. "Bein' kind to him won't bring 'ta other back."

Tears welled at the corners of the elven woman's eyes, but she didn't turn away, nor did the tears fall. Khiri rose up to her full height, which wasn't much compared with the two men facing her. Still, somehow, Estan felt as though her presence easily outweighed them both. "Don't you *ever* presume to tell me how to remember Micah."

She turned and left the room, slamming the door behind her. Neither one of the men she'd turned away from mistook the gesture as a finish to the argument.

"I don't understand what it is about this one that she canna leave alone," Fennick scowled. "Should've just dropped him back in the woods."

"Khiri is Khiri," Estan shrugged. "I don't think I've really understood anything since our paths crossed a few weeks back."

"Aye, we're all still followin' her, even when her goal is null. Seems to me, we need a new plan," Fennick said, letting a breath out through his teeth. "Not that I'm putting myself forward. I've got no leanings, one way or 'ta other. Just, her judgment lately is questionable."

"Then what she needs, now more than ever, is support," Estan said, crossing his arms and leaning against the wall. Out of the corner of his eye, he thought he saw something move from the assassin's direction, but he refused to take his gaze away from the ex-soldier.

Fennick glowered contemptuously at the younger man, "It's hard to believe you be a blooded shield carrier. She's not ever seen a proper battle, and you hide behind her like a player what never seen a stage."

"While you sit back and criticize from the shadows?" Estan asked, barely managing to keep his tone level. "You think we don't notice how often you disappear when conflict starts? What do you do? Wait until it looks like we may possibly pull through to throw in?"

The expression on Fennick's face darkened until he barely looked like the same man. He took two steps, closing the distance between Estan and himself, "I'd have a care, lad. Some wouldn't let you walk away from an accusation like that."

"Some wouldn't deserve to hear it," Estan bit.

He watched a parade of emotions roll across the ex-soldier; anger, resentment, loathing, and finally one he couldn't place. Relief? Triumph? Constipation?

"You don't want me here. She no longer needs me. Fine. I'll be gone by tomorrow," Fennick turned on his heel, opened the door to the room Estan was sharing with the assassin, strode out into the hall, out the main door and slammed that door on the way into the gardens.

Estan loosed his arms from his chest and bent at the waist, sighing to release tension in his back. Finally, the headache of Fennick was close to being resolved. They'd reached the place he was leading them. Surely, Khiri wouldn't mind that he had pushed the man so far... Maybe she'd wanted to ask him to leave herself, though. Well, she had the rest of the night. If she wanted to mend things or contradict Estan, there was still plenty of time.

A maid of the estate knocked on the door jamb, gazed unconcernedly at the unconscious man on the floor and moved her eyes to Estan. She seemed older, maybe older than Fennick, thought it was hard to tell with her smooth, dark skin. It was impossible to determine if her hair was graying beneath the opaque white scarf that covered her head and hung down her back. Her service frock was a dusty rose, trimmed with gray ribbons, that set off her wise, hazel eyes.

"His lordship awaits you in the Main Hall. Dinner will be served in fifteen minutes" she stated, her tone one that would brook no delay.

"I'll be right there," Estan nodded.

For a long moment, they watched each other, then with deliberate motions, the maid turned on her toe and headed down the hall to inform the others. Mid-spin, a folded parchment fell from her pocket and drifted into Estan's room. He casually walked to his door and shut it before picking up the scrap of paper.

"You and those with you do not know me,
 but I am a friend. Maleck Dorell hasn't died,
 but a few weeks ago, he disappeared. He left
 with one your party knows well.
 Heed my warning: Harish is not what it seems.
 Master Dorell placed a few of us in Harish
 to keep an eye on things. I am the only one
 left. They claim to be a city of war refugees.
 In fact, this is a city of Gray Army survivors.
 At night, Flayers wander the city streets.
 Anyone found on ground level is offered as a

sacrifice to appease the demon-bound appetites.
The middle city even has buildings on the ground
to house the unwary. They brought you up
here, but make no mistake, they have foul
intentions. Be wary, be ready."

Estan folded the scrap and stuffed it down his boot, wishing there was a lit fire in his room so he could burn the note to cinders. He'd known something felt off the moment they'd stepped into Harish. This was too big for him to keep to himself, but Khiri wasn't speaking to him. There was only one person in the whole party that Khiri seemed to trust when it came to advice, so perhaps that was the best place for Estan to start.

37

~Ullen~

ULLEN LAY ON THE BED that took up the entire center of his room. It reminded him a bit of the beds he'd grown up with in Eerilor's royal palace. Far too large, far too soft, and far too dangerous.

As much as he'd travelled, Ullen hadn't let himself get this close to Harish before. Maleck was the one they'd left to guard the Burning Valley, and that seemed like more than enough protection. *I should've kept better tabs on the others*, Ullen thought as he heard the door slam in the room next to him.

Walking through the lower city and riding the platform up into the suspended fortress, Ullen felt the bars of a cage bending in around him. He shouldn't be here. Ullen knew that Maleck Dorell wasn't dead. There was no way that one of the others could've died without Ullen's knowledge. *Just about anything else could happen to them though*, the dwarf sighed. *What I wouldn't give for a bit of foresight right about now.*

But foresight was Genovar's gift.

Ullen wished that he'd talked to Khiri and Estan about his past before they'd gotten this far. His princehood had caught up with him, and now it seemed that the gods were about to catch up with him, too. The Flayer Mage's tomb wasn't far from this city; powers that had faded in the twenty-year gap were itching beneath Ullen's skin. He shouldn't be here, and he shouldn't have let Khiri come here, either. It was too dangerous.

A second door slammed somewhere else in the guest hall.

Emotions were running hot, it seemed. Maybe it would be easier to talk to everyone after dinner, once things had settled down. As much as Ullen wanted out of Harish, he didn't think that they'd be able to leave before morning without insulting their host. If they were to make it out of here without stirring up the hornets' nest, they had to be careful.

Soft tapping on Ullen's door drew him to his feet. "Who's there?"

"It's Estan," the knight's voice was hushed. "I need to talk to you about something."

Ullen opened his door and the knight slipped in before the gap was quite wide enough, scuffing the chest plate of his armor. Estan shut the door behind him, and even once it was secure, he kept his tone hushed. "Normally, Khiri'd be the first person I'd go to with something like this, but she's not going to want to talk about anything until we wake the mage up."

"What's going on, lad?" Ullen asked. "Ya seem distraught."

Without saying a word, Estan plunked down on Ullen's mattress and began pulling one of his boots off. The knight turned the boot over and shook the boot out like he was dislodging a pebble. A small scrap of parchment with spidery writing drifted onto the bed beside him.

It took Ullen a moment to walk over and pick the paper up. Trepidation washed over him when that scrap fell out of Estan's boot. Pinching the note delicately between two of his meaty fingers, Ullen read the rushed scrawl. "Someone risked a great deal to warn us of a trap we already blundered into," Ullen sighed. "It'd be one thing to have had this before'n we were hauled onto this elevated slab of Arra's bone, but now we're here, I'm not sure how we're to get down again."

"What do you think we should do?" Estan asked.

As much as Ullen wanted to act, he knew the only council he could give. "Right now, lad? We wait. Not much the lot of us can do until someone else makes their next play. In the mean ways, yer gonna want to find a way to dispose o' that scrap bit. Even in yer boot, there's too much risk."

38

~Khiri~

DINNER WAS MADE UP of things that Khiri found fascinating: cheese, venison and mushroom pie, a pastry filled with custard that had a burnt sugar shell, and a drink that tasted like stewed apples and spices. As intriguing as the banquet was, so much tension hung in the air that she found it hard to give the food her full attention. Lord Rethos peppered her with questions about growing up in the Life Trees. Most of them seemed innocent enough, but she was uncomfortable with the sheer volume of interest. His zealousness intensified any time she started a sentence with "My father..." but waned when she attempted to change the subject.

It was obvious that Estan and Fennick were at odds. She wondered what happened between them after she'd left them with Kal. Fennick was still fuming at his plate. Estan seemed strangely distant, though there wasn't a single movement that he didn't follow with his eyes. Ullen, Dewin, and Resmine were seated on the opposite end of the massive table, as though they were less interesting to Lord Rethos. Considering Ullen's heritage, Khiri was almost amused that someone would consider her more fascinating. Almost.

She was so relieved to make it back into the guest hall that she flopped onto the lower bunk in her room with her boots still on. Part of Khiri still insisted that she needed to get back up. Something was unfinished. The exhausted portion of her continued to fight the feeling, weighing her limbs down, and whispering to her about how cozy the bed seemed. Dropping in and out of consciousness, Khiri snapped awake at the sound of footsteps in her doorway.

"Lass, we need to speak," Fennick's tone was hushed, but urgent.

"What's going on?" she whispered. Somehow, he didn't seem sullen anymore. He seemed more like the man she'd first agreed to travel with, back when she saved him from the Venom Guild at the bottom of the Life Trees. Back when she hadn't felt she had any reason to doubt him.

He shook his head, "Not here. I need you to come with me."

Uncertainty gripping her chest, Khiri halted outside Kal and Estan's room. She glanced inside and saw that the knight wasn't there, but Kal's eyes flashed in the dark. *He's still supposed to be pretending to sleep*, Khiri thought, though it was hard to focus. She didn't want to alert Fennick to Kal's awareness. Not when the messenger man was being so much nicer than usual. "Where are we going?"

"I got a message from Dorell's old caretaker. He's holed up outside the city, but we have to move now. The two of us can slip out and be back before the night's over. Apparently, the mage and the city have been at odds for years. When Bral... that is Lord Rethos... told us about looters, what he meant was raiders. They thought the old mage died, he was that messed up. He still wants to see you," Fennick urged.

Questions that were starting to form pressed against a sudden wall of fog in Khiri's brain. The fog made everything seem hazy, but Fennick seemed completely reasonable. Why hadn't she listened to him before? He made sense. Nothing else seemed to make quite as much sense anymore. Numbly, Khiri felt herself nod.

Fennick took her wrist in his hand and dragged her out the door into the gardens. He seemed to be fiddling with something in his pouch. "Hold this," he told her. "But don't look at it."

Meekly, Khiri took it in her hand and gripped it with all of her might. She was going to hold on really well. It seemed right that she should. It was small and smooth like a pebble, but she didn't feel any need to look at it. She trusted the man that gave it to her.

Walking through the buildings, Fennick told her to keep quiet. Though they passed by several people, all in attendant garb, not one of them stopped to see if they could be of any help. Khiri was proud of herself for keeping so very silent. He led her to a rope ladder, like the ones that she had grown up using to get in and out of the Life Trees.

At the bottom, he whispered to her, reminding her how important it was that she held onto the thing that he gave her. She nodded again. The fog didn't seem to let her talk, but that was okay. After all, he had told her to be quiet.

Flayers hissed and swayed in an odd kind of dance. The creatures didn't see Fennick and Khiri, the same way that the servants hadn't. In the second section of the city, Khiri thought she heard someone screaming in one of the ground houses. If only Fennick had told them to stay quiet, maybe the Flayers wouldn't have seen them either.

Why aren't we fighting them? The thought drifted through the all-consuming haze coating her mind.

Because she didn't have her bow, of course. Or her knife.

Isn't that odd? the thought persisted. *Shouldn't you have those things? Aren't they important?*

Not as important as holding onto the pebble-thing that she was not supposed to look at, or as important as being quiet, her fog-brain said, shutting out the thought. The thought was not important, it told her. Khiri nodded at her fog-brain's logic.

Fennick dragged her through the city, ducking this way and that to avoid running into the Flayers as they wandered the streets. Once they were outside the gates, he guided her downhill and to the north. They came to the edge of a blackened ravine, and despite her trust in

the man, she paused, not wanting to set foot on the ashy soil. It felt...
wrong.

"Come now, lass," Fennick urged. He sounded edgy, probably
because he was worried about how well she was holding the pebble-
thing. She gripped it tighter, just to be sure.

The black surface sifted like sand beneath her feet. A few yards
into the ravine, the dark scorch marks rose above her head and they
were still climbing. Tree-like sculptures of ash rose out of the surrounding hills. Khiri shivered as the temperature seemed to drop a
degree with each step she took. She wished that Fennick had decided
that they needed warmer clothes, but maybe they weren't important
either.

Deeper and deeper he led her into the blackened heart of what
had turned from a ravine into a valley. A burned valley. The thought
came back and told her that this was very important, no matter what
her fog-brain would have her believe. First Flayers and now a burned
valley. Something was very wrong.

Khiri's fog-brain fought back. There was nothing to worry about.
She was still with Fennick. He was taking her to the dying mage man.

*Why would a dying man, mage or not, crawl through this world of
dust?* the thought argued. *It's far too cold here. He would want to find
somewhere warm and clean.*

While Khiri's thoughts and the fog-brain discussed things, Fennick continued to pull her farther into the heart of the valley. He
finally stopped at the mouth of a cavern that was rimmed with ice.
Moonlight reflected from it, making the cavern the only spot of
brightness from the ground to the stars. Khiri felt like she was suspended in the sky with darkness closing in around her.

Telgan Korsborn, echoed throughout her being. The volume of it
shocked her into dropping the pebble-thing. In a heartbeat, the fog-
brain vanished. Thoughts, no longer blocked, screamed in alarm.

"Finally snapped out of it, did ya?" Fennick snarled. "Too late, now."

He yanked her into the cavern and threw her forward. *The scent of rime, sharp and metallic, hung in the air. Thick frost crunched beneath Khiri's feet, reminding her of crushing bones. The large pulsing crystal in the center of the icy chamber seemed to beckon to her, even as a thin cackle rolled off the walls...* Khiri knew this place. Only this time, she wasn't dreaming. She walked toward the strange, glowing crystal, extending her hand, but dreading the crystal's touch. Only one thing was different from the dream...

A sheath dropped into the frost behind her, even as the dream-like cackle was rising in volume. Khiri turned and pulled out a wicked looking blade, coated in something that glistened greenish-black in the large crystal's pulsing light. *She held a knife that was not her father's...*

A shadowy figure grinned at her, wielding a blade coated with a grisly, blackish-green light, only the figure was no longer shadowed. Fennick was standing in the entry to the cavern, holding a knife identical to the one she had just unsheathed.

"Why are you doing this?" Khiri asked. Though the fogginess had evaporated, she still felt a veil of falseness was cast over her vision.

"Why? Why did I pledge myself to the Gray Army at the age of seventeen? Because the world needs change! It craves it! Do you have any idea how hard it was to grovel at your feet for over a month!" Fennick's eyes gleamed madly in the flickering glow. "I was sent to smoke out the location of your father, to trick him into Harish and then bring him here. We needed the presence of one of the Great Mage's binders to undo the spell. It doesn't matter which of us dies here. All we need is a Fortiva and a life."

Reaching into his belt pouch, he withdrew a rune and tossed it over his shoulder. Blue flames leapt across the entrance to the cavern, cutting off any thoughts Khiri had of just ducking past him. "What if I refuse to kill you?" Khiri asked.

There was no warning. Fennick lunged for her stabbing with such ferocity that Khiri barely managed to raise her guard in time. She rolled down the outside of his arm and swung the butt of the weapon into his back. His odd cackle bounced off the walls, robbing her of even a momentary sense of victory.

"If you don't kill me, you'll die. These knives were made for this moment. One taste of your blood, and they eat your life," Fennick's voice cracked. "Either I defeat you and see the awakening of my master, or I die in his service and he crushes you anyway! You've lost, lass! Before you've even begun!"

Khiri longed to drop the knife she was holding, but her instincts screamed at her not to leave herself open like that. There was no reasoning with the mad man in front of her. Thinking back to the moment she saved his life, she regretted loosing the arrow. If she had just waited a few more... No, but that wasn't true, was it?

"You hired the Venom Guild to chase you," she stated.

Fennick turned and lunged at her, swiping at the exposed skin of her arm. Dancing away from the deadly blade, Khiri tried to land a blow to the ex-soldier's head. If only she could knock him out, then maybe she could prevent this insane plan of his.

"They were only supposed to make it look convincing," he spat as he ducked under her reach. "We waited out there for days, looking for a lone elf to emerge so we could pull that stunt. But you went and killed that idiot's brother and nearly spoiled everything. She swore vengeance and tried to take your life. We couldn't have that. No, I needed you alive. Alive was the only way. Arad, though, thrice-spawned traitor, backed out of our deal."

Khiri hissed out a breath of cold fury and self-recrimination. If she hadn't allowed herself to be led by this fiend for so long... *Micah*.

She grabbed Fennick's knife-wielding wrist and twisted, digging her fingernails into his flesh in an attempt to make him drop his weapon.

He ignored the pain, in the way only a madman could. Instead, he brought his head forward and hammered it into her shoulder. The deep wounds that had been left by Liren the Flayer still hadn't completely healed and the shock wave of agony caused Khiri to release her grip. She had to stay focused. No one was coming to help her this time. Even if they managed to find this place, the blue flames cut her off from the rest of the world.

Falling back, she raised the cursed blade into first-guard position. If she killed, the Flayer Mage would rise, and if she was killed, the Flayer Mage would rise. What the forest spirits was she supposed to do?

As Fennick leapt at her, lines of motion seemed to blur. She felt a rush of ethereal wind rise up in her lungs, lighting a fire that she recognized but couldn't quite remember. The wind took shape, exiting through her chest without waiting for her to exhale. An acolyte moth fluttered through the air in the closing distance between Khiri and the insane ex-soldier.

"*Only by igniting the darkness, will you find the light*," the goddess Petora's voice echoed through her being.

Igniting the darkness. Khiri shifted her grip ever so slightly and launched herself to meet Fennick, blade to blade. *Igniting the darkness...*

Yes. She could do that.

39

~Estan~

DEWIN WAS WAITING FOR Estan in his room after a very un-comfortable dinner, "We've gotta have a conference, love. There's a fair bit that needs speakin', and we've a need for you to be in it."

"What's this about?" Estan asked.

"You'll see," the thief tugged on his arm. "Now be a love, and follow."

Estan threw a look over his shoulder at the sleeping assassin. "What about him?"

"Takin' a page from Khiri, now?" Dewin raised an eyebrow. "You received sommat, yes? Then you've a taste of what it's about. Move your finely-toned rump out that door. You're the last invited not to show."

The note. It was practically all he had thought about while Khiri fended off Lord Rethos's barrage of questions. Ullen being seated so far across the table had been an unintentional blessing from their host, as Estan was certain he would've slipped up and whispered something damning within earshot of one of the servers. He grabbed his cloak off of the four-posted bed and hurried after Dewin.

She led him out of the guest hall and down a row of fruit trees. Pausing, she touched his arm and pointed up into the trees with a big smile. "Act as casual as possible, love. Everyone here is watchin' for sommat to report back," she said through her teeth. "They be watchin' Khiri closer than any. Afraid we have to leave her out this time and catch her up when we've a chance."

Estan couldn't think of an argument, so he followed Dewin's lead. He continued to act the part of a sightseer without a care in the world. If Fennick decided to say something about the pairing, it might arouse suspicion, but he and Dewin were careful to only portray a friendship. They talked about unimportant things: the approach of autumn, the coolness of the mountains, and how soft the beds were in their quarters.

Once through the fruit trees, Dewin guided him down a path through a lawn of flowers and the conversation took a slightly more serious turn. It was probably inevitable that the subject of Resmine would pop up eventually, since Estan was practically her family and Dewin was her lover. Still, Estan would've preferred to put this conversation off for a bit longer. Perhaps he'd have been ready for it in a few more years...

"Estan, love... I been meanin' to ask you," Dewin started.

Here it comes, Estan thought. He tried to relax, but he could feel the muscles in his arm twitch as though he were bracing for impact.

"Do you think she could maybe ever be a serious love, or am I hopin' too hard?"

"I really think this is something that you should talk to Resmine about," Estan said. "It's really none of my..."

"Please," Dewin's eyes seemed to glow in the waning light. Sunset painted all of the petals shades of orange, pink and deep purples. Under different circumstances, the raised platform of gardens would have been breath-taking.

With a sigh, Estan looked at his feet. It was easier than watching the flicker of hope fight the shadow of uncertainty in Dewin's soul. "Has Resmine told you about Syara?"

"Is that the name of her love what died?" Dewin asked.

This really isn't my place, Estan sighed. "She was our friend for years... She taught me to hold a sword, she taught Resmine about, well, everything. There was such a light about her that she made the entire world seem brighter, and Resmine... Resmine was the moon to Syara's sun. As brightly as Syara shown, Resmine glowed in response. When Syara died... It was like Resmine went out."

"I see," Dewin said. Her shoulders slumped and she looked as dejected as a puppy denied a steak. "So there's me answer, I guess."

"That's what Syara was to Res," Estan said. "I never thought I'd see someone that could make Resmine even think about moving on, but she *likes* you, Dewin. I think if anyone has a chance to break through her walls, you're the one to do it. But that's just my opinion. This is really between you and Res."

They fell silent after that. They were still walking through the gardens, but it felt like they'd run out of things to talk about. Dewin dragged him into a bush maze. He thought they would find the others there, but to his surprise, they headed through it without pause. "Where exactly are we going?"

"The place they'd least expect. We had to get everyone out so that we could go back in," Dewin said. "They're wanting us to sneak around, reveal that they've a traitor. We all leave, they'll watch where we flock and wait to see which of theirs skulks out when all's quiet. They be watchin' us, not people goin' bout their chores and such."

Estan thought about it. All of them except Khiri leave the building, no one would really remark on the staff that enter and exit during that time. Especially if they were already inside... He sighed. It was a good thing the others had worked these things out. Estan felt even happier that he'd gone to Ullen with the note than he did before; sneaking around was not his strong suit. Dewin was towing him around to attract attention, not avoid it. By Taymahr, he felt dense.

Slowly, they made their way back into the guest hall. Several maids and footmen bustled from one part of the courtyard to another, as though they were trying to appear unobtrusive. They'd been waiting to report a meeting place. Estan hoped their dispersal meant that they'd accepted the ruse that there was no meeting.

Once inside, Dewin led the way to a narrow stairwell that was hidden off of the main sitting room by a thin door that he had assumed was a broom closet. An attic, full of paintings and old bits of furniture also housed an unhappy Ullen, a squashed Resmine, and now Dewin and Estan squeezed in to join the cramped space. At first, Estan thought that it was just the four of them, and then the maid from earlier detached herself from a painting on the far end of the attic.

"How did you..." he started.

"Nothing too complicated," she said. "People often don't see what they aren't looking for, but you're all here for a different reason."

"Aye. You dropped sommat that seemed plenty suspect, but how are we to know you're on the side of the gods and Arra," Ullen asked. "There's plenty of shadows here in Harish. Wouldn't take much to hide in 'em."

The maid nodded as she reached up to pull off the bright white maid's scarf. Without it, she seemed taller. Her hair was black, trimmed close to the scalp with strands of silver here and there catching the scattered light. She dropped the scarf and waited for several seconds before she began to speak.

"My name is Ardi Vorden. I was a member of Master Dorell's household ever since the War of the Burning Valley. Prior to that, I was a lieutenant under General Fortiva's command in his personal scout unit. We were responsible for locating the Flayer Mage's hiding place. I come to you now because your party is in grave danger. You must leave tonight," the woman began unbuttoning her rose-colored frock. Beneath it, she had on cloth armor dyed to a darker black than her hair. "I can guide you to an emergency rope bridge that Bral

Rethos installed in case the Flayers ever made their way onto this haven of his."

"What about my horse?" Estan asked. "I can't just leave Catapult."

Ardi Vorden considered the knight for a moment in the dark attic. The silence was thick with tension.

"I... couldn't leave that horse either," Resmine agreed.

"No more, I," Ullen said, though he didn't sound very happy about his admission.

"And I wish luck to them that tries to convince Khiri," Dewin smiled, though there was little humor in her voice. "She won't let us leave the former Guildy. There's no chance she'll leave our steed."

The maid-lieutenant let out a great huff of air, "There's a way, but it will take a great deal of courage and even more luck. Seems more than a little foolhardy to me. You'll have to lower the drawlift and fight your way through the Flayer riddled city. It takes two people to lower the lift, and I doubt your horse could carry more. If you insist on this course, not only will you be on your own, but you'll also be acting as a diversion for the rest of us."

"What happened with Fennick?" Resmine asked suddenly. "I know we don't trust him, but should we just leave him?"

"That man has been in and out of this place for years," Ardi sniffed contemptuously. "If I were to have invited him into this meeting, the lot of you would already be in chains."

Estan thought about the confrontation between Fennick and himself earlier that evening. Assuming Ardi was telling the truth, then that entire argument was likely another set up. What would Fennick have been hiding when he'd already led them into his...

"Khiri!" Estan yelped. "Once we all gathered... By Taymahr!"

Rushing back down the narrow stairwell, Estan burst through the small door. Within moments, he was in front of Khiri's door. It was wide open. Khiri's knife and the bow-that-was-Micah were both sitting at the foot of her bed. Estan gazed at his own open door across the corridor. Kal sat on the floor rather than on the bed he'd been set on. His unusual eyes were open and his lips were twisted in a mocking curve.

Two steps brought Estan to the mage. His thoughts finally caught up with him after his knuckles slammed into the side of the Odlesk's face. "Where is she?" he demanded.

"That messenger took her. He's got her under a control rune... I can track her, but we have to hurry," the assassin rubbed his jaw against his shoulder. "And considering where we are and who she is, it's not hard to guess where they're going."

"Like you care! Why didn't you stop them!" Estan demanded, shaking the assassin by his loose, black tunic.

The mage met Estan's eyes, unblinking, "There is the little matter of my being tied up, not to mention that man wouldn't hesitate to kill me. Khiri probably saved my life again, not mentioning that she saw me even as she went under. Those control runes are probably part of why he tried to convince the lot of you to kill me, no? But if you release me, we can go get her. Preferably while she's still breathing."

Cursing, Estan turned to find Dewin and Resmine flanking him. Ullen reached the doorway and gripped the frame to prevent himself from barrelling into Resmine. Ardi paused outside the room, as though she was just waiting for their group to figure out their drama before moving on. Every second Estan hesitated, Fennick was leading Khiri farther away.

"Okay... Okay... Here's what we're going to do. The three of you are going to take the escape with Lieutenant Vorden. I'm going to take Catapult," Estan reached down and yanked the ropes off of the assassin's hands. "Kal and I are going to make the run."

"What is this that you suddenly trust me to do?" the mage asked, rubbing his wrists.

"A suicide run through a city of Flayers," Ardi muttered. "You are of the Venom Guild? What's your specialty?"

"Mage," Kal said. "Though my spells are limited. I can't do much without components... Unless you happen to have a staff?"

Ardi disappeared without a word, back down the hall.

"How's a staff supposed to help?" Resmine asked, leaning against one of the bed posts. She looked tired and forlorn, as though the latest development had drained her of her reserves. Estan couldn't blame her. The last time they'd really paused for a rest had been interrupted by a Flayer attack.

"A mage's staff is like a rune, but instead of storing one spell and enough power to cast, it stores many spells. The power is entirely supplied by the wielder," Kal explained.

"The better the mage, the better the staff they can make. Not always true though. Some of 'em got so much pride in the craft, they wouldn'a risk sommat runnin' off with their spells. Ran with a fella, years ago, that only stored a buncha cantrips," Ullen said. He barely seemed to be listening to his own ramblings, though. They were all running tired.

Ardi returned. She held a long, carved walking stick with a crystal wedged into its tip out to the assassin. Kal grasped it in one hand and his eyebrows shot up. "Whose was this?"

"One that Master Dorell left in my keeping, for emergencies," she said curtly. "Now, I suggest that the lot of you gather whatever you need to gather. We've got to move. We're out of time."

There was a sudden bustle as people rushed to grab their own belongings. Dewin strapped Khiri's weapons to her own pack. Lieutenant Ardi Vorden supervised; she tied straps with black cloth to make sure nothing clinked or jangled, and rubbed a dark polish on their metal clips that might reflect too brightly and draw attention.

Estan turned to Kal, a mixture of resentment and resignation turning in his stomach. "If I had my way, we'd be leaving you here," he told the mage.

"If I had my way, we'd have left already," Kal countered. Estan found he couldn't argue with that.

"YOU'RE SURE YOU CAN do this?" Estan asked. It was maybe the twentieth time he'd uttered that exact question in as many minutes, but he still couldn't believe that he'd elected to trust the man behind him.

Catapult was twitching beneath his thighs, clearly as anxious to get moving as the two men riding him. Though the rest of the group had painted their faces with streaks of the dark polish, Estan and Kal had done nothing to disguise themselves. With the Odlesk's gleaming skin and light hair, he was practically a beacon on the back of the gray gelding.

"With a staff like this, I could probably take on the whole of the Gray Army," the assassin said. "Are you ready?"

"Past ready," Estan said, gritting his teeth.

Kal raised the staff to the sky and called out a word that seemed to be nothing but garbled syllables to Estan's untrained ears. Red sparks hissed from the clear crystal and split into clusters. They swarmed the large wheeled mechanism that controlled the drawlift, causing it to spin. The platform teetered for a moment, before swinging into motion, lowering itself at a speed that barely seemed safe. They leveled out before the lift reached the ground, and when they still had almost five feet to go, the platform started to reverse its spin. "I think they've noticed that we're leaving," Kal hissed. "They're fighting me for control."

Sparing a brief thought for the others, Estan kicked his heels into Catapult's flanks and charged into motion. Catapult didn't hesitate and jumped off the platform before it moved any further off the ground.

Surprised Flayers turned to fling themselves at the rampaging warhorse. Estan brought his sword to bear on the right, where a particularly large Flayer waded toward them, yowling with an inhuman blood lust. Its mottled skin split beneath the sword's edge, and it fell away just to be replaced by another. Kal was tagging Flayers on the left, but there was no way their small party would make it to the gate this way.

Catapult reared, flailing his front legs, cracking Flayer bones but to little effect. Warhorse tactics that worked on men and dwarves didn't intimidate the hungry demon-bound. The poor animal was being clawed on his hindquarters even as he clobbered those in front of him.

Kal scrabbled to stay on Catapult's back as one of the creatures grabbed his right hand and sank its teeth through the thin tunic sleeve. Flayers swarmed in on the left, sensing the opening in Estan and Kal's defense. Estan struggled to kick one of the demons in the head and it clung to his leg. The tips of its talons pricked the flesh beneath his armor. Its claws dragged down his thigh, leaving trails of puckered skin that itched like the prickly spines of a nettle bush.

"Do you have anything stronger in that thing?" Estan screamed over his shoulder. Being torn apart by things that were keening in high-pitched wheezing voices for his blood was not the way he wanted to die. And Khiri... Khiri was still in danger.

"Since you mentioned it," Kal called back. "I just need a minute to concentrate!"

Estan looked out at the sea of Flayers. More seemed to be pouring out of the shadows, attracted by Catapult's panicked neighing and the thrashing that indicated cornered prey. "You've got maybe twenty seconds!"

The mage altered his grip on Estan's waist to favor his gashed arm, and squeezed, "Close your eyes and when I give the word, get your horse moving."

Not bothering to answer, Estan did what he felt was the dumbest thing he could possibly do in this moment. He closed his eyes.

A light flashed, bright enough that the knight saw white through his eyelids; Flayers uttered death screams into the burst of hot air that surrounded Catapult and his passengers. Estan opened his eyes and saw a ring of fire hovering in the air around them. Catapult, trained for war, was trembling with the concentrated effort of an animal that wanted to panic, but wasn't allowed.

"Go!" Kal shouted over the roar of the floating fire.

As soon as Estan's heels connected, Catapult launched through the empty space cleared by the flames. The ring of fire followed them, pushing back the Flayers and licking at the stilts of Harish's houses. People ran onto their porches and the wooden bridges pointing at the rising blaze. They hurried to find ways to extinguish their homes without descending, as afraid of being consumed by their Flayer allies as they were of being consumed by the growing inferno. Kal's staff, raised above his head, shown over all like a fallen star.

They made it through the gate as the first building collapsed. The blaze of absolute carnage and the chorus of screams followed them into the chilled night. Letting the fire ring spiral away, Kal lowered his staff. Catapult dropped into a canter, his alarmed energy having dissipated in the shedding of any immediate threat.

"You're the guide," Estan snapped at the assassin. "So guide."

"What? Before you thank me?" Kal rolled his big mirrored eyes. "Just my luck you're the one with the horse."

Estan opened his mouth to retort, but was interrupted by a sparrow of moonlight fluttering out of the assassin's staff. It flew downhill, toward the mountain range to the north, then hovered like it was waiting for them to catch up.

"Follow the bird, Sunshine," the Odlesk said. Bristling, Estan bit back his urge to kick the assassin off of Catapult.

I'm coming, Khiri, he thought, hoping somehow it would reach her. *Hold on.*

40

~Khiri~

SPARKS FLARED AS KHIRI's blade skidded down the edge of Fennick's knife. Surprised at her sudden aggression, Fennick's leading foot slipped back half a step. Khiri reversed her weapon's direction and pressed her advantage. The ex-soldier avoided taking her knife across his arm, but he was now sporting a long slash through his sleeve.

Fennick slid a finger down the cut, a smile twitching at the corner of his mouth, "I knew all that elven nonsense about not taking a life was so much smoke. Finally acknowledged the futility of it all, did you?"

"Maybe I just decided that I'm tired of your treacherous face," Khiri said. Her heart was beating erratically. Despite her conviction, she wasn't sure she could do it. It would be the end... Of everything. The Life Trees: it wouldn't be a matter of choosing not to go back anymore, they would be forbidden to her. All of Mytana could be consumed in a cloud of Flayer fog. She had nothing to go on but a feeling, an instinct, that she was correctly interpreting the words of a deity that hadn't been able to say anything directly.

Her doubts slowed her momentum, allowing Fennick to regain the offensive. "Why fight it, Khiri? Either way, you're going to die here," his smile was wider now, flickering in and out of view with the erratic pulses of the glowing crystal.

Fear threatened to choke her.

Despite the knot growing in her chest, Khiri met Fennick's rush with a swift kick to his shins. Like the wrenching of his wrist, he seemed to be unaware of any suffering that would've slowed down a sane man.

A crazed laugh clawed its way out of the former soldier's throat. Spittle flecks were flying out of his mouth as Fennick backhanded Khiri with his free hand. The blow was enough to knock her back into the wall of the cavern. She rolled away just in time to avoid his cursed blade as it plunged toward her torso.

Pushing off the icy stone, Khiri brought her elbow up and hammered Fennick's weapon arm. A cracking sound echoed throughout the chamber as the ex-soldier's bone snapped.

His screech of agony tailed the grotesque pop. For a brief shining moment, Khiri thought it was over. Fennick's knife clattered to the cavern floor, it's greenish-black blade casting a foul shadow on the ice. She followed up on her attack, slamming her fist into the ex-soldier's jaw. Fennick fell away from her, clutching his broken arm to his chest.

"No," he whimpered. "No... I'm going to kill you... Or you, me... It's not going to end like this..." He began scooting across the ground, slowly making his way to the enormous crystal. "Master! Master, please! It's time... I brought the Fortiva."

Using the crystal to steady himself, Fennick pushed his way to his feet. Sick, cruel, twisted laughter welled up from somewhere deep within the man's chest, flowing out into the cavern like flood water. The manic glee was thick, leaving a coat of slick scum over Khiri's skin. "You... or me..." he cackled.

A sweeping fog of mist rose up in Khiri's mind. She recognized it and struggled against it, "No!" she cried. She fought to let go of the weapon in her hand. "No! I dropped it! It's beyond the barrier!"

Fennick reached into an inner pocket and pulled out something, but was careful not to let Khiri see it. "Then it's a good thing I brought two," his voice still crazed, even with the fog rising in her mind. He was alternating manic laughter with aching gasps, "Got a new one, a better one, off Bral when we stopped. Gave you the spare to enhance effects on the way here... Knew it wasn't enough after you... kept the knight."

Somehow, the control he had now was worse than the grip he'd held over her during the journey to the cave. Then, she had the comfort of not really understanding what she was doing. This time, the fog prevented her from controlling her actions, but her cognitive abilities remained. Khiri watched herself make each slow, deliberate step toward the giggling, panting Fennick.

"You... Or me!" he cackled. "Me... Me! ....ME!"

Once she was within his arm's reach, Fennick dropped the control rune and grabbed her wrist. The controlling mists evaporated from her mind even as the cursed blade drove into Fennick's heart. With an expression of absolute rapture, Fennick leaned in and stammered his final words, "S...s...say h-hello to the M-m-m-master for m-m..."

Horrified, Khiri dropped the ex-soldier's body.

Fennick's blood pooled on the frosty ground, flowing uphill to anoint the fervently pulsating crystal. The glow changed color, from the soft green-white that had been flickering over the ice to a brilliant crimson. Crackles of bright white and spidery black splintered over the crystal's surface. Pulsing slowed, solidified. Rays of incandescence threaded their way through the growing web of fractures, growing until Khiri thought she'd go blind.

Light traded itself for darkness as images began to swim through Khiri's vision.

"THIS IS IT! MALECK, keep up that shield!" Genovar's voice rang out through the bare cavern. Khiri barely recognized the place without the crystal and the crunch of hoarfrost. Seven figures surrounded her, including her father, the knight Quinton, and... Ullen! How had he gotten here?

"Ullen, what's going on?" she asked.

The dwarf didn't acknowledge her. In fact, no one seemed to have heard her at all.

A deep baritone voice reverberated from in front of her father's team. "Have your armies already fallen, Genovar? Is this the best your side can produce? A handful of misfits?"

Khiri moved to the side so she could see her father's adversary. The man wore shadows as though they were a cloak, making it impossible to see his face.

Something seemed off about this place. It was almost transparent—unreal. Running her hands over her arms and across her stomach, Khiri felt nothing. Either her body had gone completely numb, or maybe it wasn't there? Even the name of her soulmate was mysteriously silent, though the place it resided was still there, reserved.

She realized that this was the portion of her father's book that he'd left out: his mysterious defeat of the invincible Flayer Mage... Somehow, she was bearing witness to an event that had occurred over twenty summers ago. So this shadowy figure was...

"This is all the help I need to defeat you," her father said, confident and sure. "Your vision of the world is far too narrow for most of us, thanks."

Peering into the darkness, Khiri got her first real look at the Flayer Mage. Trusting in whatever separated her from the past, she walked up to the figure and studied the face behind his veil. Pale blue eyes, so transparent that they were almost clear, gazed through her. His face, so unlike any Flayer she had ever seen, was obsidian black; his skin even had that slightly translucent quality that chipped obsidian possessed. Though he was far too tall to be an elf, his ears were pointed, both at the tips and the lobes. She could barely see his hair. It was jet black against the volcanic glass of his features. Her curiosity sated, Khiri backed away, sensing that it was unwise to tempt fate too long.

"Too narrow, is it? I offer you perfection. No more loss, no more greed, no more desperation..." the Flayer Mage's deep voice rang against the stone cavern and tried to worm its way into Khiri's thoughts. She shook herself and wondered how it was that the seven people facing him stayed so resolute.

"What you offer is oblivion," a man stepped forward. Khiri's breath caught when she saw him, for he bore a striking resemblance to Evic. He must have been Dewin, Corianne, and Evic's father. "Some of us would much rather experience the bad things than never experience anything."

The Flayer Mage laughed. "Enough! I have heard enough! Your petty desires have nothing to do with my vision. Soon this will all be finished."

Maleck Dorell seemed to be the short, pudgy man with long blonde hair, given that he was the only mage on Genovar's side of the cavern. He held a short, silver staff over his head. The shield dividing Khiri's father and friends from the Flayer Mage increased in power enough to be visible, drawing a thick curtain of light in the air.

Starting so low that Khiri felt it in her feet before she ever heard it, a baleful humming sound trembled through the ground.

"What's he doing?" one of the two women in the group asked. She was willowy, tan, and had hair redder than sunset.

"We've no time," Genovar said. "While he's gathering his power together... Quickly!"

Black flames leapt up around Maleck's shield, moving out through the cavern entrance. Khiri leaned out of the passage to watch the black fire progress. Once out of the cave, it shot through the valley. Soldiers and Flayers alike were consumed by the ravenous flames. Islands of humanity were guarded by bubbles of light, but the flames guarded these spots like wolves circling a wounded elk. Many warriors fled before the path of fire, seeking higher ground as the flames flowing along the ravine seemed slow as it struggled to climb the slopes.

Turning back to her father and the others, Khiri rested her hand where her knife should have been. Even if this was the past, she needed to do something. She couldn't let the world become that barren waste of ash that would haunt her nightmares. It made her ill to think that she'd marched through the people's remains and hadn't even known.

Genovar held out his hand and sliced across his palm with the knife he'd given Khiri. Each of the others in his group did the same, except Maleck who had someone cut into his empty hand for him.

"I call on the Goddess Adari, to honor our pact," The man that looked like Evic called out. The blood on his palm began to glow an icy blue.

"I call on the God Locke, to honor our pact," the tallest man said. His palm, too, flared to life.

"I call on the Goddess Numyri, to honor our pact," the willowy woman smiled without humor. It was a smile of goodbye.

"I call on the God Tharothet, to honor the pact," Ullen stated. He seemed upset.

Quinton stepped forward and added his voice, "I call on the Goddess Taymahr, to honor our pact and pledge myself forever to her service."

"I call on the God Shydan, to honor our pact," a short woman with dark hair and eyes said.

"And I call on the Goddess Imyn, to complete the pact!" Genovar's voice rang out, echoing the way that the Flayer Mage's had before. The glow from his hand shot forward, followed by the light from each of the others.

Screaming in unintelligible, guttural rage, the Flayer Mage tried to hold back the streams of icy blue, but they passed through his shield as though it wasn't there. Crystal grew over every surface that the light blazed over, frosting into ice against the walls. Once the Flayer Mage was completely encased, the light dimmed to the constant pulsing that had first greeted Khiri when she entered the chamber. The only difference was the Flayer Mage's prison was bright blue instead of the sickly green shade she'd encountered.

"So that's it then?" Ullen said. "The end of Irrellian Thornne?"

"No," Genovar flexed his now-healed hand and sheathed his knife. "No, he sleeps, but he will wake again. Even the High Gods won't hold him forever. Those that followed him will find a way. When that day comes, spirits help us."

The small, dark woman stomped on the ice coating the cave's floor. "So what do we do?"

"Watch, and wait. Make ourselves scarce. We tell no one what we did here," Genovar said, moving to the cavern's entrance. "The longer the people believe the gods still watch, the longer this cell will hold."

Khiri longed to go with them, to see her mother, but the darkness was already demanding her return.

OPENING HER EYES, KHIRI nearly jumped out of her skin. The Flayer Mage stood over her prone form, an expression of exaggerated patience on his glass-like features. "I thought it only polite to thank you before I kill you, but you don't seem to be the elf I was expecting."

TELGAN KORSBORN, the name rang out, demanding that it be recognized.

Understanding made Khiri's chest contract, making it difficult to speak over the sudden knot in her throat.

"Tel... Telgan Korsborn," she choked out. There was no question in her mind.

The Flayer Mage's eyes widened, his expression a mixture of fear and displeasure, "How do you know that name?"

Khiri mutely extended the hand with the ring that had led her down this path. She was shaking so hard that it was difficult to keep her hand raised. It was either from fear or exhaustion, maybe a mixture of the two. Tears threatened to stream down her grimy face, but she didn't dare show such weakness to the villain before her.

Taking her hand lightly in his, he took the ring off her finger with a surprising gentleness. Turning the ruby back and forth, the stone began to glow in the Flayer Mage's fingers. As the glow faded, the Flayer Mage slipped the ring over his own slender knuckles. The low chuckle that she had heard him utter in the past once more rolled off the walls of rock. "This? This trinket led you to me with that name on your lips?"

"Wh... what do you mean?" Khiri hadn't thought she could feel a dread deeper than the one she'd woken with, but the hand of fear that seized her in that moment proved her wrong.

"Child, this held nothing but a seeking spell. Something much stronger was at play to give you my name. Compounded spell work, with a touch of the divine... Trust me, after twenty years in a shell of crystal, I'm *quite* familiar with that flavor of magic."

The dagger... Khiri's mind jumped back to the day of her Name Breathing. Her father's dagger, the dagger she'd never been allowed to touch, the dagger that'd been used to bind the Flayer Mage in his crystal coffin... *No...* "No... I... it had to be..."

"I think I'll let you live, after all. Incidentally, I wouldn't use that name too often. It awakens the beast within, you know. Harder to let you survive, and I should enjoy allowing you to walk away. Only fitting for my destined mate!"

"What?" Khiri said, not sure she heard him right.

"Dear daughter of my enemy," he laughed, "elves can't fight their destiny. You and I are bound!" He began walking toward the cavern's mouth. "I am free and bound to Genovar's daughter! I feel like celebrating. I don't suppose you're ready to come along willingly just yet?"

Khiri's mouth worked, but no sound came out. She scurried backward on her hands, trying to put some distance between herself and the Flayer Mage.

"No," his dark lips curved. "Not just yet. But you will come to me. One day. In the meantime, I have an army to rebuild and a world to fix." With that, he vanished into the shadows, going spirits knew where.

Drawing her knees up to her chest, Khiri sat alone in the dark, icy cavern. The light had vanished sometime during her visit to the past. She felt like crying. Her father had protected the world for twenty years, and she'd just unleashed their destruction.

But her father had also given her the dagger that destroyed her life...

In the silence of her heartache, a new voice approached her, whispering into her mind.

Yes, you'll do.

41

~Estan~

DRAWING CATAPULT TO a halt, Estan watched as Kal's bird flew straight into a barrier of blue flames. The blackened valley of soot wasn't like normal ash. Though they had ridden hard and fast, the dust didn't leave a cloud trail, nor did it cling to Catapult's legs. As still and silent as the valley of ash was, Estan felt like he was going to suffocate if he remained here too long.

"Got anymore tricks in that thing?" Estan asked, refusing to turn around and look at the assassin. It galled him to no end that the assassin was steadily proving his worth. If Khiri hadn't dragged the man along, Estan wouldn't have made it this far. Worse, the mage knew it.

"Breaking a fire barrier?" Kal sounded uncertain. "I'm not sure. The man that made this staff had some major defensive magic, but there are far more spells geared toward using fire than halting it."

"We've got to try," Estan urged Catapult forward, as close to the fire as the horse was willing to get.

"No arguments," Kal said. He slipped off the warhorse and walked up to the cerulean wall of flames. His shadow danced over the gritty black sands as he raised his empty hand against the heat. Estan heard him hiss as the assassin's Flayer bite wound met the extreme temperature barrier. "Almost forgot about that."

Estan couldn't help the small thrill of pleasure at the Odlesk's discomfort. The knight swung his leg over Catapult's back, and then let out a strained hiss as he remembered his own set of injuries. Schooling his expression, Estan approached the fiery boundary. Kal was muttering to himself, a constant stream of what may as well have been gibberish for all Estan understood of it.

A momentary gap in the gyrating flames allowed Estan a glimpse of Khiri and Fennick. The elven woman had just hit the wall hard, and Fennick was charging toward her with a wicked-looking blade.

"Khiri!" Estan screamed, rushing forward without thinking. "KHIRI!"

Agony like he had never experienced before shot through his entire body, building through his lungs and filling his eyes. Every inch of him felt exposed, raw. The sound of something sizzling pounded inside of his ears. A cool grip found his arm and suddenly he was back out in the cool night air.

"You moron!" Kal snapped. "What in the Demon Realms were you thinking?"

"Fennick's trying to kill Khiri," Estan gasped. Even the cold felt like needles on his raw flesh. He wasn't sure whether he was blind or his eyes were just closed. Estan tried not to think about it. There was plenty of pain to distract him. "Had to stop him..."

"Well, you're going to stop yourself permanently if you try that again. Khiri can handle herself. We've got to believe that," Kal's voice told Estan the worst possible news. The assassin couldn't find a way through the barrier.

"How bad is it?" the knight asked.

"Bad enough. I suppose leaving you like this would anger her... Pity," Kal sighed. "I rather think it's an improvement. Lucky for you, this Maleck fellow did some healing. Unfortunate for me."

For the first time since they met, Estan thought he might have misjudged Kal. Had the Odlesk really wanted him gone, he would've just let Estan burn of his own stupidity. "I suppose I should..."

"No," Kal said. "Don't thank me. I saved you because the others will be here soon, and I'm in no mood to be labeled a traitor. I still hate you."

Estan shut his mouth and tried to relax as he felt the needles of exposure pull away and his skin began to firm. It was an odd, not entirely unpleasant experience, though not one he ever wanted to endure again. Instead of pain, he felt like he was cloaked in a blanket of warm snow, or maybe damp feathers. The sensation enveloped him, dragged at his conscious thoughts, until he felt like he was sinking through Arra's surface. During the whole procedure, all he could think about was Khiri, thrown against that icy wall with Fennick coming at her.

"Estan!" Resmine knelt next to him. "What happened to him?" He still refused to open his eyes, as the healing energy hadn't yet swaddled his head, but he could feel her presence. It helped him unclench those muscles that still didn't trust the assassin not to try... something. Not that it would've made sense after Kal had gone to the trouble of pulling Estan out of the fire, but there was still no love lost between himself and the mage.

"The idiot jumped into that barrier," Kal said. He sounded strained. "But we're about to have much bigger problems."

Ullen shuffled forward, presumably toward the scorching blue wall. "Aye. The lad's right. We're about to land in a whole heap of trouble. That's enough with Estan... His eyebrows will just have'ta grow back on their own... Assuming they get a chance. Everyone, huddle up 'round the knight and mage, get us the best shield what's in that staff! Right quick!"

Estan opened his eyes, curious enough to risk the possible repercussions. The first thing he noticed was darkness. The blaze of the barricade was much dimmer; the middle of it had evaporated entirely and the rest of it was melting away as he watched. Khiri stood in the center of the inner chamber holding a limp Fennick, whom she quickly dropped.

No one spoke. Despite his eagerness to break out of the circle and run to her, he didn't dare. He'd never seen Ullen's face wear that expression before and it scared him more than the prospect of walking through a thousand of those fire barriers.

"Khiri's outside of the shield, though," Dewin said, clutching her hatchet until her knuckles showed white against her skin. She shifted her weight nervously from one foot to the other. There wasn't much that any of them could do, hiding within Kal's shield.

A new glow was rising in the cavern. As it grew, Khiri fell to the ground. Estan worked to find his voice, but the pulsing crystal beyond the elven woman's body had him enthralled.

"She'll be okay," Kal said. "We have to believe that."

Estan broke his gaze with the crystal to look at the mage. He was holding Maleck Dorell's staff in front of him, steady and focused, appearing every inch the hero that Estan had wanted to be once he earned his shield. A twinge of bitterness coursed through the knight, next to his rising concern for Khiri.

There was a flash of searing light that lanced through Estan's still aching eyes as the crystal shattered. Shards of rock bounced and ricocheted throughout the cavern, making sounds like clacking teeth. A dark, sinister figure rose from the remaining shell of the transparent coffin. Estan could make out nothing but shadow, but he *knew* that this thing in front of them was Irrellian Thornne, the Flayer Mage.

Irrellian moved toward Khiri's prone form and seemed to be gazing at her. As she began to stir, the imposing figure bent in closer. It was almost a parody of a concerned parent checking on their child. Estan thought he even sensed a moment of tenderness pass between the Flayer Mage and the unconscious elf.

The moment Khiri awoke, she jumped back, startling everyone watching her. Estan had never heard her scream before, he realized. He thought now would've been the perfect time to make an exception, but Khiri kept as quiet as ever. Genovar needn't have bothered sending him after her, Estan sighed. If anything, he was Khiri's burden.

Khiri and the Flayer Mage were speaking to each other. As hard as Estan strained, their voices were impossible to make out at this distance. Ice faded from the walls of the cavern and the shards of the deserted crystal shell began to sublimate into nothing. Soon, it would be as though the Flayer Mage had never slept within the tiny cavern.

"There's no way this shield will hold him," Kal said over his shoulder. "If he wants us dead, we're breathing our last."

"Patience," Ullen said. "We'll be alright, so long as they've still enough left in 'em."

"Who?" Estan heard himself ask.

Ullen didn't respond. The quiet starlight cascaded like a fine dust from the heavens, reflecting off of the clouded breath that escaped from their lips in their little huddle on the dark, ashy ground. Estan watched the Flayer Mage slide toward them once, then turn back toward Khiri. The knight held his breath, waiting for Irrellian Thornne to notice them or attack Khiri, or whomever it was that Ullen had mentioned to show up. Waiting for something. Anything.

And then... *Estan, Knight of the Protective Hand,* the voice echoed inside of his mind. It was someone he'd never before heard, and yet he recognized her immediately.

"Lady Taymahr," he breathed. In all his time as a student at the temple, he had been told hers was a voice he would forever serve, but he would never hear her. Hearing was reserved for the priestesses alone. But then, the priestesses were traitors...

Taymahr, I stand to serve, he responded, realizing that the goddess was waiting for a response.

Be my vassal. Carry me with you when you leave this place. There will be much to do and I will need assistance, Taymahr's plea sounded more like a command, but Estan was every inch her servant. His life was already bound to his goddess; he'd honor the oath he'd pledged when he'd earned his shield. With the Flayer Mage within his sight, it didn't seem like a good idea to turn down his most powerful ally, either.

You have but to ask, he told her.

Then our bargain is thus: You will speak with my voice when I require it, you will be my legs when I need them, and you will be my sword when is necessary. In return, I will grant you those powers that are mine to bestow, and should you be in need of assistance, you will always find aid, Taymahr promised. *I shall finish the healing that was begun by your friend.*

Estan didn't argue with the goddess over semantics. He figured with Irrellian Thornne's awakening, even Kal was as close to being a friend as necessary.

No longer nervous, Estan watched as the Flayer Mage stepped out of the shadows of the old battle and toward the dawning of the next war. Estan could tell from the ageless depths of his friends' eyes that each of them had also just been tapped as a vassal, an avatar. The greatest evil the world had ever known may have just returned to the world, but the power to stop him had awakened as well.

"Let's go check on Khiri," Estan said. He smiled to himself, pleased to have beaten Kal to the suggestion.

~Acknowledgements~

This book was the result of many long hours and late nights of effort, but I definitely didn't get to this point on my own.

First, I'd like to extend a huge amount of gratitude to my father. Even though he's not the biggest fan of fantasy any more, I know he'll read this and love it because he's proud of me. He's provided a lot of emotional and monetary support throughout the years, and this book wouldn't exist without him. Thanks, Dad. I love you.

Next, I'd like to thank Stephen and Mom. They also have provided a lot of emotional and monetary support through the years, and if they hadn't convinced me to move to Texas, I might never have met some of the other people on this list. I love you both. Thank you!

A big, heartfelt hug goes to my cousin, Michelle, whom is one of my biggest cheerleaders, and has been after me to publish for years. Sorry it took so long, cuz.

I'd like to thank Becca Lynn Mathis, Wendy Nelson Sinclair, Ingramspark, Draft2digital, and anyone that's put their how to publish information out on YouTube. This process comes with a lot of questions, and having people that have gone through it helps immensely. Thanks for being there for me.

So many thanks go out to my amazing beta readers! I'd like to give special shout outs to Wendy and Katja, for their extremely detailed feedback and encouragement.

Thank you to brosedesignz for my fantastic cover art. I'll be back for sequel art.

Thank you to the rest of my friends and family. There are so many instances where you guys helped me with book stuff or just general life stuff, I'd like to name each and every one of you... I'm not going to, because that's probably its own book, but I hope each one of you knows just how important you are to me. Much love to all of you.

And finally, I'd like to thank my best and only husband, Terence. You constantly astound me with your love, support and generosity. You helped me go back to school, you've helped me concentrate on my passion, and you always see the best in me. I love you so much. *Thank you.*

For more information about Christina Dickinson and her upcoming works, please feel free to visit her website: christinadickinsonwrites.com